KEEPER OF THE DEAD

A NOVEL

Published in the United States by Puree Publishing, an imprint of Falling Pear, LLC.
www.pureepublishing.com

ISBN 979-8-9862212-0-5
eBook ISBN 979-8-9862212-1-2

Layout design by Tigaboys
Cover and segment design by Ryan Young
Cover photography by: Cottonbro, Valeriia Miller, AveCalvar, Waldrebell, David Selbert

*For mom and dad, who worked tirelessly so that
I could selfishly dabble in creativity.*

KEEPER OF THE DEAD

FALL

ORIGIN

Frank can hear every step of the second hand. It moves in a jagged fashion along its endless loop around the antique grandfather clock that belonged to his late mother. He is aware of what each tick represents and restlessness more than desire drives him up from the kitchen table, his bones and chair creaking in unison. The man of seventy years hobbles toward the foyer and to the base of a modest, wooden staircase before leaning across the railing and looking up to the second-story hallway.

"Franny, I'm headed off to bed." He waits for a response. Somewhere upstairs a door handle rattles and opens. A woman's voice calls down to him.

"Okay, Pop. See you in the morning." As usual, her tone is warm but distracted, as if her frantic lifestyle is being interrupted by small conversation.

He doesn't hear any sounds of movement so Frank is at least comforted that she's awaiting his response.

"Oh, and Franny?"

"Yeah, Pop?"

"First day of buck tomorrow so I'll be out in the woods when you wake up. We'll have lunch though?" He taps his wrinkled, stiff fingers on the worn but smooth handrail.

Frank looks forward to the few chances he has to share a meal with his daughters. Both now in their forties and no children on the horizon, they're all he's got. When they're home the house feels right. But when they're gone, he feels like he's living in his own coffin.

"I thought you gave up hunting. Didn't you sell your guns?" the voice upstairs responds.

"Just going out with my binoculars."

"Alright, then. Take your cell phone!"

Frank sighs, loud enough so she can hear.

"Goodnight, then." He steps away from the stairs and toward his bedroom on the first floor. Boards creak above as footsteps move to the top of the steps.

"Hey, Pop?"

Frank stops in the dining room and turns.

"Yeah?"

"I've got to run to the DMV in the morning, I still can't find my license. But I'll be back for lunch."

He smiles so wide that his cheeks hurt as they resist the stretch.

"Oh, and I talked to Cat. She's on leave this weekend and will be home. We should do something!"

"That sounds good to me. We'll see you tomorrow."

"Night, Dad."

Frank walks to his bedroom and closes the door with a soft latch. He falls asleep fast, eager for the hours and days to pass to reach those rare enjoyable moments with his daughters despite knowing that the moving hand of the clock is synonymous with his own mortality.

The morning is a crisp bite against his face as he exits his truck and steps heel-toe over the tall, brown grass on the side of the remote back road. It's still dark by most measures except for a faint blue tint of dawn that gives just enough light for Frank to see where he places each boot. The binoculars bounce off the chest of his tan coat and orange vest with each advancing stride into the Bucks County, Pennsylvania woods.

After thirty minutes of sneaking into his favorite spot, which is a large oak tree with a rooted base perfect for sitting, a woodland version of his home recliner, Frank gets comfortable against the rough bark of the wide tree. Aside from the binoculars and his mandatory cell phone, he carries an old green metallic thermos full of piping hot coffee.

Steam billows from the mouth of the container and he's quick to pour a cap full. This was his favorite part of the hunt. Sitting silent among the trees as the sun woke up the forest while sipping on coffee and listening to the sounds of nature all around him.

Two hours and as many bathroom breaks later, Frank's legs grow restless and his rear develops a soreness that requires him to move. With no signs of deer, or so much as a squirrel, he pulls himself to his feet and decides to walk to another spot deeper in the woods. This was his typical routine as an open field a mile or so from the road was his preferred lunch spot, though today he'll be leaving early to have lunch with Franny. The morning hours can't pass fast enough.

Somewhere between his tree and the field, a loud snap of a branch freezes him in place. The excitement returns as if it had never left. He imagines raising his rifle and scanning the trees for a deer. Instead, he looks with naked eyes until a flash of movement catches his attention. He brings up the binoculars but can't seem to focus on the moving animal. A blurry brown shape hops and gallops and stops.

"Come on, stupid thing." Frank fumbles with the focus dial of the binoculars.

The image becomes clear. All he can make out is the flashing of a white tail, the rest of the animal obscured by overbrush.

Leaves crack and twigs snap behind him.

Frank lowers the binoculars and turns to the new sound, as not to spook the animal up ahead. He's shocked to see a fellow hunter, meandering a dozen feet behind him. Something about the man is off. He has no rifle and his camouflage and orange vest are tattered and stained.

"You...you okay, buddy?" Frank whispers. He fondles his pocket for his phone which he's now glad he remembered.

The man sways in place, head down with scrappy hair covering his face. Frank can't quite see his features, but he appears dirty and unkempt.

"Do you need some help?"

A rustle in the distance as the deer bolts from cover and disappears into the forest. Frank's attention is drawn to the fleeing deer.

"Darn it!"

As if triggered by the startled animal, the man roars an awful growl and lurches toward Frank who spins around and stumbles backward.

The man's face is covered in blood and grime, the whites of his eyes and teeth are bright among all other features. Frank loses his footing and falls onto his back among the cold, wet leaves. The impact takes his breath away as pain jolts his spine. Groaning and biting, the man lunges at Frank. Frail arms hold the weight of the man above at bay. Horrific sounds accompany the swipes and snaps of a predator.

He's able to draw up his binoculars as the madman chomps down on the rubber eyepiece. Using his entire strength, Frank rolls the flailing body from off of on top of him and scrambles to his knees. He's never been so conscious of his fleeting youth than at this moment, but he's determined to fight. While still trying to get to his feet, he manages to pull the phone from his pocket.

Frank is hit from behind and his cell phone vanishes among the leaves. Pain surges through his neck as the man bites down on the soft skin above his collar. All he has now is his thermos and so he whips around, slamming the canister into the face of the man who's clawing at his legs and back. A bit of Frank's skin dangles from the open mouth.

He can feel blood trickling down his neck and into his coat as he pulls himself across the forest floor, his fingers grasping the cool dirt and leaves. With one last valiant effort, Frank pulls himself to his feet. The sound of the man, unrelenting, ignites a reaction that he hasn't felt in decades. With a swift kick, Frank plants a boot into the head of what used to be a man crawling toward him. The body rolls to its side and squirms, growling and disoriented.

Moving as fast as he can with one hand holding the back of his neck, Frank forces one foot in front of the other while checking behind him for the deranged attacker. His bleeding isn't life-threatening so he knows he just needs to get back to the truck, get home, and get cleaned up. Then he will call the police.

As he reaches the edge of the woods and sees his truck, a sensation overtakes him. A feverish warmth combined with the weight of something on his back. But nothing is there. He's lost the man and is alone, staggering to the driver's side door. A hot flash and the feeling of bearing something heavy strengthens as he fumbles for his keys.

With a crank of the ignition, vertigo fights his vision to stay focused on the road. He blinks it away.

"Come on, Frank."

He coaches himself the whole way home, unsure if he's having a heart attack or what is wreaking havoc on his body and senses. Pulling into the empty driveway is a blur and he isn't sure how he makes it to the door, let alone inside.

"Franny!" he calls out but is greeted by silence.

His heart races as his blood pressure plummets. Frank can feel his knees go weak as the floor approaches. He doesn't feel the impact.

Sprawled out across the foyer rug for hours, his mind battles an unknown assailant as his cells fight the ravenous, microscopic intruder. Up until this point, he's prayed that someone will find him. But now, as the last of what can be recognized as Frank fades away and a violent appetite overtakes him, his final coherent thought is a hope that he'll never be found.

As if overheard in a distant room somewhere deep in the house, the sound of a door opening and a voice screaming penetrates the fog in his mind, though he has no clarity who it might belong to or even the concept of what the noise means. Sirens wail somewhere far away. A muted voice echoes closer. A shape kneels at his side and he can sense the pressure of their touch but there is no detail. It's as if all of his nerves have fallen asleep.

It's not relief he feels, but hunger. An insatiable and immediate urge. And so, it happens.

Frank eats.

THEN

DAY 1 – WESTERN NORTH CAROLINA

"Viktor Hamilton, I've got a nine o'clock with doctor Baker," Viktor states while tapping his keys on the counter and looking around the room as the young woman behind the desk in sky-blue scrubs clacks on the keyboard.

A dozen or so patients sit reading or watching the sole TV in the large waiting room. Tall, tinted glass windows span from the tile floor to the twelve-foot ceiling. The news is on, which some people appear to be invested in, but there is no audio, only subtitles, and he can't make out the words from the check-in station. When one of the patients waiting looks up from her phone at him, he realizes he is still tapping with his keys and raises a hand of apology.

"Alright, Mr. Hamilton, have a seat and fill this out. We'll call you back shortly," the nurse says, handing him a clipboard and pen.

Viktor thanks her but instead of sitting he leans against the wall next to the counter. She looks at him for a moment and returns her attention to the computer. The form is one he's filled out countless times and he goes through checking off boxes and scribbling what answers he can recall. It's not until he reaches the emergency contact section that something gives him pause. It also reminds him to check his phone, but that just brings disappointment when he sees there aren't any new notifications.

Caroline should be awake and headed to school by now.

He sends a text, hoping for a response:

Hey sweetie, have a good day!
Looking forward to this weekend!

His typing is cumbersome and loud. Viktor hits the send icon and begins to slide the phone toward his front pocket when it vibrates in his hand. Serotonin courses through his brain, but it evaporates when the screen displays:

SENDING FAILED
TRY AGAIN WHEN SERVICE IS AVAILABLE?

He clicks the send icon again and tucks the phone into his pocket. After a few minutes and a half dozen more papers, Viktor returns the clipboard and pen to the front desk.

"Mr. Hamilton?" a nurse calls from a hallway between the counter and the lobby. Viktor limps around the station and through the door, exchanging a polite smile as she gestures inward.

The floor is cold on his bare feet. Compression socks, worn to improve circulation, were one of the items on the removal list before entering the scan. Everything about the sterile room is chilling, including the draft that carries upward into his loose bedgown. Viktor tightens the knot of the rough fabric robe around his waist. After locking his phone, wallet, clothes, and car keys in a numbered wooden cubby, he pauses for a moment, not quite sure what to do with the orange locker key that dangles from his wrist.

He rubs his thumb against his ring finger, ensuring he's not still wearing the wedding band that has been absent for several months now. The smooth, naked skin just under his knuckle still doesn't feel right without it. As he looks around for a dropbox, or any place to store the locker key, Viktor thinks it might have been nice to have someone here with him, if only for this purpose. After all, it's just an MRI and there's little to be worried about, but the solitude of a solo visit is another unfortunate reminder of his current station in life.

I'll hand it to the nurse, what was her name? he thinks hard, as he exits the small dressing room. His bare feet transition from tile to carpet and back to that frigid and pristine white marble stone.

"Mr. Hamilton?" The MRI technician surprises him as Viktor rounds the corner into the hallway.

"Uh-huh," Viktor scans her name tag as she gestures him forward.

"Cathy is it?" he calls out as he struggles to keep up.

"Yes?" She doesn't look back as they arrive at the room labeled MRI-4. Viktor reaches out with the small key.

"I still have this," he says as if he's broken a known rule.

"Just don't forget it when we're all finished. Unless you want to be in that gown all day!" Cathy laughs, snatching the key from his outstretched fingers and placing it in a small white bowl next to the line of computers and equipment that cover the technician side of the screening area.

She escorts him into the large room, empty save for the giant coffin-looking tube that he is about to crawl into. It's not his first

MRI, but it has been years and he doesn't quite remember how it feels. A faint memory of noise, and horror stories about earrings or loose pens finding their way into the brains of unwitting patients. Just stories, but of course they flood his thoughts at this most opportune time.

"Alright, what brings you in today?" She's already read his report but is making small talk as she preps the room. Viktor is relieved when she retrieves a giant bath towel from a heated container.

"I'm uh, having some leg pain, mainly my hip. Comes and goes," he dismisses, still not coming to terms with the inevitable fragility of aging.

"Work related?" Her tone reminds him of an insurance adjuster.

"No, no, I'm out of work at the moment. But I'm an electrician by trade, and that's nothing more than a minor unexpected jolt now and again."

"I see. Well, you're too young to be lamed up like this so we'll see if we can find out what's going on," she says.

"I guess 40's the new 30, they say." Though he doesn't know who *they* are.

She shares a polite laugh and adjusts the pillow on the outstretched table, still holding on to the warm towel. Viktor can feel the heat radiating from there and he's anxious for her to hand it over.

"Lie down here, carefully. Head back against the pillow."

Viktor does so, trying not to wince at the pain of having to raise his right leg. Once he's situated on the table, the stark white tunnel looming just beyond his feet, Cathy lifts his knees and places a foam brick under.

"How's that feel?" she asks.

He nods. She unfolds the hot towel and drapes it over his midsection and waist, it goes all the way to his knees. The reprieve from the coldness of the room is almost magical.

"Okay, last thing. Date of birth, name, and no metal objects or anything left on you right?"

Viktor recites his information and pats his sides for his keys or anything he may have forgotten, which of course he hasn't. The cheap robe has no pockets. All he feels is the seam of his boxer briefs, the only property he has with him.

"How long will I be in there?"

She checks her chart. "This scan will run a total of forty-five minutes, broken into seven intervals. But I've got some headphones for you and here's the squeezer, just give it a press if you need anything. I'll be able to hear you in the other room." She places the rubber bulb in his left hand, which he can just make out in his peripheral. He feels the hard lines that run around it.

If I press does it stop automatically? Would it reset the whole test and I'd need to start all over again? Would I be the only one today to push it?

He's pulled out of his thoughts as loud music slams into his eardrums. The too-small headphones clasp over his ears with an uncomfortable pressure. He can sense Cathy walking into the next room and thinks he hears the two-way door close, then open, and settle on closed again.

"Starting now. Just relax Mr. Hamilton, it'll be over before you know it." Her voice interrupts the piercing music and is blown out once she clicks off the intercom.

He'd rather her talk the whole time as he can't even tell what genre of music is pouring out of the cheap and treble-heavy earphones. The table starts its slide into the plastic tube. It stops with his head sticking out of the end. He can't quite see the edge but a soft white shape at the bottom of his vision lets him know it's there. The visual barrier is somehow comforting.

This machine probably costs more than my house. My old house.

Viktor squeezes his lids shut and allows himself to succumb to the sounds. The blaring of the music that's so loud he can't even distinguish the beats. The repetitive jack-hammering of the magnets within the machine, both digital and penetrating. The eventual overwhelming silence in the sensory-deprived space, as a symphony of noise that is only discernible in its randomness and chaos, becomes normal. He rests his eyes, somewhere between awake and asleep, counting down the minutes in his mind.

Forty-four.

NOW

DAY 1,809 – EASTERN TENNESSEE

The musty smell of damp leaves and the airy crackle of fresh ones falling among the branches toward the soggy earth may as well be the alarm clock of the wild. It's been almost five years since waking up in the comfort of his home. It has been almost as many nights since he's had trouble falling asleep. Something about survival instincts that never switch off is a great recipe for falling asleep fast, his mind taking the rest whenever offered. For a moment, he allows himself to contemplate what it must have been like for early humans, waking in a dark cave, not knowing if the fire has lasted the night or if a clever beast is about to clamp down on their throat.

I'm up. Viktor props himself on his elbows, boards creaking under the shift of his weight. Shards of light dance in through the branches and gaps in the walls that surround his canopy shelter. This isn't his first treehouse, though it is quite a step up from the long-forgotten hideaway he started some thirty years ago as a child. He has dozens now that are located within a single day's walk of each other, but none stand as sophisticated or homelike as this one. The diameter of his circular shelter network spans almost 100 miles in all directions, extending his ability to scavenge and never be too far from a safe nighttime retreat.

Living in houses or buildings would be easier, but the lingering memories that live on within, both before and after the collapse, combined with claustrophobic interiors that offer little means of escape, proved too much for him to bear. *There's safety in the trees*, he tells himself when jaded by the struggles of living outdoors. Viktor has grown to admire the ability of the human body to adapt, finding comfort in even the most harrowing of situations. Like soldiers finding rest in a trench, thankful to have their heads down and still attached.

The idea of tucking himself into strangers' sheets, placing his head on pillows that still contain their sweat and saliva, is far too unsettling. The sights and smells of people lingering long after they've gone. But his mind told him it was safe. *They can't open doors. They're loud and slow.* Or so he thought.

The old world meant safety, but no longer. *Dead traps*, he calls them, the buildings and homes of the past. Now he enters for as long as he must and never stays the night. There are other reasons for his dedication to this particular tree, but he allows fear to be the excuse, a common trait in the world of the dead that needs no further self-explanation. Safe from the grasping fingers and chomping teeth. Safe from the rabid beasts with their sharp, impaling antlers. Safe from the roaming pillagers seeking survivors as their prey.

He stands, shaking out his limbs. The floor is hard and his bedding is soft enough, but this does little to prevent kinks and aches during the night. The thick thermal blankets keep him from changing positions, causing further pains to attend to each morning. Stretching out his joints as he walks, Viktor crosses the twelve-foot length of the floor from the bed to the opposite end. Four half-walls rise from each corner, stopping in height just below his shoulders, allowing for an unobstructed view out into the trees. The main support is a massive oak, several feet in diameter, its thick branches supporting the weight of the shelter that rests ten feet above the ground.

Stacked along the floor in an organized line, several labeled plastic bins serve as his clothing, food, and electronics storage. Viktor navigates around them as he reaches a power strip and flips the button, feeling satisfied when the orange light glows. A dirty, nicked power cable runs from the strip, along the base of the floor, up to a small side table and ending at a plastic single cup coffee maker. He checks the filter and turns it on. Grabbing a metal thermos from the floor, he pours drinking water into the top of the machine and presses a button. It begins to spit and steam. The whir of the pump dies as a few drops of coffee make it into the pot. He presses the brew button a few times. Nothing. He traces the cord back to the power strip where the orange light is now as dead as the coffee maker. He toggles it off and then back on anyway.

"Shit," he mutters, looking upward.

Moving to the other side of the floor next to his sleeping roll, Viktor pulls down a hinged step attached to a large vertical branch. After sliding into his worn boots, he steps onto the first rung and reaches up to the slatted metal roof where he slides a lynchpin out of place. Pushing up, the hatch opens outward and drops adjacent to the opening with a bang. He pulls himself up and out of the treehouse and onto the roof. The sheeting has proved invaluable during the rainy months and while it looks disjointed, not attached to the walls or floor, it's secured to the upper branches. It's his proudest achievement of the entire build. Most of the canopy branches have been trimmed away so that he may slide over to the rope ladder that lies coiled next to the edge. He kicks the ladder over the side and it unravels down to the ground below. He waits, listens.

Silence. Good.

He'll still wait a few more moments before peering over the side to confirm a safe descent. The thought of being attacked while climbing down the swaying rope ladder is a frightening one, a simple snag of the heel could mean a certain and horrible, inverted death. It's been a long time since any have stumbled on this particular tree, but that doesn't keep him from acting as if a whole crowd is standing by for any indication of his presence.

Once on the ground, Viktor walks along a thick black cable that runs from the base of the treehouse, down along the trunk, over a thick root jutting from the dirt and then into the earth via a small conduit sticking out a few inches from the soil. Buried a foot underground, the cable travels straight into a clearing to the northeast. The possibility of needing to dig any of it up to troubleshoot the outage raises his blood pressure. He tracks along the narrow but defined dirt path that leads from the tree to the small open field. Bark and stones have been trampled into the dirt over the years under his own feet, forming a pavement-like surface.

Just outside the reach of the far trees' shadows that are cast from the rising sun, the cable flows out of a piece of conduit and ends at a large contraption of scrap metal sitting on elevated feet in the center of the square, open acre. The tall grass and weeds have been beaten back just enough to access all points around the structure, and still act as a semi-camouflage when looking at the clearing. Nested on top of the rectangle, and the only part visible above growth, is a six-foot-wide solar panel. Viktor examines the surface, brushing it with his hands. Dirt and grime smear as his fingers slide across the dark blue squares. Pieces of the membrane underneath peel away with the motion. He looks at his hand and back to the panel.

"That'll do it." He pats the solar panel and wipes his hands together.

Viktor checks the cables leading from the panel to the wooden box below that houses four car batteries. No corrosion or dead animals zapped inside, all connections look secure, no evidence of any issues there. This particular unit has lasted almost four years so he's not very surprised when it's determined to be the fault in the system, though he's disappointed in himself that he didn't check the battery depletion the day before. *No harm done,* he thinks. *Time to get a new solar panel.* And he knows just the place to find one.

He grabs his walking stick, capped by a burnt and sharpened point, as well as a matte-black hand axe with a silver-tipped blade and a trident punch-out. He slips the handle into his belt.

It was by chance that his old rusty hatchet had fallen apart and so he was on the lookout for a new tool. The young boy's bedroom where he found the upgrade was decorated with a folded flag and a shadow box with dog tags and various military patches. On the wall above the shelf was a proud display containing the axe. At the time he wondered about the boy, and what the weapon meant to him. Viktor often finds himself daydreaming of the dead, especially when it comes to their belongings, every item containing a story of a life that now seems as far away as fiction.

He exits the tree the same way as before. From the ground he pulls on a rope that coils the ladder back to the roof, tying it off in the branches of a large bush. The combination lock on the roof hatch would require bolt cutters and the overhang of the roof would be almost impossible to slip in over the walls.

Viktor plots a course on an old road atlas map, red circles dotting several locations as well as his current spot, with symbols for supplies and scribbles for places to avoid. He heads due south through the forest, the top of the treehouse shining like a candle behind him as the morning sun breaks through the canopy and projects a glare off of the aluminum roof.

THEN

Whirs, *buzzes, pops, eerie mechanical adjustments, horrendous music.* Somehow the cacophony has just about tranced Viktor to sleep. The repetitive banging of the magnets scanning his lower back and hip for the mysterious villain that has been the cause of great discomfort, creates a different kind of agony while lulling his mind to that weird plane between awake and dreaming.

The beat of the music competes with the rhythmic thud that surrounds him. He tries to make the two sounds sync tempo in his head, as he often would while driving: the wiper blades, the turn signal, and the beat of the radio, always just a fraction off from one another. Now the slight variance is almost as torturous as the volume itself, but the effort to align them is interrupted when he struggles to hear something else. Something outside of this contraption, outside of this room.

Knocking? Pounding? It sounds like a fist on glass. The screech of a desk moving across tile. *Maybe a scream? Can't be.* He doesn't hear this so much as feels the different frequencies penetrate through his body. Then a click. The MRI has stopped. He thinks he still hears the music but that has also quit, all that remains are the echoing leftovers that his cochlear hair cells are struggling to expel from his auditory memory.

Viktor tilts his eyes as far up into his head as he can manage, attempting to see the room behind him. He's trying hard not to move his body in case the test restarts. Half an hour into the total scan he's not about to risk causing a do-over. After what seems like several minutes, but is closer to just one, Viktor decides to squeeze the bulb that is still clenched in his left hand. He expects Cathy's voice to patch in asking if everything is okay, or explaining the delay but no response comes. There's also no beep to confirm he pressed the bulb hard enough to register, so he squeezes it once more, holding it all the way down for a moment to ensure it worked this time. Still, silence. He allows the buzzer to fall to the side, dangling from the cord that runs the length of the table.

Reaching up, trying not to disturb his position, feeling for the outside of the headphones, he carefully removes them from over his ears, and places them on his chest. His ears ache as the blood returns to the outer cartilage that was being pinched by the tight cushions. There's tension in his shoulders and neck as he's anticipating a loud, chastising burst over an intercom for ruining the test. He'll make up an excuse, bathroom break maybe, as any moment Cathy will scold him from the other room. But it never happens.

"Hello?" Viktor listens. "Miss Cathy? Are we finished?"

He tries to roll onto his side to have a look, but he's still buried within the tube with little wiggle room beyond what extends above his shoulders. When they asked about claustrophobia this isn't what came to mind. In a pre-panic, Viktor forces his arms in front of his face to try to find traction on the lip of the entry. Not quite as limber as he once was, and his forearms now damp with sweat from the heated towel, the skin on his arms slide against the inside roof, sticking to the smooth plastic and pinning his biceps and elbows around his face. Like a boxer trying to avoid a punch, Viktor writhes left and right with his elbows until they break free and land back on his chest and knock away the headphones that bounce and fall toward the floor outside of the tube. The audio cable tightens across his neck as the headphones swing a foot off the ground.

You're a bloody fool, he thinks, mortified at how embarrassed he will be if anyone is watching his inept struggle from the other room. As he positions his arms back flat against the bench to his sides the silence is broken. A hinge.

Was it the door?

"Cathy?" he says like a child about to be berated by an angry parent, expecting her to come to his aid as the mess of cable and towel and gown are a far cry from how he started the procedure. The sound of a rubber sole sliding. Then a heavy step. The door is still open as Viktor can hear a commotion somewhere outside his MRI room. The thick door bounces against something soft as it swings to close under its weight. Another *slide*. Another *thump*. The noises from outside the room strobe as the door swings through and then settles, closed.

"Is someone there? Can you help get me out of this please?"

That sound. For the first time, Viktor hears the noise that will haunt him every day and night for the rest of his life. Like a baby taking a long breath mid-sleep, but the airway is obstructed by a sludge of mucus and sharp, gravel-like material. Deep and visceral. Primal and terrifying. He would call it a growl but it's more human than animal, and void of any modern recognizable traits. Something instinctual fires within him. An ancient voice passed down thousands of years lying dormant until this very instant. A beast is in the cave and the fire has gone out.

Move!

Viktor's head pounds with adrenaline as his eyesight narrows into a spotlight of focus. He pushes and jabs his arms against the sides of the walls. He's able to inch himself backward on the table, gauging his progress by the amount of ceiling he can see beyond the lip of the tube. He's not alone. The drag, the thump. Drag. Thump. Horrible, guttural, wheezing.

He throws his hands up to the top of the tube and pulls, lifting his upper body off the table. He repeats the move, this time pushing with his feet and moving his ass back. Almost out of the machine, Viktor throws off the headphones that still hang from around his neck and rolls himself out of the scanning device and onto the cold tile floor. An instant stab of pain shoots through his right leg and into his hip.

"Fuck!" he howls.

Using one hand to prop against the table above, he pulls himself up to his knees. From overhead, a shadow falls toward him and his instincts make him cower back toward the tile. As he puts his weight on his right hand that braces the floor, it slides on something wet, sending his face and body downward. Looking at his outstretched hand, the simultaneous realization of blood on the floor and the monster above him hit at full speed. Viktor flips onto his back in a defensive position with arms up.

Caught on the MRI table above him, Cathy's distorted face hangs down inches from his own, her teeth gnashing, the same deep, unnatural growl flowing from within. Her arms swing and slash as he kicks and moves on the floor. He's able to get a foot against the base of the table and drives himself back to create distance. Cathy's painted nails slice at his gown. He can feel the searing cold stone mixing with warm blood against the bare skin of his back where the robe parts, the knot poking into his lower back as he squirms.

Rolling over on hands and knees, Viktor crawls toward the door, stumbling in the trail of dark red. Metal and plastic clank and snap at the tube behind him. He reaches the door and uses the frame to pull himself up, bare feet sliding in the gore beneath him.

What used to be Cathy is now free of the table and staggering his way. He struggles to gain footing so he can launch himself through the doorway.

"Come on!" he yells as his heel slides out, causing his knee to smash into the door.

She's closer. It's only now that he burns the picture of her in his mind. Torn flesh missing from her neck. Half of her face hanging to one side. Blood staining her blue scrubs that have turned black with saturation. He can't even remember her real face, just the awful nightmare that's chomping toward him.

"No, no, no, no, no!"

He drives himself forward, pushing into the door as she lunges onto his shoulder, her weight pulling on the robe as she collapses, almost taking him to the ground. From the floor, she snaps and bites at his bare legs. Holding himself up by just the frame, he kicks at her, somehow avoiding the clenching of her teeth.

Realizing he's done for if he doesn't make a move, Viktor steps onto her writhing body to gain traction and uses the leverage to dive through the door. Without an inch to spare between his body and the opening he lands in the next room, scrambles to his back, and kicks the door closed behind him. It bounces off of Cathy's face and pops open again on his side before closing altogether.

He's on his ass with hands propped behind him. Cathy's body falls against the other side of the door with a loud thud and it drifts open. Without hesitation, he throws his shoulder forward and slams the door shut against her. The tip of a severed finger flies past as a moan erupts from the other side.

Cathy is inches from his face, separated by only the thickness of the wooden door. He cringes at the sight of Cathy's wretched, polished index finger lying next to him. He can feel her weight on the other side and responds with equal force.

Viktor pants with little control, feeling every heartbeat like a hammer to the chest. Trying to catch his breath, he rests one hand on his heart while glancing down at the shadow moving underneath the gap of the door. A soft, repetitious thud accompanied by what is now nine scratching fingers, taunts from the other side.

"Wake up. Wake up. Wake up," he chants between breaths.

NOW

Desolation. Streets, buildings, and hastily built military installations, all share one thing in common: emptiness. Walking among them feels like exploring an ancient civilization, akin to the Mayan ruins or historic cities of Athens and Rome. Though this experience is much different than the honeymoon abroad he shared with Sandra almost twenty years ago. He isn't elbow-to-elbow with tourists fighting for the perfect photo, or dodging street sellers and beggars among plump vacationers. Now Viktor is as ancient and archaic as his surroundings, a vestige of the past, soon enough to be a relic like the faded buildings of this quaint main street of which he strolls down the centerline. But unlike the great structures and humans of history, he will not be remembered, not in the world as it exists now. It's as much a blank canvas as modern society has seen and destined to be erased forever, washed away with whatever comes next.

What could possibly come after this?

Viktor had grown accustomed to being alone, even before everything went to shit. He never expected that the pure absence of human contact, like the brush of a stranger walking by or the ambient coughs in a crowded room that before would go unnoticed, are now painful in their absence. His mind wanders to the thought that this is nothing like the movies, books, and shows that had fantasized about the end of the world. It feels more like living in an unfinished tale. A book with half the pages torn out, a film where the projector dies leaving the audience aghast and clamoring to find out how it all ends, a show canceled before it could wrap up its character arcs. There are no answers to be had, no possibility of continuation or closure, it's just over and the hopelessness of that reality far outweighs the prospect of rebuilding society anew.

As he walks down the barren street, he pictures the abandoned and rusted cars with their drivers at the helms, commuters, people fleeing, all dead the same. He's traveled this road before and doesn't take the time to loot the cars that he's already checked as today the search is for something specific.

Wildlife, of all kinds, have become the new rulers of the land, if not the dead. While most are still scared of his presence, he's careful to avoid large predators. Bears and coyotes are common enough. More abundant and curious now that humans are scarce. With no shortage of food now that they have free reign, they seem to be less aggressive, but he still takes no chances. One thing is certain, none of these animals seem to be affected by the disease, if anything they're flourishing. Except for one species.

Patient zero.

Viktor freezes at the sound of hooves clacking on the pavement somewhere in the street behind him. With as little movement as possible, his hand slides to his belt, the other gripping the staff. He pulls the axe out of the loop and wraps his fingers around the handle. Looking over his shoulder, he turns with a calculation to each degree that he moves. Like navigating a minefield, he carefully places his foot first, then pivots his body to face the direction of the sound that was behind him, ready in case such a beast has found him.

He exhales a sigh of relief.

"Just a pig."

A hundred feet or so down the street, in the middle of a crosswalk, a dark gray and white pig sniffs and scratches at the pavement. The animal is massive, standing what looks to be three feet to the top of its ears, and seems to not mind Viktor watching it scrape at the defiant grass and roots that thrive in the cracks of the asphalt. Its hairy back and tail twitch in the wind, low and eager grunts blow out of a wet snout as it huffs at the dirt.

Viktor calls out a soft whistle through his thumb and finger.

"Hey boy, hey!"

The pig's ears perk up, but otherwise, it pays no attention. It scrapes the ground again and continues walking along the crosswalk. Viktor takes a few more steps toward it, extending an arm out and waving.

"Come on, boy. Over here." He has not the heart to kill it, nor the desire to slaughter and prepare it. There's enough to scavenge that such efforts seldom pay off. But he does desire a momentary connection with something alive, maybe a pet on its back or a wet kiss of the snout as it smells an offered hand.

Closing the distance with caution, Viktor continues stepping toward the grazing animal. It snorts in the dirt and tugs at the roots of a weed with large white teeth. Mid chew it throws its head and ears up. The hair on Viktor's neck stands. He recognizes the behavior as his own.

A threat. Viktor scans the area. To his horror, he sees what the pig has yet to witness: scurrying into the street a young boy moves toward the animal. His clothes are tattered and stained dark brown and crimson. A single arm is outstretched as he moves with speed, the other shoulder has a gaping hole saturated with blood. In a matter of seconds, the boy has closed the distance on the pig. The black and white face looks to Viktor, as if just now noticing his presence, its snout wiggles as eyes read his body language. He whistles again, louder, trying to spook the animal to run. Its ears perk up again and locks eyes with Viktor's. He takes a step forward thrusting his staff in the air.

"Get out of here, go on!"

The pig scuffs a hoof on the pavement, a defensive move to get Viktor to back off. From the other side of the street, a group of the dead staggers into the road. They converge on the animal. By the time the pig realizes that Viktor isn't the real threat, it's too late. The boy is first to lunge at the hindquarters. A fierce kick knocks the child back with a horrific *crunch*. The five other attackers surround the pig, pulling it down, biting, scratching, pulling out its hair. The boy crawls toward the pile, his hips and legs twisted outward. He crawls atop the other dead and tears into the pig's flesh. The animal squeals and cries below the flailing of arms and hands. Bodies rise and fall on top of the struggling prey.

Viktor cowers at the death throes of the animal. The screams fade but the animal still thrashes on its side. As one of the ravenous dead pulls what looks to be the pig's esophagus toward a decayed mouth, the sharp end of the staff gets there first. It groans and falls motionless to the street. The other dead growl and swipe at Viktor, but with speed and precision he executes them one by one. First with the staff and then with the swift, precise blows of the axe blade to the skull. In a heap of blood and gore, where pieces of human and animal are now indistinguishable, the boy crawls to the summit of mount death. Viktor wipes his brow, watches the dead child for a moment, then drives the staff straight down through his eye socket and into the exposed rib cage of the pig. The pile looks like a sandwich of macabre, complete with a toothpick to top it off.

After he catches his breath, Viktor rummages through the stack of bodies. He examines every pocket he can discern from the blood-soaked clothing. With each wallet that he finds, he removes the driver's license, places it in his top chest pocket, and tosses the leather back into the pile. He even finds a purse among the spoils, doing the same with the license, but ensuring nothing of use remains inside before he tosses it aside. Once he's done searching, he counts five IDs and three cell phones.

Not a bad haul.

Viktor steps around the pile and places a hand on the staff, with a firm yank upward, he releases it from the grip of carnage. As it slides from the boy's skull, the bottom half splinters and falls to the ground. He examines the broken staff and throws it to the pavement.

"Son of a bitch." He liked that particular weapon.

Now armed with just his axe, and the proof of existence of a few dead strangers, Viktor walks down main street. He checks the road atlas with the intersection sign overhead and steps toward his next marker. With his staff now gone, he'll need to make a quick detour.

THEN

edge the door. Before committing to giving his legs a rest, he scans the room for anything he can use to block the entrance. Viktor spots a rolling desk chair that is lying on its side, a dried-up fountain centerpiece in a lake of blood. Still applying light pressure with his feet and being careful not to open it himself, he stretches to grasp the chair wheel hovering in midair. After some struggle and compromising a single foot position and a good amount of leverage, he's able to get his fingers around the wheel and drag the chair toward him. He takes a second to analyze the chair and figures he can wedge it under the counter with the seat lift.

He spins the legs like a game show wheel, looking between it and the door. The noises from the other side have grown louder, closer. From underneath, a faint shadow fills the space under the door. He's got to get out of this room and get help, but to do so means leaving the door insecure while he searches for his locker key among the upturned room.

There's no door to the hallway, just an opening in the wall where up until this moment little sound has been heard since he escaped the chamber. Breaking the silence is a wretched scream, that of a man, and something metallic sliding across tile.

Fuck. One threat at a time.

He springs to his feet, wincing in pain having forgotten what brought him there in the first place. Viktor lifts the chair into the air and throws the feet down against the edge of the desk. Wheels snap and fly off, bouncing around the room. He turns the chair upright, spins the legs so the wheel-less stubs touch the floor, and jams the back of the seat up under the counter and in front of the door. Yanking up on the lever, the back of the cushion rises into the overhang. A loud crash rattles against the door.

The opening cracks a fraction of an inch, but the chair holds. Growling penetrates through the door from the other side. Viktor steps back, eyes fixed on the chair as the door bounces against resistance. He scatters around the room, opening boxes and containers, drawers, and cabinets. It's all he can do to keep his balance against the blood-covered tiles. He flips over anything and everything, but there's no sign of the small brass key or the orange wrist strap it was attached to.

"Key, key, where's the damn key?" Hearing his own voice brings a sense of comfort.

Another bang on the door and the chair moves. It's all that stands between Cathy's insatiable hunger and the meaty buffet of his trembling body. Somehow, it holds. If even by accident she can wedge her fingers between the door, it won't take long for her to get through. He has felt her unnatural strength and it was almost as unsettling as her grotesque appearance. Viktor checks the last of the room but finds no key. The dish that it was placed in lies upturned on the floor but is also empty. On the counter, hanging from a broken lanyard and smeared with someone's blood, Cathy's ID badge stares back at him. He grabs it, not knowing if he might need to access a locked door.

In a tall cabinet, door bent and hanging by a single hinge, Viktor finds a pair of dark blue scrubs. He checks the pockets just in case, but there's only lint. Realizing that he's underdressed in the loose-fitting exam gown, he holds the pants up to his legs. They're short but the waist looks like it will fit. He pulls his gown over his head, standing in the center of the room in only his gray boxer-briefs. With some pain, Viktor manages to get both legs into the scrubs and ties the waistband knot. They're loose in the midsection and about a foot too short. They look more like capris than pants. He slides into the top which fits a little better. It's baggy in the chest but tight on his biceps and also too short, ending above his waist but just covering his navel.

The next crash does the trick as the chair falls to the floor. The door surges toward him before retreating and stopping without warning. Stained fingers and torn nails creep around the crack, pulling the door inward. He can make out the severed stub along with the others that now create an opening. His flight instinct kicks in as he hurdles over the chair and makes his way toward the hallway. In an instant, Cathy lurches forward and is through the door, but she's tangled in the chair. Her twisted body spasming, grasping for him as he escapes the room.

Sliding on one foot, Viktor glides out into the corridor. The aftermath of whatever took place looks like a grenade went off in every room. Holes in drywall, blood, and flesh scattered in every corner and walkway, but there are no bodies. An odd thing to notice as he runs down the once sterile path, the patter of his damp feet echoing on the hard surface.

"Help! Anyone? I need help!" he shouts as he runs.

He sees the lobby up ahead and beyond are the main office doors, propped wide open. Outside, the concrete overhang lies in shadow, a breezeway between office buildings on the first floor. If he can make it outside, he can try to call the police.

Maybe they're already here, he hopes. *There has to be a SWAT team outside waiting for the order to enter. If he can just show them that he's alive, they'll quickly come to his aid.*

His brain and upper body stop, but his feet don't receive the message. Viktor almost hits the floor again but stays upright by planting a hand to the tile. Huddled just before the exit, a group of the dead is feasting where patients and their families once sat while waiting for their turn to be called back. Tearing flesh and organs, gnashing and growling, unaware or unencumbered by one another, but all shredding. All ravenous. He notices some of the dead in scrubs, others wearing gowns, some still in plain clothes. One man is naked, his testicles hanging down from a crouched and predatory stance over a poor soul, like a hyena scavenging a stolen kill. Jeans and fabric clutter the floor, tatters of clothing from the victims left scattered around the lobby.

Is that a badge?

On the floor just past the dead, a shiny object lies on a square of the bloody fabric of the doormat. Beyond, he now realizes what's holding the main doors open. The bottom half of a person, black dress slacks, a shoe off and scattered aside. A belt with a gun still in a holster. Entrails lead from the lower half in a horrible spaghetti pattern that points back to the attackers.

They haven't seen him yet. Viktor creeps beside the nurse's station, planning his path to the door. The naked man stops feasting for a moment, turning his head toward the counter with clouded, empty eyes staring in Viktor's direction. After a tense moment with Viktor cowering behind the counter, the man snaps his head back to the body before him.

Not wasting a second, Viktor sprints for the lobby door then slides along the floor until he stops at the disconnected body. He yanks the gun out of the holster and draws aim at the feasting nurses, doctors, and patients who were something else entirely not an hour before. The polymer grip of the gun feels awkward in his hand, unable to remember the last time he held one and surprised by its weight. His hand trembles, nervous of the kick should he have to fire.

By some miracle they haven't noticed him. Strands of human flesh still fly about in the frenzy. He takes a step back out of the entrance, but hesitates as his bare feet make contact with the rough concrete of the sidewalk. Viktor kneels alongside the body and removes one of the victim's shoes. He grabs the mate that was already cast aside and with soft footsteps runs out of the office, into a world that he could have never imagined.

NOW

The doors and windows to the storefront are locked and no signs of break-in or disruption. Above, GUNS & PAWN in large red letters, holes and cracks marking each one, spans the rectangular sign that hangs over the door. It's been years since he even held a gun, preferring the proximity and silence of the staff. Like vehicles, the noise firearms carry may as well be a dinner bell to any flesh-eaters within a couple of miles. Not to mention the trained ears of survivors with nefarious intent that could pinpoint his location as soon as a second round is fired. While ammo is a bit easier to come by than clean fuel, Viktor still prefers the quiet simplicity of hand-to-hand combat. A single jam or bullet miscount could prove fatal, where a pointy end stabs equally every time. Until it splinters in a heap of dead bodies, anyway. He rubs his hand along the axe in his belt as if weighing the pros and cons of evolving his medieval weapons.

More untouched places like this gun store exist than he would have expected. Everything went south so fast that looting didn't take place until after it all went to shit. He figured people were either eating each other or being eaten and had no time to grab supplies for such measures. Now, with so few people left in comparison to the goods available, some stores are still somewhat intact as if shuttered for a storm. On occasion, they're unlocked and ripe for the picking, though none within his circle remain untapped or unsecured. He contemplates this as he examines the chain wrapped around the door. This particular store owner must have anticipated coming back at some point.

Poor bastard's likely digested by now.

"Hell with it." Viktor slides the spike end of the hand axe into the loop of the padlock and begins twisting the handle. The rusty chain turns and coils until it snaps against the torque of the axe. The weight from the chain unravels itself and falls to the ground, clanking at his feet. Readying the blade face to strike, he places a hand on the door pull and cracks it open just a few inches. An odor hits him square in the face causing an instant gag. He shoves his face into the sleeve of his arm.

Is that a dead smell or a dead, dead smell?

The world is rotten and Viktor knows the aroma all too well. Every dead smells the same, but they typically carry more of a fresh death scent than that of a decaying body. The dead smell like a butchered animal strung up in a cooler. Cold blood, with a hint of sourness, to the contrast of spoilage from a rotting corpse. Perhaps this is the result of continuous exposure to the fresh human flesh of their victims. Either way, it's a pungent odor he has yet grown accustomed to, as if recognizing the extinguishing of human life and the instinctual danger it represents.

This time he can't be sure as the exposure was so brief, but if he had to guess it was closer to long decay, the preferable option. With the axe poised, he pulls the door all the way open toward the street, letting the thick, foul air billow out in a mass escape from years of confinement. He struggles not to breathe through his nose.

After a few moments, Viktor cocks his head back and forth, peering into the dark shop before committing to a single step inside. Once the air has had a chance to dissipate, or dilute, since the smell of death is perpetual after it hits the nostrils, he creeps into the shop and allows the door to shut behind him. It's confirmed by a bell jingle, one that he hadn't heard the first time as the warm blast of stink had hit him in the face.

Heel, toe, heel, toe, Viktor moves deeper into the store. Shafts of daylight reach in through the barred windows that face the street, adding just enough ambient light to be able to make his way around the space without knocking into anything.

"Ah, fuck!"

He jumps back. A shotgun is pointing inches from his face as he stares down the double-barrel like the reverse end of binoculars. A cobweb dangles from the end of the gun, swaying so close that it almost touches his nose as it dances in the drafty air.

Lucky for him, the person behind the trigger is a shell of a threat. What appears to once have been an older, bearded man is now just a hollowed and decayed skeleton with thinned skin pulled taut over the jaunt edges of bones, looking more like transparent paper than flesh. Seated by the counter, the long-dead shop owner has the gun propped up and aimed at the door. His right arm grips the shotgun, bent and withered fingers looking like they would snap like twigs if Viktor dared to move them, the gun itself resting on the arm of the chair.

In the man's left hand hangs a large, silver revolver, holding on by a fingertip. The sunken eye sockets rest in front of the bullet's path through the temple that ended his life. Viktor notices the entry point and the large exit wound on the other side that blew out a chunk of skull the size of a baseball.

"Poor old nut."

He wonders who locked the man inside, or if it was on request, a captain going down with the ship maybe. That seems unlikely, but the whole picture looks unusual.

He looks around the store, now taking stock of all the dusty guns that still line the walls and glass cases. Rows of rifles, hunting and semi-automatic, shotguns, and crossbows fill racks on both walls. The cases are filled with handguns, large and small. A compact, pink-camouflage one catches his eye. A sign stands upright on the counter above:

LADIES CONCEALED WEAPONS COURSE $50,
SEE AN ASSOCIATE

Viktor hops over the counter, careful not to disturb the body, and pulls down an intimidating tactical shotgun. He's only ever fired a handgun, but he likes the no-aim defense this one has to offer. After looking it over he finds a lever that extends the stock. He pulls it to his shoulder to get a feel, aiming around the room at the stuffed animal mounts that line the tops of the gun racks. Viktor grabs the vertical foregrip tight and snaps left and right. It feels solid and firm in his grasp. It's a weird calming sensation to him, the sense of safety it brings even knowing full well it's empty of any ammunition. There's danger in that reliance, he's quick to recognize.

This will do.

He vaults back over the counter, shotgun in hand, and combs the display in the center aisle of the store. He pulls off a large plastic package and tears it open. The sling dangles out and he straightens it between both hands. Clipping it onto the shotgun stock, he tosses it over his shoulder and lets the gun hang down to his waist, uncomfortable with how close the muzzle rests next to his groin. His insecurity prevails as if a dozen gun enthusiasts are watching him fumble with the weapon, pretending like he knows what he's doing.

On the way out of the door, he grabs several boxes of shells. He loads the gun to capacity and stores the rest in his backpack. The added weight is substantial. He stops at the glass counter that holds the handguns. Using the back of his axe, he smashes the top glass and clears out the shards. For a moment he doesn't know which to select but then he finds the perfect one. The pink-camouflage handgun is lighter than he expected as he mock-aims with it buried between his hands. He laughs to himself and sets it back inside the shattered case.

With utmost respect for the dead, Viktor unhooks the revolver from the shop owner's finger with a gentle tug. The last bit of moist skin is stubborn and the peeling snap of separation gives him a shudder. It's heavy in his hand and gives him a second thought. For a moment he considers putting it back among the rigid fingers but instead leaves it on the counter.

"Sorry amigo, rest easy." Feeling the pockets of the hollow body, Viktor finds a wallet and cellphone. He pulls out the man's ID, giving it a once-over.

"Leonard Mon—Monsalt-- Monsaltier?" he stutters.

The Tennessee license is in impeccable shape, though the heavy-set man in the photo with the salt and pepper beard and thick-rimmed glasses can't be the Halloween decoration that rests before him. On his way out he stashes the driver's license in his upper pocket and the phone in his bag.

"Later, Len!" he calls as he steps back out onto the street.

For a moment, the brightness blinds him as he emerges from the darkness of the shop and into full sun. He picks up the chain and wraps it back around the door handle, even though the lock is busted. Only serving as a visual barrier if anyone wanted to get in, but at least enough to keep out the dead should he ever return this way.

Each of his interactions with the gun that he now carries is cumbersome and clumsy. Nervousness, combined with the undue adrenaline that courses just from handling it, makes him feel inept at self-defensive by firearms. He tries to calm his nerves with controlled breathing and worries about the day when he might have to shoot it. For now, the shotgun hangs to his side as he opens the road atlas, tracing his next path that leads out of town. He walks the rest of the way down main street to the last intersection and takes a left.

THEN

Red everywhere. Shades of crimson, bright stoplight red, some pink with flecks of white. There's so much blood that Viktor can hardly focus putting one bare foot in front of the other as he runs along the concrete sidewalk that leads out of the office breezeway and into the main parking lot. He's careful to step over chunks of flesh and large pools of dark blood that have begun soaking into the porous pavement.

A small, white hatchback with a thick, blue paint stripe along the doors sits parked at an angle facing the doctor's office. Its LED headlights are dim in the daylight but shine onto the large glass windows of the building. Screams and shouting echo elsewhere in the parking lot. The blare of a horn in the distance.

Viktor hobbles to the vehicle as it's the closest thing to him. Without his car keys, he makes no effort to go into the lot for his own. He can come back for it later when they find his wallet and phone, after everything goes back to normal. For now, he just needs to get home, his old home, he couldn't care less about the apartment. At the moment it could be ablaze and it would not deter him from his mission.

The driver's side door is still ajar and the yellow lights on top flash on and off. A streak of red has smeared across the security company's logo that sits inset on the blue stripe. He peers into the backseat before hopping in, an old habit he used to badger Sandra about whenever she would go shopping alone. *Always check the backseat*, he would say, which in turn was met with a dismissive nod or little acknowledgment.

Nearby, screams followed by gunshots reverberate off the four-story building, but it's all peripheral. Viktor finds it all but impossible to focus on such directional things in the moment, it all feels so heavy and close. He fights against tunnel vision as the car seems to be the only thing he can see. The scrubs ride up his legs as he steps down into the car and tosses the shoes and gun into the passenger seat, yanking the door shut behind him. He winces in pain as he drops into the low bucket seat of the small vehicle.

Grabbing the shoes, he crams his size ten feet into the size nine sneakers. They're damp against his arches and toes and he hopes it's only sweat. Something told him the car was already running but it's silent on the inside. There are no keys, just an ignition button, but a quick look at the dash display and it suddenly makes sense.

"Electric!" he chants as he shifts the car from park into drive. It kicks forward with more pep than he expected.

The gun slides on the passenger seat and Viktor snags it before it can tumble to the floor and out of reach. He fumbles around attempting to put it barrel down into the cup holder as he weaves and accelerates through the parking lot, dodging other cars left driverless in the middle of the lanes. Something obstructs the gun and he looks down between swerves and sees another ID lanyard and a cellphone taking up the space. Using the tip of the gun, he bends the ID just enough to see the picture and read the name as his eyes dart between it and the obstacle course of the parking lot.

Sammy Hernandez, A.C.E. Security Solutions.

"Unlucky," he sighs.

Registering that there is a phone next to him, Viktor jams the barrel into the crease in the passenger seat cushion to prevent it from moving.

He picks up the phone and presses the side button, praying it isn't locked. The screen illuminates, displaying several missed calls and an endless list of text messages and voicemail notifications. While managing to turn out from the parking lot and onto the main road, he dials 10 digits in desperation and hits the large green call icon. He has to yank the steering wheel hard to avoid a truck flying by that takes up both lanes. A moment later he realizes the driver of the truck, a blur of a shape, was the first person alive that he's seen since he crawled into the MRI tube. He's relieved that he's not alone. It lasts but a moment as a loud collision and flash come from behind him. In the rearview mirror, he sees pieces of metal fly through the air and a small fireball that was once the truck.

It's the ceasing of the internal ring that brings him back to the phone. Not a voicemail system or a dial tone, but dead, silent air. He double takes the screen which displays a connected notification over a timer counting upward from zero minutes and zero seconds.

"Sandra! Sandra! Are you there?" he gasps, eyes darting back to the road. "Can you hear me? Say something. Please!"

"I-,-ere. He---, --n -ou--her- me?" A woman's voice is barely distinguishable.

"Hey! You're breaking up. Sandra!

"-elp, -fect --ing t- ki--. De--. HEL--!" the voice screams in a cracked and choppy transmission before the phone beeps and the call is ended.

The bar on top of the phone flashes with a no service indicator.

"Oh, God. Oh, God. Hold on, baby." Viktor tries to floor it, pounding on the wheel. "Move, you piece of shit!"

There's little traffic to contend with as the small electric car zips down the four-lane street, no gridlock or pile-ups to impede his top speed of sixty miles per hour. The few vehicles that drive past are erratic, keeping him vigilant to avoid a crash. Traffic signals and signs are all but ignored as the free-for-all on the roads worsens the longer that he drives. The congestion and panic he expected to encounter, filling him with anxiety as he hung up the phone, is scattered to the shoulder or just abandoned in the center of the street, doors left open. It's all he can do to navigate around them and it's slowing him down. Several emergency vehicles sit abandoned as well, pulled off onto the shoulder with flashers still strobing, no signs of the first responders that left them there.

A shape and blur of a person stumbles from the tree-lined median into his lane. Viktor has no chance of stopping and the front bumper clips at mid-leg, sending the body up and over his mirror and windshield. He catches a glimpse of the jawless face and long blonde hair as it streaks over the glass and disappears behind him, leaving a faint red swoosh across his view. Lasting a fraction of a second, the image of the horrific face still lingers in his mind. The brief guilt of not even twitching toward the brake pedal evaporates with the realization that she was already dead.

For fifteen minutes Viktor drives on, not knowing what he'll find at the home of his ex-wife, imagining every scenario and praying that at the very least Caroline is safe.

Did she make it to school? Maybe they've sheltered in place.

He needs answers and can't get to them fast enough. For a moment he even thinks of Sandra's new husband, Max, hoping the man who is so different from himself is still capable of protecting his family. *His* daughter.

Fewer and fewer vehicles obstruct the road but there are a growing number of people. Dead people or people soon to be dead. There's an overwhelming desire to help each of them but one thing is on his mind, getting to Sandra and Caroline.

A deafening *whoosh* shakes the vehicle and rattles Viktor's insides. He peers up through the windshield as two jets fly over a hundred feet above the road. They're gone just as fast. He's confused by the lack of police or military on the roads, no checkpoints or barricades, no sign of any official resistance to whatever is going down. It doesn't take him long to understand why. They're probably doing what he's doing at that moment, looking for loved ones, trying to get home themselves. After all, what could they possibly do against something so inconceivable? The brave stayed to fight the dead, but now they *are* the dead.

He slides onto a side street and weaves around more bodies and parked cars. Taking a left and then a right, he navigates through the neighborhood that he used to commute through every morning and night. The familiarity is unsettling among the chaos. He's made the trip only twice since he was asked to leave his own home.

Viktor pulls into the driveway and the first thing he notices is the front door is wide open. He throws open his door and feels for the gun in the seat but can't find it. He digs around the edge and on the passenger floor. It must have dislodged during one of his many reckless maneuvers. As his fingers find the cold metal resting on the passenger floor mat, he feels a violent tug on his left leg. With a growl, a large man is pushing himself into the car. Viktor feels a warmth dripping onto his legs and arm.

Max. Shit! He recognizes the dead man as his replacement, though he has never faulted him for it. He inches the gun closer to his grip using the tips of his fingers while fighting the man back with his left forearm. Lucky for Viktor, Max's large frame obstructs his head from pushing further into the tiny car. Bloodied hands stretch out and swipe at the air. Viktor gets a hand around the gun, points it at Max, and pulls the trigger without hesitation. It doesn't go off, just a soft clink. He pistol-whips Max across the face and pulls himself into the passenger seat, wincing at the pain shooting down his leg. He's able to pop open the door and scramble out and onto the ground. Staggering to his feet, he sprints to the front door and slams it behind him, latching the deadbolt for good measure. He checks the gun and releases the safety. He feels stupid but is thankful the mistake didn't cost him his life.

"Sweetie? Sandra?" he calls out. "It's Dad. If you're hiding you can come out, it's safe."

Viktor carefully steps through the foyer of the house. The living room is in complete disarray and the realization that someone fought for their life here hits him like he hit the woman on the street.

"Sandra? Sandra? It's Viktor. I have a gun," he says, hoping to bring them out of hiding.

A low gurgle emanates from the kitchen behind him. From around the island counter, a single hand reaches out and digs into the carpet. Shaking, Viktor aims the gun and steps toward it. He knows the hand but needs to check it out anyway.

"Sandra?" Another hand reaches out, pulling itself forward. One hand, then the other. Blood-soaked hair emerges from behind the low wall. Then the head turns with a crunchy moan.

Sandra. Drawn to tears, Viktor covers his mouth, still aiming the gun in her direction. The body on the floor inches closer, one reach at a time.

"No. No, no, no, no, no," he cries.

Sandra's hollow eyes and distorted face hunger for his flesh.

Her teeth snap open and shut as she creeps closer.

"Caroline! Caroline!" he screams out.

A man of great composure any other time, Viktor can feel the walls now closing in around him. The house, his house, is suffocating him as he watches what was once his wife, the mother of his only child, move closer. He wants to crawl into Sandra's arms and let whatever this thing is take him so that he's no longer alone. The gun shakes in his hand as tears flow free down his face.

Banging and scratching at the door. He looks back to see Max's figure pushing against the glass insert. Then back to Sandra who's just out of reach.

A few moments of pain and it will all be over.

"No, baby. No," he bumbles, snot and spit dripping down.

The gun waivers in his hand.

A loud crash behind him shakes him from the despair of Sandra's blank gaze. Viktor swings his arm around and fires blind, expecting Max to fall at his feet having broken through the door. The smell of gunpowder and ringing in his ears is the only thing he can process. He's dizzy. When he blinks back the tears, he notices the front door is still closed.

There's a body at my feet.

Still seeing Max's silhouette behind the glass, it doesn't register. Nausea and clarity come at the same time, like the head-on collision he narrowly avoided, and now wishes he hadn't. He dry-heaves and doubles over at the sight before him. In a moment of frenetic instinct that will consume every thought and action for the rest of his life, he realizes that he mistakenly discharged a single round into the chest of Caroline.

NOW

A bright orange sign depicting hammers and saws hangs over the store at the end of the strip mall. When he found this place there weren't many useful items that he could salvage from the hair salon, the layaway center, dance studio, or the bakery, which was the biggest disappointment. The hardware store, on the other hand, has proved invaluable many times and worth the round trip.

Glass crunches under his boots as he enters the store with the shotgun draped over his right arm. With careful steps, he makes his way to aisle seven. Among the cheap tools with unusual brand names that were once shipped from a factory on the other side of the world are the specific boxes that sent him on his day quest. He picks up the largest one and looks it over. The eight-foot solar panel, while dusty on the outside, seems to be in the same condition as when it was put on a boat half a world away.

One of the few reports he heard suggested that the outbreak began in a village in China when the disease jumped from the native water deer to humans. A type of chronic wasting disease that emaciated the population while turning them rabid. As he heard the report, he pictured the small deer attacking people with its unique fangs and sharp hooves.

At least ours don't have fangs, he thought at the time. It was little consolation when he remembered the massive antlers of a North American whitetail. In reality, the only thing he fears more than the dead are the rabid deer that stalk the woods and vacant cities. Though far fewer seem to exist than before as he suspects the infected animals don't reproduce, they are still a fast and agile predator and he makes every effort to avoid a chance meeting. Especially with the male antlered variety. It's been over a year since he last saw one and hopes that they have finally died off, but also knows he doesn't have that sort of good fortune.

He places the large solar panel box in a shopping cart, its corners rubbing against the plastic sides of the red basket. Roaming the aisles like any other day. Throwing in a bundle of rope, a new hand saw, it could almost be the old world. A tune comes to his head that he imagines playing over the speakers in the ceiling. Maybe he'll run into an old friend and talk shop. *Dad business,* as Caroline would call it.

He passes by the rotted corpse of the intruder he killed on his last visit. The young man had a similar thought to get supplies, but he didn't account for getting attacked in the parking lot. By the time he made it inside, he was more interested in taking a bite out of Viktor than grabbing a generator or shovel. He did take the man's ID with him before leaving, which offset any guilt he felt about how he left the remains. The crowbar still protrudes from the sunken skull.

Time's up, you can't linger.

Viktor scans his watch and looks around the store one last time.

"That should do for today," he says, enjoying the sound of his voice in the space.

After walking for five hours, he's spent no more than fifteen minutes at his destination. He's continued his dedication to time management, maybe the one thing that's carried over into this new life, besides the utter loneliness. Viktor knows he needs to leave soon to ensure he's back to the treehouse before dark. He takes few chances traveling at night. After all, deer were often nocturnal feeders he recalls, and there's always the dead. And the *soon-to-be* dead.

With the atlas sticking out of the front pouch, he takes new streets on his way back. It's just another measure to avoid undue risk as only in the rarest of circumstances does he retrace his steps when he goes out on runs.

He's seen the worst in humanity since the fall and has concluded that all of the killing of the dead has made the killing of the living seem normal, even essential. It's one thing to be robbed, but to be killed for sport in a world without consequence leaves little desire to take chances, so a new route home prevails. The cart squeals and shakes. His biceps burn from holding it steady as he steers along the paved yet bumpy surface.

There's always one broken wheel.

THEN

A thick haze drapes over the living room, backlit by the sun streaming in through the blinds. Max's shadow breaks up the shafts of light as he stumbles along the exterior of the home, back and forth, grunting along the way. Viktor stares down at the barrel of the pistol as a bit of smoke tapers away, the scent of metal and burnt paper is as thick as the air inside. He lets the gun fall to his feet.

He can't bring his eyes to focus on the body that lies in the center of the floor. They travel to every object, light reflection, speck of dust, but he won't allow himself to look down on her, to see what he's done. Had she cried out, or made any sign of struggle, Viktor would have been on the floor trying to save her by any means necessary. But the sickening, lifeless thud, followed by the haunting silence void of breath, including his own, confirmed that the sole shot through the heart was instantly fatal.

Caroline is dead, and by your own hand.

The thought is impossible, like a foreign language he can't comprehend, or a memory someone else planted in his mind. The truth is she's at school and if he just dares to look closer, then he will see. His eyes travel as slow as he can manage from a random section of carpet to a piece of clothing. Then up to an outstretched arm. It's still not enough, so he forces his eyes to go right to her face and take it in. He prays for relief, to not recognize the person in his living room. But there, in the center of the beige carpet next to the matching sofa and love seat that he and Sandra argued wouldn't fit when they moved in, lies Caroline, still as a photograph and as beautiful as a painting. A small red dot the size of a quarter pools just off-center of her flowery shirt. Her eyes are open but empty, a stare traveling far beyond the confines of the ceiling.

Kill yourself.

As if someone else flipped a switch in his mind, he goes from disbelief to undeniable reality and the accompanying anguish hits him like a freight train. Viktor drops to his knees and without looking, feels for the gun that landed somewhere next to him. His fingers find the grip and lock it in his hand.

Pull the trigger.

The muzzle is still hot from the first shot, but he welcomes the pain to his temple. He rubs his finger up and down the trigger, his stare a blank fixation on the motionless body of his ten-year-old girl. All of the memories flood his mind. Viktor slides his index finger into the trigger guard and rests it against the trigger itself. All it will take is a small squeeze and he'll be dead without even hearing the blast. His eyes are red, blotting out any signs of white, his face contorting so hard that the sweat and tears mix. Blood vessels pop in his eyes and forehead.

"I'm sorry."

He pulls the trigger. Once again, the gun *clinks*. He can't believe it. Viktor checks the handgun over, ensuring the safety is still off. Then he sees the gun's magazine a few feet from his knees. In the course of dropping it he must have hit the release button, which ejected it from the gun when it bounced off of the carpet and rendered it safe.

A shooting pressure drives through his heel and into his Achilles tendon. Sandra has crawled across the kitchen and living room and sunken her chipped, bloodied teeth into him. All that prevents her from breaking the skin and tearing the muscle off of the bone is the leathery backing of the too-small security shoes that he still wears. The pressure and pain of the moment shake Viktor from his immediate state of utter shock. An instinct to survive emerges that moments ago he suppressed to depths unknown.

He kicks the foot free and jumps to the floor for the magazine. Loading the weapon, he swings it toward his ex-wife and lets off a round. It pierces through her right ear, taking most of it away. She continues to crawl forward pulling herself up his legs. He fires again hitting the shoulder blade. The bullet bounces around and exits her body before burying into the kitchen island. The shots enrage the dead man outside as Max pounds and scrapes at the glass insert beside the door. It spiderwebs but doesn't shatter.

Viktor steadies his hand with the other and focuses on her empty eyes as she inches closer and closer. He squeezes the trigger and the bullet travels straight between the two, connecting her eyebrows with the small round dot. The back of her head blows out, scattering brain and blood across the kitchen wall. She falls motionless at his feet.

Viktor scurries backward to create space. Panting hard, he struggles to catch his breath. Other sounds begin to fill in his peripheral. Scratching and growling still occupy the front door, but it's the new sound that frightens him most. Like a child taking a puff from an inhaler, he can sense Caroline rising behind him.

Don't look. You can't look.

Terrified of what he might see if he turns around, he would

sooner die than remember his daughter as one of the dead so he holds firm. He will always picture her as alive and perfect. The wheezing turns into a gurgle. Reserved to sit there and let her feast on him the way Sandra would have if given the chance, he deserves it after all. The slump and slow draw of seventy-something pounds sliding across the carpet invokes a horror that is unlike anything he's felt to date.

Viktor shakes his head. "No. Stop it," muttering to himself.

He can only look into the lifeless face of his former lover, former mother of his former daughter. It makes him gag as a tiny red drop rolls down her face to her chin. In the light of the room, he struggles not to see the dead monster that desperately tried to kill him but to see Sandra. Behind the blood and horror, a face asleep. At peace. A small hand slides up his back sending chills and goosebumps everywhere. His hairs stand on end. It grabs at the scrubs and pulls itself up, the strength more unsettling than anything else.

"I love you baby. Daddy's so sorry." The words don't sound right as they sputter almost silent from his cracked lips.

What could he say that would vocalize his guilt and pain? No thoughts come to his aid. Viktor pulls away from the grasp and holds the gun over his shoulder, resting the barrel inverted and facing at an angle downward behind him. He closes his eyes tight, forcing a fresh stream of tears down his throbbing cheeks. Another grab and pull from behind before the dead child bites at the pistol that hangs in front of her. He waits for the sound of her teeth against metal.

"Forgive me."

In a calm, smooth motion he squeezes the trigger, not to save his own life, but to free her from the monster that she's become. The monster that he made her. His eardrum ruptures and his head rings as he slumps forward, trying to crawl deep into the carpet, below the floor and into the dirt, gone forever. His empty hands fill with the low pile yarn as it pokes out between clenched fingers. Dizziness overtakes him and all that can be heard is the hum in his head, alongside Max's methodic pacing outside the front door.

NOW

Wisps of white smoke curl upward in the distance. There's a bend in the road that prevents Viktor from seeing the source and he's reluctant to continue, as a fire could be the sign of many ill scenarios. The two-lane highway is surrounded by tall trees and a steep embankment on the left side that disappears below the guardrail. The sun is descending to the west and few clouds break up the warm rays that bask the road in front of him, creating highway mirages that dance milky-gray in the distance.

The smoke is closer than he expected, so retreating would have done little good had any real danger been present. At first, it appeared to be large columns of a plume, but it was only a trick of perspective. Just around the bend in the highway, the narrow shafts of white swirl up from the base of the embankment down below. The scent is industrial, but the all too familiar smell of melted, rancid fat sours the air. He leans over the guardrail, peering down the grassy slope for the source.

A large swath of gray ash encircles the charred bodies lying in the black grass. They surround a burnt-out SUV that's pinned upright between the bank and a tree. He's unable to tell the make, model, or color as it's now just a melted skeleton of metal, rubber, and fabric. It sits on blackened rims and there's no sign that there were ever any tires on the vehicle as the rubber has flowed and congealed with the carcasses on the ground.

Leaving the cart on the shoulder, he steps over the twisted guardrail where the SUV presumably went over and weaves his way down the embankment toward the wreck site. Viktor left the shotgun on the cart so he draws the axe, tight-gripped and ready to strike. From what he can guess there are twelve bodies or so surrounding the vehicle in a melted and tangled mess.

He covers his nose with the axe handle and his right forearm, wafting away the remaining smoke that trickles up from the bodies. Using the axe, he pulls and pokes at the now very dead corpses. There will be no looting of these poor souls, he realizes. It's impossible to tell the difference between burnt flesh, bone, rubber, and who knows what else is mixed into the wreckage.

As he moves closer to the SUV, Viktor can make out the remains of the passengers inside. The bodies are still burnt but in various stages of doneness. The driver is slumped over and fused to the steering wheel. The rear passenger is bent over the front seat, the cavern of its face sunken into the back of the neck of the driver. Out of the corner of his eye, he notices a car seat in the back and just as fast he looks away, afraid of what he might see.

Carefully stepping over the bodies outside the wreck, Viktor makes his way to the front passenger side window. There, as if pulled from Pompeii, is a sleeping girl forever preserved in ash. She's older, judging by her height in the seat, the head slumped forward with chin resting on her chest. What remains of her hair hangs down on each side of her charcoal face.

He gently prods her shoulder with the top of the axe. The heat has melted her to the seat. When the body doesn't move, he leans in further and notices a small, burnt handbag at the girl's feet. It's still intact, the char looking no more than a soft coat of black paint. The brand insignia on the buckle is still recognizable but matching in an ash color. He tries looping the strap with his axe, but it's just out of reach. Viktor steps back and tries the door handle. He howls as it's still hot, shaking his hand in an attempt to relieve the burn. The door is locked or jammed.

"That was stupid," he admits.

Eyeing the girl once more, he leans in further. Her hair tickles his neck as he stretches out the axe to hook the purse. Reluctant to commit too far, he keeps looking up at the girl's face, expecting her eyes to be open and staring back at him. He needs to reach a bit further but going on his tiptoes makes him vulnerable. Shaking under the strain of full extension, the axe nudges against the handle of the bag. He tries several times and at last hooks it, then shimmies back out of the window opening. Viktor is almost out of the SUV when he's caught on something. He looks down at whatever is keeping him inside and sees his shirt pocket is snagged on the inner door handle. He drives his feet into the ash below, trying to pry himself loose as he can't reach the handle with his free hand.

Did she move? Can't be.

Viktor is frantic, panicked by the predicament he has thrust himself into. The body sways in the seat. *Or did he move it?* With the bag still looped on the back of the blade, he jams the head of the axe into the console trying to push himself up, but the leverage isn't enough. He is stuck, upper body inside and lower body dangling outside. The heat of the door frame begins to seep through his shirt, burning his stomach. He convulses, trying to free himself.

With a snap, the girl's head breaks from the neck and rolls to her lap. It lies motionless just inches from his face. He can feel flecks of her skin flowing into his nostrils as he takes in deep breathes. Once again, he pictures her eyes springing open, but they never do. Still kicking his feet in wild circles, he's able to thrust a foot into the dried carcass of one of the victims below. He uses the leverage of his anchored boot to pull himself out of the window. The shirt pocket tears free of the handle and the button flings somewhere into the SUV. His backward momentum carries him too far and he lands on his back, creating a mushroom cloud of ash. Viktor coughs and looks to his axe that is still gripped in his left hand. The handbag dangles from the blade.

"This better have been worth it."

He coughs again as the snow-like cloud of human remains falls all around him.

Brushing himself off as he staggers away from the SUV, he looks up the embankment and inhales a deep breath. The struggle was exhausting and he climbs back up the grassy slope and over the torn guardrail. Viktor tosses the handbag into the cart with everything else and pushes it along down the road. Cool water from his canteen does little to clear his airway of all that he inhaled. He may not have been able to collect their IDs, but he suspects he carries their crispy DNA inside his lungs. Viktor smirks at the thought and coughs the entire way back home.

THEN

The only movement in the entire house is the slow crawl of shadows cast by window blinds as the sun travels across the sky. Hours have passed and an orange glow has replaced the vibrant blue light. A wide range of sounds have come and gone outside the home, none even so much as stirring Viktor from his current position, hands and face buried in the carpet. He hasn't fallen asleep but neither is he awake. He's in shock and the weight of everything doesn't allow him to move from a semi-fetal sprawl. Screams, sirens, and shooting did nothing to draw his attention. The deep boom of explosions that rattled the glass and walls barely caused a flinch.

It's not until Max begins scratching, an awful pitch of fingernails on the cracked glass of the door insert that Viktor regains the presence of mind. Something about the scraping is an annoyance he cannot ignore.

"Quiet!" he yells, face still planted in the carpet fibers.

Bits of spit fly from his swollen lips. As if mocking him, Max begins scratching the glass with both hands, accompanied by a furious gurgle on the other side.

Viktor squeezes his eyes tight, trying to wish it away but doing so just makes him more aware of that which is bothering him.

"Shut up! Shut up! Shut. The. Fuck. Up!" More blubbering than commanding.

Max begins tapping his forehead against the glass, a soft patter of flesh with a wet reverb. It's rhythmic and even covering his ears does little to drown out the persistence.

"That's it."

Viktor pushes himself onto his elbows and then up onto his knees. Everything hurts, his entire body aches from lying in the same place for too many hours to guess. He grabs the gun where it landed beside him and staggers to the glass insert. Not even bothering to open the door, Viktor presses the barrel of the gun to the glass where Max's gnarling silhouette is outlined. As if waiting to be tested he looks away and listens. With a soft thud and scratch of the nails, his finger squeezes the trigger.

Glass shards explode in all directions, nicking him in the arm and neck. The thump of Max's heavy body on the door stoop shakes the remaining pieces of glass from the casing and onto the floor. With a sigh of frustration, like a child waking from a nap, Viktor unlocks and opens the front door and peers outside. Max is folded over, his upper body bent over the single step that leads up to the house.

Grabbing Max by both feet, he uses all his leverage to drag the man into the house. Pain travels up his leg with every step. It takes several minutes but Viktor is finally able to lay the body alongside Caroline's. He never looks though, allowing the shape to be nothing more than a blur in his subconscious. He fears that a single second of looking at her lifeless body will replace a second of memory from when she was alive. Doing the same with Sandra, and as gentle as can manage, he pulls her to rest next to her family.

Her family.

Pulling blankets off the back of the couch, he drapes them over the bodies in the center of the living room. Only now that they're covered does he look down at the three ambiguous figures. They could be anyone. Blood soaks through the fabric, taunting his memory of what lies beneath.

He exhales long and slow as he sits on the couch with the corpses at his feet. The hum of the ceiling fan catches his attention and after looking up, notices it still spinning overhead. Viktor tries to ignore the blood pattern that was cast out over the white ceiling from each of its blades.

The power is still on.

He turns on the television. A sports channel comes on first as he can identify it by the station icon, but there is no programming being played, only what looks like a screensaver. Fumbling to remember the channels, he changes over to find a news station. The sound blares on before the channel can even register a picture. It's cutting in and out, a digital pixelation that looks like a video call from another planet, but he's able to get the gist. Mass panic. Mass casualties.

Mass fucked.

The feed steadies enough to read the lower thirds that scroll across the screen. He's able to decipher something about China, the images behind the caption are shaky cell phone videos sent in by viewers. Death on full display during daytime television with no censor or warning. People attacking each other, eating one another. Then, if that weren't enough, a video rolls that he thinks can't be real.

A woman is being filmed running in an open yard. She's blindsided by a large deer, goring her through the neck and side. The person recording gasps and screams. The buck plants the woman onto the ground as she struggles to get free. The footage zooms in and distorts, but Viktor can see the mangy fur of the animal as well as the outline of its rib cage beneath the skin. The woman claws at the ground trying to get free, but the animal shows great strength as it pierces the woman in the back and lifts her off of the ground. He thinks of a bull goring a bullfighter. She lies writhing on the ground after being slammed down again. The deer tramples her as it gallops away.

A bystander rushes from a car to check on her, looking around with eyes of desperation while calling for help. Within seconds the woman reaches up and bites into the good Samaritan. People scream and stampede in front of the camera, knocking the person filming over. Feet and bodies fill the frame as muffled cries crackle the speakers before it all cuts to black.

It's surreal that even this imagery can become monotonous. Viktor watches the news, eyes glued to the TV for a few hours, the coverage becoming more and more sparse, the captions increasingly truncated, then just b-roll footage without narrative or text, and finally the station goes off the air altogether. *No signal* error messages now duplicate across all of the channels that he checks. He leaves the television on in case one of the broadcasts come back.

Viktor realizes that he's sitting in the dark. That the sun has set and the pale streetlights fill the room. He doesn't dare go outside, but the idea of staying doesn't sit well with him either. The decaying stench that grows in the closed-off home will drive him mad soon enough. He suspects it's already worse than it is, like spoiled garbage that goes unnoticed, only evident when coming inside after time away.

Even though he locked the deadbolt, he pushes a table against the front door and blocks the broken insert, barricading himself inside for the night. A few boards from the garage go up across the windows. He hopes these measures will help him sleep, but knows rest won't be found anytime soon.

Unable to bring himself to sleep in any of the beds, Viktor pushes a comforter from the closet into the bathtub and tries at the very least to close his eyes. He stares at the opening of the bathroom as he refused to close the door. Being able to hear and see the darkness was a compromise to his fear.

Sometime during the night, the power began to flicker on and off. Now from what he can guess it's been off for more than an hour, by far the longest stretch, and he fears it has no intention of coming back. Viktor's grateful when dawn begins penetrating the house, raising the ambient light out of the clutches of night.

Viktor rummages through Max's closet and manages to find something other than scrubs to wear. This time too big but still a welcome change, the jeans, work boots, and flannel button up fit as good as he could hope for. He searches through the rest of the house for anything worth taking, and makes his way to the kitchen, stuffing anything edible into a large duffel bag. He manages to find and fill three large containers of water that he hooks onto the bag through the shoulder strap. It's heavy, but he just has to get it to the car. There will be a single trip from the house to the vehicle, no back and forth, so if he can manage to carry it, it goes.

Stopping at the wall of photos that overlooks the bodies on the floor, he scans each one. His fingers glide down an image of Caroline. A school photo with a solid background. He pulls it off the wall, removes it from the frame, and places it into the bag. He takes half a step toward the door, but turns back to the photo collage and grabs one of Sandra and Max together. Out of the frame and into the bag, which he zips tight.

Viktor makes his way to the front door, dropping the bag and water with a thud on the carpet. After nudging the table out of the way, he examines the pistol in his hand. He looks from the gun to the bodies and back to the gun. Viktor tosses it to the floor and moves back to the kitchen. He finds the largest knife he can and slides it into his waistband. Hopping across the living room, he yanks the wooden curtain rod off the wall. Driving one end into the floor and slamming his foot down on it, the rod splinters into a sharp point. He turns it in his hands, impressed with the improvisation. With one last look around the house, he slings the heavy bag over his shoulder and is out the door. He pulls it closed behind him and doesn't look back.

NOW

Dust flies up from under boot and wheel alike as Viktor hustles along the gravel and dirt road. Trees tower and sway overhead, jutting up from forests that flank him on both sides. Branches crack and break in the distance. He curses under his breath at the sound of snorts and hooves scratching somewhere in the woods. The clearing is a short distance up ahead and he only needs to make it to the safe harbor of his tree. The shopping cart bounces off the potholes and it takes all his strength and focus to keep it from tipping.

Dusk is a distant memory as only the faintest of orange can be seen in the deep blue of night overhead. Turning sharp from the rocky surface, he pushes the cart down a worn, dirt path and breaks into the clearing. He doesn't stop pushing the cart until he's made it to the power station. It tips on its side, spilling everything to the ground. He snatches the backpack, pulling out his emergency lantern. He slings the bag and the shotgun over his shoulders and digs for the charred handbag. The new solar panel lies in the cart at the base of the station. It will have to wait there until morning.

Viktor wastes no time getting to the ladder. After untying the coil of rope that holds the whole thing overhead, it rolls down and lands at his feet. He places hand over foot as the darkness creeps into the forest. The only light is what's left of the western sky fading through the canopy.

Once on the roof, he moves to the hatch. The combination lock seems unmolested and he fumbles through the numbers until it pops open. He slings his shotgun into an aiming position, placed tight into his shoulder. Using his boot, he nudges the hatch open and thrusts the barrel inside.

"Honey, I'm home," he says between exhalations as his breath catches up.

Viktor drops down into the treehouse and closes the hatch overhead. He twists the knob on the lantern and the LED light illuminates the interior with a bright, white glow. He hangs it from a hook in the center, sending his shadow dancing around the room as it settles.

From a bin on the floor, he pulls a ration of energy bars and a can of mixed nuts. A small refrigerator sits in the corner. He opens it, takes a small box, and slams the door just as fast. Viktor hasn't forgotten the power was off but hopes the drink is still cool at least.

"What do we have today? Grape Berry Bounty," he reads the label with a mock of sophistication. The purple box is a kid-size juice drink, complete with a plastic straw glued to the outside.

Pulling up a wooden crate to lean against, he sifts through the contents of his backpack. He also retrieves the collected IDs from his chest pocket and lays them out on the floor like a proud hand of cards. He's lucky to not have lost any with the ordeal in the SUV. The phones he pulls out of his bag and piles them in a neat brick stack next to a power strip that's riddled with phone charging cables.

"Tomorrow night we'll have a look at you."

One by one Viktor picks up an ID from the spread and reads every line of it, front and back. Every detail he concentrates on, and he's seen the same lines all before, but it's the differences that draw the most scrutiny. He traces a hand over the picture, then the name, pressing the holographic stamps like buttons as they glow in the lantern light. With each plastic person he analyzes, Viktor is lost in the what ifs and scenarios of their past. Most of what he conjures, if not all, is a fabrication of the mind, but he finds comfort and purpose in giving them a story.

From the bin he retrieves a large binder, four inches thick, and opens it three-quarters of the way to the end, leafing forward a couple of pages in search of the next blank spot. The pages are clear plastic meant for trading cards but they suit driver's licenses and various IDs perfectly. After dwelling on each new one for a moment he then files it away in the sleeve next to the previous. He always says their names out loud as he puts them to rest.

"Steven Thompson, Tennessee. Jane Griffin, Tennessee. Ali-Ali-b, Alibra Shakayan. Hope I pronounced that one right, sorry Ali. Washington state. Wow, you were far from home."

This is how it goes for the nine people he's collected today. The nine souls he hopes he's preserved for something, or someone. That part he hasn't figured out and doesn't expect he'll live to know. They'll probably die with him he's almost certain, but at least for now, they live on.

Someone has to remember.

The monumental task weighs on him each night that he reviews the lost. Viktor thinks of the magnitude of people, thousands, millions, hundreds of millions that will long be forgotten as if they never existed. But these nine continue living, in a book, in a bin, in a treehouse.

He almost forgot the burnt handbag. Viktor retrieves it from the floor and slides it over to where the IDs are displayed in front of him. Going through it, piece by piece, he sets everything out neat and organized. Surprised by the number of items that are contained inside, he has to push the now empty bag off to the side just to make room.

"Lip gloss." He places it next to the bag.

"Ah tampons, nice." These go to a new pile of their own. They have many uses outside of their original intent and he's resourceful if nothing else.

"IDs and more IDs." He collects three rectangular cards and shuffles them in hand before taking a closer look at each one.

The first is the most common and the one he'll likely store away as her keepsake. The driver's license features a beautiful, striking woman, and close to his age based on the DOB. Neat black hair, straight and shoulder length. Her eyes are bright green and her summer top is atypical for a government photo. *This could be a dating profile picture,* he thinks. Viktor reads the rest of the license but his eyes keep shifting back to the image. He feels something he hasn't in a long time and it's as unwelcome as it is unsuspected.

She's dead, he reminds himself.

Viktor shakes himself out of whatever unsettling notion was beginning to take hold and brings forward the next ID. It's a health insurance card, numbers and information that he doesn't care to read at the moment. He shuffles it to the back with a sigh as he brings the final card to the front. Something isn't quite right. This one is a student ID and is in good shape compared to the license. It's not the condition but the photo that throws him off.

The girl in the school picture appears much younger, maybe nineteen or twenty. The image doesn't match either. The facial features are different. The hair is black, the eyes are green, but the smile is wrong, as are the cheekbones and jawline. This girl looks unhappy, yet her driver's license is all smiles.

"Who's happier at the DMV than college?"

He thinks the student ID must be old, but he can't explain why it's in better shape than the other. The date on the bottom confirms his suspicion. Then it hits him like a warm sledgehammer to the chest.

Check the name, idiot.

Had Viktor not been in such a hurry to bury the attraction he felt to a stupid picture then he would have spotted the differences. Viktor holds both photo IDs side by side and as he reads each one, a smile grows on his weathered face.

"Andrea Gall. Virginia Tech University," he says, scrolling across the school ID with his thumb.

"Francesca Hawthorne. Pennsylvania!" he all but yells. He shuffles the two IDs back and forth, again and again.

As if assembling a puzzle and discovering the missing piece, he realizes why a college student would be carrying an ID of someone else, especially someone who is almost twice her own age.

"Fake ID! Fake ID!" He's almost dancing in place on the floor.

Viktor checks the insurance card for good measure and sure enough, it also belongs to the student.

"Andrea, sorry my dear."

Trying to maintain the same amount of respect that he did for the others by stifling his excitement, he files her student ID into the binder.

The driver's license he keeps for himself. He reaches up to the lantern and twists it off. The battery indicator goes dim along with the light. He gets comfortable on the floor, just a blanket above and below. In the moonlight that barely shines through the break in the wall and roof, Viktor flips the ID between his fingers, rubbing his thumb over Francesca's face on the worn plastic card. He doesn't want the feeling that he's experiencing, but it's new and exciting. He tries to convince himself of the work to be done. More dead to be slain, and more people to be remembered, but his thoughts keep falling back to the woman in the photo.

You'll get yourself killed.

He tries to tell himself what little the different IDs mean in reality, and that this woman is, in all likelihood, long dead. It's no use muffling the thoughts that battle in his mind as he drifts in and out of sleep. Like a splinter that's lodged deep down, there is a pain he hasn't known for years and is one that he is as afraid to feel, as he is to ignore. *Hope.*

THEN

The vanishing yellow meter representing the remaining battery, along with the dropping mileage toward zero, makes Viktor increasingly anxious. He had checked Sandra's gas-powered car in the garage but the needle was sitting on empty. *Some things never change,* he thought at the time. For several reasons, he would have enjoyed taking Max's truck but the keys were nowhere to be found and he's kicking himself now for not looking harder.

After driving for eight hours he's managed to cover almost 300 miles, but the road has been a slog of frustration. Remnants of civilization in various forms of disarray extend from every turn. Some areas just coming to grips with what has happened, evident by the panic, looting, and violence, while others are empty of life and only flooded with hordes of the dead. In those close-call moments, he was thankful for his silent car, humming as it whizzed by smoking towns and overrun communities.

Viktor made a quick decision after leaving his home to avoid the interstate, afraid of the potential gridlock or running out of juice with few places to hide. He stuck to back roads, going what he presumed to be north.

Government is north. Canada is north. The extreme cold is north. All sound like better options than where he started that morning and apparently, he wasn't the only one. Viktor had passed countless vehicles along the way, often needing to swerve and maneuver around them. Most were stacked to the brim with belongings and passengers, others were abandoned with doors open and no one to be found. The frantic survivors he did see paid no attention to him as he flew by. After the first few he began doing the same. *What good is making eye contact with someone you can't help?*

He was halfway up an on-ramp when the smoke from stacked vehicles caught his eye. Then he saw something that terrified him. A horde. Hundreds. Not just milling about but swarming like bees over and between cars. It looked like they had all gone mad in a coordinated frenzy. This was the first glimpse of the mob mentality that would be the biggest threat from the dead. The larger the group, the faster and more aggressive they all seemed to become. In those instances, avoidance is the best chance of survival.

Now somewhere in Eastern Tennessee, the low battery indicator on his electric dashboard begins to blink red. The mileage is in double-digits and a flutter of panic surges through his arms and chest.

"What the hell do I do now?" he sputters.

He's passed dozens of gas stations along the way, but in this rural section of the country, a charge station is a long shot, let alone a functioning one. Viktor considered stealing another gas-powered car, but any contenders he saw were in precarious positions, and the unknown fact if they were empty was enough to pass them by as it was just safer to keep driving.

Another hour passes, along with a handful of gas stations, but no power stations to be seen. Traveling no faster than forty-five miles per hour, Viktor has managed to slow the battery drain. It still flashes red and has for some time. The mileage indicator now displays eight miles worth of juice left. He's starting to wrap his mind around having to go on foot.

The idea is better received in this moment rather than before as almost everything now seems to have gone quiet. Maybe he's just headed in the opposite direction of everyone, but his encounters with other survivors have dissipated to almost none. As he considers taking every turnoff and driveway that he passes, he tries to justify the absence of chaos.

It either had to go one way or the other.

The outbreak had to be slow enough that it could be stemmed off and managed by a massive military intervention, or so fast that as news spread so did the infected and by the time a plan could be implemented, those in charge were chewing on each other's body parts. And then it all became nothing but the few lucky survivors searching for a place to hunker down.

An audible warning chime lets Viktor know he needs to make a decision and fast. The reality of getting stuck on this rural stretch of road is not appealing. He stops at a four-way intersection and contemplates his next direction.

"Where can I find power?"

He analyzes the road straight ahead, which wraps around a bend. *Who knows what's in that direction?* Looking to his left, the paved road turns to dirt and winds up a hill. *Not promising.* To Viktor's right, the paved road splits into two lanes leading down a tall, well-groomed canopy of pine trees. A large sign sits adjacent to the intersection.

"Pine Castle Estates," he reads. "Sounds elite."

Glancing each choice once more, he then makes an abrupt turn to his right into the community entrance.

A half-mile down the entryway, a landscaped round-about and security gate split the roadway. The exit side has parking cones and heavy equipment, it appears asphalt was being poured. On the entrance side, where he idles for a moment, the barrier arm is down but has been broken from the inside, wood scattered along the grass and blacktop.

Someone was in a hurry.

The car glides around the broken arm and through the community gate. Houses spring up among the wooded development. Two and three-story goliaths stacked isolated in their own large, grass lots. Many of the houses have missing front doors and construction lining on the exterior walls. Garages are empty, many without doors, their openings like a mouth screaming in the face of the giant homes. As he follows the road there are no signs of life anywhere. Somehow more unsettling, there's no sign of death either.

"Where is everyone?"

He takes a loop around the community, but it's more of the same. The houses look as they did the day before, he's certain. Undisturbed and forgotten. He's beginning to doubt anyone even lived here. *Maybe the residents are holding up inside,* but he isn't sure if that would be a good or bad thing. The alarm dings once more and the indicator reads zero miles.

"I'm trying, alright!" he yells at the dashboard.

He rolls past another home, this one appearing different from the rest, more finished he would guess. The lawn and front facade are both perfect. The garage has a door and it's wide open. He has to do a double-take and squint to believe his eyes. On the back wall of the garage interior is a large panel with a green glow around its border.

"You're shitting me!" he exclaims.

Viktor yanks the wheel and pulls into the empty garage.

He waits inside, half expecting a homeowner, dead or alive, to burst through the door from inside the home. It's not like he could go anywhere as the car doesn't have the juice to make it back out of the driveway. The threat never materializes, so he kills the electric motor and steps out. He's stiff and sore, his right leg far worse. The knife is still tucked into the front of his jeans and he holds the sharp staff in his right hand, though it was awkward and cumbersome to remove from the vehicle.

After a few moments of circling the car, he places the makeshift spear onto the hood, and yanks open the charging port on the wall. A plug sits coiled inside. The light remains green and that's reassuring. Yanking the plug out of the box, he walks it back to the rear of the vehicle but can't find where to put it. It takes a moment to find the cover, which is located on the front passenger side of the car just below the hood, and connects the power. He hears a chime from inside the car. Bars on the wall panel blink.

"That's probably a good sign."

From the comfort of the garage, he analyzes the surrounding neighborhood. *Doctors, lawyers, these are million-dollar homes.* Something doesn't add up about the emptiness of the neighborhood. The homes look like fortresses, so the feeling of solitude doesn't sit well. Not that he's eager to meet the neighbors, but if any place could make it, a secluded community likes this would be it.

He moves to the yard and walks across the new grass, thick rectangular chunks of fresh sod, toward the front door. Viktor expects it to be ajar or broken, but it appears solid and untouched. Then he understands why it's undisturbed. A large combination lock hangs from the door handle. Viktor lifts the heavy device and shakes it to see if it pops free with a key. It doesn't. Looking back toward the lawn, he sees what he missed the first time. A colorful advertisement swinging on a tall wooden post.

"Come see our model home!" he reads. "You've got to be joking."

He looks around the neighborhood and notices similar colorful signs that display square footage and leasing terms. He can't help but laugh to himself.

Viktor retraces his steps back to the garage and tries the interior door to the home. The knob turns without resistance and drifts inward. As he walks inside, he looks back out onto the street and presses the large white button on the wall next to him. The garage door drops down, smooth and silent and new, cutting the sunlight with a harsh edge as he enters the model home. He closes the door behind him.

NOW

As he wakes up to the crisp morning of singing birds doing flybys, he regains his bearings of last night's delayed task that still awaits in the nearby field. He puts away the binder and bins he was digging through, but something is missing. The ID. Viktor remembers falling asleep with it enveloped in his hand but after sweeping the entire treehouse, there's no sign of it anywhere. He pats himself down, feeling all pockets and folds in his clothing. Much like the unwelcome feeling of hope, anxiety now flushes his system with a similar uninvited disruption. Then, as his face contorts in frustration, he realizes where it's gone. His hand slides up along his neck and feels for the plastic rectangle.

"Nice one, you old fool."

Stuck firm to his skin just below his splotchy beard, the ID of this mystery woman hangs against his neck, face down. He must have fallen asleep while reading it over, memorizing every dot of ink and color. Viktor peels it away and gives it a rub as if the woman will appear and grant him three wishes. There's no question what his first wish would be. Opening the top pocket of his backpack, he stows away the ID for safekeeping. Peeking through the divide between the wall and the roof, Viktor gauges the hour of the morning and checks it against his watch.

"Time to get to work," he says, gazing into the canopy all around him. Viktor changes his clothes from the tactical pants and flannel shirt, still covered in ash and dirt from the day before, and pulls on a white V-neck and a pair of tattered jeans. *Work clothes,* as he likes to call them. Rolling on a fresh pair of socks and sliding his feet into worn-out sneakers.

Viktor grabs a plastic water bottle from the small counter that runs half the length of the wall. From a bin underneath the shelf, he retrieves a pack of nuts and an energy bar. It's mundane but quick. Eggs and meat or fish would be his go-to starter, though he's short on both and is eager to get to work.

The axe goes through his belt loop and the shotgun hangs over his shoulder. Balancing the food and water in one arm, he pulls himself up and out of the hatch. Navigating his way down the rope ladder, careful not to misstep, he lands on both feet with a thud. He doesn't bother to draw it up as he won't be leaving the vicinity.

The grass and underbrush around the tree are worn away, as is the path leading toward the clearing. Viktor follows this for several feet but turns at a fork in the path, the branching section barely noticeable and less trafficked. A short distance from the main path, a plastic shed sits hidden in the thick brush. He makes his way to the doors and draws the axe with his free hand. Using the blade, he pulls open the black heavy-duty plastic door. It wobbles as he drags it through the sticks and pine needles that bunch up against the base.

"Let's do this!" he shouts. Not because he thinks something is inside, but he's learned to make noise in a situation like this rather than giving the dead a silent advantage.

Just as he left it, the shed is empty of threat. Light pours in and illuminates the tools that line the walls. Viktor slides the axe back through the loop and grabs a shovel leaning upright in the corner. He also grabs a tool belt that he slings over his right shoulder. Out the door, he kicks it shut behind him with his heel and heads to the main path and toward the clearing.

The shopping cart lies on its side in the field next to the solar structure, an eerie sight he thinks as if it willed itself there on its own. He abandoned it in such a hurry the night before, he's not sure it was him at all. Aside from a moist covering of dew that's already begun to dry, everything is in order. Viktor puts down his shovel and shotgun, leaning them against the cart, and unboxes the solar panel, setting it upright against the old one. Pulling a wrench from the tool belt, he climbs onto the structure.

A couple of years back a terrible storm, that he suspects were the remnant of a hurricane, swept through and demolished everything, including the original treehouse and solar setup. It had been in place for a year, and much less substantial than the one he resides in now, but it was uninhabitable after the storm. He survived the long night by hunkering under a nearby bridge, convinced he would become trapped and drown if the river rose any higher.

Once the new panel is up and the work has been completed, he throws the trash into the shopping cart and places the tools in the child seat basket. Pulling down on the main lever attached to the underbelly, he activates the solar panel. Moving to the power converter below, he hits a switch and the juice runs through the unit. The large car batteries that line the base of the structure begin to charge.

"That a girl. A few solid hours and we'll be back in business." Viktor brushes off his hands and pushes the cart back toward the woods. He'll burn what trash he can that evening, and bury what he can't another day. Many scraps will be recycled and reused somewhere in the treehouse.

As he re-enters the tree line, the solar structure sits alone in the clearing behind him, a perfect ray of sunshine beating down hard on its surface. Photocells agitate as the electrons are knocked out of their sandwiched layer of phosphorous and boron, generating the electricity that will light a treehouse, keep a small refrigerator going, and he hopes brew a cup of coffee.

There was still six hours of direct sunlight after the solar panel was up and running, and it took that entire time to get enough juice in the batteries for Viktor to bother sending the power back to the treehouse. From the time it took for him to walk from the switch to the tree, the smell of coffee permeated the area. Having forgotten to turn the coffee maker off when the power died, it kicked on as electricity surged through the cables. While waiting for the final drips to splash in the small pot, he was quick to unplug the refrigerator as it would take several full days of sun to charge the batteries to a capacity of uninterrupted operation.

"No point wasting a cup of good coffee," he said while enjoying a hot mug of the brew.

Now, after a dinner of more coffee, canned vegetables, and a tuna pouch, Viktor slides a plastic bin to his feet and retrieves a beat-up laptop from inside. He opens the screen and is eager to power up the device.

From a port on the right side, a portable hard drive hangs down from a short cable connected to the computer. Almost forgetting, he hurries to connect the power cable that runs to a nearby power strip. The computer used to stay charged for an entire day, but after years of unreliable charging and seasonal temperatures, it now needs to be plugged in at all times. He hasn't done the math, but he thinks the current charge of the main system should let him run for a few hours at least.

The start-up chime of the laptop surprises Viktor and he returns to the screen. Digging in the bin, he retrieves three cell phones and looks them over with a careful inspection. A dongle of power cables is tangled inside as well, but he finds the ones he needs for the phones and dumps the rest back in the box. Connecting the first phone to the computer, the charging icon appears on the cracked screen.

"Aha! Today is our lucky day!" After hundreds of phones, the success rate of turning one on is hovering somewhere around thirty percent. And that doesn't include the ones that are locked and inaccessible. He spent the better part of a month reading books on how to jailbreak or bypass the security but was never quite able to make it work, and the effort proved fruitless.

The other two phones both display their respective charge icons, and Viktor is excited that he'll have not one but three devices to sift through, should his power hold out. The computer is a mess of accessories with devices hanging from every port and he positions it on top of the bin while sitting on the floor.

It takes a few minutes for the phones to have enough charge to power up, so in the meantime, he navigates the touchpad mouse to the portable hard drive icon on his desktop.

"Archive thirty," he reads the name of the drive. "Has it been that many?" A piece of masking tape on the drive displays the same title, written in black marker.

Double-clicking on the drive icon brings up a list of folders, each named for a state and followed by a two-digit number that represents the year. He scrolls down to Tennessee and double-clicks again. This folder contains another list of folders, each with a person's name as the identifier, last name first and first name last. Right-clicking on the touchpad, Viktor creates a new folder and pauses to type in the name.

Reaching to the first phone he plugged in, he holds the power button and waits a moment, hoping it will obey his command. The screen goes black, then the logo of the phone's manufacturer lights up the display, followed by the network carrier's logo, both companies are now as dead as the owner of the device.

"Bastard," he says under his breath as the lock screen appears. Viktor tries a few different number combinations but of course nothing works.

Depending on the type of phone, it's not a complete loss. After seeing every brand and model, Viktor's become quite an expert on each device. He's lucky, this model has a removable microSD card and he's able to retrieve it using his fingernails to pry it from its harness. Careful not to drop it between the slits in the floorboards where it would be lost in the darkness below, he clicks the card into the side of his laptop and waits for the folder to pop up on the desktop. Navigating through all of the card's system folders, he finds the one he's looking for and opens it. A long list of photos and videos displays before him. Crosschecking with the IDs that he retrieved at the same time as the phone, Viktor identifies the man in the first photo with the corresponding driver's license. The stranger with salt and pepper hair smiles at the camera in front of what appears to be a bar in the background. The bartender, a cute young woman leans in, also smiling.

He opens the window on the computer with the named folders and types in the man's name as he reads it from the license.

"Herschel, Simon." He drags the entire contents of the media folder over to his newly created archive of this man's life. Another window pops up showing the transfer details.

"Three-hundred and thirty-eight files."

The transfer time lags before producing an estimate.

"Approximately two hours." It's slow-moving but time he has, and he hopes the power system got the memo.

As the files transfer, Viktor scrolls through the images and video files of the man's life. From trips, to food, to downloaded images that represent his specific sense of humor, all the expected content of someone's digital life is there. Including the personal content. At first, he felt guilty about looking at a stranger's private, intimate images, but loneliness and the repeated mantra that they're long dead tends to be all it takes to bypass his conscience. The first of these photos he finds is of a woman, a few years younger than the owner of the phone. She's beautiful, posing in front of a bathroom mirror, bearing everything for the man to see. Her large, fake breasts sit perfect on her thin frame.

"They've aged well."

He clicks to the next image, the same photo but a slightly different pose. Viktor glances between the image on the phone screen and the transfer bar, which hasn't changed since it started at still two hours to go.

Viktor hesitates at first, but as he scrolls through the images of this woman, he does what any man might do. Any man who hasn't seen a live person in years, let alone a naked woman. The guilt comes in small waves but the urge to release overpowers his better self that tells him he shouldn't. *She's dead and will never know,* battles with: *this is gross.* The distraction lasts not more than a few minutes as it doesn't take long for him to complete the task.

The wave of shame returns with it, and he can't scroll off the image fast enough. He knows the hypocrisy of this justification but once the files have moved to the hard drive, he'll go in and delete those specific photos from future eyes. An absurd amends by acting as a censor for her dignity.

While the files transfer, Viktor powers up the next phone that goes through a similar pattern. This time there's no lock screen and he's into the phone. He swipes a few times and sees an icon that looks promising.

"Alien Defender," he reads in a theatrical voice. Low-budget graphics fill the screen as a small character falls from the top and is surrounded by attackers. Tapping the screen with forceful thumbs, he passes the time throwing grenades, knives, and even trash cans at the alien onslaught. The moon on a cloudless night illuminates the forest outside of the treehouse as the soft blue glow of electronics extends beyond the wooden walls of the treehouse.

THEN

The smell of fresh paint is somewhat masked by the fresh-scent plug-ins staggered around the outlets of the modern home. A plate of stale cookies, meant for prospective homebuyers, is the only imperfect and non-staged item. Viktor eats them anyway. As he sheds crumbs across the marble surface of the otherwise pristine kitchen island, he reads the business cards and pamphlets left behind by the realtor who was in all likelihood showing the home just the day before. After searching the entire space, it seems the cookies are the only thing of any use.

When he first arrived, Viktor gave himself the grand tour and was impressed at the sheer size of the place. Five bedrooms, as many bathrooms, including a master suite ripped from the pages of a design magazine. Tile spanned the floor and walls, thoughtfully matching the fixtures on the sinks of the stunning dual vanity. After spending an exorbitant amount of time using the brand-new toilet and a functioning shower that could fit ten people, he moved to investigate the rest of the house, finally landing back in the kitchen. He still dries his receding hair with the sole decorative towel from the bathroom. It's heavy and embroidered, but soft against his face and much nicer than the three-dollar discount towels that he's used to.

As in his former life, he finds himself chomping on the complimentary cookies simply because they're there. His appetite hasn't reached the point of hunger just yet, a feeling he suspects he'll have to learn to live with, but the cookies exist and therefore should be eaten. Even if they do taste like little burnt frisbees. The sparse chocolate chips make them palatable.

Viktor grabs a glass from a see-through cabinet and turns on the faucet. He fills it almost to the brim but before taking a sip he stares at the clear bubbles swirling inside. He thinks on it for a moment, the dryness of the cookies telling him to risk it. He turns the glass over the sink letting the contents splash into the stainless square tub. The glass clanks and rattles on the marble countertop where he sets it next to the faucet. Spinning around to the range cooktop, he turns a knob and it ignites.

"No shit."

The flame dances blue among the black grate. He rifles through the tall ceiling height cabinets, all of which are empty. The ones with clear doors at least have glasses and bowls for showing purposes, but those won't do. Then he looks up. Hanging over the vast island is a large pot rock. Viktor unhooks a massive 3-gallon stainless pot and somehow fits it into the sink. He taps on the handle and water again spews out, this time filling the pot. He taps his fingers on the rim while looking around the kitchen, admiring the tile-work backsplash and attention to detail. He steps back to the range and plays with a long metal arm that protrudes from the wall above it. It has knuckle joints and folds in and out like an accordion. The end of the arm has a valve. He turns it. Water flows out and splashes down onto the range surface. Steam and sizzle as droplets hit the flame. He's quick to turn it off all the while laughing at himself.

"So, this is how the other half lives," he admires.

His work provided a comfortable living, even before the split, but neither he nor Sandra had much desire for refined things such as over-the-range pot fillers. Caroline seemed to follow suit, never so much as asking for anything of fluff as a child would be expected to do. He was most proud when she offered to donate one of her Christmas presents and continued to do so each year following.

Shutting off the island faucet and moving the pot out of the sink and over to the range, its contents sloshing high up the metal edges, Viktor positions the metal arm again, this time over the pot, and turns it back on. He stands back with a sense of accomplishment as the water fills with surprising speed. Then the doorbell rings.

Pounding, frantic beating on the door. It reminds him of Max, but this is rapid and intentional. *Don't even think about it.* He kills the spigot as the pot is almost full and cranks the dial, increasing the flame to the max.

"Hello! Is anyone there? Let me in, please!" The voice is youthful, maybe a young adult or teenager.

Through the windowpane he can see the silhouette moving.

"Please! I need help!" More pounding on the door and glass. Viktor steps closer, still mulling what he should do. It could be a trap.

Don't.

"Come on! I can see you moving inside, please!" Viktor freezes in place. More knocks and a gasp from the other side.

"Fuck!" As quick as the banging started, it stops and the shape vanishes.

After a moment of silence, he leans closer, listening first, then unlatching the deadbolt. With the staff aimed and at the ready, he cracks open the front door. The porch step is empty, as is the neighborhood beyond the yard.

Movement catches the corner of his eye. Down the street now several homes away, a boy darts from one entryway to another. Viktor squints and confirms it's a young man, maybe a teenager. The boy's hooded sweatshirt bounces as he runs from door to door, repeating at each home what he had done right here on this doorstep.

Meaning to call out, Viktor's mouth hangs open as he can no longer see him. Then, from the last house, the boy runs into the street, holding his hands over his head. It looks like he's gasping for air.

"Hey! Hey!" Viktor yells. The boy rests his arms on his knees, hunched over. "Hey, down here!"

Looking to both sides of the street, the boy darts up the road and then off into the woods. He didn't hear him. Viktor calls out again, this time waving his staff in the air.

"Come back!"

He tries to whistle, but his dry lips release a squeak. The figure in the hooded sweatshirt bounces into the trees at the end of the street and disappears. Viktor steps back into the house and locks the door.

He lies down on the stiff couch. Viktor rolls onto his side and stares at the open, empty fireplace. It's still spotless without a hint of grime or ash. The faux wood logs are elegant and realistic, molded in the center of the dark square among the refined stonework.

He imagines a roaring fire and glasses of wine. Sitting next to Sandra on the couch while Caroline plays on the floor. They laugh and toast each other. He looks down to a younger Caroline who scoots across the floor playing with a pink race car. She looks up at him, smiling. Except something isn't right. As her hair brushes over her face, terror chills his whole body. The dead eyes. Teeth blown out from a point-blank blast of the gun. Her hair is matted with red. She roars and growls as she lurches on all fours toward him.

Wake up!

Viktor jolts upright on the couch in the now dark home. First relief, then sadness falls over him at the memory of his dream. Except the dream has carried over into reality. A growl echoes throughout the spacious and open floor plan.

"It's inside," he sputters while grabbing at the cushions of the couch. *Clawing* and *scratching* from somewhere within the house.

Without another thought, he's to his feet and dashing toward the kitchen. Viktor grabs an empty pot he sat aside and meant for boiling more water. He left the jagged curtain rod upright against the counter and manages to snag it with his opposite hand. Rushing through the foyer and to the door that leads to the garage, Viktor slides from one wall to another. Only now does he feel the knife hanging at his waist and remembers keeping it there while he slept.

With both hands weaponized, he fumbles with the door handle lever. He steps back and uses his foot to push it down. As soon as it's ajar, a body pushes through the opening and knocks him back. The ravenous man lunges forward, biting and slashing at him. Viktor loses his staff in the fall but slams the metal pot into the gnashing jaws. Teeth clamp down making an awful sound against the rim, the pot now the only thing between the bite and his throat.

Pinned down by the weight of his attacker, Viktor struggles to move his arm, feeling for the staff along the floor and baseboards. The smooth glossy finish of the curtain rod is a welcome feeling to his fingertips. Wrapping them around the staff, he jerks the rod up and jams it up into the ear of the dead man. The body falls slack.

Hearing more sounds from the garage that now fills the house, he kicks off the corpse and pulls himself to his feet. Using the sole of his shoe, he pushes the skull off of the end of the staff like an impaled pumpkin and readies it again with the sharp end forward. He's thankful to have put his shoes back on before lying down, though at the time he could hear Sandra yelling about the furniture.

The dead's now limp body holds the door open and Viktor can see the dim cabin light of the electric car as well as a section of driveway beyond. The garage door is open no more than two feet off of the ground, and the sight baffles him. He knows it was closed as he watched it block out the sun with his own eyes. The light inside is faint, but he can make out three moving shapes in the garage. He contemplates making a run for the car, but another dead flings itself against the wall, reaching through the open door. Before he can jump past and make a dash for it, another body stumbles forward from the dark.

Viktor jabs the woman who attacks first in the gut and she falls but is no less a threat as she throws wild swings on the floor at his feet. A younger dead man blasts into the house in a rage. The agility of this particular one is shocking and sends Viktor retreating into the kitchen. He can hear the growling and swiping of hands chasing behind him. Over his shoulder he sees the mangled face, shards of glass protruding like horns. They dance around the island. The man sprints at Viktor. Using his staff, he thrusts the pot of water that still sits on the stove at the man. It does little to slow him down as the face howls and shakes in fury.

Surging forward, the dead slips and trips over the water and kettle. Viktor darts around the island and beelines back to the foyer. He sees an opening and jumps over the gutted woman that claws at his legs. He bursts into the garage but knows there's at least one more, his eyes bouncing around in the darkness. The white button on the wall is within reach, and he punches it with the side of his fist, but it doesn't comply. The garage door hangs in place, partially open to the outside. Then something else moves.

There, on the other side of the car, a silhouette stumbles along the wall. He keeps the vehicle between himself and it. Snarling, the figure counters, and moves around the back. He goes for the driver's door and pulls it open. Viktor throws himself inside as the dead slides across the trunk and thrusts its arm into the door before he's able to close it. Fingers swipe at his face. With one hand Viktor pulls out his knife, kicks open the door, and drives the blade deep into the hollow face of the attacker.

"No. Fuck. Please no," he stammers. The lifeless body that hangs on his door is that of the young boy that he was too slow to help.

Guttural moans bellow from inside the house. Viktor slams the door shut and starts the car. Throwing it into reverse he floors the pedal, sending pain straight through his leg. He winces and watches in the mirror, anticipating the whole garage door tumbling down. A loud clank and a jerk forward. The car stops in place. It barely bent the door. He accelerates but all that produces is a violent shake.

The dead woman flails herself onto the windshield, intestines spilling all over the glass. She bites and slaps her hands as if on the other side of an aquarium. Viktor now recognizes her face as the real estate agent from the business cards. Tires squeal in place with another failed attempt to break through the door. He grabs his duffel bag off the passenger seat and makes a run for it. He skips over the boy's body on the floor and dives for the opening underneath the garage door. He pulls himself forward, scratching at the brick-paver driveway. The man and woman slam into the inside of the door above him at the same time as he drags his feet across the concrete of the garage floor. They swipe at him, sneering as they pull at his shoes. He's able to get free and into the driveway. The banging inside the garage carries into the night.

On the street outside the home is a damaged SUV, steam billowing from the hood. The windshield is missing a large section and a body lies underneath the rear tire. Growls and wailing in the distance as more figures move in the darkness of the neighborhood. With his staff in one hand and bag in the other, Viktor makes his way to the trees and vanishes into the night.

NOW

Sometime in the early morning hours, Viktor gave up on the video game and finished transferring the files. Even with a late night, he doesn't sleep much past dawn and wakes up to another hot cup of coffee. The coffee maker is what spurred the initial idea to build his solar structure. It was no more than an intense desire for something normal, or familiar. Campfire coffee wasn't doing the trick so as soon as the treehouse was built, the first iteration, boredom set in and he decided to lean on his vocational training to make it a reality.

After figuring out the solar system, Viktor's ideas grew from there. He soon added the small fridge. It was summer at the time and being able to chill water and other drinks, outside of submerging them in the river, was a godsend. In winter months he does unplug the refrigerator to conserve power as less sunlight is available, reverting to a submersion bag for chilling as the river water flows frigid and on occasion freezes solid on the surface.

The garden he once had next to the solar panel provided fresh potatoes and corn. One thing he didn't anticipate was the kind of animals the garden would attract. It took a single run-in with a rabid deer that was tearing down stalks of corn for him to dig up the entire plot and commit to canned vegetables. Once he built up his supply it wasn't so bad, and he suspects he'll need to return to gardening one day, but he'll wait until after the infected deer have died off. His tree saved him during that encounter and he didn't come down for two days. Viktor hasn't seen the animal since.

It was a sole dead woman who stumbled into his clearing that inspired him to begin downloading the contents of found phones. He couldn't say why, but something just told him she needed to be remembered and not forgotten.

A single trip to an electronics store scored him everything he needed to set up his laptop storage device. He still doesn't know his final plan but at the moment it's a purpose. The task also provided him with a job. A mission. A reason to leave the treehouse. But now, there's a new mission. For the life of him, Viktor cannot get the woman on the Pennsylvania driver's license out of his head.

"Francesca." And he tries different pronunciations. "Fran-CHAY-sca." Hours disappear as he obsesses over the details of her ID.

Sprawled out on the wooden floor, Viktor now examines the road atlas. He has marker tabs on several pages as he flips back and forth between states. A hot cup of coffee steams next to him. Using a yellow highlighter, he traces lines and roads, plotting a course north. Some lines go along roads, but most cut through off-road areas, both to save time and avoid cities. He also circles potential intersections and areas that are likely to have supply stations, but also aren't good candidates for hordes of the dead. Backwoods, railroads, small towns, that's his path north to Pennsylvania.

Using a ruler and scratch paper, Viktor does the math between each dot that he makes. He cross checks the ruler with the key on the corner of each page, determining the mileage. The routine goes on for the rest of the day. With a final scribble on his scratch paper, he makes an eccentric circle and underlines it for emphasis.

"That's it. 628 miles."

You've got to be joking.

"Let's see, doing 2 miles per hour for 14 hours a day…"

He scratches down some numbers and lines and then reads aloud his work.

"Say 28 miles a day, divided by 628." More scribbling. "Point zero four…what?"

Jesus, you're going to die out there.

He scribbles out the equation and starts again. "Damn it. 628 divided by 28."

Smiling, he crunches the numbers. "Twenty-two days," he says through a grin. "I can do that, it's less than a month."

It's an estimate he knows and doesn't account for terrain, sickness, scavenging, anything other than walking. But even rounding up to a month sounds good and just plausible enough to ignite his dream into a reality.

Viktor begins compiling a list of what he'll need for the trip. He cross-checks it around the space with what he already has, taking a deep inventory and putting a lot of thought and effort into every item he'll need to complete the journey. It will be the longest he's been from this treehouse since his arrival, by hundreds of miles, and that thought is both exciting and terrifying.

A mystery woman, far more likely dead than not, in a distant state, in which he's going to travel on foot more than 600 miles through the wilderness.

Across the Appalachians, really? he thinks, looking down at his lines across the map.

It's an absurd notion, he's more than aware, but he's exchanging one hope for another. He can continue to survive in the daily monotony of his current existence, or he can have a purpose. Even if he dies a horrible and vicious death, which he pictures with vivid clarity, he still checks off the supplies list.

"Frawn-chess-ka," he lets it roll off of his tongue as if meeting this woman for the first time in some bygone cafe.

THEN

Branches swat against the raw skin on his face and neck. A drop of blood slides down his forehead but is diverted at the last second by a bushy eyebrow. The moon casts a blue glow that gifts just enough light to be able to navigate through the dense forest. Viktor gulps for air, darting between trees and over creek beds, limping and staggering with every plant of his bad leg. The pack of dead has grown in pursuit and with it their speed and intensity have magnified.

The direction and course are unknown, *escape* is what guides him. He believes he's headed back toward the main road, but he can't be sure. Even if he was, he doesn't know if that would be a good thing. Without a car, there would be little advantage to an open road. Up ahead, a clearing provides a beacon of hope with the gentle grass swaying in the night.

This will be a great place to dig your own grave.

Stumbling toward the middle of the field, he listens and looks for anything to use, anything to make a last stand. Viktor throws down his duffle bag and leans against his one real weapon, the makeshift staff. He can run no further.

"These fuckers don't get tired I'm guessing," he says between gasps.

The sudden silence sends a chill down his spine. An unbearable sound of the dead crashing through the woods, screeching and chomping, was all he heard for what could have been an hour of chase. But it has vanished. A cool wisp of air whistles through the trees and over the grass. Insects chirp a short distance away. Viktor spins in a circle, squinting into every shadow in the forest, waiting for a mob rush to break through, but it doesn't come. And then he hears it.

For the first time, he hears the creature that started it all, the one sound more frightening than the dead. A *snort*. Then the *scraping* of hooves, *pounding* in the dry dirt. It repeats but he can't pinpoint it, as now the sound surrounds him. Then from behind him, a *gallop* and the vibrating of the ground with every step. Whipping back with his staff pointed forward, he sees it. Charging at what seems like an impossible speed, a massive deer heads straight toward him, head lowered and antlers down. Breath shoots out of its nostrils into the cool air, like exhaust from a roaring engine.

Viktor stands his ground. Until he doesn't. With the great buck bearing down on him, he gets a glimpse of its eyes, dark red and hollow, then its coat and antlers, mangy and rotted, falling to pieces like old furniture with fur hanging in shreds. He dives to the ground and balls up in a fetal position, holding the staff over him in desperation.

The animal can't slow down but lowers its antlers further and hooks Viktor's right leg as it barrels over him. They both roll as he shrieks in pain. Immediately, his right leg goes numb. With a tremendous exhale from the beast, he feels the dirt blast against his face, warm and sour air right behind him. The animal staggers to its feet and rears up. It slams down on top of Viktor's side. He screams in pain again, but no sound comes from his lips. The wind has been knocked out of him. He gasps for air. The deer rolls him over with its antlers and huffs into the dirt. Rearing up, it then slams down on his lower back. He's convinced his spine is broken.

Lying motionless, face buried in dirt and grass, he thinks about how the cold blades feel good on his face and to be this close to the earth is somehow soothing. He forgets the agonizing pain that's pounding from all over his body. Viktor senses the animal moving around him. It bites at his clothes, first his pants and then his shoes. A yank at his foot feels like his whole leg has been dislocated. Another tug. He's convinced this rabid thing is going to start eating him. It snorts and stomps on his leg. It takes everything inside him not to wail and thrash around and to remain balled up and still.

Viktor slips the knife from his waistband with as little movement as possible. The deer has a large section of his shoe between its teeth and begins jerking his foot around like a dog with a toy. He sees his window and takes it. Raising the knife as far in front of him as he can, he swings it down along the grass and slashes through one of the buck's front legs. Blood and fur fly forward as the knife dings against bone.

The screeching call that follows is one of nightmares. Without hesitation, as if waking a hive of bees behind its eyes, the beast rears up and kicks down beside him. Lowering the antlers, it drives into his side, rolling him over and over. Once Viktor's belly is exposed, it rears up again and drives straight down. An antler pierces through his rib cage. As the animal shakes its head, he feels and hears the crack in his lower side as an avalanche of pain overcomes all other senses in his body. He tries to scream, but the surge of anguish is too great. Retracting its antlers, the deer steps back and aims to drive the final blow into his chest and neck.

Mustering whatever survival strength that he can find, Viktor grips the knife as if it's a lifeline hanging over a thousand-foot drop. Somehow, he rolls his body toward the animal as it steps in toward him, then grabs an antler with his free hand and pulls himself up to its raging and rabid face. The eyes aren't even looking at him, the lights are all off and it's as if he can see the entire universe in the soft emptiness of the fully dilated pupils. A snort of warm air blows against his open wound, reminding him of his pain. He drives the knife deep into the neck of the animal, just below its skull, and gives it a twist for good measure.

With no change in the animal's eyes, the whole beast goes limp and collapses to the ground. A final exhale and the mouth falls slack against the dirt. Viktor senses every torn muscle, broken rib, and bruise that torments his body. He lies there, unsure for how long, staring up at the stars trying to catch his breath and slow his heart rate as it pounds in his chest, pumping the life from his body through the hole in his side.

Each inhale comes with a *wheeze* and sharp pain. The numb tingling in his leg has given way to a throbbing sensation, consistent with his previous injury except much, much worse. Viktor may very well spend the night in that exact spot until the thought is interrupted. Lurking, cracking of branches in the edge of the forest. Moans grow in the darkness. The horde of the dead have found him, and how could they not? His screams and struggle must have been like an airhorn, advertising his exact location.

Now more dispersed and moving slower, they trickle into the clearing one by one, stumbling over holes and ruts in the grass field. He's got to get up and he knows it, but has no energy left to move. The weight of the animal lays square on his left arm. He hadn't noticed as it must have gone to sleep. He pries his arm from underneath the carcass. Every movement is a repeat of the attack, lightning bolts of pain hitting every nerve.

Viktor can hear them stepping closer, their grotesque sounds getting louder and more directional. With a strong push of his good leg, he's able to dislodge the arm and use the animal as well as his staff to pull himself to his feet. As blood moves down his body, it hits all of the pain points that have been torturing him. What he thought was a level ten is now a welcome callback. His whole body is on fire.

One foot after the other, he's able to hobble to the edge of the clearing. The dead converge and move toward him. Viktor skips to the first viable tree he can find and starts climbing. Using just arm strength, he's able to sit on the first branch. He pulls the bad leg up into a seated position. Again, using only his arms, he grabs the branch above him until he's standing on the first branch. This is the method he uses to go up another ten feet until a large, thick branch welcomes the size of his body.

He lies flat on his back as careful and quiet as he can manage. He uses the staff to bridge to another branch so he can spread out his bad leg. With growls and snarls passing below him and the contrasting peaceful sky above, Viktor gazes into the stars counting every heartbeat as the timekeeper of immeasurable pain.

NOW

Leaving the safety of the treehouse took several days of planning and gathering. While it could have been done quicker, a level of confidence was being built to take the first step in the journey, and part of that was making quick runs to nearby homes. Viktor used these structures as caches for overflow supplies knowing that if anyone came raiding, he would be out just that loot and not risk his life by residing in the same locations as his valuables. He collected by day and prepped by night.

Wanting to carry a single pack and keep the weight as light as possible, he filled the large hiking bag with enough food to last three weeks, mostly dried fruits and meats, nuts, and candy bars for their high calorie-to-weight ratio.

The one non-essential task he focused on was making sure all of his files were backed up and secured. Viktor packed all of the drives, their backups, and binders in the waterproof bins that line the walls. He secured them with a combination lock that both prevents them from being opened as well as holds them to the legs that support the counter overhead. Someone would need bolt cutters and a lot of resolve to steal them and would be most disappointed when discovering the contents.

With the brand-new, extra-large hiking backpack strapped to his shoulders, the shotgun hanging around his front, axe looped into his belt, and trusty atlas riding in the front pocket of the shoulder strap, Viktor set out from the safety of his treehouse at first light on Halloween. A sense of abandonment was hard to ignore as the weight of leaving all that he's built and collected loomed behind him. He made a stop at the solar station and shut everything down to preserve the moving parts and pieces. Returning home to a few days without power was worth the sacrifice to avoid a full-on equipment catastrophe.

Now well on his way and having memorized the first few days by heart, Viktor rarely glances at the map that plots his course. Only when a street sign has collapsed and he second-guesses his direction does he peel the page open to double-check, not even removing it from the pocket sleeve. He does know that he needs to reach a certain point before dark, some twenty miles northeast of his treehouse. A big blue circle on the map identifies the location. A few more circles are scattered outward and beyond at similar intervals in space.

"Should have waited until spring," he says as a chill of air blows leaves across the empty dirt road. This gust is cooler than the last, and it almost makes him turn back. It will get colder as the days pass and the further north he travels, but he anticipates he'll reach his destination before the first major snowfall.

What if there's nothing to find?

He can't make the trip back with winter in full tilt.

If she's alive, will it matter?

He continues walking.

The first day is uneventful, to his liking. A single dead here and there, slogging along in the woods to his flank. The ones he didn't feel like avoiding are dispatched with a quick swipe of the axe and collection of any identification. It's done with such efficiency that it doesn't impact his pace. He's allotted space in his pack for any IDs he will come across, but the thought of hauling them hundreds of miles is less than appealing, especially as the stack grows.

While the shotgun bounces off of his stomach and hip, he has yet to draw it. He carries it as a backup, with a heavy amount of spare ammo that he regretted from the start, knowing that the sound often brings more trouble than by evading or plunging the blade. The movement of the barrel off of his upper leg has become rhythmic in his subconscious, and he catches himself keeping pace based on the tactile tap against his thigh.

Stopping along a creek bed for lunch, Viktor unrolls a portable solar panel meant for charging his phone and small electronics. He lets it top off in the sunlight and attaches it to the back of his backpack to collect more sun as he walks. He retrieves a phone. It's one he's kept for years. This device didn't belong to anyone as he yanked it from an electronics store as it advertised the largest storage capacity. On it, he's loaded what he hopes is enough podcasts, audiobooks, and music to last the trip. All these files came from various strangers whose phones he cleared out months and years prior. This vast library of media, of which he carries a fraction, is also stored back at the treehouse.

He's often transported to thinking about who and how these things had previously been consumed, silencing out the very content being played and daydreaming about it being amplified through a girl's headphones while running, or a guy's pickup truck while driving. As he scrunches up the wrappers of his lunch and shoves them into a designated trash pouch, Viktor slings the bag back over his shoulder. He places one earbud into his left ear and lets the other dangle over his collar. He prefers the wired variety to conserve power.

Browsing the phone, he finds something interesting and selects the play button. With one ear free to listen for danger, Viktor resumes the route with some in-flight entertainment. The financial times podcast spouts information on gold and silver commodities that goes way over his head but he listens for a different reason. The memory and feeling of a time that no longer exists, like a looking glass back to an era of happiness. The encouragement of what life was before, and the feeling of nostalgia that is along for the ride. There will be plenty of time for music but, at the moment, he's lost in years-old financial advice.

Anxiety grows as the blue circle on his map approaches slower than anticipated. As the late afternoon hours set in, Viktor recalculates in his head. He estimates he can reach the dot in another hour or so, and with that assumption, he picks up his pace along what appears to be an endless train track.

Foot over foot along the railroad, visual fatigue begins to set in as the scenery changes little. The ties pass at perfect intervals and it almost makes him dizzy. The weeds are high in some places as an absence of train traffic has caused spots to grow a few feet above the rails, but he's quick to stomp them down with a hefty boot.

The one downside to traveling along the tracks is bearing the sun overhead without the relief of shade for long sections. Luckily, the rays have now sunk below the tree line and given him some comfort for the past hour or so. Viktor shakes his head and bats his eyes to try to maintain focus. He's been on the tracks too long, a strange vertigo from the repetition-induced eye strain.

He takes a knee as an idea stems from the impairment. From the bag, he retrieves a section of rope, maybe three yards in length. Holding it outward, he measures the distance between the rails, tying a knot in the rope over each one to represent their distance from one another. He uses his hand to approximate the width of the rail itself. In his mind, the lightbulb moment will work, and he has the information he needs to take a swing during his next stop.

He continues on and up ahead cross street bisects the tracks. Checking the map, he's just a half-mile from the blue circle. Viktor steps off the tracks and heads north up the single-lane, paved road. Cicadas chirp in the tall grass. A burnt-out car sits off the shoulder with litter scattered around it.

A dirt road designated by a single mailbox leads off to his right. Dense woods line both sides of the driveway as far as he can see. Tucking the map away, he turns onto the dirt patch and walks several hundred yards in the only direction it travels. After a short bend, the old white house emerges from among the trees. The faded siding and ominous screened front porch hang the same as when he was last here. Tall grass has taken over the once trim lawn but the dirt pathway leading around back is still visible.

Without more than the initial glance at the home, he bypasses it and walks around the back and further into the woods. Along a clearing, he follows the worn, but almost overgrown trail. Still within view of the old house, and the familiar clearing on his right, Viktor finds the tree that's circled on his map.

The towering tree that once saved his life stands in front of him. Bent and weathered boards hang horizontally, still nailed to the face of the trunk. He slides out his axe and climbs board after board toward a large flat wooden platform several feet off the ground. As Viktor makes it to the base, he peeks over the edge of the floor. With nothing more than a few leaves cluttering the planks, he pulls himself up and over onto the very first treehouse he ever built.

Viktor unpacks his bag and sets out a rolled sleeping pad and blanket. A small LED lantern sits next to him that he switches on. It's not much light, but as darkness takes the forest it will be more than enough illumination. If he were staying more than one night then he would risk a fire, but the warmth of his kit should do well enough for now.

He sets out a few packs of food, jerky and nuts, as he likes to save anything with carbohydrates for breakfast. Before enjoying the modest dinner, he shuts off his phone and plugs it into the portable solar panel to charge.

The food is satisfactory enough. At this point, it's all about going through the motions as little enjoyment is derived from the consumption of a meal. It's a task, like any other, and it's been months since he's had a craving for the unlimited offerings of the past.

By the light of the lantern, he pulls out the single magazine that he packed for the trip. While filling supplies from a store he saw the dusty cover staring back at him from the cashier line. A very muscular man beaming a smile on the cover.

"Be the man she's always wanted. Speak the language of her dreams!" he reads.

He flips to page nine and reads the article, rolling his eyes more times than he can count. He wonders what Sandra would say about it, or if Caroline would have shared a laugh with him over the nonsense. Then his mind wanders to Francesca, and there it battles between meaningless words on the page and imagining fantastical scenarios of their future.

THEN

Sleep was elusive as even the slightest movement jolted his body awake with the sense of plunging to the ground. The bark of the tree was rough with sharp edges and a knot protruded into his bruised and broken ribs. The pain throbbed and worsened as the night went on, so much that out of pure exhaustion he passed out.

Dawn comes and goes and gives way to mid-day. The thick canopy shields much of the direct light, and it's the change in temperature that causes him to stir. Viktor rolls to the right but the belt has him secured in place, a moment of confusion causes him to overcorrect the other direction, and he almost rolls off the other side of the branch.

The sudden fall panic takes care of any grogginess. The agony burns all around his body but he can now comprehend his injuries with more clarity. Peeling up his torn shirt that's stuck to the gaping gore hole in his ribcage, Viktor bites his bottom lip and cranes his neck to get a good look. He knows he needs to get it cleaned as soon as possible or risk infection. The puncture looks mostly superficial or he would have otherwise bled out in his sleep.

A hell of a scar and story to tell.

Not that there will be anyone to hear it.

After several minutes of examining each wound, Viktor casts his eyes to the ground below, remembering what chased him up there. The leaves and needles are scattered and disturbed, but the horde of dead is long gone, save for one. Half of a man is bent upright at the trunk of the tree, scratching and biting at the bark. Its lower half is a trail of intestines and sinew. A path of red in the dirt illustrates the manner of arrival.

He understands the need to get down and find a proper shelter if there's any chance to mend, but he's in no mood or condition to fight for his life right now. Undoing the belt and struggling to sit upright, Viktor gathers up his staff and places it across two branches. Using it as a pull-up bar, he lowers himself down to the next branch praying it will hold his weight. Once his footing is secure, he twists the staff and slides it through the branches, down to rest next to him against the trunk. A mere six feet off the ground he stands up, wobbling, contemplating how to navigate the biting teeth and snarls coming from below.

"Fuck it."

Placing both hands on the staff he holds it out in front of him, pointy side down. With a single step, he's off the branch and falling feet first toward the ground. With all of his weight behind it, he drives the sharp end through the dead's mouth and out the back of its neck, spiking it to the earth as he falls. The rod breaks in half and he tumbles over the entrails and rolls across the worn grassy patch. The pain shoots everywhere in a renewed intensity but the snapping of his weapon helped to soften his crash.

Viktor staggers to his feet and makes his way into the clearing. He finds the deer carcass, which looks even more hideous in full light, and retrieves his knife that's still embedded in its neck. Wiping it off on his pant leg and tucking it into his waistband, he then gathers his duffel bag from where he dropped it among the matted grass and trampled earth. It has some blood and dirt stains but is otherwise intact. He double-checks for the photos of his family inside, just to be sure.

Carrying the bag by his fingertips, he walks along a faint trail along the edge of the clearing. A flash of white through the trees catches his eye, except it's not moving. It appears to be something stationary that comes into view between the blowing of the branches. As he gets closer, he realizes that it's siding and that the white is a wall, part of a small two-story house.

A narrow dirt driveway leads away from the home and deep into the forest. A single power line runs along the road and ends with a hanging line down to the front porch roof. No vehicles are in the driveway and the home appears undisturbed. Leaves are scattered and piled on the edges of the porch. A piece of paper hangs from the front screen door, blowing in the gentle breeze. He looks around once more before calling out.

"Hello, is anyone home?"

Viktor eyes the surroundings to be sure no surprises are lurking in the woods.

"I'm badly hurt. Er, not bitten or anything, but I could use some help and I just need to clean up."

He makes a point of holding his palm against his wound in case someone is peering from inside, selling the severity of the injury. He steps up onto the porch.

"May I come in? Hello?"

He taps a few times on the door, the hollow frame and loose hinges rattle with a familiarity of his grandparent's home, comforting in its modesty. The note shifts again in the wind and he lifts it off of the screen.

His lips move as he reads the small sheet of paper.

Janice, your dad and I drove into town for help.
We haven't much supplies here and his medication is low.
The news didn't say a whole lot before we lost signal so hoping
we will make it back soon. Please wait here for us to return.
I'll keep trying to call from my cell but doesn't seem to be
working anymore. Don't come looking for us, please stay put
until we get back.

Love ya,
Mom

Pressing the tape, Viktor reapplies the note in the same place where he found it and opens the unlocked door. The porch has the smell of mothballs and dust. A pair of sneakers sit next to the door, the kind with two Velcro straps in place of laces. The tops are worn ragged and have stains of mud and grass. He steps onto the doormat and knocks again.

"Is anyone there? May I come in?"

After waiting a few seconds, he tries the doorknob. The small white orb with chipped paint and loose screws turns without any resistance. The glass door rattles as it opens inward. Without committing, Viktor leans his head in and calls out once more.

"Hello."

With no sound returning from inside, he steps off the mat and enters the home. The smell of food still lingers in the air. Once a pet peeve, the experience of entering someone's home only to smell cooked onions or fried bacon was enough to make him cringe, though he was always polite and pretended otherwise. Now the faint smell brings a hopeful feeling that the dead haven't taken over everything, just yet.

He traces the smell to the kitchen. Simple, flat cabinets painted green with peeling brass knobs. Linoleum flooring that's probably older than he is. Appliances that look to be out of a museum and in no way operational are proven to work by the scent that lingers. A stack of papers and envelopes sit on the small, round kitchen table, the top bordered by a corrugated metal ring and metal chairs with taped tears in the cushions, also an off-green color.

Taking quiet steps around the kitchen, he listens to every creak that calls out from the old floorboards. The character of this house reminds him of something from his childhood, a combination of reading old books and his grandparents. There are a few cans of goods that he's reluctant to take.

What if they return?

He takes half of them and places them in his bag, leaving the rest behind.

The rooms of the home are all small and quaint, with dated wallpaper and dolls or animal statues occupying each dresser and shelf. A girl's room, a boy's room, photos of children in each, though the beds look like they haven't been slept in for years. If he hadn't seen what he has over the past forty-eight hours it would all look haunting, but in comparison it's endearing.

Making his way back to the kitchen, Viktor opens the back door and looks out into the small backyard. A rusted swing set still supports two flat swings that sway back and forth. The faintest squeak from the chain matching its movement. A patch of dirt still owns the space beneath, where feet pushed and jumped and climbed onto the seats for who knows how many years. A shed is to one corner of the yard, and he notices a large stack of vertical barn planks resting upright against the side wall. Grass and weeds grow up thick around them. It's these wooden boards that give him an idea.

The moment he stepped foot into the house, he knew he

wouldn't be spending the night inside. Worst-case scenarios looped through his mind that extinguished any ideas of staying in the confines of the home. Having looted all of what he could in good conscience from the owners, including the supplies that he plans to use to clean up his wounds, Viktor now steps out into the backyard and makes his way to the shed. He examines the wood planks, cobwebs peel off as he flips them over, nails stick out with rusted points, but the boards are in good enough shape for what he's thinking.

He unhooks the shed latch and looks inside. A riding lawn mower sits centered in the middle. On both sides, plastic shelving rises from floor to ceiling. He finds a hammer and a box of assorted nails. Pulling two boards at a time, he drags them from the shed to the tree at the edge of the clearing where he spent the previous night. Viktor stacks them at the base and goes back for more. It takes over an hour, but he's dragged the whole bundle of wood to the tree.

Carrying a couple of plastic bottles of warm soda, the hammer, nails, and a small hatchet he found in the shed, he makes a final trip to the tree to begin working on the platform. He hacks a dozen or so foot-lengths of wood and then tosses the hatchet aside and grabs the hammer along with a handful of nails. Shoving most in his pocket and a couple between his lips, Viktor lines up a small board just a short distance off of the ground. It takes a few tries, but he's able to sink a first and then second nail into the center of the board. Letting go it hangs firm on the face of the tree. He gives it a good tug for assurance and it doesn't budge.

Measuring the same distance between each rung, he repeats the method up the tree until he's reached the branch where he spent the night. The work slows with each new foothold as it becomes harder to hold up his body weight while hammering the rung in place. He lost count of how many trips he's climbed up and down, but each seems to aggravate his aches and pains. Upon nailing the last rung, Viktor pulls himself up onto the large branch that he'll use for the base.

After several minutes of rest, he manages to motivate himself back down the tree for his first large plank. Viktor stands it up next to himself and holds what he guesses is the six-foot mark before settling it back down. He organizes the boards according to size. They'll go up uncut so he'll need to work with what's he's got. The organized piles of wood sit at his feet.

"Well, looks like you're not going to build yourself."

Viktor picks up the longest piece but lugging the board to the top isn't as easy as he had hoped, limping with every step upward. He takes another rest on the branch with the large board spread across his lap. Hammer and nails sit like a dinner plate in front of him. He rolls his eyes at the stack of boards below and then looks through the trees to the white house, contemplating if any of this strain is worth it when there's a perfectly good home nearby.

"Hello?" a woman's voice calls out.

Viktor can't believe his ears.

"Mom! Dad!" she cries out again, from somewhere beyond the house. He stares through the trees, squinting for any sign of movement.

"It's Janice! Hello?"

Holy. Shit.

NOW

With the first sign of dawn peeking through the trees, Viktor checks his watch and wastes no time packing up his things and descending the ladder rungs. He still remembers the day he hammered them to the face of the trunk, in constant agony from the previous night's attack. And then the visitor. *What was her name? Janice.* He hadn't truly forgotten.

He places an earbud in one ear, positions the solar panel hanging off the bag, and then he's headed back toward the train track and onward to the next blue circle on his map. Viktor calculated it would take about eleven hours between these two spots, and he's eager to get back on schedule.

For the next mile or so he grants his mind to be transported by the feelings of some nostalgic songs, allowing himself to miss those that are gone, and welcoming the mental images of a past that he believes are remembered only by him. Doing so invigorates his spirit and determination. He convinces himself this mission isn't for himself, not a self-serving attempt to find someone who's been long dead, but the task of collecting identities. Preserving the past.

After half a day of walking the tracks, he makes a scheduled exit. Dirt roads give way to single-lane paved roads that lead into small towns. Viktor stops a couple of times to re-check stores that he's visited before. An extra bottle of water here, scrap of food there, and he's on his way. The smaller roads grow larger, which he expected based on his navigational plan. The next blue dot is not far from a city, its name illegible from the streak of blue ink. He has a plan to avoid the larger population centers and in the next town, before his rest stop, he'll look for the supplies he needs to put that plan into action.

To his relief, the hardware store is still standing, without any signs of forced entry or dead ambushes awaiting him. This city bypass opportunity that he considers hinges on him being able to build what he needs and it working out to offset the time of going around instead of through the city. Had the store been gutted or overrun, Viktor would be scrambling for a plan B. Navigating to an aisle with large wheels, intended for lawn mowers or wheel barrels, he compares the width of one of the wheels to his hand, trying to remember the exact size he needs. Deciding they will do, he grabs four wheels, brackets, hammer and nails, and a large chain.

Using the chain, he threads the four wheels and slings them over his shoulder like an ammo belt. It's heavy, but this is the best opportunity to get what he needs for the project. The hammer and nails go in his bag. Behind the buildings and next to a dumpster he finds a stack of junked items. Washing machines, a shopping cart, and the prize: a bicycle frame. It's missing a front tire, and the back tire is still intact, but flat. He inspects it for any tears or holes but it looks to be undamaged.

A pool supply store caps the end of the plaza. There's no glass left in the windows where the front of a car smashed through. He steps up over the bumper and through the empty window casing.

It's a small store and he can gauge from the outside that it's free of threat. Next to boxes containing animal-shaped pool floats, Viktor grabs a rectangular package that hangs from a wall hangar. It's an inflator and should work fine for his bike tire. It takes a few minutes to pump the tire by hand, but when he bounces it on the sidewalk and it springs back, he lets out a howl of achievement.

His arms grow tired as they support the bike upright, rolling along on just the back tire as he walks along the road. Viktor continues another two hours down a scorching highway, without a single cloud to block the sun. After a hard right turn down an embankment and into the woods at the mile marker that he's designated on the map, it takes a short hike to get to the hidden pond surrounded by tall pines. Algae has overtaken a large part of the water's surface and flies battle mosquitoes for superiority. The treehouse that he's heading to is far enough beyond the water that the pests are kept in check.

Exhausted, Viktor dumps his non-essentials to the base of the tree and begins a very high climb up a sophisticated rope ladder. This shelter may very well be his favorite, not in scope but location and view. Halfway up the trunk he stops and reaches out against the bark. A deep engraving is almost unreadable, but it's still there. *AJ & MD*. A large heart outlines the letters. Another sign of humanity that brings him a little comfort.

As he hoped and was counting on, several cases of bottled water remained stacked in the corner, covered in dust but ripe for the taking. He uses a bottle to quench his thirst, and another to brush his teeth. With each location he's built, he made a point to stock it with as many emergency supplies as he could not knowing when the time might come. And thinking if anyone might stumble across it makes him feel good, imagining how happy they would be upon seeing the stash and taking what they needed. His old faded sign granting as much is still secured to the tree above the water, though it appears nobody has been close enough to know it was even there for the taking.

Having spent the better part of four years branching out, building, foraging, stocking, there's more than enough to last him his lifetime. But none other than his primary place has a solar setup as the rest aren't as sophisticated. He determined it would be unlikely that a power setup would even be functional upon his scattered visits.

After a peaceful night's sleep and an early rise, he enjoys a quick breakfast. Viktor then climbs down the ladder as he is eager to begin working on his contraption. In his head, it will function as designed, and save him both time and energy as well as give him a safer route, but he knows there's little time to waste if he's to make it to the next stop by nightfall.

Gathering the wheels and tools, he lays out the design on the ground. Four wheels sit on each corner. He pries a few boards off of the top walls of the treehouse and lays those perpendicular to the wheels. Digging through his backpack, he finds the rope he had marked for just this purpose. Two knots identify a specific length and he sets the wheels at their exact points. Using the nails and hammer he secures each wheel to a corner of the makeshift platform.

Spinning each for good measure, Viktor is satisfied with their balance. Upon flipping the whole thing over he lines up the half bike on the right side, matching the good tire with the tires of the new cart. The Y-shaped frame is attached where the front tire would be, fitting snug over a section of the wood. It's not as easy to secure, but using several nails and tension from the chain it holds steady. He even sits on the bike seat to ensure it doesn't tip.

One more nail goes in the center front board and he hammers

it to bend it down to form a hook point. Now using the same piece of rope, he threads the nail and it catches on the knot. A hard tug on the rope pulls the cart and bike forward. The bag and weapons go on the cart and he tows it out of the woods. It takes just a few minutes to reach the railroad from the treehouse.

Using a spot where the road bisects the tracks, Viktor moves the cart to the rails and, as somewhat of a surprise, they line up. The real test will be if they spin. Using the claw of the hammer, he peels the rubber from the tires one by one, exposing the metal rim. This takes longer than the rest of the build as the wheels are new and stubborn.

Ten bucks this doesn't work.

Viktor realigns it to the track and adjusts the cart until it clanks down onto the rails. Using his foot, Viktor pushes the cart back and forth to test the resistance.

"Ha, would you look at that!"

The cart rolls along the track under the guidance of his foot. The back tire of the bike doesn't quite line up with the rail but he's able to bend the frame until it's just right. He had considered centering it but the rugged planks bouncing under the wheel didn't seem like a fun ride. If the wheel can stay on track it'll be smooth riding. He reloads the cart and mounts the bike, being cautious not to mess up the balance. It holds steady and even rolls forward under the weight.

Viktor begins to pedal and the momentum builds. Once the platform gets going, he estimates his speed at almost ten miles per hour, outpacing his walking pace and making up for the planned detour. He lets the bike coast every so often to check the atlas, rest his legs, and take a swig of water. He was so engrossed in the project that he forgot to put in his earbud when he got going. The solar panel lies flat on the cart sending a full charge to his device.

Viktor will save the battery and reward himself with a movie or TV show tonight, though there aren't more than a couple of titles to choose from.

Aside from a few sections of overgrown weeds where he slowed down to avoid derailing his setup, Viktor makes great time and pedals at a steady pace. An hour before dusk, he arrives at the cross street where he needs to disembark. It's not until he steps off that he feels the throbbing pain in his hip from the repetitive motion of pedaling.

A short trek through the woods takes him to the furthest treehouse of his network. It's also the simplest. Viktor rolls his eyes as he gazes up at the tree, remembering the build. Five boards weave between thick branches. Thin wood makes a sorry railing surrounding the floor. Small blocks of misshapen scrap wood compose the footings to climb.

"Up we go."

Viktor settles in and is quick to realize why he had chosen this location. The soft murmur of a river not far off soothes any discomfort from the modest shelter. As the sun descends well below the canopy, Viktor passes the time reading more of his magazine. Once it's dark, he turns on his phone and navigates to the videos folder. He finds a film and hits play.

With an earbud in place, he reflects on the peacefulness of the starry night overhead, enjoying the familiar dialogue of the movie that he's seen countless times. He quotes along in the open air just above a whisper.

THEN

A figure moves between the trees. Viktor can't believe his eyes. From the perch of the unfinished floor, he peers through the branches as the mystery person circles the white-sided home. He loses track, only to pick up the bright shirt again on the other side of the house.

"It can't be," he whispers.

The person is out of sight, maybe back to the front of the home. Viktor lowers himself down the tree and retrieves the hatchet. He approaches the home, stealthy and agile, peering around the corner before advancing. With soft footsteps, he makes his way to the front of the house. Leaning at a severe angle to keep behind the wall and out of sight, he examines the front yard and driveway. He takes another step forward, moving past the wall and along the front porch.

In the driveway, a small silver car has been parked in what appears to be a hasty arrival. A shiver is cast over his body as his arm hair perks up over goosebumps. A *sniffle*. Stifling of tears and wiping against a sleeve. The soft breathing that he hears seems unreal. Sitting on the porch steps, face in hands that grasp the note of paper, a woman sobs, unaware of his presence. Viktor is frozen, unsure of what to do. He can only think to flee. He puts one foot behind him, an attempt to backtrack the way he came. A scuff of gravel betrays his plot to sneak away. Startled and frightened, the woman jumps back against the wall, screaming at the sight of him.

"Who are you!" she yells.

He can't even open his lips to breathe.

"Stay the fuck back!" the woman demands.

She's on her feet, slamming the screen door between them. With her sleeve, she wipes her face of any sign of sadness. Fear and anger are the only emotions on display. The woman glances to each side of her, probably looking for a weapon to defend herself. Viktor sees this and tries to deescalate the situation.

"I won't harm you," he says, emphasizing a soft tone.

"Who are you, where are my parents!"

Before he can answer he's interrupted.

"If you hurt them, I swear to God I'll kill you. You'll wish you were found by one of those things instead of me!"

Viktor raises an empty hand, lowering the hatchet with the other that he now realizes he was holding up in a defensive posture. The woman stares back, eyes wild, darting between him and the car. Her dark brown hair is in a fuss, but still holds the shape of the tight curls that don't quite touch her shoulders. The bright yellow shirt she wears is stained with tears. She appears not much older than himself, but her round face is worn and tired.

"I promise I haven't hurt anyone. I was just passing through, saw the home, and planned to stay for the night. Nobody else has been here since I arrived. I swear it."

"You saw the note and didn't leave? What kind of person snoops around someone else's home?" Tears begin to replace the redness of anger.

"Ma'am, I've been almost eaten alive more times than I can count in the past two days. I was attacked by some sort of rabid deer that tried to tear me to shreds" He lifts his shirt to show the wound, but if she cares she doesn't show it. "And I haven't seen another person alive since…" Letting his shirt down, he trails off. He leaves out the boy in the neighborhood.

"Well, since my own daughter. But she's…"

The woman has the slightest change in body language, but she still holds the screen door closed.

"If I thought anyone would be back here, I would have been on my way. I swear it."

"What's your name?" she asks.

A sigh of relief that he tries to hide, escapes his lips.

"Viktor. I suppose you're Janice?" He motions to the paper in her hands. She nods in return.

"I'm sorry but I helped myself to some things from inside, and grabbed some food as well. I've got it all in the woods out back, I can return what I haven't used." Janice shakes her head and cracks open the door. "Keep it. I'm not staying myself. Despite their wishes, I've got to find them." Her voice breaks as she says the words, unable to look at the note that she still holds.

She opens the door all the way and gestures. He hesitates as she nods to his shirt. Looking down, Viktor notices blood has stained through. He applies pressure and winces at the pain that responds.

"Come on, I'm a nurse. Not the first wound I've dressed today." There's a hint of kindness with her offer. He manages a small smile and accepts her invitation.

Janice pulls out a chair at the small dining table and insists he sit. Viktor does, using the tabletop to support his weight as he eases into the seat.

"Lift up your shirt. Don't be shy," she says as if he's just seeing the school nurse.

Viktor lifts the side of his shirt to expose the injury. She stretches her lips acknowledging the ugly nature of it all and takes a close, hard look.

"Sit tight, I'm going to need to clean it up a bit. A bandage and some antibiotics and you'll be good as new." Her voice trails as she leaves the room.

Viktor can hear her clanking around in the bathroom adjacent to the kitchen. He hopes she doesn't notice what he's taken for himself already.

"Thank you, Janice. I mean it, you don't have to help me," he calls out, loud enough for her to hear from the other room.

No reply, but a moment later she returns to the kitchen with a clear bottle, gauze, tape, and a little orange prescription canister.

"Don't thank me just yet, this will probably sting a bit."

Without warning, she splashes the liquid on his dark, oozing wound. He bites his lips, trying to suppress the pain that comes from the cool wetness that stirs the injury and aggravates the nerves.

"Tough guy, I see."

Janice dabs the area with the gauze and tosses the used pieces aside.

"Normally I wouldn't use straight rubbing alcohol but I don't trust what's coming out of the faucet right now." She examines the small puncture. "We're not quite done yet."

She retrieves a pair of tweezers from a small dish where they were resting in the same clear liquid. When she did that, he can't say, but she's good he can tell. Viktor rears back in pain as it feels like she's stuck her whole finger inside his ribcage and is poking around.

"Almost got it."

His eyes are closed as tight as he can manage as the sharp pain subsides. A metallic clank in the dish beside him as the tweezers drop.

"Is that bone?"

"Antler," he replies, opening his eyes to see the small shard lying on a towel next to him.

Judging by how it felt to have it removed, he would have guessed it to be the size of a quarter, but the fragment is no larger than a fingernail. Janice places a few clean patches of gauze over the area and tapes them in place.

"There you go, good as new." She opens the pill bottle, spills a couple into her hand, and then closes the lid.

"Take a couple of these every day until they're gone. They're expired but should be okay. Lucky for you, Mom never threw anything away."

"Thank you, really," Viktor says.

Janice gathers the used gauze and triage kit and moves toward the bathroom. As she brushes by Viktor, he notices a bandage on the back of her neck.

"What happened there?"

She stops halfway out of the kitchen and places a hand on the back of her neck.

"Oh, this? I told you, you weren't my first patient today," she chuckles and walks into the bathroom.

Viktor pulls himself to his feet, his hand sliding off of the table.

"You sure you're okay?"

It's hard to hear her response through the bathroom walls. Cabinets closing and the doors creaking step over her words. He struggles to make them out.

"I finally got the courage to leave the safety of my home and

    Ryan Young

come check on my folks, who of course weren't answering the phone. While I was running to my car, a man came out of nowhere and latched onto my back, I thought he was trying to grab my purse or steal my car."

Viktor takes soft steps, navigating toward the back door. He doesn't like where the story is headed and feels the need to be outside, in the open. The house feels claustrophobic and stuffy.

"That's when the fool bit me. Tore right into my shoulder and neck. You should have seen it, you thought yours was bad. He took a nice chunk outta me."

More banging around the bathroom accompanies her voice. He's almost to the door, reaching behind him, feeling for the handle.

"I kicked him off and jumped into my car so fast I thought I was going to drag him with me. I did a couple of loops around the block until the man was gone and went back inside to clean it up."

Janice emerges from the bathroom, wiping her hands.

"Then I got back in the car and came straight up here."

She looks at him with uncertainty as he stands against the door, his knuckles white as he grips the doorknob.

"Everything okay?"

"Yeah, I'm fine. Just think I'm going to finish up my little shelter and spend the night out back. Never felt good about staying in a stranger's home."

"You're staying out there?" She gestures to the woods beyond the door.

"I know, it's weird but I insist. I could be a crazy person and you've done more than enough."

She laughs. "Well you're crazy for wanting to sleep outside, but suit yourself. Come by the house if you change your mind."

He nods thanks and walks out of the back door, minding the

broken steps.

Janice holds the door open with a hand on her neck as he walks through the backyard. As he looks back, he thinks she's gone pale.

Has she always looked this way or is it only now?

"I'll be gone in the morning, you're welcome to whatever you need," she says as he steps into the high grass of the clearing.

He waves with gratitude and turns toward the trees.

Viktor can't help the uneasy feeling of leaving her inside. Still not quite sure of how the transition works, Viktor thinks about how fast Caroline changed, but he's yet to deal with a bite victim. Of the little news he saw, some mentioned transmission and fever leading to infection within twenty-four hours, but who knows what was real and nonsense, or if bites were even fatal.

He's able to finish the structure before it's too dark to work. Lying bundled on the floor, sleep doesn't come easy. The glow from a window nags at him through the forest.

"Goodnight, Janice," he whispers.

If she hasn't left by morning, then he'll check on her. Viktor comforts his decision with that rationale over and over again. If she hasn't turned by then she could be fine, and he'll worry about it in the morning. Best case scenario she drives away, turns somewhere down the road, and crashes her car where she can't eat anyone for breakfast.

He nods off and on, glancing up into the trees to see if the light is still on in the window. It stays lit through into the darkest hours and it's then that Viktor falls asleep, but the cold dampness of the morning brings a too quick rise. It's almost dawn, and there's no more light from the house. Perhaps she turned it off, or better yet, maybe she's already gone. Not wanting to stick around any longer than necessary, he makes his way down the tree and back toward the home. He goes around the front and there's no sign of anyone there. The car is not in the driveway, so she must have left at some point during the night. It must have been while he was asleep but he's surprised it didn't wake him, though he remembers he also didn't hear her arrive.

Dodged that bullet.

Eager to be on the way, Viktor walks past the house without any intention of going back inside. But hunger convinces him otherwise, he should do one last sweep for anything useful now that she did give permission to take what he didn't grab the first time.

He enters the house as if it were his own. A light is still on in the bathroom, which was unexpected but he pays little attention.

Remembering the house still has power, he looks to the dated, square TV in the center of the small living room. Viktor had meant to check it the night before until the interaction with Janice sent him fleeing to the trees. After a little searching, he finds the remote. Deciphering its controls, the TV *thunks* to life with that old but familiar sound of an aging set. Bunny ears stick out of the top and he manages to find a channel with some digital static. He adjusts the antennae and a signal breaks through, but it's far from anything informative or useful. An audible tone fills the room and a solid blue image with counting numbers appears on the screen. They repeat one through ten. Underneath the counter the sole text reads:

EMERGENCY BROADCAST ANNOUNCEMENT - SEEK SHELTER

"No shit."

He places his bag and hatchet on the floor and grants himself a seat on the couch, propping up his boots on the wicker coffee table. Flipping through the basic channels, pixelated signals come as expected. The sound of the TV drowns out the soft drag of fabric across the hardwood floor. From the kitchen behind him, a scrape and bump of metal against metal. Viktor looks over his shoulder but seeing nothing more than an empty kitchen, he turns back to the set. Flipping channels back to the announcement and the tone breaks the noise.

The flickering of the TV lulls him into a trance. A violent tug on his pantleg startles Viktor out of his place on the couch. Decayed arms flail with a throaty growl. He hops over the armrest and stumbles into the kitchen, bumping into the microwave cart.

He yanks the cord from the wall and moves to the couch. As a hand digs into the fabric of the seat cushion, Viktor lifts the microwave overhead and then slams it down onto the skull of the dead. It pops against the floor like a red balloon. Brain matter splatters the outside of the microwave, the corner implanted into the back of its head.

"Jesus. Janice..." he sighs with his hand over his mouth.

The sight before him is grotesque.

That was a bit much.

The now-motionless corpse oozes onto the floorboards and area rug. Her legs are twisted below the waist at an unnatural angle. The fabric of the couch absorbs the blood as it travels upward from the floor. He hurries to grab all of his belongings and notices the back door, bouncing open in the breeze.

With bag in hand, Viktor stops in the kitchen, seeing a purse on the counter. He digs through it searching for her keys. He stops when he sees Janice's cell phone and wallet. At that moment he isn't sure why, but he feels an overwhelming duty to take her phone. Not stopping there, he slides her driver's license out of the wallet, pairs it with the device, and shoves it into his bag. No keys are found within the purse and so he grabs what food he left behind and they go with the rest of her belongings.

The silver car sits parked in the back just off the stoop. He can see the trunk is open and there are boxes in the back seat. There's blood covering the broken stairs where dead Janice must have plunged through. Her mangled and broken legs now make sense as he hops down from the house.

He closes the trunk and gets into the car. The thought of her parents returning home to find her body makes him sick, as does the hope that they're already dead so they can avoid such horror. Sorrow and guilt are abandoned for relief. The keys still dangle from the ignition as the door open chime dings inside. He climbs in and gives the ignition a crank. Viktor pulls around to the front of the house, giving the front door one last glance, and accelerates down the driveway. The house shrinks in the rearview mirror. It disappears in a brownish-red fog as the dirt kicks up behind him.

NOW

A crab apple tree on the way back to the tracks provides an unexpected but welcome impromptu breakfast. He packs his bag full of the ripest ones, not worried about the extra weight as it will soon be off of his shoulders and riding on the cart. The small apple is sour, but he doesn't mind the tartness.

The morning is still young as he arrives at the railroad, but the contraption he built is nowhere to be found. For a moment he thinks he dreamt even building it, then readies his shotgun, convinced someone has stolen it and is now watching from the tree line. He even pulls out his atlas thinking maybe he went the wrong way after detouring for the apples. Then, in the distance, a peculiar sight allows him to lower the shotgun as he furrows his brow. A few hundred yards down the track, he sees that the cart is rolling away. His eyes must be playing tricks but it looks as if it's being pushed.

Was the apple already bad? It tasted fine.

Viktor shakes his head and squints, trying to make sense of what's taking place before him. Re-slinging the shotgun, he picks up a quick pace to catch up to the cart. After fifty yards or so the reality of what's happening seems impossible. A dead is lying face down on the cart, with armless pits oozing from the shoulders. Without any arms all it can do is move its feet, driving back and forth, unable to right itself. This motion propels the cart further down the track. He wonders how far this guy would have gotten and how close he was to losing the cart altogether. Like an untethered row boat lost to the sea.

Walking up behind the dead, it becomes aware of his presence but is unable to turn or move in any direction other than forward.

"You gave me quite the scare, fella!" he muses.

Whipping out the axe, Viktor raises it high but doesn't bring it down. Not only due to the challenge of a moving target but he's also humored by a concept that pops into his brain. The thought alone makes him chuckle. He resets the axe into his belt and skips ahead of the cart.

Once aboard, he plops down cross-legged facing the dead's upper half. It bites and growls but is stuck by gravity and its own propulsion pushing forward. The cart rolls slow with his weight, but only for a moment. The enticement of Viktor acting as a carrot enrages the dead to drive harder and harder against the ties in the track.

"Nobody would believe this."

He snaps a photo with his phone before hopping off the slow-moving ride. He moves around to the back of the cart and has to step on the dead's legs to stop it from moving forward. It writhes, trying to figure out how to turn around. He raises his axe once again but this time doesn't hesitate. The blade splits the dead's head in two and exits through the jaw. It sticks into the cart.

"Goddammit."

Wasting more time, he struggles with trying to remove the blade and keep the cart from rolling forward. After many failed attempts, he decides to pry the body off the axe. Viktor grabs the dead's head like a split cantaloupe and using a boot to push the cart, lifts the head off the axe. The handle hits the top of the spine and further connects the body to the cart.

A moment of levity has turned into legitimate frustration as he yanks at the corpse. With a forceful kick of the boot against the cart and a jerk with his hands, the crunch and crack of bone releases the cart and axe from the body. Viktor rolls the corpse over and digs through the pockets. No phone or wallet, but he finds a name badge and lanyard tucked into the back of the jeans.

"Earl Schwarsky. Head of Maintenance, Chatham Railyard Services."

He stuffs the badge into the designated pocket of his bag and catches up to the cart. Resuming yesterday's routine, he drives himself along down the track with vigor. Eager to make up time as he's unaware of where he'll sleep tonight. Viktor has now gone beyond the furthest point of his network and the lack of safety from his treehouses weighs on his mind.

The grade of the track changes as he can feel the resistance against his thighs. He pedals uphill for hours and almost regrets building this heavy burden. It's not until he reaches the leveling point and sees the valley below that he reconsiders. The grade changes just enough that the cart begins rolling on its own.

"This should be fun."

Viktor gives the pedals a few hard turns and lifts his feet as they spin freely. The momentum picks up as gravity pulls him down the grade. He's not going fast enough to cause concern but enough to enjoy the breeze and not do any work to keep himself going. Every couple of minutes he gives himself a good hard pedal to keep the speed consistent. He travels miles down the slope into a valley of dense trees.

From up high he can see towering industrial stacks and office buildings, maybe a small town off to his right. Once the cart comes to a stop at the level of the track, he'll hike through the wooded area and try to find a shelter near the town.

The cart slows and he allows it to come to a stop without pedaling any further. It is here that he'll have to spend the night, in a place he's never been. He looks at his atlas and pinpoints where he thinks he's stopped. Looking ahead at the forest, he traces a straight line to what he hopes will be a place to camp. Tucking the map back into his pocket he walks into the ever-darkening woods.

THEN

The silver sedan pierces through the shafts of sunlight that split the trees, creating a strobe effect within the car. The glove box bounces open and closed. An irritating and faulty latch is to blame. As it hangs open, something inside catches his eye. He applies the brakes, stopping in the middle of the road. The plume of dust he created catches up to and surpasses the car.

Digging into the glove box, Viktor retrieves the pamphlet and shakes it loose. It's a Tennessee state road map and he unfolds it across the steering wheel. He traces his fingers along the roads, trying to pinpoint his exact location. Peeking over the map he can see an intersection up ahead. The dirt road meets a paved road with a rusted and faded green sign that rests titled off the shoulder. He lets the car coast forward to get within reading distance.

Finding the intersection on the map takes several minutes, and he almost gives up by choosing instead to pick a direction and try for a locator sign. He continues to search, trying to follow his tracks from the previous days to where he assumes that he might be. Once he's found the paved road that crosses before him, he traces it along until discovering the dirt intersection where he now sits. Viktor grabs the blue pen that rests in the console cup holder and circles the house he left behind.

It's either left or right. The car sits just above a half tank of gas and he's concerned with how far that will take him. Viktor considers the routes and makes a plan.

"Over toward Knoxville, then straight north," he decides.

Viktor knows the risk of nearing the city, but the thought of being stranded in the dense backwoods of Tennessee without much food, drink, or fuel isn't enticing either. His map doesn't show much nearby, so he has to go toward the population if he's to refuel. He rests the atlas on his bag, draped over the top on the seat next to him. Taking his foot off the brake and pressing on the gas, he accelerates onto the main road and hooks a hard right. The smoothness and quiet of the paved road are a nice change to the chattering of stones and dusty air vents. A sign flies by indicating the distance to where he's headed.

"Knoxville, only 50 miles."

He watches the fuel gauge, imagining he can see it move toward empty. The paved road twists and turns through the woods and up and over rises in the earth.

After almost two hours, the meter sits between a quarter of a tank and empty. As he passes over a drop in the road, the city of Knoxville lies in the distance below. Smoke rises from the tallest buildings among the condensed skyline. Fires burn in the streets, their blaze flashing off the reflective glass facades. The Sunsphere, a structure that resembled a golden golf ball on a tee that was once an iconic symbol of downtown, smolders. The remnants of what appears to be a military helicopter stick out from one side. The globe now looks like a deflated, charred ball. Viktor navigates the approaching decline, letting his car coast most of the way.

A highway on-ramp appears on the right as the road flattens out, and he recognizes the number as the exit he needs to take to head north of the city. He estimates he has enough gas to get beyond it and then search for fuel. Most newer cars are made to prevent siphoning, so he'll need to find something old or swap for another vehicle with more fuel.

Abandoned cars are off the shoulder. One is burnt out after what appears to be a collision with a support column. He pays it little more than a glance before taking the ramp and then merging onto the highway. Viktor slams on the brakes. The smell of rubber and smoke fills the interior of the car.

A few hundred feet ahead, the entire highway is blocked. Military transport trucks still burn behind Humvees that are scattered among the wreckage. Civilian cars are folded into one another, making it hard to see where one car begins and the other ends. A massive wall of tangled metal spans the entire width of both directions of the highway. But it's not the junkyard on the highway that frightens him. A massive horde of the dead mills about the wreckage. It looks to be hundreds of meandering bodies.

They don't move with the slow drudge of the ones he's seen. For a moment he even mistakes them for people as their movements are snappy and agile. He yanks the wheel to the left and attempts to do a U-turn so he can drive back down the on-ramp, even though the red wrong-way signs warn against it. Viktor slams down on the gas but a loud crank and thud sputters from underneath the car. It drags for a moment and then brings the car to a halt. He presses down harder on the gas but the car just rocks and the RPMs go red. The tires screech but don't move forward.

The noise from the tires pierce into the car, and he knows he's made a grave mistake. His eyes go to the rearview mirror. To his surprise, the dead are gone. Smoke dances where they once gathered. A motion in his side mirrors draws his attention. The dead weren't gone at all. They've already discovered his presence and have closed the distance in half. A mass of sprinting corpses closes on him. Somehow, he can make out their teeth and eyes even though they're still little more than specks in the glass.

"Fuck, fuck, fuck."

Viktor shifts between drive and reverse, trying to dislodge whatever he's on, but the car shakes in the same place. Despite every instinct saying otherwise, he jumps out of the car and drops down to his stomach. Underneath the body of the car, a large bumper is wedged high into the rear axle. One tire off the ground and the other skims the pavement. Terror fills every cell of his body as he feels the vibration in the concrete, the sound of the dead bearing down on him. The high pitch of their shrieks and murderous growls amplify as they descend on him.

His eyes bounce around, looking for any means of escape, but there's nowhere to go. He can outrun them for a bit but there are so many he won't be able to keep up. Viktor moves to the edge of the highway and looks down. It's a forty-foot drop at least, and the landing is sheer rock and shrubs. The dead don't seem like a better alternative, but the thought of him breaking his legs or back and lying there in agony, just to be eaten anyway, doesn't instill confidence. He steps onto the ledge as the dead are almost upon him.

In the distance, the roar of a motor builds. A horn blaring rings out, further inciting the dead mob's pace. Viktor squints to the south side of the highway, the opposite direction of where he was headed. A camouflaged Humvee races toward him. Like something out of a video game, the vehicle power slides into a one-hundred and eighty degrees turn and comes to rest just a few feet away from him. Viktor can't believe it, but the man behind the wheel, in full military garb, gives him a nod as if he came upon a hitchhiker.

"You bit?" the man says, deadpan.

Viktor manages to shake his head no.

"Then get the fuck in!" the man screams.

The tone and ferocity in which the stranger bellows the command forces Viktor's limbs into motion without consent. He's moving toward the Humvee before he even realizes it. The dead are so close he can smell their stench, and the whole highway moves under their stampede.

"With some urgency, pal!" the man yells again. He runs to the front of the vehicle, but before he opens the door he turns and sprints back to the silver car.

"Hold on!" Viktor shouts.

"You've got to be shitting me."

Yanking open the passenger door, Viktor grabs the duffel bag off the seat sending the map airborne, it floats away like a loose kite. The shock of seeing the horde so close almost freezes him in place. They're feet away. He throws the bag into the backseat of the Humvee and jumps to hold the roof rack. There's no time to get in.

"Go! Go!" Viktor cries.

Smoke and shrieks as the engine takes off. The first wall of the dead slam into the back of the vehicle. Viktor's legs fly backward from the acceleration and the dead swat at them with mangled hands and fingers. Bodies fall behind and under the rear tires, it's all he can do to hold on and not fall himself. The speed of the dead seems impossible, but that sentiment is short-lived these days.

Once they've put some road between themselves and the dead, the man slams on the brakes, sending Viktor's feet in the opposite direction. Once stopped, he releases his grip on the roof rack as blood returns to his hands.

"Let's go," the man says, once again cool and calm. Viktor

hustles to the passenger side door and hops in.

"Thanks."

The man doesn't acknowledge, applying the gas as if they were out for a leisurely drive. As the dead fall further behind, Viktor takes his first full breath since he got out of his car. His lungs burn and his heart pounds in his ears.

NOW

The cold barrel of the shotgun feels smooth in his palm. He's yet to pull the trigger, so he's unsure of the kick and a bit nervous should the moment come. Dusk has fallen, more so amongst the trees, and it's becoming harder and harder to see. His palms begin to sweat, causing him to re-grip the gun between wiping them dry on his pant legs.

He pulls the stock tight into his shoulder, but his aim is sporadic and twitchy. He's being followed, hunted, and the coming darkness elevates the fear. Twigs snap, leaves rustle, but at least he hasn't heard anything to indicate it might be a deer, which puts his mind somewhat at ease.

A loud snap echoes through the trees very close by and Viktor whips the shotgun in that direction. He can barely see the figure approaching. It's almost full dark now, and the outline of the single dead stumbles toward him. Then a second, third, and fourth emerge from all around him. He considers going for the axe, but it's too dark. Getting so close is risky, but so is setting off a small explosion that will carry through the forest, alerting any other dead to his whereabouts. As if sensing the other dead nearby, the closest becomes invigorated and steps toward Viktor.

"Looks like you're up first, Rambo."

He leans into the stock of the gun and discharges the weapon. A bright muzzle flash illuminates the forest. The image is seared into his brain. Four has become eight or maybe ten as the head of the first shreds to pieces, brain matter casting outward and all over the tree behind it. He tries to recall the image that flashed before him, identifying where each threat stood.

Moving backward, being careful not to stumble, he pumps off more rounds at each of the advancing dead. After the sixth casing pings and ejects out of the shotgun, a clank of the firing pin indicates he's empty. Three more dead stagger over the bodies and around trees. One's neck is already halfway severed, the other looks as if it may have been alive a few hours ago. The last one that lurks behind is the most unsettling as it gets closer with burnt, peeled skin contrasting against a bright, flowery dress stained with blood and earth. All of the images are seen through the horrible strobe of the muzzle flash.

Viktor looks behind him to calculate his path. Above the trees, a bright red light pulses. It could be a radio tower, that won't do, a power line, also bad, but as he steps through the trees, the moonlight casts a glow off a bulbous and white sphere.

"Water tower."

He's relieved at the sight. While hustling backward he struggles to reload the shotgun with shells from his cargo pocket. Once six more shots have been loaded, he again aims. With vigor, he dispatches the remaining dead, some with two shots, others with just one well-aimed blast to the head. He closes his eyes as he cuts the woman in the dress in half with two shots to the gut. It growls and squirms on the ground. Viktor stops for a moment, takes aim, and puts a shot to her head, ensuring her final and true death. He'll collect what he can in the morning, as the noise will attract some unwanted guests.

Making his way to the base of the water tower, he climbs the metal ladder as fast as he can, his pack bouncing with each step. As he feared, he can hear the rustling and snarling below as more have gathered. Once to the top of the catwalk, he looks down over the railing that spans the circumference of the tower hull. There are still a few dead below, and Viktor decides that it's a problem for the morning. The air has gone cold as the adrenaline wears off. He's chilled to the bone. Digging through his pack, he retrieves his thick blanket and sweatshirt. He bundles himself and places the bag as a pillow. The metal grating is rough but he's able to rest, listening to the repetitious movements of those waiting below.

The next morning, he's woken by a violent shake. It's as if someone has stirred him out of sleep. But it is his own body that causes the tremor. The temperature must have dropped during the night. Frost clings to the outside of the water tower and the sun has yet to crest the horizon. Noises still bellow up from below. Viktor needs to move and regain his body heat or he'll get sick, and getting sick is an easy death sentence nowadays.

Jogging in circles he moves around the tower, lap after lap, he jumps up and down, rubs his shoulders, anything to heat up. It's not until the sun peaks over the trees and that first ray hits him that he feels any relief from the cold. Though it's subtle, the first kiss of the sun is like opening an oven door and Viktor must bask in it. After several minutes of absorbing the radiant gift, he's feeling less concerned about his lasting health but knows it could have been much worse. If anything, it serves as a rude awakening of what's to come.

First, he's got to deal with what's below. With the axe in hand and the rest of his gear slung over his back, he makes his way down the ladder. The cold bites at his fingers as the whole metal structure has drunken in the cold as the temperature plunged during the night.

Several feet from the ground, Viktor stops to assess the danger. To his delight the pathway down is clear. There are three dead and they appear slow and lethargic. An odd sight as they don't move from their places, only swiping and reaching as he touches the ground.

"No way!"

He examines the nearest dead with the axe at the ready, the right half of its body is stuck to the large metal support leg of the tower. Viktor can see the frost and ice meld the decaying skin to the rusting I-beam. For a moment he's confused as it doesn't seem that cold out, but then it clicks. His body still pumps warm blood through his veins. These goons are glorified reptiles. Without any source of heat coursing through their bodies, any moisture on their skin has stuck them to the metal like a freezer-burnt popsicle. As he gets closer, the agitated dead lurches toward him and the skin begins to peel and tear away.

"Alright, alright, cool your jets."

Viktor executes them one by one with a swift blow of the axe. He makes quick work of retrieving the IDs, one cell phone, and a cigarette lighter. Overall not a bad collection. Retracing his path, he finds the bodies that he cut down the night before. The carnage is a bit shocking as the darkness hid much of his handiwork. Another cellphone and a single ID go into his bag.

The girl in the flower dress lingers on his mind. He can still see her among the strobe of gunfire, the visual printed onto his brain. The dress even looks familiar, like the one Caroline wore to her first piano recital. Suddenly the girl on the ground isn't some stranger, but his daughter. Each body that is strewn across the thick undergrowth at his feet is now someone he once knew. Looking from the mangled corpses to the empty faces of the dead that surround him as if they're praying to the god that struck them down, Viktor begins to weep.

THEN

Cool air flows throughout the Humvee, circulating like a tornado in the center and venting with a violent howl out of the open windows. Gusts knock against Viktor's head as if he's taking blows in the ring, his hair flapping in every direction. Even if it weren't for the roar of the monster diesel engine beating against his chest, he still wouldn't be able to hear anything over the wind slamming into his eardrums. The bearded man at the steering wheel thrusts a hand down into an open bag behind the driver's seat and rustles around.

"Jerky?" the man asks.

Viktor wants to respond with a question, but something about this man demands careful examination of his speech. He knows what he heard and instead of forcing a repeat offer he cracks the seal on his lips.

"Uh, yeah, sure. Thanks."

The stick of dried meat wrapped in bright red plastic lands in Viktor's lap. As he struggles to tear it open, the man next to him has torn off the wrapper with his bright white teeth and spit the corner out of the window. He mimics the process, not quite as graceful, but it does the trick. The man doesn't notice while chomping at the rectangular slab of beef.

"Good thing you're not vegan. Pretty much just got the meat. Maybe some nuts back there but you're probably allergic. Everyone's allergic to everything nowadays."

"No, thankfully not." Viktor takes a bite. "It's good. Thanks."

"You said thanks already."

The driver's eyes don't leave the road.

"Ah right, well I appreciate it. Haven't had much to ea--"

"What's your name, pal?" Followed by a large bite, tearing at the stick.

Viktor stops himself mid-bite so he can answer. The passive-aggressive tone is becoming awkward and he'd almost rather leap from the vehicle and take his chances with the dead.

"Viktor."

In an instant, the man clasps the beef jerky between his teeth and extends his right gloved hand, palm upward. Viktor fumbles with his own snack trying to free up his right hand. It seems like an eternity to find the man's hand. The return squeeze is quite a bit harder than anticipated, but he tries to match the pressure with his own.

"Name's Tom." The man doesn't let go. "Army Captain Tom Becker. 278th Armored Cavalry Regiment," Tom says as if reciting his re-enlistment oath.

Viktor begins to pull his hand away but Tom tightens his grasp.

"Nice to meet you, Vik. Must have some balls to still be alive out here."

He finally releases the grip.

Viktor's hand is pure white and he stares at it for a moment as the red fills back in the empty spaces. He wants to rub it, but there's no way that's happening.

Not in front of Army Captain Tom Becker.

"Just did what I had to, only been a few days."

"Well as you can see most of the world has completely gone and fucked itself and that was within the first 24 hours."

"Good point."

Silence hangs in the air and against his better judgment Viktor has to break it.

"So, uh, where are we headed? Are there others, like you?"

Tom doesn't answer right away. He checks the mirrors for a moment, which gives an uncomfortable suspicion to Viktor that he's calculating his response.

"Oh, there's others, quite a few of us actually."

"That's good to hear. I didn't have much hope that there was anything resembling organization left."

Tom ignores the interjection and continues his thought.

"We were in a convoy, just left base and headed down to old Fort Hood, Texas for some good old-fashioned, ball-sweat field training."

He tosses the empty jerky wrapper in the backseat and it spins through the air current before wedging itself between the seat and the frame.

"On the road maybe an hour and we come across a big ole' traffic accident." He nods in the direction they came from and Viktor understands this as the roadblock they just escaped.

"Few of our boys get out and see if they can help. We pull up one of our flatbeds in case we need to off-load the tractor to move anything off the road. But you could tell right away this wasn't no normal accident, it was bad. And we all had seen plenty of piled-up vehicles overseas and those were all fender benders in comparison. This was something different.

"That's when we hear some screaming. Not civilians mind

you, that's common enough in our line of work so you can tell it apart. But grown men, screaming. Boys from our convoy. Then the first shots."

Viktor resists the urge to participate with a question.

"Now gunshots to us are about as second nature as your own breathing but when you're not expecting them, you see it trips a fuse in the mind of a soldier. You're instantly in battle mode. All the training kicks in, adrenaline pouring through your veins like ice water."

He rolls up a thick loogie with his throat and tongue and hocks it out of the open window.

"So we grab our rifles and advance on the pile of cars, smoke makes it hard to see but we still hear the gunshots of our boys. We push hard, the shots lessen and then cease, but the screams grow. That's when it went from fuckin' weird to fuckin' insane."

Tom waits. He wants Viktor to ask, he's building to it, Viktor suspects.

"What happened?"

"Eerie fucking silence. Eight of us push through the smoke between cars. A couple of civilians run out and pass us. Then there, a few meters ahead, just bodies writhing around on the pavement. Pools of blood everywhere. Five or six of our boys lie there motionless, civs on top of them tearing away at their uniforms and flesh. Fucking unbelievable. Of course, I'm sure you've seen your own brand of shit, seeing as you're still tickin'."

Viktor nods and his mind is flooded with the horrors of the past few days, but they vanish as Tom continues.

"We holler at em' to get up and back away or whatever but they just keep at it. One of our guys, Private Madones--Maddie, he's real close to one of the men being torn up on the ground and he blasts a few rounds off on one of the civs. Well, they all turned around, riled up like a beehive. We took em' down quick enough but the image of those people with our teammates' blood dripping off their faces, charging at us like wild animals, man that's some shit you'll never forget."

Viktor gulps hard, he's afraid Tom may have even heard it.

"How'd you guys get out of there?"

"We're professionals. Won't pretend it was easy but we stayed in line and took as many down as we could. Once our numbers were at a disadvantage, we huffed it back to the vehicles and evac'ed our asses on down the highway. There were thirty-two of us altogether in the convoy, twenty-five got out. Couple more fell on the way back to the trucks, Maddie included. You don't expect to eliminate one of your brothers in the middle of a U.S. Interstate."

"Shit."

"Shit's right."

This time the silence is welcome. The heaviness of the story and the images they conjure leaves Viktor with little else he wants to say at the moment. But his curiosity does get the best of him.

"Why'd you come back to save me?"
He doesn't look at Tom, almost wishing he wasn't heard over the noise of the vehicle.

"Well, truth be told I came back to collect the bodies of the fallen, if possible, and if not at the very least grab what supplies we left behind. Couldn't risk any more of my men though, so I was scouting from that overlook up there."

Tom points through the windshield toward the side of the mountain in front of them.

"Almost called it off due to that nasty horde that showed up and that's when I saw you knee-deep in a shit sandwich." Tom chuckles, which takes Viktor off guard, the only sign of levity since he got picked up.

"Well thank you, again."

"Once is enough. Get some rest if ya like, 'bout an hour back to camp."

Viktor nods and tries to get comfortable against the door frame, the seatbelt bounces against his temple, but he chooses to endure it. He doesn't sleep, but he does stare off at the scenery rushing past. He stews in the irony of a buddy road trip, intertwined with glimpses of carnage passing by at 80 miles per hour.

WINTER

NOW

New socks. Viktor could come across a full-functioning pizzeria serving hot slices and cold Coke but he'd walk right on by if there was a single pair of new socks to be found. The miles of trekking and fast approaching cold have done a number on his feet. Sitting on a guardrail just off the shoulder of a road, he rubs his tender big toe between kneading thumbs.

Viktor has noticed that he's lost several pounds as the constant walking has proven to be more than his limited food supply can keep up with. He doesn't feel weak, quite the opposite, leaner and more able-bodied. Despite walking every lighted hour of the day, his body has adapted to both the exercise and the calories available.

"Shall we," he mutters to himself.

Shaking out both socks and getting his boots tied up, he's back on his feet and ready to move. With the map under arm and pack slung over his shoulder, Viktor's determined steps take him along the two-lane road that bends into the woods and around a tree-covered mountain that rises ahead of him.

The current plan takes him northeast for a few days to the Appalachian Trail where he'll take that as a path into Pennsylvania. As the afternoon wanes, a slope in the road reveals an off-shoulder hut up ahead with a large yellow and tattered sign. He can't quite read it yet, but it puts a kick in his step. The lack of urban areas has brought both a sense of safety and sadness. Every moment Viktor spends in the woods or on a desolate road he's reminded that he's alone and the old world is gone. He squints to make out the patchy, worn sign text.

"Fresh ears of corn. Tulson Family Farm Co," he reads.

Pieces of the material hang down and wave in the wind like a flag of the farm, complete with a husked corn sigil.

He's well aware there won't be any fresh corn to be had, but there may be some dried corn or cornmeal he can scavenge. The axe hangs from his fingertips as he steps into the open-air hut. There isn't much to be found outside, most of the bins have been picked over by wild animals and only the decayed husks remain. A few kernels line the bins along with animal droppings, probably mice, maybe bats. He looks up at the canopy ceiling just in case.

The enclosed section of the building has a double wooden door with a padlock. Using the back of the axe, he knocks the lock off the handle in one swing, something he's become quite good at. Viktor shakes the latch loose and the door moves a hair. A waft of stale, dry air flushes through the opening and disappears among the cool air outside.

"Jackpot."

To his delight, there are several barrels of packaged corn products and shelves of confections and sweets, many of which are well-conditioned and still as good as the day they were stocked. He yanks a bag of Corn Nuts off the clip and almost bites a finger as he funnels them into his mouth. Behind the counter, a few cases of bottled soda and water are stacked next to a moldy, upright glass cooler. As he struggles to tear away the plastic wrap and get to a bottle of warm Coke, he sees the only thing that could pull him away from the highway oasis.

Along the wall, next to a row of corn-themed T-shirts and corn comic strip paintings, is a single row of socks. The long socks hang down in a neat line, each pair held up by a small clip. They're bright red and decorated with ears of corn, kernels bursting off into popcorn upward toward the rigged seam of the upper elastic.

"Socks!"

Viktor throws down his bag and pulls the entire strip off the wall. He yanks at his boots, unwilling to yield the time it would take to loosen the laces. His old socks hit the corner of the floor and he rolls on the new ones. A type of ecstasy flows over him as the clean, soft fabric touches his skin. He falls onto his back, wiggling his toes in their warm, new homes. He might even pull up his bag and take a nap right here. Until he's interrupted.

Voices.

The low-end bass notes of two separate people deliver a spike of fear. They're getting louder, but not yet inside. Someone, or a couple of someones, are moving around the back of the hut. He can't make out what they're saying, but how they speak feels malicious. He reaches for the axe on the floor. The double doors creak open.

"I thought you said this wasn't hit yet," a man's voice whispers into the dusty room.

"I swear it wasn't. Passed by two days ago. Was all locked up, didn't have anything to break the lock," a second man's voice says louder, without the sense to whisper.

"Doesn't look like they took much. Maybe it was a bear," the first man suggests.

"A bear? I don't want to go in there, what if it's still in there?"

"Get your ass in there and check it out or I'll lock you in there myself."

Boards creak and feet shuffle against the dusty planks. Viktor holds his breath.

"What do you see, Mike?" the first man calls.

"Nothing. Ain't nobody or no animal in here. Maybe they spent the night and skedaddled? What do you think, Jack?" the second man, who is now inside, retorts from the far side of the shack.

Jack, the alpha of the pair, stands outside the door. He's a middle-aged man, scuffed up and dirty. He squeezes through the doors and into the space where Mike confronts him. Mike is younger, rail-thin with hollow cheekbones and a mop of hair.

Viktor watches them both, now peering between boards from the outside. As they argued about who would enter, he was able to slide underneath a gap in the wall behind the checkout counter. His gaze travels from Mike to Jack and back to the floorboards where he stashed his bag. He considers reaching in for it and making a run, but the two men meet in the center and take stock of the room. It's now that he sees that they both carry weapons, Jack with a pump-action shotgun and Mike with an oversized handgun. Viktor left his only weapon, the axe, in his bag as his shotgun had malfunctioned the day after he spent the night on the water tower.

Viktor examines both men, considering what he might do if it comes to a fight. Both wear coveralls, once blue but now pale and tattered, the name badges long ago peeled off but the oval fade still present on the fabric above the chest.

"Why and the hell would they leave all this food behind?" Jack mutters, tapping the end of the shotgun on a wooden post along the counter.

"Maybe they didn't plan on leaving? You think they heard us coming?" Mike's tone suggests he's proud of his deductive reasoning and awaits Jack's agreement.

"Yeah? And how come we didn't see 'em? Where could they have gone?"

Mike shrugs. "I don't know--I just thought--"

"Shut it!" Jack barks.

His eyes train on the wall where Viktor has taken refuge.

"You hear that?"

Jack raises the barrel and points it at the wall, just to Viktor's right. He moves his aim closer and closer toward Viktor who's frozen, afraid to make any noise that would give away his position.

"Shh. There."

Jack steps closer, the shotgun moving and pointing right into Viktor's face.

KABOOM.

He doesn't hear the gunshot so much as feel the shockwave and see the bright fire flash from the end of the barrel. Wood splinters in all directions, a sharp needle flies into his cheek as a large section of wall blows out right beside him. A cold liquid runs down the side of his face as he cowers on the ground. His fingers reveal its blood, but not his own. At his feet, an almost headless corpse oozes into the dirt, half its head blown clean off. Daggers of wood stick out of its shoulder and neck like porcupine quills. The ringing begins to subside just as he hears feet shuffling and murmuring voices from inside.

The loud creak of the shack's doors sends adrenaline into his legs, in a moment the two men will round the corner and find him disoriented. If he's to escape he has to run, now. Viktor is just on his feet when a shout causes him to throw his hands in the air.

"The fuck are you?" Jack commands.

"I told you they was here!" Mike interjects, only to be silenced by a steely-eyed look.

"Start speaking or you won't have a mouth to talk with."

Jack points the shotgun at Viktor who stammers to respond.

"L, l, look--"

"Go on spit it out, where you come from?"

"Be, behind. Behind!" Viktor stammers between deep breaths.

Jack exchanges a look of impatient anger with Mike and aims at Viktor's head.

"Your funeral buddy!"

Jack's finger moves down the trigger, beginning to squeeze.

Mike screams as a dead bites into his neck from behind, the flesh tearing away with muscle and arteries alike. Blood sprays all over Jack and the side of the building. He whips the gun around and with a single shell disintegrates both Mike and the dead's faces into a mushy abstract painting that runs down the length of the wall.

Before he can get the gun back around, Viktor disappears over the bank, sliding on his ass and out of view. Branches whack him across the face, slicing his arms and hands as he grabs for traction while sliding down the loose gravel. He comes to a stop in a grove of thick bushes. From above, four loud gunshots ring out. *Pump-bang, pump-bang, pump-bang, pump-bang,* followed by curdling screams as Jack is overcome by what must be a substantial group of the dead.

Beat up but otherwise okay, Viktor creeps down the hill toward the wooded area below. He's dizzy and disoriented, but some buildings in the distance give him a bearing and that's enough. Night is settling in and he's got to make it to the safety of those structures.

It's almost pitch-black when he arrives at the edge of the woods. Two and three-story buildings make up a small gathering that doesn't quite look like a town. There's a clear road in and out, but there aren't any stores or signs that he can identify. Viktor scans each building before taking a step into the clearing.

A light catches his eye, sending him to his belly in the wet grass. A window in one of the buildings illuminates. Then another. One after the other several windows come to life. He begins crawling back to the protection of the trees when a shout rings across the yard.

"They headed north, this way. Up to the highway!" a man calls out.

A flashlight beam bounces as footsteps and voices echo through the settlement and off the brick exteriors. The mechanical sound of large lights kicking on causes Viktor to grasp the wet grass so tight that mud squeezes between his fingers. He can't lie low enough. The blades are cold and damp against his face.

The whole of the yard is now illuminated, including Viktor lying face down in the flat between the trees and buildings. He glances from the grass to the trees to the voices.

"Hey over here! There's a body!" The person calling out gets louder and he can feel the vibration of footsteps running nearby.

Viktor releases the grass and extends his dirty hands upward. His eyes travel toward the light now shining in his face.

"Don't shoot. Not dead," he pleas, just above a whisper.

THEN

Twelve-foot fences topped with horizontal strands of barbed wire surround a sprawling industrial complex. Once a distribution center with dozens of loading docks lining the length of one side, it appears to now serve as a military base and refugee camp. Viktor perks up at the sight of the massive building, the soft orange glow of dusk outlining the rectangular shape of the structure as if a forest fire rages somewhere far off in the distance.

Trailers have been lined up along the chain-link fence for added support and security. Guards patrol the wide concrete parking lot that's illuminated by beaming floodlights atop the walls of the building. Half of the concrete lawn has been dedicated to some sort of construction. He can't quite tell what they're building aside from the forklifts and movers working in unison.

"Not bad for a few days' work," says Tom, his choice of timing to break the silence always startling Viktor.

"Looks like there's a lot more than twenty-five soldiers down there," Viktor notices as they descend the paved road toward a heavily-fortified entrance that leads into the business park.

"Keen eye, and you're not wrong. We were lucky enough to

bump into another national guard unit evacuating a university. Similar situation, they lost a bunch of guys and the rest bugged out before becoming someone else's lunch."

They roll to a stop at the front barricade where two heavily-armed soldiers approach them, one with a rifle at the ready and the other with a hand up, his rifle slung in front.

"All in we've got seventy-five soldiers and last I heard three hundred civilians and change." Viktor's always respected and supported the military, but as the guards approach a sense of danger overwhelms him. He has no reason not to trust the man who saved his life or his friends, but being thrust into a base without so much an examination, or say in the matter, leaves him feeling trapped.

"Any bites?" The first guard shines a bright flashlight into the Humvee, gesturing at Viktor's arms and legs. Again, Viktor shakes his head no.

"Clean as a whistle," answers Tom. "Otherwise, one of us would be dead by now."

The guard shines his light on Tom, who doesn't appreciate the thoroughness with which the man is doing his job.

"I'm good, dipshit. Let us through would ya, need to refuel and grab a bite." He chomps his teeth at the guard which is an unwelcome joke.

Viktor grabs at the door frame. The second guard aims in with his rifle.

"You're a real prick, Tom."

The first guard fist bumps him through the window and waves them through.

"That's Captain prick to you, Scully!" He bellows a laugh and taps the gas.

The second guard keeps the rifle trained on the vehicle until it passes through the entrance. They wind through a parking cone-designated road on the concrete lot to an open bay door at the far end of the complex. Viktor notices now with clarity the work he saw from above on the way in, large solar panels are being unboxed and constructed in a tremendous area. A soldier lays down thick cables running toward the main building.

"Our former OIC lived a couple of miles from this place, knew they assembled and shipped solar units here. Not a bad plan, eh?"

Viktor nods in agreement. "What happened to him?"

Tom doesn't answer, and it's as if the question never occurred. They park along a row of other Humvees and military trucks, some mounted with large machine guns.

"Let's hit it. We'll get you situated with some grub and a bathroom break and I'll get you off to your entrance exam."

"Exam?"

"Worry not, highway dancer. We just want to know who we've got here and what, if any, specialties they carry so we can put everyone to good use. Not everyone can shoot a rifle or build an advanced communications setup, right? But there's still plenty to be done to keep the whole thing operational."

Viktor follows Tom like a child following a parent on the first day of school. They make their way up a loading ramp and through the towering open bay door. It takes a second for his eyes to adjust to the bright lighting, as it was all but night outside. The area inside is almost unbelievable. His eyes can't focus on any one thing as the room seems endless. Giant fans spin above, moving a great amount of air and providing a nice breeze.

"Power is still up, but our engineers don't think we've got more than a couple more days at most before the coal and hydro plants go offline."

"Can they fix them?" asks Viktor, feeling like he must ask

questions to show interest.

"Unlikely, but even so doesn't seem much use to keep the lights on for the whole city. Not yet anyway. Be decades before we're back to that point."

Decades.

Viktor's never really thought about the future until now, but it's true. There's no way the world could ever return to how it used to be, not in his lifetime anyway. They cross the main floor toward a line of tables with a queue of people snaking along stanchions. Bypassing the refugees standing in line, he avoids eye contact with those waiting patiently.

"Two plates if you would," Tom says to a volunteer behind the table.

A generous helping of rice and beans are scooped onto each plate.

"Apple or banana?" asks the volunteer.

She's a younger woman, rather cute if Viktor is being honest but he's overwhelmed by the whole thing that he doesn't even answer.

"One of each," Tom answers, grabbing both plates and handing one to Viktor.

"Gotta eat the fruit up while it's still good."

Tom doesn't wait to dive in and shovels in spoonfuls as they walk toward round tables with folding chairs. He plops down and continues to scoop the rice and beans into his mouth. Viktor feels the need to speed up just to keep pace. It's no use as Tom is done in a matter of seconds. He tosses the plate and plastic fork into a bin and shoves the banana into a mag pouch in the front of his uniform.

"Finish up," instructs Tom as he stands from the chair, moments after sitting.

He steps close to Viktor and places a hand on his shoulder.

"When you're done, head straight to that tented area over there. Tell them who you came in with and they'll get you all squared away. Got it?"

Viktor nods, trying to swallow a bite so he can answer.

"Good, I'll see ya around. Make yourself useful or you won't last long!"

At first, the comment sounds like a joke, but there's a threat in Tom's tone. Viktor can't quite put a finger on the exact reasoning, but there's a stir of paranoia brewing inside of him. He tries to reassure himself that he's alive, with a hot meal, among dozens of armed guards whose job it is to keep him safe.

Choking down his food, he manages to belt a reply before Tom is out of earshot.

"Thank you."

"That's four." Tom doesn't look back, instead just holds up four fingers as he marches out the bay door.

He takes his time before tossing his garbage and heading to the tented area. Viktor stands there, drinking in all the details of the building, the moving pieces and designated areas, as busy as a shopping mall on Black Friday.

"Name?"

A pen taps against the plastic table that runs the width of the curtain backdrop of the processing tent. Large cards stamped with rules hang on the backdrop. He has made it through a portion of the first card when he realizes the tapping is directed at him.

"Eh-hem. Name please."

He looks down to see a woman, around his age. She's dressed the same as the other workers seated at the table. A stark blue t-shirt, few are the correct size to fit the person adorning the makeshift uniform. A prominent golden necklace dangles in front of the cheap cotton shirt, a contrast that doesn't go unnoticed. An unfamiliar pendant bounces while the woman speaks.

"Haven't got all day, sir. I need your name."

"Yes of course, sorry--" Viktor catches her paper name tag just in time. "Sheila, is it?"

"Mm-hmm," More taps of the pen.

"I'm Viktor."

She begins writing on a clipboard. "And do you have a last name, Viktor?"

"Hamilton!" he stutters and blurts it out, causing those around him to side glance.

"Sounds like a first name to me." Sheila continues writing and before Viktor can respond, reads another question. "Trade?" Viktor doesn't answer, unsure. Sheila doesn't look up just awaits his response. "Trade. Skillset. Job," she says, rushed, but not impatient. She's kind, he thinks.

"Uh, I'm good with wiring. Used to work as an electrician, some home installation stuff, nothing major." Trying to be quick on his feet, he adds some less than true experience. "Uh, solar. Had some jobs doing solar install as well." He looks around the room as if someone might know him and call him out.

"Good. Very good. As you probably saw on the way in, that's going to be our lifeline here."

Viktor nods. Sheila shoves the pen into the top of the clipboard and passes it over the table. Her eyes are still fixed on the paperwork before her as she gestures with it again until finally, Viktor takes it.

"Step aside, finish filling that out and hand it back, completed. Don't leave anything blank. If you have any questions, read it again. Oh, and don't keep my pen."

Before Viktor can respond, Sheila calls on the next person, an older woman who he didn't realize formed a line behind him.

"Next! Name?"

He tries to block out the other woman's answers as he concentrates on his questionnaire. Viktor can't help but think about standing in the doctor's office a few days ago doing this very thing, unaware of the atrocities to come. It was the last normal interaction he had before everything went to hell. The pen traces each question, standard health stuff that he fills in as best he can recall. It's not until he comes to the family section that he stops, feeling as if he's been hit with a bat right to his stomach. The pen hovers over the blank answer sheet.

SURVIVING IMMEDIATE FAMILY:
LAST KNOWN LOCATION(S):
DID ANY FAMILY MEMBER TURN?: (Y/N)
IF Y, HOW WAS IT RESOLVED?:

Viktor turns to Sheila and opens his mouth but is cut off.

"No questions. Re-read, answer best as you can," she continues without skipping a beat.

He puts pen to paper and details what he dares recall. Leaving out some intimate details he scribbles in the final questions and places the clipboard down next to Sheila. As if a cordial light switch were hit, she looks at him with a smile.

"Thank you, Mr. Hamilton." She files the paperwork away without even glancing at the answers provided.

"Head behind this curtain and into the tent. They're going to do a full medical evaluation and get you your residence assignment. Welcome to FOB Zero!"

Viktor makes his way around the small group that has formed at the welcome tables. He hears snippets of the same answers he just gave and the reality of his surroundings begins to settle. A refugee camp. Militarized in every way. He bends low and ducks into the tent with a large red cross above the flaps. A sign to the right of the door identifies its specialty.

LEVEL I - SICK BAY

Before entering, he looks to the right where a large arrow is pointing to the other side of the long floor. At the end of the expansive corridor above a large, closed bay door, red lights strobe in a continuous circle, casting crimson shadows around the wall, roof, and sign.

BUILDING 4 – TRAUMA/INFECTION
MILITARY PERSONNEL ONLY

Two armed guards stand adjacent to the door. Nobody is within 100 feet of them, which is identified by a yellow-painted square, and he doesn't plan to be the one to change that. The tent flap closes behind him. Magnets lock the privacy flaps into place. Smoke-colored plastic sheets obscure the silhouettes and dark shapes that move about inside.

NOW

Streaks of light flicker between the woven fabric of the canvas bag covering his head. The wisp of night bites at his arms, but the hot air from his own breath gives a feeling of suffocation. He tries to exhale through his nose to direct the air downward. It helps, but only a little. Viktor is led along, hands bound in front by zip ties, through what he believes is the paved streets between the buildings of this unusual compound. Voices and shouts disorient his bearings.

They're looking for someone.

Catching a foot on a curb, Viktor almost face plants onto a sidewalk.

"I said step," a man retorts, pulling on the link between his hands.

It's not long before he's led into a building, a solid metal door clanking behind him. His eyes have a hard time adjusting to the dim hallway seen through the fabric of the bag. The sound of footsteps on linoleum is familiar, as is the smell. Musty and mildew, with a hint of mothballs, ammonia, and rotting books.

A few confusing turns and he's pushed into a room just off the hallway. *Screeching* as a metal chair slides on the floor, all while he is spun one hundred and eighty degrees, facing back the way he came in. A forceful but careful pressure as two hands push down on his shoulders. Viktor has no choice but to sit and for a moment his stomach flutters, unconvinced he'll hit the seat and not the floor. Alas, the rigid plastic catches his fall and the chair cries out under his weight. The bag is whipped off, but his hands are left bound in front, resting on his legs.

The room is lit by the smallest of standards, lanterns flickering along the perimeter and in the hallway. The door is wooden, with wire glass on both sides. The thick, square metal frame around it is a chipped, sky blue. A cracked and peeling whiteboard is all that is left on the walls.

"Where's Jack and Mike?" The voice of a man behind him makes him jump in his chair.

"I don't know. I don't know a Jack and a Mike. I travel alone," Viktor offers in defense.

Footsteps travel from one ear to the other as the man moves around him and to his front. A small man, a bit younger than Viktor he surmises, muscled and stern. All the appearances of a soldier without the uniform.

"Why did you sneak into our camp?"

He stutters, trying to recount the escape through the forest, down the hill from the highway, the corn shack, and the two men, now dead, but can't produce a single word.

"Jason."

Viktor looks up and the man looks back, waiting.

"Viktor."

"Okay, Viktor. I need to know. Why were you sneaking around our camp, and where the hell are our guys?"

"How should I know? Look, I was being chased by some dead up by the highway. I stumbled down the bank, saw trees, and just kept running. Once it got dark and I saw these buildings I had no choice. It looked abandoned. I didn't see any lights." Viktor gestures with his hands, hoping he'll be unbound, but Jason pays no attention.

Instead he moves to a chair beside him and leans against it.

"And you didn't see any men out there? Just the dead?"

He shakes his head in earnest, hoping not to oversell it.

"You with a group? Maybe one of these wolf packs that likes to go around sacking other communities?"

The look of confusion is enough to make Jason elaborate, but he can tell the man is not convinced Viktor's game isn't an act.

"Bearded, scruffy bastards. They're raping and pillaging all over this area. May as well be Vikings." Jason stands again. "I'll admit, you don't look the part. But maybe you're a new recruit?"

"Look, I--, I don't know anything about your men, or these other men. I just needed a place for the night." Jason's eyes study Viktor's, unwavering. "Let me go, I'll even travel in darkness, please just let me out of here."

The young man seems to consider it for a moment when a guard bursts through the door.

"Sir."

"What is it?"

"We found Jack and Mike--"

"Well good, get them in here. See if they recognize our guest."

The guard stammers but doesn't respond.

"Spit it out, Fez."

"They're dead, sir."

"Dead, how?"

"No, like dead, dead. Jack stumbled onto the grounds with a few others, we had to cut them down. Backtracked through the woods and up onto the highway and found Mike's body, or what was left of it." The man called Fez pants as he tells the tale.

Jason turns to look at Viktor but still addresses the guard.

"This wasn't up by that corn shack, was it?"

"Yes, sir."

Jason walks around behind Viktor. He can hear rustling behind him before he's thrown into darkness once again. With the bag again over his head, Viktor pleads with a muffled voice.

"No, no, wait. I'm sorry. I did see them, I just, I just wanted to go. They were attacked and I ran, I swear." Viktor's voice catches as he pleads.

"Fez, get him outta here. Throw him in a cell. I'll figure out what to do with him in the morning," Jason's voice commands as he's pulled from the room.

The guard grabs him up by the hand ties and yanks him into the hallway.

"Please, please. You have to believe me."

There's no acknowledgement or response from either man. He's led down more hallways, outside in what he imagines is a courtyard, then back inside and into a large open space. The echo and sounds of the footsteps on smooth wood is familiar. A basketball court.

The hood is pulled from his head as fast as it was applied. A loud chain-link door slams behind him and a padlock is clasped as Fez walks away. Viktor finds the corner of the cage and sinks to the floor. The gymnasium bears enough reminders of the past to be surreal, torturous even. The faded mascot logo on the wall, a great antlered deer on its hind legs, *Bloomington Bucks* scratched and chipped, above.

In the adjacent cell, a body stirs on the floor with a tattered mattress underneath, as the form rolls from one side to another. Long brown hair, clumped but not matted, messy but not dirty, sways with the repositioning figure. A woman's voice stabs like a dagger in the dark.

"Please don't start crying. I just want to fucking sleep."

Viktor wants to reply, ask a hundred questions, but for some reason, he sits in silence. He doesn't expect to sleep, not here and not like this. After hours of watching nothing more than the moonbeams as they cross the walls of the gym before vanishing, sleep overtakes him. He nods off in this strange place, feeling calm like he's right where he's supposed to be.

THEN

The months after his arrival flew by as repetition set in, almost like it was before the world collapsed. Almost. Wake up, go to work, sleep. Viktor soon found himself pretending he had expertise in solar power and installation until he began grasping it after weeks of trial and error.

Luckily for him, nobody else knew much about it either, save for Army Specialist Ramirez with whom he'd developed an amicable bond. If not for him, Viktor may have been outed as a phony right off the bat. Perhaps it was an act of kindness or Ramirez just didn't care, but it was obvious from the start he knew of Viktor's ruse and still took it upon himself to show him the ropes. Ever since, they've worked side by side almost every day, only breaking the norm when the soldier was called out on retrieval runs with an expeditionary squad led by Tom.

It was after one of these outings, lasting several days and causing rumors to fly through the compound like the cold winter wind that had also descended on the base, that Viktor noticed a change in his work friend. The day started as any other had since the chill set arrived. Viktor awoke to the community horn, at 7:00 a.m., or zero seven hundred.

A quick rinse in the public shower, one minute per resident, and a starchy towel to dry off with and hang up at each person's bunk. He didn't mind the hurried pace of morning, all the better to get busy. The water from the showers was warm enough, thanks in part to Ramirez and Viktor's handiwork on the roof structure. Sun-heated pipes that are gravity fed to the cleaning stations. He knows they'll need to come up with something different now that the temperatures are dropping and snowfall is imminent.

That was to be the focus of his day, brainstorming with Ramirez about winterizing the grid and water systems. It was something he was looking forward to, problem-solving and mental work was the best blinder to the new world. A quick breakfast of cereal and canned apples while reading the morning memo was nothing special. By 7:30 he was walking the outer lot and headed for the solar panel yard.

As Viktor scrubbed at his first row of solar panels, a daily task to keep up efficiency, he heard Ramirez's approach and could tell from his gait something was different.

"Morning, specialist," Viktor said as he had every shift since they began working together.

"Hey."

He fought the urge to whip around as the curt response added to his inclination that things were not normal on this day.

"We were worried about you. Two days beyond plan, a lot of people started thinking the worst," said Viktor.

"Well, they wouldn't be wrong."

Viktor heard Ramirez open his work bag and retrieve tools. A socket wrench tightened bolts on the corners of panels. They worked in tandem, panel by panel, as they always do.

"Everyone made it back, right? I didn't see any names on the memo this morning."

The talkative specialist was being short, and it drove Viktor mad the longer he resisted blurting out "Tell me what happened!" He always enjoyed the stories that Ramirez brought back from outside the compound since he hasn't stepped foot beyond the fence since he arrived. He suspected these stories were inflated and falsified for color but it didn't matter. Viktor relished in their ability to transport him somewhere else if only for a few minutes.

"Yeah, all accounted for."

Work progressed through the morning void of casual conversation as they finished the preventative maintenance right at the lunch call.

As they now sit across from one another tearing into a modest meal of fresh flatbread and some canned meat and rice casserole, Viktor sees an opportunity. Ramirez's mood has improved and it's enough to bring the courage to ask what's been on his mind all morning.

"I didn't see Tom yet today."

Ramirez nods, tearing into a piece of bread.

"Yeah, Becker is in debrief all day."

Viktor stirs, carefully choosing his next words. "Must have been a lot to download. Anything unusual out there?"

"Come on Vic, you know I can't talk about it."

Fearing he blew his chance to find out what happened and also alienated the one person in the compound he talks to, Viktor backtracks.

"Of course, of course. I'm sorry, you've just been quiet all day and I was just trying to loosen ya up. My fault. I know the rules." Viktor can't take his next bite fast enough just to shut himself up.

Ramirez stares at him for a moment before placing his fork on the table next to his plate.

"Not a word?"

He forces down the mouthful he shoveled in, trying not to blurt out with eagerness. This is how the stories would start, a soft reluctance then a spilling of great detail, but in this instance, he didn't want to press his luck.

"Nothing. You're the only person I talk to." Viktor laughs to sell the sincerity behind the words.

"Alright, and I mean it, you can't say anything. This isn't our usual buddy banter, feel me?"

Viktor nods, hiding the worry about what could have happened to change his friend. Ramirez gauges the room before leaning in to speak, his voice little more than a whisper.

"Just before we were supposed to head back to base, our convoy rolled up on what looked like an abandoned encampment. Campers, trailers, tents, what have you. We followed procedure, hopped out, searched for anything usable, food, supplies, the usual."

"Sure." Viktor isn't sure active listening is the best play but he can't help himself.

"Well, there wasn't much to find and after maybe five minutes we load back up. But then Staff Sergeant Roberts hollers out 'Hey hol up!' The rest of us dismount and circle around him. 'Y'all hear that?' he says, and we listen intently. *CRYING* right! A baby, maybe two of them, wailing but muffled. We can't pinpoint it. That's when Becker has us all flush out and try to find where the noise is coming from."

Viktor tries to tear off a piece of bread, his hunger for the story generating a real hunger inside him. Ramirez goes on, unabated.

"Finally, Roberts waves us over but is shushing us and pointing toward the ground. The crying has gotten fainter at that point, but we're there when it goes quiet. Someone, one of the guys I forget who, grabs the branches from the ground and there's a wooden door underneath."

"No shit."

"Becker doesn't hesitate a second. He steps in and yanks up on the wooden door. Screams and crying make us all jump back until we can see maybe fifteen, twenty people all crammed into a space the size of a small bathroom. 'Come on out, don't be afraid' Becker extends his hands down. Some of us have our guns drawn, some don't. It was all really confusing and unexpected." Ramirez takes what seems like forever to take a sip of water.

"We get 'em lined up and Becker is asking a bunch of questions. They're scared, kids crying, a couple didn't speak English and they're screaming. Whole thing seems to be escalating for not much reason at all. Out of nowhere, four guys ambush us from the trees, luckily, they're a shit shot and our guys dispatch them pretty quickly. The women and children run to their bodies, everyone's screaming. Becker's pissed.

"After we gather ourselves, Roberts comes up from the ground hide with a weapon and some canned food. Becker sends me down with Roberts and we end up retrieving a bunch more stuff. One of the women falls to Becker's feet, pleading that it's all they have. That's when shit went south."

Ramirez takes a long look around the meal hall before continuing, maybe considering if he can still back out from telling the story. Viktor gulps hard, his mouth dry from heavy breathing.

"Something in Becker turned, he crouched down and grabbed the woman by her hair and says 'where the fuck is the rest?' She pleads and screams that she doesn't know. Without warning, he pulls out his sidearm and wastes her. Just blows a hole out the back of her head. Moves on to the next. This woman, maybe even a teenage girl, tells it all. Another camp just down the road, a lot of food and more guns. No security, the guys they killed were it.

Becker gets this demonic smirk and just says 'good', ya know? We're all looking at each other like this is fucking nuts and that's when he gives the order."

"Order?"

Ramirez speaks so low that Viktor has to stare at his lips to understand.

"Well first he pulls the young girl and a couple other women from the group and then says, like he's ordering a coffee, 'execute'."

He watches Viktor, looking for a reaction and when none appear, he continues.

"I don't know who shot first, but blasts come from all around as the people in the main group start falling lifeless to the ground. I fire a couple of shots into the dirt out of fear ya know, I don't want to be seen disobeying orders, but I can't fucking believe what I'm seeing. The three girls wail and scream and it's all the guys can do to hold them down.

"Just like that he orders the bodies dumped back into the hole and covered. Men, women, babies. A tangled ball of dead civs piled back in their hiding hole."

Ramirez sits back, almost as if a storm has passed and the calm has overtaken him.

"We spent the next two days at their other camp, drinking, gathering shit. God knows what Becker and the others did to those poor girls. Never heard or saw them after that. I just loaded gear and stayed out of sight. Couldn't get back here soon enough."

Viktor lets a reaction slip, realizing he was nothing more than a statue this whole time.

"That can't be. You're joking right--"

"I like you Vic, but if you say anything you know I'll have to kill you. Like no joke. Becker will hang me from my balls for everyone to see. It's all fucked and we just have to play our part."

Staring into his half-finished casserole, Viktor's appetite is gone. Ramirez excuses himself and stands, tray in hand.

"Gonna take a shit. I'll see you at command in ten to go over winter prep."

Viktor nods. He spends the rest of lunch planted at the table, a pit sinking in his stomach like he hasn't felt since that first day of mayhem.

NOW

For a moment, Viktor can't recall where he's at, his mind feels muddy and divided as he tries to reason his whereabouts. The low morning sun shines through the upper glass windows of the gymnasium. Voices echo off the walls and it sounds as if a basketball practice is taking place and all is normal. The shuffling of feet and talking comes into focus as he rolls from his side to sit upright.

"What's going on?" he asks the woman, squinting between the bars at the commotion on the court.

When he receives no response, he looks to her cell and is surprised that it's empty. Viktor can't believe he slept through them taking her. He can't help feeling somewhat disappointed. Granted she was a bit cold, *a bitch even*. But the hope of hearing her story and maybe what this was all about, along with the cascading list of thoughts he couldn't even begin to vocalize, all vanishing in the night, leaves a feeling of profound sadness.

"Alright, fall in line."

Viktor snaps his head back to the court. Some sort of training is taking place, he gathers. From across the gymnasium, the bang of metal and wood rattles across the space as Jason burrows through the doors. He's walking straight toward Viktor's cell, eyes locked on him. Before Viktor can mutter an ill-fated question, Jason jams a key into the cell door lock.

"You gonna be a problem?" he asks.

Viktor shakes his head no.

The door wobbles free and Jason gestures with his left hand. Feeling every pain in every joint, he manages to pull himself to his feet and step out of the cell. Viktor follows Jason's lead out of the gym. The hallways and rooms look different than he pictured when he was being led through, masked. The sounds played tricks as he was guided left and right. The school, or maybe some sort of community college is, for the most part, intact even though it does show significant signs of age and neglect.

They push through a door and into the room that he suspects was where he was questioned the night before. Though, again, he's unsure as it's difficult to remember with the darkness and disorientation.

"Shall I assume the position?" Viktor breaks the silence.

Not amused, Jason gestures to the chair across the table. Once Viktor is seated, Jason steps out of the room for a moment, but returns with something in his hand. He tosses Viktor's bag down on the table between them.

"This yours?"

Viktor stammers, not expecting to see it and trying to come up with some sort of explanation. He digs at the cloudiness of his memory, struggling to think of everything inside of the pack. Trying to figure out Jason's angle and what he might be thinking.

"Better start talking, it's an easy question. Your bag, yes or no?"

He knows it's his own, but he touches it with a bound hand, rolling the fabric between fingers but not examining the contents.

"It-- It is," Viktor says.

"While we were recovering our guys, we checked the stand and saw the floorboards disturbed. Oddly enough we find this." Jason sits across from Viktor, locking eyes. "Now there's some unusual stuff in here. Care to explain?"

"It's just my supplies. I didn't know if they were going to rob me so I hid it and was going to come back for it later at night."

"Yeah, sure. There are some supplies in there. But what are you doing with all this?"

Jason dumps the bag upside down as IDs, and phones spill onto the table. Cables tangled around devices. Faces scatter like a deck of cards. His food is not among the pile.

"These the people you killed? You some kind of sicko who gets his jollies off the people you've murdered?"

Viktor is shocked, he didn't expect the questioning to go in this direction at all. He stammers for a response. "What? Fuck. No!"

"Start making some sense then buddy. Two of our guys are dead and this doesn't look good for your future here." There's a threat in his tone, Viktor believes Jason might pull a gun and shoot him on the spot.

"Look. I didn't have anything to do with that, I told you. I don't know. I collect things."

Jason's eyes squint almost shut. "Things?"

"People. I mean, their identities."

Jason sits down across from him and props his elbows on the table.

"No, I know how that sounds. I mean for memory. Like a memorial. When I come across the dead, I collect their IDs, phones, whatever. I don't know why. Trying to preserve their memory, I guess. It started with my family right after everything happened and it's just been a habit since. Look, I don't have an answer more than that because honestly, I don't know. I just thought somebody needed to do it."

Jason leans back, but his expression is unchanged. The awkward silence hangs in the air. His sudden *guffaw* makes Viktor jump in his seat.

"So, what, you're like some historian?" Jason laughs. The tension isn't lessened by the outburst and Viktor can't figure out what to say for some time.

"I mean, maybe? I don't know. Like I said I just thought someone should be doing it," he concedes.

"Alright, alright. You're a weird shit you know that, Viktor was it?"

He nods.

"But there ya go, keep your things. Gotta keep your weapon though. For now. I'm sure you understand." Jason stands up.

Viktor begins shoveling the IDs and gadgets back into the bag. He stops and raises his wrists that are still joined to one another.

With a quick flip, Jason thrusts a blade at Viktor and cuts the ties, his hands parting before he knew the knife was out. He shakes his hands and scoops the rest of the contents off the table without any regard for organization. Two more IDs land with a clack on the metal table in front of him. He stops packing and looks from the faces to Jason, who's looking back at him from the door.

"Put those in your book or whatever you do. They weren't angels but they deserved better than what they got."

Without waiting for a response, Jason is out the door. Fez steps in after him but says nothing. Viktor slides the two faces closer to him and looks at the men, recognizing them from the night before. He slides the cards together, taps them on the table, and places them inside his bag. Slinging the bag, he walks to the door but is stopped by an outstretched hand.

"Aren't I free to go?

"Not quite," replies Fez. "While you're not a prisoner at the moment, I do have instructions to keep you on site for the time being."

Viktor looks around the room and back to Fez. "Looks like prison to me."

Fez opens the door and nods for Viktor to walk through. "Go on, I'll show you around."

He moves through the door, Fez following just a step behind. Viktor is guided out of the main entrance and into the campus yard. Hanging garden baskets adorn several of the wall spaces, box gardens line the sidewalks, fading fruit trees and winterized vegetable plots sprout from the earth. Each building has a sophisticated rain barrel system. Some solar panels dot the structures. The roar of generators is loud enough that Fez raises his voice to speak.

"We tried solar in the beginning, but we quickly found we had to choose between the trees and the sun."

Viktor looks around the span of the campus. Towering, bald cypress trees surround the compound. No border fortification is in place except that which mother nature planted hundreds of years ago. They stand tall like soldiers on a garrison, overlooking the residents below.

"At max, we were getting three to four hours of good sun which could barely give us enough light to read, let alone sustain the colony."

"Colony? How many people live here?"

"172, as of this morning." He looks at Viktor.

"I thought I wasn't a prisoner?"

"Merely a census, Jason insists on thoroughness above all else. Every calorie of food, gallon of fuel, calculated to exactness for each member."

The generators grow louder as they walk closer to the power field, as pointed out by a crude wooden sign and orange netted fence.

"The biggest challenge hasn't been finding enough fuel to run these. Hell, there was enough gas just sitting in abandoned cars to provide power for hundreds of years."

Viktor nods, somewhat surprised he hadn't come to a similar conclusion during his years in wooded exile. "I imagine capture and longevity are your primary obstacles?"

Fez stops a moment, apparently surprised at the insight from the new stranger.

"Precisely. We've got a brilliant scientist here though, used to work for big oil or something. Figured out a way to take old gasoline, run it through some sort of franken-machine he built, and out comes pretty fine burn-juice. Something to do with hydrocarbons and excess water vapor. Thankfully, not my area of expertise."

The rattle and grind of the generators begin to fade as they walk further down a curving sidewalk toward a lone brick building at the end. The concrete curls in both directions around a dried-up fountain with overgrown weeds in the center and connects back to itself on the other side. Fez opens the boarded glass double doors that lead into the brick apartment building. A cracked, dirty plaque hangs over the entryway. *Jefferson Hall.*

"It's a bit dated, but likely better than what you're accustomed to judging by your appearance."

He can't help but feel a bit self-aware before Fez corrects himself.

"No offense of course. Just a warm shower and softish bed will probably be a nice change."

"Indeed," says Viktor.

They ascend the stairs and walk the dusty hall in silence. A hint of mold and decaying carpet fills the air but it's by no means overpowering. Floorboards creak under their feet as they reach a door.

"Three-oh-seven, this is you." Fez turns the tarnished brass handle and pushes open the door. "No keys, means no locks."

A blast of warm air fills the hallway from the room but settles.

"Been vacant for a while, box AC in the window. Feel free to run it as needed but be mindful of the power. Jason's got meters on every building and if you abuse it you will surely lose it."

"I expect I'll be just fine."

Viktor walks into the room thinking of all the cold nights he's spent outdoors in the open air. He sets his bag on a small entryway table. The lamp vibrates as if it might tip with the added weight, but settles as fast as it took off.

"Showers and toilets are end of the hall. This was a single sex residence so just the one. Respect your neighbors. Like I said, showers are warm, not hot. Those are solar fed from the roof during summer and pumped through the generators during winter to prevent freezing. Don't drink it, all of our water is from collection or snowmelt. We save the well for drinking only."

Fez begins to let the door close but remembers one last thing. "Meals are 8, 12, and 5, no exceptions. If you need anything, follow the lone sidewalk back to the main courtyard. Curfew is 8 p.m. unless you're on official business."

"I think I've got it," Viktor interjects. "Curfew, set meals, yard time. Not a prisoner though, right?"

Fez smirks. "I like you, Viktor. Watch yourself though, you may find you like it here!"

With that, the door closes and Fez's footsteps carry down the hall. The room is old carpet, worn bedding, and not a single item hanging on the walls. He lies on the bed staring at the ceiling, but it doesn't take long for cabin fever to set in. After spending the last few years with almost every moment in the open air, the room feels small and confined.

Viktor explores the entirety of the hallway and finds his way to the bathroom at the end of the hall. He's startled as the door lurches open as he reaches for the handle. A woman, beautiful and somehow familiar, is as surprised to see him as he is her. Her brown hair drips of water and she's wrapped tight in a stained, off-white towel.

"What are you doing? Get out!" she shrieks.

He hobbles back into the hall and stammers an apology. After a moment she re-emerges from the bathroom, paying him no attention. Viktor loiters in the hallway, feeling too awkward to retreat to his room and not wanting to seem too eager to go in, so he admires the empty wall. Once he hears her door latch and the hallway is empty, he enters the public bathroom. It's bigger than he expected based on her reaction, a dozen stalls and as many showers line the wall opposite the row of sinks. He finds a stall and takes a seat.

A couple of unseen people enter, flush, and leave while he sits there contemplating everything about his current situation. He can't stop picturing the brief glimpse of the woman's face. He recognized the hair and her voice. It was the woman in the cell next to him, that much he knows. But there's something else familiar that sits deep in the recesses of his conscious.

Then his mind completes the puzzle, connecting two obscure thoughts as one. He doubts the very notion of what he suspects. Reaching into his jeans, Viktor digs for his wallet. His hand snags on his pocket, turning it inside out. The leather bifold drops and bounces on the grimy octagon tiles. A shot of pain jolts through his hip as he extends to grab it off the floor. He can't open it fast enough. In the center flap is the ID he's looking for. Viktor fumbles it in his thumbs and flips it over. Francesca stares back at him.

His heart sinks at the same moment the stall next to him flushes. Viktor hadn't even heard the person come in or do their business. He rubs his thumb over the picture. The variations between the woman he scared to death leaving the bathroom and his mythical *Francesca* are minor but undeniable. He marvels at the similarities, uncanny for certain, but his eyes move to find the absolute differences.

He glances at his watch and sees that it's almost noon. May as well eat, even if he isn't feeling all that hungry. Making his way back to his room, he passes the woman again in the hallway. His heart jumps. Viktor wants to utter another apology or do something to get her to make eye contact, but she walks too fast, now clothed with a jacket clenched tight in her arms and held across her chest. Her eyes stay down as if he wasn't there.

Viktor can feel her melt into the wall as they pass one another, trying to create as much distance between them as possible. He returns to his room and for the first time in years, Viktor checks himself in the mirror. His age and weathered features are obvious. He fusses his hair and gives himself a smell check. Then he's out the door, exits the dorm, and heads down the narrow sidewalk as an early winter breeze settles in over the campus.

THEN

Not a single word was absorbed during the winter prep meeting as Viktor could only think about the story Ramirez had told him over lunch. It wasn't until Tom burst into the conference room halfway through that he even looked up from his technical binder. He watched as Tom paced the room, his left arm bandaged, before stopping at the head of the large oak table.

"Now I know what you're all thinking, and no I haven't been bit. Sorry, looks like you're stuck with me a bit longer and none of you lucky fuckers are gonna get to put me out of my misery." He chuckles until the others join him.

"While we were stuck out there, one of our Humvees got caught in a ditch and I burnt my arm on the exhaust trying to get the damn thing out."

Viktor looks to Ramirez who seems to avoid his gaze. A moment of panic flutters through him as Tom notices the exchange but doesn't miss a beat. Tom slides a binder toward himself from another technician, he raps on it with his knuckles.

"I cannot emphasize enough that you all learn this like the back of your hand. This may sound dramatic but our lives depend on it. Winters can be hit or miss around here, but none of us have had to endure it like this. It's our first winter and we best get it right."

The thought is an uncomfortable one. Viktor realizes the holidays, traditions, feelings that this time of year usually brings, will now be vastly different.

"We've been increasing our energy consumption and it will only grow as the days and temperatures shrink. We'll use wood for heat but we'll still need our units running at full efficiency if we don't want to sit here in the dark, picking our asses and waiting for spring." He shoves the binder back to the technician and walks to the door.

"Carry on. Ramirez, a moment." He doesn't look back for confirmation.

Ramirez exchanges a glance with Viktor, who shrugs. He's up and out of his chair and through the door. Viktor can see them through the glass and observes their back and forth exchange.

At first, it starts with a light tone and nodding, but then erupts as a dark redness fills Tom's face, the veins bulging in his neck, though his voice does not rise enough to carry into the room. None of the other technicians are even paying attention, their noses buried in binders. Ramirez continues to nod and Tom's color returns to normal. He gives a large forceful pat on Ramirez's shoulder and disappears from view.

Ramirez returns to his seat but doesn't make eye contact with Viktor. He does offer a quick shake of the head but Viktor's not sure if that was to say "it's all good" or something else. They continue with the meeting as if the interruption hadn't taken place.

After the session has ended, Ramirez catches up to Viktor in the hallway leaving the conference area.

"Where you going? You got early leave?" Ramirez asks. He looks surprised when Viktor responds.

"Yeah. Therapy session."

"Your hip?"

Viktor nods. "Getting better."

"Alright, well I'll catch you tomorrow." Ramirez slaps him on the back, peeling off and walking down another corridor.

At 4 p.m. a woman in uniform enters the makeshift rehab room. It's just another conference room free of any meeting tables or business chairs. A few large inflated balls, rubber bands, and small weights line the floor. Viktor sits on the lone bench with his back against the wall.

"Viktor. How are you feeling today?" She's young and fit, a first-generation American he remembers her saying from a previous conversation.

"I'm doing alright. Thanks, Doctor."

"You can just call me Chan. Not a doctor, remember?" She points to her Medical Specialist insignia.

"I won't tell if you won't."

She laughs at this and it's a nice feeling. There isn't an ounce of tension, just the conversing of two people as if everything is normal. It feels good. Chan works him through the routine of stretches and movements, testing mobility and points of pain. After thirty minutes of a little small talk and painful therapy, a soldier has arrived for his appointment. Viktor avoids lingering and waves on the way out.

"Thanks."

"See you next time," Chan replies, as Viktor is out the door. A voice surprises him in the hallway.

"Cutie, huh?"

He turns and sees Tom coming out of another room, a fresh

bandage on his arm. He gives it a light tap with his fingers. "I'm stuck with Doctor Zhivago in there." Tom points to the room behind him with his thumb.

"Looks like you've got it made in the shade though."

He cocks his head as he passes the therapy room where Chan is bent over, examining the other soldier. Once past the door, he looks back to Viktor.

"Hip still giving you trouble?"

Viktor slows down a bit allowing him to catch up.

"Doing better, thanks."

"Yeah, me too."

Tom places his hand on Viktor's left shoulder as they walk in tandem. His fingers dig in, but just light enough to not be aggressive.

"I bet you heard we had quite the escapade out there."

Viktor doesn't respond, just shrugs so Tom can feel it in his hand.

"Come on, I know you and Ramirez are close. He's a good guy. And you're a smart cookie yourself."

"No, sir. Captain. Er-Tom. He hasn't said much. Only what you said about getting stuck out there is all."

Tom doesn't respond at first, causing Viktor to pick up the pace.

"How long you in that bandage for?" he asks, trying to break the silence.

"Ah, Dr. Big Nose thinks the cut should heal fully in a couple of weeks. Best to keep it wrapped to prevent infection."

"Cut?" He can't help but blurt it out and regrets not letting it slide.

Tom squeezes deep into Viktor's collarbone guiding him to turn around so they are face to face. Tom's expression isn't the rage-filled depiction that Viktor had witnessed earlier and had expected was coming his way. Tom holds up his arm showing it off.

"Yeah, damn sharp edge of the frame got me while I was hooking up the winch."

Had he forgotten what he said earlier or was this some game to catch Viktor in a lie of his own?

"Well, I'm glad it wasn't anything worse and that you all made it back safe and sound." Viktor tries to break off and leave, but Tom's grip is back on his arm. He hasn't lost any strength from his injury.

"The world is an ugly place now, you do realize that don't you, Vik? I mean I know you saw it for yourself, with what happened to your family and all."

Viktor forces an amicable nod.

"Sometimes, things happen downrange that aren't always on plan and you've gotta be a tough sonofabitch and think on your feet. You with me?"

Viktor feels like a bobblehead as Tom's hand guides his shoulder as he speaks.

"I appreciate what you've contributed to this community so far, I want you to know that I value that you're a part of it."

Stammering, Viktor manages to squeak out a thank you.

"No one is irreplaceable though, don't forget that. We've gotta keep things running tight around here or what's out there will surely kill us all." Tom points to the walls with his bandaged arm.

"Loud and clear, sir."

This time Viktor breaks away and sighs in relief that the interaction is over but Tom's low, crooked voice has a grasp of its own.

"One more thing."

He waits for Viktor to look back, eyes locked and unwavering.

"Your boy Ramirez, he's not as innocent as he lets on. Out there you're either alive or you're one of them. There ain't shit in between. Not anymore." Tom breaks off his searing look and heads back in the direction that he came.

"Carry on, Vik!" He waves his injured hand over his head. Tom angles his head to catch one more glance of Chan as passes the rehab room once again.

Viktor doesn't linger. He can't wait to get back to his tent but knows there will be no rest for his mind. He fights the urge to track down Ramirez and interrogate him on what was said by Tom just now. The small pieces inside him that started to make the routine and scenery all feel normal, resembling something of a home, begin to deteriorate.

The next few weeks were business as usual, and Viktor was thankful as he needed a reprieve from the tension of that hallway meeting with Tom. Ramirez has seemed off as of late and, as if shadowing the status of their friendship, the first cold snap of winter arrives earlier than anyone expected. Light frost covers the pavement and solar panels, but it melts away as the sun rises over the surrounding mountains. It's only after a particularly cold afternoon, where they both shiver among the steel structures that support the hundreds of panels, that he catches Ramirez off-guard.

"Tom came to me," Viktor says.

Ramirez stops ripping a piece of electrical tape mid-tear and gauges Viktor's expression.

"A few weeks back, after my therapy class. Same day he ripped you a new one in the hall."

"That so?"

Viktor returns to his task of putting the insulation around the pipe that runs along the base of the support legs on the ground. Ramirez still has the tape hanging from one hand.

"I suppose that's why you've been all business lately," Ramirez adds, and to Viktor's relief, he's back to taping up the insulation as they move down the line.

"Just a lot on my mind. First holidays coming up and all," replies Viktor.

He can tell that Ramirez doesn't buy it.

"Take it from someone who has spent most holidays away from family on a base or in a shithole somewhere. Just have to make the most of it. It doesn't take much time for the surreal to feel normal."

Ramirez works faster, forcing Viktor to do the same. He rushes to lay down more insulation.

"Is that what happened out there?"

Viktor hadn't planned on cutting right to the chase but why not. The dancing around and curiosity were becoming unbearable.

"I told you what went down, Viktor. And I trusted you not to say a word."

"And I haven't," he's quick to defend himself.

"I know. You wouldn't be here if you had."

Viktor isn't sure if that was a threat, the tone didn't feel like one, and he is right. Tom would see to it.

"But what you said about normal. I bet it's gotta be hard when such barbarism becomes the routine." Viktor knows it's forced, almost cringing hearing himself say the words.

"I've got a job to do, same as this."

"Keeping the lights on by babysitting solar panels has never killed anyone."

A darkness begins to emerge from Ramirez, a familiar look he's only seen in Tom thus far. He knows he's getting somewhere.

"You never know what can happen out here."

The glint in the soldier's eye punctuates the threat.

A *snort* from above the perimeter distracts both of them. A light dusting of snow covers the pines and hillside above the barbed-wire topped fence. A puff of steam between branches catches Viktor's eye. He tries to point it out for Ramirez without moving too fast. A hundred yards up the slope, a massive buck stands statuesque, looking down on them. He can tell from Ramirez's change of expression that he also sees the beast.

Mangy fur hangs like burlap from its sides. The antlers are grotesque, maybe fifteen points, many snapped at the end with shards reaching out like daggers. The animal snorts again then scrapes the ground with a hoof and rears its head. Both front hooves slam into the ground. Another puff of steam as it blows air out of its flaring nostrils. Neither men retreat, but they can't suppress the fear in their eyes.

"Fucking hell, would you look at that thing," Ramirez whispers. "I've heard stories, but goddamn. I kinda thought it was all bullshit."

Viktor gulps hard. He rubs his side where the scar from the antler still marks his midsection. "Wish I could say the same."

Ramirez looks back, noticing Viktor caressing the old wound. "Nah, you're playin'."

"First week after it started, couple of days before I got here. Took a spike to the ribcage. Even now, still never seen anything like it in my life. Not even in horror movies. The ferocity, empty, hollow death in its eyes." Viktor shutters at the retelling.

A loud outburst of laughter startles Viktor as well as the deer. It skirts along the slope but doesn't leave. Another *snort* and *scuff* from above.

"You're crazy man. But you've got some good stories."

They watch the buck take small steps to both sides, pacing. With a loud exhale of steam, the animal rears up again and charges down the slope in their direction. The fence is in between them and the galloping beast, but it doesn't stop the men from scrambling backward and up against the structure. They retreat, following the cold steel frame as the deer rages toward them, down the slope a few feet away from the fence. It slams into the chain-link wall at full force, causing the whole section to wobble. But it holds.

"Fuck!" Ramirez yells.

The deer's antlers are caught in the links and it rattles back and forth. The fence shakes with horrible violence. The noise is a piercing metal and bone scraping as the animal shrieks and huffs in frustration. Air blasts from its nostrils and hooves kick at the fence.

A single shot rings out through the compound and a small cloud of dirt and snow kicks up from behind the buck. It shakes free of the fence and bolts up the hill as fast as it had charged. Another shot blasts through the snow just below its feet. In seconds the animal is in the trees and has vanished. They look down the row of panels toward the base. Tom stands firm, slinging a large caliber, scoped rifle over his shoulder, his free hand still bandaged.

"Sorry!" he shouts, raising his damaged wing as if to give an excuse for missing. "Told you boys, nothing good out there!"

Ramirez gives an acknowledging wave as Tom walks back to the building.

"Fuck this. I'm taking an early lunch." He pushes past Viktor. "You coming?" he asks.

"Yeah."

Nothing good in here either.

Viktor can't be certain, but the faint echo of something moving in the trees quickens his pace back to the safety of the compound.

NOW

"Dear Lord, we're gathered here before you to enjoy this bounty you have provided. In these dark times, Lord, let us not take for granted the provisions which you continue to bless us with on a daily basis. Watch over our community, its members, our land, and our souls. Help us to defeat the dead and any who would rise up against us for matters of evil. All this we ask in your name, Lord Jesus. Amen."

"Amen," the crowd murmurs. Jason brings his chin back to level and opens his eyes. His arms, which were outright with palms upward, return to his side.

"You a religious man, Viktor?" Jason asks as he pulls up a chair next to him, a food tray in hand.

"Uh, in my youth. Now I'd say I'm probably agnostic more than anything."

"Only thing worse than an atheist. At least they have the courage to believe in something. Even if that something is nothing." His tone isn't judgmental, more humorous, and Viktor takes it as such.

The woman from the hallway sits a few seats away. Viktor catches her rolling her eyes at Jason's spiel and goes back to eating by herself.

"I'm just joshing you. To each their own. So long as you don't object to how we operate, everyone is welcome here, regardless of faith, creed, orientation, what have you."

"Good to know." Viktor tries to end it there and shoves a spoonful of something far tastier than he expected into his mouth.

"Hey uh, Catherine was it?" Jason asks down the table.

The woman looks up and nods.

"Come on over here and join us, would ya?"

She hesitates, looks to Viktor and back to Jason, then slides down, still keeping a seat between herself and everyone else.

"You two are the newest additions to this little experiment in community building we have going on here. Now I apologize for our initial treatment, but we can't be too cautious. And with two of our own missing, later to be found dead, we needed to cross our T's and such."

Jason begins eating and a sense of relief can be felt between Viktor and Catherine. The food is superior to anything he's had in quite some time. Some sort of game stew, with a side of fresh skillet bread and even a cold glass of Coke.

"Ain't that a kicker?" Jason gestures with his fork to the bubbling soda in front of him. Viktor's look of non-comprehension invokes an explanation that he immediately regrets instigating.

"You see about a year ago all the bottles of pop we started to come across were flat. I guess their expirations finally started kicking in. Bummer, right? The end of something great. No more pop. Like movies, books, new cars, art, what have you, another thing to add to the list of bygones." Viktor takes a big gulp and lets the bubbles dance on his tongue before swallowing.

"Some genius on staff here accumulated a few of those pump soda machines where you could just make your own back in the day. Pours flat bottles of Coke into 'em and boom, fresh bubbly pop. Forget power and medicine, this guy gets a Nobel prize in my book." Jason smiles and takes a sip of his own, letting out an audible lip smack and *ah*.

"How long do we need to stay here?" Catherine interjects, taking both Viktor and Jason by surprise. Jason puts down his fork and wipes his mouth with a napkin.

"Like I told you both yesterday, you're not prisoners here. All I ask is you stay a few more days and see if it grows on ya. If you still want to leave, by all means. We'll even give you a care package on your way out."

Catherine cleans her tray and excuses herself from the table. She exits the cafeteria, a blast of cool air from the open metal door sends shivers to those nearby as she vanishes into the darkness outside.

"How long has this, have you all been here?" Viktor decides to strike up a conversation. After the shower incident, he'd like to avoid the perception of following Catherine back to the residence hall by leaving at the same time. Sitting in silence won't do for Jason, he guesses, so he'd rather himself steer the topic.

"Three years, give or take."

"You've managed to fight off the dead for that long without much fortification. Impressive."

"Don't need it. Got God on our side." Jason points to the ceiling, smirking. "You see this place happens to sit in a pretty substantial valley, surrounded by steep inclines and shale-faced cliffs. Any dead or delinquents have to funnel down the way you came and we've got watchers. And firepower."

"What about deer? Seems it would be pretty easy for a rogue infection to spread if just a single animal came rampaging through the campus." He tries not to sound too inquisitive.

Jason appears impressed by the keen observation. "It was a problem at first. But to be honest we've done a good job clearing the east from north to south for miles and haven't come across any in over a year. Zero infiltrations, as you put it. I think they're finally dying off, honestly. Unable to breed is my guess."

"Makes sense."

"We just started clearing the west this summer. Hence our two boys running into you up at that road market or whatever it was. Shame really, I sent them out there myself."

"How can you still see God so clearly, after all this time? Doesn't it just seem like a fairy tale now, considering?" Viktor asks.

Jason doesn't miss a beat. "I don't see God, Viktor. But I see the devil. Every damn day. And you can't have one without the other." Jason leans in on his elbows and speaks softly. "You see, humans need to have faith in something more, beyond all this." He waves his hand around his head. "If not, how can I ask these people to muster the courage to face the dead, or worse?"

"So, it's a ruse to generate obedience?"

"If you told anyone in the past world that this is how civilization would fall, wouldn't you have been called crazy? You see, the real ruse is living life like we have the slightest clue what's to come or what exists beyond our pale understanding. It's simply a message of hope and love, Viktor. And there's no greater friends to survival than those two things. Best you remember that."

Viktor nods and stands from his seat. Jason downs the rest of his Coke and taps the empty, plastic cup on the table.

"Come see me tomorrow. I've got a job for you, Mr. Collector."

A job? You mean prison labor?

The next morning, after a restless night in a too soft bed, he made his way to breakfast at 8:00 a.m. Viktor can't help but rub his neck as he woofs down a hot serving of scrambled eggs and fried potatoes. As soon as he's finished, he tracks down Jason who leads them down into the building's basement. *Please don't be the morgue.*

"Here it is." Dust plumes through shafts of light from the hallway as Viktor peeks his head around the door. Jason feels along the wall for a switch and toggles it several times.

"Bulb must be out. Anyhow, prop the door open for now and have a look around. I'll be back with a bulb in a few." Jason's steps patter down the linoleum hallway.

Viktor steps into what appears to be an old custodial closet. Metal racks line the walls and are filled with office boxes that are marked in alphabetical order with large letters written in thick, black marker. He pulls the closest box, lit by the dim light coming from the hallway, and flips his fingers through the folders inside. Each file folder contains at least one ID or photo of some stranger he doesn't recognize. Some folders have phones, memory cards, and other personal effects as well. Each is topped by a tab with a scribble of the name it contains, as well as large capital letters, *COD.*

"Cause of death," he whispers to himself. Reading this particular description makes him feel sick to his stomach, the taste of the eggs creeping up his throat.

"Kevin died fighting off the dead while on a run. He is survived by his wife and three children." The only thing in his folder is a photocopy of the man's driver's license.

"We let the families keep everything of course, but he deserved a file nonetheless." Jason's voice from the doorway makes Viktor jump, with a shadow now cast over the box.

"What do you want me to do here?" he asks as he flips through more folders.

Jason unscrews the bare bulb with his hand and twists in the new one. The LED light fills the space, causing Viktor to take in the scope of all the boxes on hand.

"These just get stowed away. We burn all our bodies here and this is where the identifying effects go. The folders are like tombstones and this is our graveyard." He gestures to the modest closet. "When you told me your story about that little pack you carry around, I thought to myself, well if that isn't some divine intervention, I don't know what is."

"I can't carry all this. I don't even know where I'm taking what I have currently. What am I supposed to do with all these records?" Viktor's already trying to find a way out of whatever is being asked of him.

"Fire up that dusty computer in the corner, should be whatever cables and gadgets you need in that drawer." Jason points to the darkest part of the room where an old desktop machine stares back, the dust piling in the corners of the off monitor.

"Like I said, I don't even know why I'm carrying what I have with me as it is, why are you trusting me with this?" To try to sell the dissuasion he closes up the folder and box and slides it back on the shelf. Jason sizes him up and pats him on the back as he walks toward the door.

"I don't know why you've taken this upon yourself either, Viktor. But the Lord has a plan for you, and the memory of all these people. And if I've learned one thing in this whole Hell-on-Earth scenario we live in, it's don't bet against the Lord."

Once again, Jason's steps recede down the hallway. Viktor spends the rest of the afternoon toying with the ancient computer.

He comes across the folders of the two men who died at the roadside shack, their photo-copied ID papers already sitting inside. Jason must have scanned them before he handed them over, he assumes. One of the folders has a phone, dried blood and a cracked screen marking the front face. Using a stack of post-it notes, a pen, and rubber bands, he starts working on the file folders in alphabetical order.

The first task, he decides, is to attach a name to any of the devices lying within. One habit he picked up on in the record-keeping process was to keep assets together. Dozens of loose phones and IDs would be madness to reconnect if shuffled. After about an hour, all forty-eight phones he counted now have names attached.

Stacking the phones and IDs in a pile on the desk he begins copying the relevant media over unto corresponding folders on the connected external hard drive. While navigating one folder he sees another labeled music. He selects a track and the computer struggles to play it.

A muffled but clear enough rhythm fills the room. The small speakers on each side of the monitor thump out a song that he's never heard. Some cross of hip-hop and rock with lyrics that would make an average person blush. He looks over his shoulder as he lowers the volume.

"Progressive tunes, for a church bunch."

He taps the pen on the desk to the beat.

THEN

Viktor has paid little attention to the restricted access area since his arrival at the compound months ago. After all, despite the new locale, this was still an operating military base so it never felt out of place. Not until the latest uncomfortable encounters with both Ramirez and Tom did a growing sense of deception begin to take hold.

Ramirez has all but cut Viktor off as of late, some shifts going their entirety without anything other than work speak between them. Once, Viktor even got close enough to the restricted area to try to catch a peek as someone with clearance entered. The guards closed the door behind them before he could get a look.

"Move along, civilian!" one had shouted. It was loud and stern enough that Viktor hadn't bothered with a response. He scurried away.

Not until a late evening after Tom and Ramirez had exited the doors together, did Viktor decide he needed to know what was going on inside. From the relative concealment of his barracks tent, he watched as the two men charged out of the door in unison. They had another exchange, similar to the one outside the classroom. He was surprised at how much Ramirez was giving back this time. Knowing Tom's superiority complex, it seemed unusual that such subordination would go unpunished. When Tom stood there and took it, Viktor realized Ramirez must have some insurance policy allowing him to speak so freely. What could he have over Tom? All of this just fueled his plans to get inside.

He planned to wait until their New Year's celebration, which was a few days out. If the Christmas meal from over the weekend was any indication, a large buffet was to be prepared and many, including the soldiers, would be well fed and distracted by the extravagance.

The morning of the New Year's Eve party arrived after two days of agonizing and overthinking. Now, as he lies in bed through the zero seven hundred call, he thinks tonight will be the night he will find out what this place is hiding. What Tom and Ramirez are hiding. With Viktor knowing that routine will be the key in avoiding any hint of his operation, he makes a point to hit breakfast at his normal time, eat his usual meal, and shower all in the same manner as any other day.

Both he and Ramirez have the day off so he gets in a little exercise and makes a trip to the media center. It took several months for the makeshift entertainment hall to come together, but now it has a respectable offering with some nice comforts.

He checks out a laptop, headphones, and a random hard drive. He's less concerned about what films are on it. Viktor spends the rest of the day reading a book and enjoying movies. Or so it would appear. While the movies play on the laptop, he mutes the volume while wearing the required headphones so he can still hear his surroundings. On a piece of paper, he marks guard rotations, noting their movements and duration.

At 6 p.m. a loud chime dings throughout the building. Everyone moves as if they know this means the meal is ready.

Simple paper decorations leftover from Christmas line the food hall, tables, and chairs. White paper table cloths dress each table with candle centerpieces. It's all very vague and could be a wedding ceremony as soon as a New Year celebration but nobody seems to mind. Viktor shows up, enjoys the meal of canned ham and chicken, instant potatoes with brown gravy, canned corn, and pumpkin pie for dessert.

By the 10 p.m. curfew call, everyone has settled in and only the night sconces illuminate the massive interior space. At the far end, the red lights still glow over the restricted door. Viktor waits another hour before dashing to the restrooms. It's out of the way but at least gives him an alibi should he be discovered out of bunk. He uses it as one last opportunity to canvas the door before making his move. With a deep breath and a fake flush, Viktor exits the bathroom and slides along the wall adjacent to the red doors.

He knows that at 11 p.m. on the dot they'll do a shift change and he has to time it with no margin for error. Too late and he'll miss his window, too soon and he's out after curfew, exposed. Each minute that passes his situation grows more perilous. Lucky for him the exchange is on time. As the guards swap out, they step away from the door. The four guards gather outside the painted box talking, inaudible from Viktor's proximity.

As he hoped, the day guard lights up a cigarette and hands it off to another who takes a long, slow drag. One guard punches the other in the chest as he tries to waft the smoke away. Viktor slides closer to the door along the wall. Their backs are turned, and he feels like this is the moment. Another step closer, his hands pressed against the wall behind him. They share a laugh and the smoker tosses down the butt and stomps it out.

This is it.

Just as Viktor is about to move to the door, it bursts open and a beam of light causes the four soldiers to react. They must have seen Viktor as the light from inside flashed across the wall. The guards scramble, one kicking away the cigarette butt as Tom steps from inside the red doors and approaches them. The doors begin closing behind Tom who stands off to the side confronting the guards.

"The fuck's going on out here?" Tom demands as he adjusts his camo pants and belt.

One soldier stammers as he tries to respond but is interrupted with an outstretched hand. The guard with the cigarettes pulls the pack from his chest pocket and places it in Tom's palm.

"Contraband." Tom chuckles as he pulls a cigarette out and leans forward, expecting an immediate light from one of them. The other soldier wrestles his lighter out and ignites a flame.

The big red door latches with a metallic thud, the light that was cast across the men and floor now returns to a dancing, dim red once again. Viktor has made it inside.

Sterile, white hallways that look more like a hospital than an industrial complex. A blue stripe marks the center of the light gray tile hall. Bright fluorescents give Viktor no shelter from view should he meet anyone else in the hallway. He moves along the wall, exposed to anyone who might come through the door behind him or emerge around a corner ahead.

With each door, he comes to he tries the lever, but they are all locked. No signage so much as identifies a room number, just a light brown wood grain rising from the floor, interrupting the bright white walls as if that was their intended purpose. After he rounds a corner, the sounds of the large red metal doors clank behind him, followed by a pair of boots tapping along the floor.

Viktor picks up the pace and is almost jogging, touching each handle as he goes by. None budge from their secured horizontal positions. He spots a set of double doors up ahead and goes straight for the handle. It opens toward him with an unforgiving squeal. He slides into the door and darkness beyond.

Feeling along the wall, he slides himself as far away from the door as possible in case his pursuer happens to burst through. Viktor clenches as the footsteps grow loud, right up to the door, but pass as fast as they came. A sigh of relief is temporary and he continues sliding along the wall. His arm touches something. The realization of what it is shocks his nervous system.

Flesh. Cold, unresponsive flesh. His mind knows it's human, even if he can't see the body. In the pitch-dark, Viktor begins to lose his bearings, shapes and shadows that aren't there play with his eyes. He searches the room for the light that peers through the cracks to try to orient himself. Alas, he sees a glimpse of light from the hallway bleeding under the door.

As he scrambles back along the wall, his hand swipes a rectangle that he had missed the first time. The room shoots into brightness as Viktor shields his eyes. They adjust and as he scrambles for the switch that he bumped he takes stock of the room. Steel tables, maybe a dozen, organized all along the floor. Blankets drape over human figures on each surface. The one closest to him, the corpse that he touched, has a lifeless gray arm that hangs out from beneath the sheet.

"We're behind but we'll get it done," says a muffled voice from the hallway.

Viktor moves to the light switch, but the voices grow louder. He sees an empty table with a folded blanket. The door opens.

"That's unusual," a voice says.

"Everything you do is unusual, Doc." Viktor recognizes this voice.

"I'm not one to leave the lights on," says the man called Doc.

Viktor has never tried so hard not to breathe, which seems to expand the desire to take a huge gasp. The blue sheet that he's draped over him itches at his nose as he forces himself to take long, slow exhalations out of his nostrils. Through his periphery and the thin fabric, he can see two shapes navigate the room. The sound of a blanket whipping off of a body.

"This one showed promise. A detectable heartbeat returned, but it accelerated so fast it blew up in his chest."

Another sheet is ripped off. "Jesus," says Tom.

"She actually got worse. Became more ravenous and almost broke our restraints. We had to put a bolt into her brain."

"Afraid of a little bite, Doc? That's what the muzzles are for."

"Indeed, but until we crack this disease, I'm reluctant to take chances."

"Who's this big, bloody fuck?" The sheet next to Viktor whips off and hits the floor beside him. The airflow disturbs his own and he can feel his hand exposed to the room as the covering settles back down on his wrist.

"You don't recognize him?"

"Can't say I do, though he looks like someone put his face in a blender."

"Corporal Stevens. Your valiant knight from the raid."

"I should hang his body from the fence as an example to the rest of them."

"Morals are a dangerous game, these days," adds Doc. "Anyhow, no response from him. Guessing the right dosage proved challenging given his...size. Plus, not understanding the metabolic rate of the dead--"

"Losing me, big brain," Tom groans.

"We'll need new specimens, but we're close." A minor feeling of relief as the footsteps and shapes seem to move away from

Viktor.

"Leave it to me. You'll have your subjects."

"Thank you, sir. I won't let you down." The room plunges back into darkness and the light from the open door begins to fade. "Getting a bit overcrowded here anyway, time to thin the herd." Tom's chuckle fades away as the door snaps closed, sealing off the light and returning the room to black.

Viktor moves the sheet off of his face and takes a minute to regain his normal breathing. He feels like he'll never catch his breath, the throbbing of every heartbeat like a hammer to his chest. He can feel his pulse in his ears, eyes, and hands. Once he's regained control, Viktor pulls off the sheet and plants his feet on the floor, careful not to make a sound. He feels from table to table, moving toward the faint glimmer of light under the door. With each body that he passes he feels as if it will rear up, sinking its ferocious bite into his arm or neck. Shuffling his feet, afraid to take steps, it seems like minutes to get to the door.

After pressing an ear and ensuring nobody is waiting on the other side, he presses the latch bar and the squeal eases outward into the bright hallway. Confident the two men traveled back the way he came in, Viktor makes a right, headed deeper into the restricted area. He passes a single metal door with an exit sign overhead. The temptation to go through is strong, but he presses on to the end of the hallway where the last set of large double doors conclude the hallway. If he was dropped here blindfolded, he wouldn't know the difference between the room he was just in and this one, judging from the outside. His suspicion is just that, another room of bodies. Perhaps a different stage of experimentation.

Just as he's about to pull down on the lever to open the door, hushed voices stir on the other side. His instincts scream to run, but something about the tone of the whispers brings his ear closer to the door. The faint sounds of female voices, some children's voices even, echo beyond the door. He has to see.

With a brave tug, he swings one half of the double door wide open, expecting to be met with a guard and a crack of a rifle butt against his skull. A hushed silence falls over the dim room. Low output, glowing green night lights line the walls. Metal bars rise from floor to ceiling. Dirty, battered hands grasp the bars. The eyes stare back at Viktor with stoicism.

Dozens of women sit, stand, and lie down in these cages that fill the space the size of a classroom. There has to be fifty of them crammed in here, he guesses. Then Viktor sees the young girls, no older than his own, huddled into the breasts of their mothers who shield them in corners. He hasn't even made it more than a few steps inside when boots approach from behind him from down the hall.

This time there's nowhere to hide. He backs out of the room, all eyes on him. Viktor lets the door latch, almost succeeding in perfect silence. The boots grow closer and louder. He's boxed in and knows it. Then he sees the single exit door but is unsure if he can make it there in time. He doesn't have a choice.

In a sprint, he's down the hall and up against the metal door. He leans into the bar latch praying it's not rigged with an alarm. It opens as a blast of cold air shoots inside.

"Hey, you feel that?" a voice shouts from behind.

Viktor plunges outside into the frigid air. A faint glow of the moon and gentle snowfall gives just enough light to see the lot of the compound. "Check the door!" he hears a voice yell from inside.

Darting across the asphalt, Viktor heads for the massive solar field at the edge of the lot. Just as he ducks behind the first row, a flashlight beam crosses in his direction.

"You see anything?"

"Who the fuck left the door ajar? Becker's gonna have our ass!"

The beam shines at their feet and Viktor is terrified his footprints will betray him. The heat of the pavement is enough to have dissolved the dusting of snow on contact, leaving behind only the moist, black asphalt surface.

"I ain't saying shit. Latch the damn thing and let's make our rounds."

The metal door bangs closed in the distance and then, in the darkness of the lot, he feels the pain in his hip and the cold metal of the structure against his hand. He's stuck outside and is going to freeze to death.

The hum of a power bank draws his attention. Viktor places his hand against it. The unit could barely count as warm, but in comparison to the air and metal, it may as well be a heater. He curls up against it, pulling his arms and hands inside his shirt, tucking himself into a ball. He can't help but shiver until he falls asleep.

Viktor dreams of dying in that spot, frozen, and then awakening from the dead. He storms the complex as an icy blue demon, tearing flesh and ripping the heart out of Tom. His wife and daughter are there at his side, helping him rip people apart. A herd of deer charges through the building like it's made of paper, entrails and body parts hanging from their antlers. He rides one like a horse in battle. A dead army, bound to his bidding.

"Charge!" he screams.

NOW

“Another poor bastard?” Catherine nods to the ID buried between Viktor's fingers.

He didn't hear her come up behind him on the sidewalk. The cold winter air and chilling concrete bench where he was lost in thought had distracted him from the surroundings. Her arrival brings back the faint hum of the generators as well as the sun's welcoming contrast to the breeze that swirls around the empty courtyard fountain.

“Yeah, someone I picked up awhile back.” He stuffs Francesca's ID back into his pocket and keeps his hands inside hoping the cold won't bring her to ask about it.

“Must be someone special.” She doesn't press further but gestures to the bench beside him. “May I?”

He agrees and scoots over, even though he had left plenty of room when he sat down. With a bare hand he swipes at the seat as if it's dirty.

“Gentleman.” She seems surprised or at least hides any tone of mocking.

Catherine sits closer than Viktor expected. She's stunning, there's no doubt about it. Her flowing brown hair spilling out from under a knitted wool cap that's seen better days. Her bright green eyes had gone unnoticed until now as they had exchanged just simple greetings prior.

"What's your plan- Viktor was it?"

"That's right, and you're Catherine?" He knows she is but tries to match her uncertainty. She extends a gloved hand which he accepts and lets go after a brief squeeze.

"Nice to meet you, fellow inmate." Viktor cringes as he says the line.

"You've got dad jokes. Great." They both share a laugh.

"So, what ill-fated decisions led you to be my cell neighbor... what's it been, a week now?" she asks.

"You remember? I was sure you hadn't, it seemed to be an especially rough few days for you."

"You're not getting off that easy, creep. I remember the bathroom too." She playfully jabs him with an elbow. "Seriously, what crazy luck cast our fate in this awful place together?"

"Well first, I wouldn't call it awful. There are definitely worst places to be *prisoner*." He air quotes on the word. She looks to him surprised as if he's got a story to tell.

"Go on."

"No, I just mean it's been a while since I've been around other people, at least for any extended period of time, and felt any degree of safety or normality. It's a nice change."

Catherine looks away, across the lawn where Viktor laid face down that first night. "I don't know, I had it just fine playing wanderer on my own. Now I'm a prisoner of this cult. I swear if he comes at me saying I need to have his babies I'm cutting every dick I see clean off!"

They both laugh. "Noted. I'll be sure to knock next time."

"You didn't answer me though. How'd you end up here?"

He shrugs. "I guess I decided to try my hand at wandering as well. Headed north, seemed to be the safest play."

"Picked a hell of a time to do that. Must be something pretty important driving you into winter country."

Viktor doesn't respond, the last thing he wants to do is try to explain or justify what he's doing. In all likelihood, he's more afraid of hearing him say it aloud and realizing how foolish it all sounds so he moves on.

"Anyhow, I don't think I'll stay much longer. Assuming they let me leave."

"I believe they will. Jason seems like a decent man."

She scoffs. "I know their kind. Decent, until you have something they want."

"Sounds like everyone, nowadays." He bites his lip as it doesn't come out as intended.

"Maybe. But yeah, as soon as we get a break in this weather I'm heading southwest."

"What's Southwest?"

"Texas, if I can get there." He considers the idea and smirks. She smiles back, trying to read his eyes. "What? You got something against Texas?"

"Haha, no. It's just far. Very, very far."

"Says the man traveling north as winter rolls in."

"Fair enough. So, what's in Texas?"

She leans forward, bracing herself with her hands on the bench and looking down at the snow-flecked concrete. "Way I figure, Texas probably had the most guns and combat veterans in the country. If any civilization survived this mess, it's gotta be in Texas. Either that or there's a lot of those dead things roaming around out there all strapped at the hip."

"I can't say I argue with your logic, but how do you know you won't be trading one idealist community for another?"

"I don't. But at least it won't be so damn cold. And it'll be my choice this time, I had little to do with me sitting here right now. This is literally the last place I wanted to be."

Viktor avoids looking at her, not because he's hurt but to make sure he shows he didn't take that as a slight. It doesn't work.

"No offense."

She looks back at him as he looks around the campus. Neither one of them speaks as the outdoor sounds fill the gap in their conversation. Finally, Viktor musters an idea.

"Maybe I'll head out when you do. Travel west a few days before we go our separate ways. Safety in numbers?" He lets but a hint of a smile curl the edges of his mouth.

She looks him over.

"Cold out here, huh?" Fez interrupts as he walks up on them. He stops, leaning against the fountain. They both turn to look over their shoulders. Visible breaths answer for them.

"Well just wanted to let ya both know the weather report is calling for a bit of a snowstorm tonight. Could be several inches so be sure to come by the supply center to get rations in case we lose power or anything. You'll also need to be assigned storm duties so best you get there early."

They look to one another and back to Fez. Catherine is the first to add her thoughts. "What kind of duties are we talking about?"

"Everyone has a role to play, and they've been assigned based on ability and necessity." Fez crosses his arms, showing his lack of desire for any argument on the subject.

"I see. And what job wasn't being done a week ago that is suddenly now a necessity?"

Viktor looks away, the awkward confrontation makes him

want to crawl under the bench until it passes. For a fleeting instant he has the desire to place a hand on her arm and tell her it will be fine but knows if he dares interject, he's as likely to lose the hand as he is to lose the only person that he can consider a friend in this place.

"First, there wasn't an impending blizzard a week ago. Second, you have no issues eating our food or enjoying our electricity so you might want to sound a bit more grateful." Fez looks to be working hard to suppress his frustration with being challenged.

"Warden telling the convict to be thankful, I get it. Except I guess you're not really the warden, are you? More like a guard with a bloated sense of duty."

Viktor is sure this is enough to make Fez crack, and it's now that he realizes Catherine is merely sparring for the sake of the fight as there's little passion in her voice. She's enjoying trading barbs and it arouses a spec of admiration in him.

She's feisty.

Fez clears his throat and changes posture, making it clear he's ready to leave. "If you don't like it, take it up with Jason. These are his orders. Don't be late."

He steps back, further indicating, almost pleading, for the conversation to be finished.

When she concedes and neither of them responds, Fez nods, heal turns, and walks away. Once he's out of earshot Catherine leans in close and Viktor fights the urge to lean back into her.

"Fucking cult, I say."

Steam puffs into the air as they share another laugh.

THEN

A cold, harsh cough awakens Viktor from the deep and dreamy sleep. His visions and obscurities were random and fleeting. They ranged from the dead to hallucinations of raging rivers of blood and melting towers of hot iron.

As soon as he's fully awake, the shivering sets in hard. His ears and nose are numb, as are his cheeks. Another cough somewhere behind him, and he leans to look down the row. Working toward Viktor's direction, Ramirez sweeps off the snow from the panel surfaces, humming along quietly as he works. He's a hundred feet away still, but Viktor can't believe he hasn't been noticed yet, lying at the base of the structure tucked into a ball. Maybe the white powder that accumulated overnight has camouflaged his presence.

Viktor stretches out his arms and legs and tries to get the blood flowing. He rolls to his side, away from the row, and squeezes under the panels. Pulling himself as low and controlled as he can, he slides his whole body out into the next row over. He gets up into a squat position, peering over the lip of a panel and watching Ramirez sweep. As soon as his back is turned, Viktor leaps up and walks briskly toward him in the opposite aisle.

"Morning!" Viktor calls out.

Ramirez turns around and nods without a hint of surprise.

"You're out here early," Viktor adds.

"Yeah. Had an all-hands-on-deck call late last night. False door alarm in trauma bay. We finally got the all-clear after the sweep early this morning so I just came out here rather than go back to bed for an hour," Ramirez talks through his work of cleaning off snow.

Viktor analyzes his tone, curious if the soldier is out of the loop or playing dumb.

"A bit underdressed don't you think?" Ramirez points with the handle of the broom.

Viktor realizes he's wearing only sweat pants, a sweatshirt, and shoes which were barely enough for being inside the compound, let alone outside. No hat, gloves, or jacket. He must look like a fool.

"Ah yeah, I saw you out here and was afraid I missed a shift change memo so I rushed out. Didn't expect it to be so cold." He feigns rubbing his arms as if he wasn't already aching from hours in the bitter cold.

"Run back inside. If you die of pneumonia from being out here like that, I don't want to have to kill you again."

Viktor looks around as if just realizing the environment they're in, trying to further sell the lie. "Uh yeah, sure. Thanks. I'll hurry back."

"Oh, and Vik, don't forget your broom. Hard to sweep panels without it."

There's something dark in his tone that makes Viktor uneasy, but he hurries down the aisle toward the compound pretending he didn't notice.

After taking a few minutes to warm up inside, change clothes, and down a hot cup of coffee, he returns to the solar structure to assist Ramirez. Trying to calm any tensions that he might be imagining, Viktor delivers a fresh hot cup of coffee for his work partner. Steam billows from the paper cup as Ramirez removes the lid and blows across the surface. He bows his head in gratitude before taking a careful sip.

Viktor starts sweeping while Ramirez takes a break. After a few minutes, they begin leap-frogging panels, brushing the light dusting of snow onto the pavement. As the sun rises over the mountain it begins to melt and becomes more of a hassle to push the mushy globs off and onto the ground. They're nearing the end of the structure when Ramirez leans his broom against a panel and turns to Viktor.

"Why don't you ask me what's been on my mind? You love playing shrink, don't you?"

Ramirez's glare is icy cold. Viktor fakes a clueless expression to the accusation.

"Don't take me for a fucking clown, alright?" Ramirez steps too close and lowers his voice. "Go on. Ask."

Viktor's smile fades and his demeanor is just as serious as the one staring back at him.

"Okay. Fine. What part did you really play during your *botched* mission?"

"Ya know, you've got it pretty good in here as a civilian while the rest of us go downrange, fighting and dying on your behalf. So what if things aren't black and white anymore. It doesn't make me a bad guy. Shit's changed and you'd better get used to it."

"What part did you play? Was any of what you said even true?"

"It's just like I said."

"And what about Corporal Stevens?"

Ramirez's eyes contract like he's been stuck by an arrow. His cheeks redden beyond what the cold has already done. "The fuck you know about it?"

"You mean, what the fuck do *you* know about it? Is this some game we're playing here, we both know that you know who's to blame for the alarm last night," Viktor says.

The soldier's posture stiffens. "I don't know what you think you saw--"

"The girls locked in cages. Is that not black and white because it seems pretty fucking clear to me--."

Viktor doesn't see the punch coming. Ramirez is on top of him like a wild animal before he hits the ground. He can taste the warm blood and rolls his tongue across his teeth to see if they're all there. His eyes are clenched shut waiting for another strike to land but when it doesn't come, he opens his eyes. Ramirez is panting over him, both hands locked on his jacket, pinning him to the concrete.

"I ought to strangle you right here, right now," he seethes, but the rage drains from his face and his grip loosens. "But fuck me, our fates are linked." He rests back on his heels. "Seems Becker doesn't buy that I didn't tell you the truth. If I kill you now, I'll surely follow suit, at his order."

"If he thinks I know whatever the fuck is going on here, why hasn't he done it himself? And why the hell would he kill you for doing it for him?"

"You don't know Becker like I do. He's got a plan and don't think for a minute we aren't both playing our part in it. If I kill you, it just confirms his suspicions. I'll be dead before nightfall." Ramirez stands, brushing himself off, the knees of his pants donning wet circles from the melted snow. He makes no offer to help Viktor to his feet. "There's no good, no bad. There's just survival. Consider this your only chance at it. You need to leave. Tonight."

Viktor pushes himself up, grasping at the panels to get to his feet as Ramirez looks down on him. "I'm not fucking around, Viktor. And I don't think I need to remind you what Becker is capable of." Ramirez grabs his broom and stomps toward the compound.

After he's out of sight, Viktor wastes no time making his way back to his barracks. He shoves his few belongings into his large duffle bag. He eyes the laptop and hard drive that he still has checked out and looks around the canvas tent, making sure there's nothing else he wants to take. Deciding that he has the room, he packs the computer and drive into the side of the bag. To avoid anyone being tipped off, Viktor hides the bag under his cot and exits into the main hall.

If it were up to him, he wouldn't wait until night, but Viktor knows he'll need the cover of darkness if he's going to get out unnoticed. That part of the plan he still hasn't worked out and it's looming like a dark storm cloud pushing closer and growing more menacing by the minute.

As luck would have it, a scheduled rehab session that afternoon provides an excuse for access to the medical facilities. While waiting for Specialist Chan to arrive, Viktor hoards supplies, bandages, antibiotics, anything he can get his hands on, and lines his pockets. Wearing a jacket doesn't even seem out of place given the temperature inside. Without it, he would be hard-pressed to take a fraction of what he has on him now.

"Alright, Viktor. How are you feeling today?" Chan asks, not looking up from her file as she enters the room. He's startled, almost caught in the act of theft, but regains his composure.

"Fine, thanks. If it's all the same to you I'd rather skip today's rehab, just feeling a little worn out. Long shift." He looks down to hide any signs of bullshit.

When she doesn't respond, he's forced to make eye contact. Her eyes pierce into his. She leans against a table in the corner of the room.

"You know you could have canceled upfront, no need to wait for the appointment to tell me in person." Her tone is inquisitive, but still polite and professional.

"You're right, I didn't mean to waste your time. I was fifty-fifty when I came in but it's really hit me in the past few minutes. And I didn't want to just leave without telling you."

Chan watches him for a moment, then closes his file folder. She crosses the room and opens the door. "Alright then, Viktor. Rest up and we'll see you next week for a double session?"

He doesn't hesitate, sliding off the bench and moving to the door. Viktor is almost into the hallway when the shattering of glass exposes his motive. A small bottle of antibiotics has fallen from his jacket and onto the tile floor. Chan looks from the bottle and up to Viktor. She pushes past him and sticks her head out into the hallway.

As her mouth opens, presumably to call for security, Viktor finds himself thrusting his hand over it and forcing her back into the room. The door snaps shut behind them and he has her up against the wall. He's pressing all his weight against her as her hands flail and grab at his jacket sleeves. As her eyes grow wide, he starts to feel sick, realizing what he was about to do. Leaving his hand in place, Viktor backs off of her so she won't suffocate and tries to tell her to quit resisting using only his eyes.

Chan appears to sense his change in body language and releases her grip on his jacket, letting her hands go wide along the wall, palms facing out as if to surrender and comply.

"Please, please you have to be quiet. It's not what you think. I'm not an addict or anything like that." Viktor looks from one eye to the other trying to gauge the level of her fear and distrust.

With not more than a beat of calm she thrusts her knee up into his crotch, but he's able to block it with his bad hip. He winces and it's just enough to give her a window of escape. Chan throws her forehead into his chin, sending stars into his vision and causing him to let go of his grip. She bolts for the door and Viktor dives to stop her. He's able to get an arm around her leg causing her to fly forward. Chan's head makes a gut-wrenching sound as it impacts the door handle, her neck snapping back at an unnatural angle. She falls limp to the ground.

"No, no, no. Fuck!"

Viktor falls to her side and with great care rolls her onto her back. A trickle of blood rolls down her face from above her eyebrow. It's already swelling. He can see the rise and fall in her chest which gives him hope and sends a flutter through his own. Viktor places his fingers on her neck and waits for a pulse.

"Oh, thank God."

He's quick to his feet, wiping his mouth in a motion of anxiety and looking all around the room. Footsteps in the hall send panic through him but they fade away. Viktor grabs a pen and begins scribbling on a corner of paper from his file. He tears it off and stuffs it in Chan's pants pocket. Moving her body and keeping her neck steady, he sets her up on the examination table.

"I'm so sorry."

He moves to the door, cracks it open just enough to slip out, and vanishes down the hall.

As he makes his way to the mess area all he can think about is them finding Chan and looking at the appointment schedule, if she doesn't wake up and rat him out first.

He knows he doesn't have long. It's now 4:15 p.m. and already the sun is going low outside. The overcast sky hastens the arrival of night. Viktor grabs as much food as he can without throwing up any alarms. The pantry is always stocked with canned and bagged snacks but there's constant supervision to prevent hoarding.

When he gets back to his bunk, he's surprised to see a blanket balled up on his cot. Unfolding a corner of it, he finds a pair of bolt cutters tucked inside. *Ramirez.* He had no idea how he was going to make it out of the compound and it wasn't going to by walking past the guards. Ramirez had to know as well, and it makes him wonder why he's helping him. Perhaps an absurd way of righting his wrongs or offsetting the soldier's complacency with Tom's savagery.

He tucks the cutters into the top of his duffel bag, along with the food and water he was able to grab from mess. Doing his best casual walk, Viktor makes his way out of the compound building and past the security guards that watch the bay door twenty-four hours a day.

"Just a quick maintenance check before dark," he says, gesturing with his bag.

Both men give a nod. His coming and going to work on the panels have become routine and since it's not yet past curfew, there's no pushback from the guards.

Viktor walks at a brisk pace to the far corner of the lot as the still-dim overhead lights have just begun to kick on. Their blue LED glow brighter as the sunlight has transformed into a deep orange and purple haze. As he nears the fence, far away from any guards or prying eyes, the hair all over his body stands on end. The gurgled, muffled growl of the dead carries through the chilled air and over the damp, snowy ground.

Just beyond the fence, at the section where he intended to make his escape, a shadowy group of the dead plod twenty yards past the perimeter. They're aimless in their direction, slowed down by the cold and snow at their feet. Viktor looks to the compound and then back to the dead. Back and forth, a decision being weighed with terrible consequence.

Guards burst from the bay doors of the compound.

Shit, they found Chan.

The growling dead stumble closer to the fence, now attracted by his presence. There are thirty or more strung out in several steps behind the first six that now begin to push against the chain-link barrier.

"Over there! I'll check the solar yard!" someone shouts in the distance.

Viktor looks down at his duffel bag and pulls back the zipper. The bolt cutters look up at him from inside as if not agreeing with what he's about to do. He wrestles it out of the opening, the wide handles catching on the edges of the flap. The struggle itself is as if the cutters and bag are pleading not to be made accomplices. Once it's free, he opens and closes the jaws to get a feel for the movement.

He analyzes the fence before him as it bends to the will of the dead horde pushing against it, the number of bodies adding to the weight. Black and decayed fingers, square voids of dark skin at the end of each digit where the nails used to be, dangle through the diamond sections of the fence like sea snakes swaying with the current while luring their next meal. He pushes the bolt cutters forward with open jaws and makes his first cut.

NOW

The storm dropped almost eighteen inches of snow in as many hours. Power and water restrictions were put in place as the generators struggled to keep up with the demand. Now, with an overdue lull in the snowfall, do the residents of the community begin emerging from their buildings. Workers shovel off solar panels and clear out piles from around the generator exhausts. Narrow lanes are cut along sidewalks so people can move from their housing to common areas.

Viktor and Catherine had spent the night together. As the snow began to fall and the lights flickered along, an announcement came that the community was cutting all but essential power. Soon after the bulletin, she tapped on his door. He was surprised to see her as he cracked it open, figuring it was just a courtesy check regarding the weather. Viktor smiled as she showcased a half bottle of whiskey in her right hand, sloshing it back and forth.

"What do you say?"

Opening the door and waving her in, Viktor was in rare silence for the lack of a clever response. They sipped dark brown spirit from the only glasses they had and talked about all things serious and silly. He had never articulated his ordeal and the death of his family to anyone, and hearing himself tell the tale made him realize they had far too little liquor on hand.

Viktor was fast to move on from the story, both to think of something else and to not endure any forced or awkward response of condolence.

"Where did you find a bottle of whiskey? Thought this was a dry community," he asked, emphasizing that he was impressed and following it with a generous sip.

"Dry for most." She laughed and took a sip of her own. "I saw it in the filing cabinet of your buddy Fez while he was dolling out our tasks."

He raised his glass as a toast to her observation. "He won't miss it. Not like he can report it lost anyway," Viktor added.

She finished her glass and was quick to refill it. They talked deep into the morning until Catherine fell asleep, tucked into the firm arm of the small, worn sofa. While Viktor may have longed for something more, once she fell asleep, he sighed a moment of relief. The unexpected closeness to another person was a welcome progression and he feared any expectation of intimacy from her.

Viktor covered her with a thick woven blanket and sat in silence, finishing the bottle while watching the snow fall outside. The orange wash of a streetlamp cast its color over the vibrant white snow. He watched until the light flickered and went out, only the ambiance from the snow illuminating the night beyond the window.

When he awoke, he could already feel that Catherine was no longer there. The blanket that was left folded on the arm of the couch confirmed as much. Snow continued to cascade outside, thick pieces sticking to the window as Viktor sat unmotivated in his room with a mild headache. His brain and body were not used to alcohol and he felt like it was his first-time drinking.

By lunch, the storm had quit and a round of door knocks let

everyone know it was time to get to work doing their cleanup duties. Viktor pulled on his thick gloves and knit hat and made his way downstairs. His task was to work alongside Fez clearing off solar panels and water lines.

Déjà vu.

As he now shovels the thick snow into mounds away from the units, Viktor almost regrets filling them in on his experience, the memories of his time at the first compound piling up with every scoop and leaving a sour taste in his mouth. *Maybe it's the whiskey.* But as he digs off heavy shovelfuls, he is at least thankful he wasn't assigned to sanitation. Two other men stand resting on their shovels across the yard. Their task of shoveling the snow off of the large septic tank is not envied.

Viktor works into the afternoon, even after Fez disappeared to take care of some clerical work, though Viktor didn't buy it. It's not until Catherine comes storming past that he stops to take a break. She is followed closely by Fez, and it's clear they are in the midst of a heated argument. He works his way closer to them as not to appear to eavesdrop, but he's desperate to hear what has her so pissed off.

"It's a bullshit task and you know it," she blurts, setting herself square to Fez while crossing her arms. Her body language begs for a response so she can swat back.

"Look, we all have things to do here that we would rather not."

"And of course, because I have a pair of tits and nothing dangling between my legs, I'm stuck on kitchen detail."

Fez scoffs and it's obvious that he doesn't have an answer to give her that isn't a complete fabrication. "So, I should put you on de-icing duty with the mechanics and stick George in the kitchen? We talked about this yesterday when I gave you the assignment."

"You called it health services!"

"Food is health!"

This is the first time Viktor hears the typically meek Fez raise his voice.

Catherine's face turns red and Viktor looks away, but his eyes drift back to the pair.

"Fuck you. I was a medic. And a good one. Clean your own dishes."

She turns to storm off but stops as Fez lightly grabs her arm.

"You've been drinking."

Catherine doesn't move. They both know the rules and Viktor worries she'll end up back in the gymnasium cell. He wants to step in but waits to see if she can handle herself.

"I can smell it on you, and I'm sure it's no coincidence my filing cabinet was left unlocked. And empty." Fez says it loud enough for effect, but quiet enough to play it safe.

Viktor can just make out what he's saying over the noise of the work and the dampening qualities of the snow. She turns, shrugging away her arm from his grasp, redness gone from her face but eyes still piercing.

"And what exactly do you think that means? If you tell Jason, where do you think I'll tell him I got it?"

Fez looks to be considering her point. He opens his mouth but is interrupted.

"What's going on here?" Jason's voice booms but doesn't carry far. He strides up behind them and stands between the two.

"Working out the task list, sir," Fez answers, not taking his eyes off of Catherine. A sense of nervousness behind his otherwise expressionless face.

"What's to work out? Delegate the list. Why isn't she working?"

"I'm not--" Catherine can't finish before Fez steps on her words.

"I was just informing her that I've transferred her to medical.

She'll be better utilized there," Fez says, looking from him and back to her.

Jason turns to Catherine, his head tilting the only thing that he needs to say.

"Right. I was just running back to my room to grab my kit," Catherine improvises.

"I wasn't aware we gave that back to you," Jason says as he throws Fez a side glare.

"Run along then. Fez, walk with me."

Jason does an about-face and leads Fez with a hand on his back. Catherine scrambles down the sidewalk, head down. She sends a glance to Viktor then back to her feet. He grips the shovel, fighting the urge to follow after her but she waves him off with a hand as she passes. The excitement has vanished and just like that he's back to shoveling snow.

Three days pass and the morning of their departure arrives. Catherine had confided in him the night of the argument with Fez that they should leave as soon as the storm work was done. Half the snow still lies on the ground as it hasn't been warm enough to melt away, but all of the community is back to functioning as normal.

Viktor had thought about their leaving all night, and as such found little sleep. Before dawn, he is now up and working in the closet, organizing files and transferring media and information onto drives. The one labeled master drive flickers in front of him. He's focused on the task at hand, trying to get as much done as possible. There's an admiration of Jason for keeping his end of the agreement and allowing them to leave. This motivates Viktor to push through to complete the mundane assignment, even though he's anxious to depart.

At nine in the morning, he does a final check on the progress of the last block of data transfer. There's still an hour to go and he decides to multitask to help expedite the process, the sooner they can leave the farther they can get before dark. He heads to the cafeteria to meet up with Catherine. She's already at the table eating, a piping hot paper cup of coffee steaming in front of her.

"Last hot meal for a while," he says, introducing himself. She nods, before blowing on the coffee and taking the smallest of sips.

"I was thinking we head north along the highway pass for a few days so we can link up with the interstate."

Viktor has begun to unfold his atlas onto the table between them. Catherine slides her medical bag forward, blocking the space.

"We'll have countless hours to plod our course along the way," she says.

"Right."

Viktor folds the map and tucks it back into his pack. "Do you have everything?"

She pulls her large personal backpack up from the seat next to her. "As much as I could fit in here. It's heavier than when I got here." She cracks a devilish grin.

"And I take it the medical bag is a bit lighter?" Viktor points with his eyebrows.

"It is *my* bag after all. But it's empty, they can keep it. I'm not going to stick around just to fight about possession laws in the apocalypse."

Viktor laughs louder than intended and is quick to temper it down.

"I'm packed as well, just need to run back to the office and shut down the file system."

They sit in silence for a moment while they clean their plates. Though neither of them vocalizes it, difficult times are ahead and the comfort of the meal and setting will soon be missed. Viktor finishes first and stands, taking his plate.

"Meet you back at the fountain in thirty?"

Catherine checks her watch and coffee cup then gives a look of approval.

"Works for me. Sooner we get walking, the sooner we put this place behind us."

"I hear ya."

In truth, he's anxious to get on the road as well, but given the past travels he's wary about leaving the comforts that this place has provided. Every time he considered making this community his home, Viktor's thoughts would wander to Francesca. He had to find out if she was alive. This place would always be here should he decide to head back south, empty-hearted.

On the way back to the administration building to check on the files, he's stopped by a shout from across the yard.

"Viktor!" Jason jogs across the sidewalk to catch up.

The concrete has dried, but the air is still cold and a half foot of snow covers the grass. It glistens and melts as the sun bakes down without a cloud to obstruct the radiation.

"This is it, huh?" Jason says as he catches up to him.

Viktor nods and extends a hand. "It is. I appreciate you letting me stay." Not all genuine but eager to be done with the formalities.

Jason squeezes his hand hard. "I like you. I'd be lying if I said we couldn't use you around here, but I respect you needing to go your own way."

"Thanks."

"If you're ever back this way, don't be a stranger."

"You bet." Viktor breaks away and tries to turn, but Jason gives one last tug to his arm.

"I promise, you won't be our prisoner next time."

He hands Viktor his axe which he produces from behind his back, then laughs and gives him a hard slap on the shoulder. Jason is off down the sidewalk as Viktor shakes his head, thankful that the interaction is over.

By the time he reaches the storage closet the master drive still hasn't finished transferring. An error has popped up on the screen. Viktor restarts the computer and tries again. The window displays a progress bar.

"Four hours?"

He curses under his breath. He looks around the room and back to the computer. Viktor grabs a piece of paper that he had scribbled on with big letters spelling out *Viktor's Office* and flips it over. He jots a note in sloppy handwriting.

> *Jason,*
> *I'll come back this way and collect the drive. Sorry I couldn't take it with me.*
> *Thanks again.*
> *- V*

With some reluctance, Viktor turns off the light and leaves the room. He knows Catherine won't wait a second longer and he'd much rather take to the road with her at his side than by himself. She's waiting for him at the fountain as he walks up.

She gestures with her hand and Viktor obliges, leading the way out of the campus. Catherine doesn't look back, but he can't help but offer a long gaze over his shoulder. The quiet little cluster of buildings and sidewalks shrinks behind them as they walk along the paved entrance road. Once they turn left onto the highway access, the community vanishes out of sight thanks to the towering trees, without so much a street sign as evidence that it even exists.

THEN

The dead funnel through the cut fence like a dam broken and overflowing. Viktor cowers under a bank of solar panels as the vicious horde lumbers through the rows, trampling over their own that have fallen to the pavement. Shots ring out as the soldiers realize they're inside the compound. They scream over their radios for backup. Viktor watches from between bars of cold steel as more soldiers line up on the edge of the expansive lot, standing in a row as a firing squad. They mow down the dead without hesitation, but those streaming in have grown too great and the gunshots attract any that are nearby.

The weight of the surge has knocked down a section of the perimeter thirty feet wide as what seems to be an endless stream of predators becomes emboldened by their numbers. Many of the dead move in fast pursuit overtaking the flank of the dozen soldiers who lined up in defense. Viktor sees this as his window to escape but looks back to the compound. He let the killers through the fence and he can't allow himself to leave without trying to help the innocents still inside.

More soldiers emerge from the large bay doors, which draws the attention of the intruders away from the back wall of the building. Viktor slides along the panels and jogs in the darkness of the compound fence until he reaches the far end of the building. He eases along to the corner and peers around its edge. A single dead claws at the wall and hovers near the security door where he escaped the previous night. The flat, handle-free slate of metal hinges outward with a *creak*. A soldier with a rifle tucked into his shoulder moves out of the door. A growl from the dead forces him to pivot for a shot, but he slips on the pavement and fires off a burst into the air as he lands on his back.

Before he can draw his sidearm the flesh-eater is on top of him, tearing at his hands and face. The screams are horrible and animalistic. Viktor eyes the handgun on the pavement next to the soldier's twitching arm. He sets down his duffel bag and makes a move. Sprinting toward the open door, he slides on the snowy asphalt and grabs the gun. Just as the dead turns its blood-soaked jaws from the writhing body toward him, he plunges a round straight between the hollow eyes and it collapses on top of the soldier.

Viktor steps over the entangled bodies when a hand grasps his pant leg. The gurgling sound is an attempt at words, perhaps a plea for help, but indiscernible among the blood pouring into the man's open throat. He looks down upon the mangled face and neck. All that remains is a skeletal stump where his face used to be. As he steps over, pulling free of the grip he lets off a double-tap into what he thinks is the forehead of the lost soldier. Using his boot, Viktor pushes the bodies just enough to let the door close behind him as he enters the secure wing of the building.

The hallway flashes red and a siren chirps in the distance. It takes a moment to gather his bearings, but he makes a left toward the last set of double doors at the end of the hall. Pulling hard on the lever he almost loses his footing, falling back when the doors don't budge. Viktor realizes they must be fire locked because of the alarm and looks around the hallway. A keypad on one side. He opens the exterior door again, which moves just a few inches before hitting the corpses on the other side. Their weight must have shifted and now blocks the door. Not being able to see the other side, Viktor reaches his arm around the door and feels along the soldier's chest. His hand lands in warm goo and tangled hair from the dead resting on top of the soldier's stomach. His fingers find a chest pocket. Inside is a plastic rectangle and a small key attached to a spiral band. Sticking his arm into pitch black and shark-infested water would have been preferable to this. He imagines teeth sinking into his arm at any moment and can't retrieve the band along with the key card fast enough.

Moving back to the keypad, he presses the card to it and hears the doors click. He pulls again, this time with less force and they swing open. A gasp settles over the room. It's the same as the night before, though it feels like there are fewer of the prisoners than he remembers. The women and children are huddled in the corners of their cells. Viktor fumbles with the key, the red spiral dangling below his hand. Without saying a word or looking at anyone, he moves from cell to cell unlocking each door. He's stunned when he realizes none have left their cages. They sit and shiver, looking at him in disbelief as if he means to play a trick.

"Go! Everyone, get out! The dead have made it inside!" Not a single person moves as there is a stir of discomfort among the crowd. Hushed whispers, a heavy sense of the terrified children.

"What are you waiting for? You have to leave now!" Viktor bangs on the bars of the cages with the barrel of the pistol.

The women and children cower and flinch at the sound.

"Nice try, Vik." The sound of Tom's voice tenses every muscle in his body.

He points the gun in the direction of the door. Tom's silhouette stands calm. He emerges into the red glow, his look unimpressed and unafraid.

"Please."

Without warning, Tom draws a gun of his own and sends off a round. It grazes Viktor's ear and pings off a cage. The bullet hits the red bulb and glass shatters to the ground. Women and children shriek.

For a moment the room is plunged into darkness. Viktor can still see Tom's silhouette against the closing door and fires off three shots. The first two miss, but the last one lands in the shoulder, sending him backward and onto the floor as the door latches shut.

Viktor sprints forward, jumping over the area of darkness where he thinks Tom fell. The groans and curses below let him know he's close. Two shots ring out from the ground, the bright muzzle flash revealing Tom's hateful expression and then blinding Viktor for a second as he lands against the doors, somehow unscathed. They fling open under his weight as he falls forward into the red hallway.

Slipping and crawling to his feet, he slides for the exit door. It's still blocked by the bodies outside and he still can't fit through the opening. The sound of the double doors causes him to spin around. Afraid of striking someone inside, he fires high rounds into the wall above the door. Tom ducks back inside but empties the rest of his magazine down the hallway.

The screams from inside the room are more than Viktor can bear and they almost mask the sound of Tom reloading. Using all of his weight, he throws himself against the exterior door until he can squeeze through. Flesh and bones tear and are crushed as the base drags over parts of the dead soldier.

"Where the fuck you think you're going!" Tom's voice echoes

off the walls, followed by two more rounds that puncture holes in the steel frame.

Viktor scrambles over the bodies and shoves the door closed, rolling the dead back up against it. A loud thump from the other side then two more shots ping off of the metal. The door moves open, fighting against the dead doorstop. As Tom sticks his head through the crack, Viktor throws himself into the door and hears a pop. Tom's gun falls to the ground as he spits blood.

"You fucker, you broke my neck," his now raspy voice absorbing into the red-stained slush below.

Viktor pistol whips Tom across the temple and his whole body goes slack, pinned upright in the door frame, only his head and arm dangling outside. A faint cloud of steam puffs from his open mouth. Viktor puts the barrel of the gun to his head and realizes the slide is locked back. He's out of ammunition. He drops down to feel around the soldier's body, first pulling at the rifle but the strap is caught and tangled in the two corpses.

Screams and growling and gunfire ring out in the compound lot. The dead are pouring into the main building now through an open bay door. He prays the people are escaping, not willing to consider what horror may be on his hands. The sounds grow louder and closer to him. Viktor finds a spare magazine and pulls it off of the body. Before he can reload, a dead staggers upon him from behind and causes him to scurry to his feet. He looks back to Tom's lifeless body and the dead trudging toward him. Viktor leaves Tom hanging in place as the ravenous creature descends on the door.

Let the dead do the deed.

He grabs his bag from the corner of the building and sprints to the fence. Bodies wander about in the soft illumination of the lot. Screams and gunshots still emanate from inside the building. As he steps through the cut chain link and looks back on the absolute chaos, the cost of his actions becomes clear. He knows many won't survive, and none of those who perish will be remembered. Viktor carries the weight up the muddy hill, forever leaving behind his first home in the new world.

NOW

Two hours into the steep upward climb, Viktor and Catherine can see the snow-dusted and grassy embankment leading to the mountainside highway. The road up had been cleared of snow by melt running downward, leaving a damp but clear path winding up and away from the community down below.

Once realizing Catherine wasn't up for chit-chat, Viktor dug through his bag and produced his phone and earbuds. Weary of the battery as sunlight will be scarce, he still proceeded to load a selection of music to accompany him on the hike. He had found, and borrowed, three more battery banks that were in the storage closet and he was able to fully charge them before departing. He's sure they won't be missed and doubts anyone remembered they were even there.

Catherine, having passed him almost as soon as they left, looks back while still plodding forward as Viktor fumbles with his phone. "Everything alright back there?"

He can hear out of his open ear but pulls out the other as a courtesy while jamming the next button on his device.

"Yes, all good. Hey, look!"

Viktor points forward as the embankment leading up to the guardrail identifies the upper highway. The road they're on snakes away from the highway and so they plan to walk up the snowy incline to reach it.

"About time," she says and picks up the pace.

By the time they reach the highway, after trudging through the knee-deep snow, Viktor initiates a rest by plopping down on the cold guardrail. Catherine sits next to him and digs through her bag. It's evident she would have preferred to keep moving. They both have a snack consisting of dried fruit and a package of nuts. Not more than a few minutes after sitting down, the sound of a booming explosion, followed by its concussive reverb, travels up the side of the hill and bounces off the mountain ridge above.

Viktor shoots a glance at Catherine, both unsure of what caused the explosion down in the valley. She packs her bag and looks around. Another boom follows the same echoing pattern up the mountain. They're both standing now, staring down the road they just trekked, trying to see anything to make sense of what is happening. Gunfire erupts in the far distance among the trees. Soon after, smoke begins rising below.

"Is that…" Viktor stammers.

"The community. Yeah, I think so."

Return gunfire blends with the originating shots. They're followed by multiple hollow and quieter explosions. Snow shakes off the trees nearby as the shockwaves travel upward.

"We have to go back!" Viktor is already slinging his bag and grabbing at his axe. He's whipped around as Catherine yanks at his arm.

"Are you nuts? We have to leave before whatever is down there comes up here!"

"What if they need our help? We can't just abandon them!"

"What are you talking about? They held us prisoner. We don't owe them anything!"

"You can't actually believe that. When's the last time you had a decent shower and hot meal? And for what? A little labor and community service?"

She shakes her head, fuming. It's clear the idea of going back down the hill is not an option for her.

"You can wait for me, or go on and I'll catch up. But I have to go back."

Viktor hops the guardrail and moves faster than his hip allows. He limps, this time not exaggerating, but moves down the embankment, arms out trying not to fall.

"Fuck!" Catherine hops over and slides down the bank, catching up in a matter of seconds. She pulls ahead of Viktor and pulls a handgun from her waistband.

"Wait, what?" Viktor hustles to catch up to her side.

"Never seen a gun before?"

"They checked all of our stuff when we got there, how did you smuggle it in?"

"I didn't. I smuggled it out."

What took two hours to do uphill they manage in forty-five minutes going downhill. Viktor's entire lower body is on fire. The pain surges through his hip, but he keeps in stride with every determined step Catherine takes.

It's been twenty minutes since the last succession of gunfire rang out. It was followed by several softer rounds of smaller caliber fire. Determined and symmetrical in sound. Twelve short pops, separated by a few seconds each. As they reach the road that turns into the community, Viktor pulls on Catherine's arm and leads her into the woods.

"We can go in the way I came the first time. More cover," he whispers.

She follows his lead. They step through the snow-filled forest floor. The trees are dense, offering enough protection that they can creep closer to the buildings from this direction. Dark smoke billows up above the canopy. They can start to see the first set of buildings in the compound. They've been torched.

Bodies lie strewn across the snowy yards and sidewalks. A commotion draws his attention. Several uniformed soldiers surround a Humvee. A deep voice emits from the center of the huddle. The man, whose face is obstructed by his crew, points out instructions and the soldiers disperse, moving down the sidewalk further into the community. The leader's back is to the trees, but Viktor can see him digging through the front seat of the vehicle.

The man turns, pulling a massive gun from the front seat. Its size looks like it more belongs riding on top of the vehicle instead of in a soldier's arms. He jams in a magazine and pulls back the slide, chambering a round. He looks up, revealing his face in Viktor's direction as he gives out a booming order to his troops.

"Let's go shit-eaters, we roll out in twenty!" shouts Tom, his voice loud but ragged as it escapes lips that are now hidden under a thick beard.

Viktor sinks back into the trees, covering his mouth with a gloved hand. "Impossible."

All they can do is wait in the wooded covering outside the campus, watching as soldiers, led by Tom, move building to building. There's no visible resistance which produces an ominous realization. They're not looking for fighters, but supplies, which means the fighters have already been eliminated. Soldiers carry cases of food, stacks of guns, and ammunition. A large military truck with a crane mounted on its bed lifts the generators onto a flatbed truck.

As the last of the soldiers mount up, Tom moves to his Humvee but detours to a nearby troop transport carrier with a canvas top. Viktor leans forward against a tree, trying to squint into clarity what's taking place.

Tom pulls open the flap and shouts some orders inside, but as he lets the canvas go it bounces and Viktor can see, clear as day, several women bound at the mouth and hands. They're seated in rows and the look of fear on their faces is unquestionable.

"We have to do something!" Viktor says through his teeth as he steps forward.

Catherine yanks him back, almost pulling him over.

"Are you fucking crazy? We have a single gun and your stupid twig splitter."

She gestures with the handgun to the axe that he didn't realize he was now gripping in his gloved hand, as if ready to hack every tree in his path.

His ambition doesn't matter. No sooner than she speaks the words, the trucks are tearing up mud and blasting diesel smoke into the air as they drive down the entrance road. They both wait a moment until the sounds of the engines are gone. Viktor is first to stand up and he crosses the snow-covered opening, the same field where he lay face down when he arrived.

"What are you doing? You saw what happened, we just need to get out of here!" Catherine emerges from the woods and trudges through the snow to catch up.

"We have to check for survivors."

As they walk along the sidewalk, they come across the first travesty. A few feet off the path, lying face down in the snow, a row of a dozen men with hands bound behind their back. He connects the image of the bodies with the sequential pops they heard as they neared the campus.

"Why would they do this?" Catherine mutters.

"Because he's the devil," Viktor retorts as if talking to himself.

"You know who did this? Were you with them? How exactly did you get here?" Her accusation shakes Viktor back into the moment.

"Years ago. I escaped their base, and killed their leader."

"They might disagree." Catherine points to the bodies with her gun.

Viktor kneels at the end of the row, recognizing the clothes of the man who is face down.

"Fez," Catherine says. "Come on, nothing we can do now," she adds.

They make their way to the main hall. The smell of gunpowder and blood hangs thick in the air, though there aren't as many bodies as he expected. Judging by the number of corpses outside, Viktor suspects they made a defensive push to meet the attackers in an attempt to protect the women and children inside. The bodies that do scatter the hall are just that, *bodies*, presumably the ones who fought back.

Viktor can't get out of the hall fast enough. He moves to the stairs and heads down a flight, Catherine over his shoulder aiming her gun at every body and corner. As they exit the stairwell and push through the stair doors, Catherine lets out a screech and the gun clanks to the tile. He whips around to see a gnawing dead biting at her pant leg, its fingers wrapped around her foot. The back half of the corpse has been blown off, the entrails leading around to the back of the stairs and a blackened wall. As it pulls her leg closer to its violent jaws, Viktor sinks the blade of his axe deep into its skull. The mouth hangs open as its head falls to the floor. Catherine wiggles free and picks up her gun.

"Are you bit?"

"No, I'm fine, just got my pants." She takes a deep breath.

They step into the hallway and walk along the wall, the overhead lights flickering as they go. Viktor passes the storage closet, but a moan from inside makes him turn back. He presses an ear to the door. Another gasp, almost inaudible. He points to the door and raises his axe. Catherine aims her gun just over his shoulder.

Viktor yanks open the door with a yell, ready to slam the axe into whatever horror awaits him. The light from the hallway is just enough to stop him from bringing it down on Jason's forehead.

"Wait!" Viktor shouts, ensuring Catherine doesn't fire.

Slumped against the wall, Jason's breath is shallow. He's riddled with gunshots to the chest and abdomen. Blood trickles from his lips.

"I would have shot you, ya know," Jason manages to whisper.

He tries to lift his arm, but only his shoulder twitches. The limb is also full of holes, leading down to his hand lying limp on the floor, a finger twitching now and again. Next to his arm, a rifle rests in a pool of blood.

Viktor rushes to his side and looks him over. Catherine covers her mouth with her arm. The site of his wounds is grotesque and the mere fact he's still alive is shocking to them both.

"Come on, we have to get him up."

"Viktor."

He struggles to move Jason, who winces at first touch.

"Viktor."

He turns, expecting Catherine to be ready to help. She's standing against the doorframe, a pale look gazing down on them.

"Why aren't you helping?" A curse more than a question.

"It's okay, Vik," Jason spits out with a cough of blood. "Just don't let me turn into one of them."

"No, no. We can stop the bleeding." Viktor looks at Jason's shirt and his side.

"Stop. I'm Swiss cheese. I can feel myself fading. Just do it already." Jason lifts his left hand, the good one, and manages to point to Catherine.

Viktor realizes he's gesturing to the handgun she's holding. He looks back and forth, trying to find words to argue. He doesn't even hear the gunshot, just feels the concussion from the barrel and the ringing that follows.

"Fuck!" Viktor exclaims, rubbing his ear.

Catherine steps across the room and picks up the rifle. She checks Jason for any spare magazines and finds one. She checks the mag in the gun and chamber. As she slides the extra mag into her coat, she hands the pistol to Viktor.

"Better if we're both armed," she says.

Viktor wipes his brow as he stands, walking past her to the computer station.

"I'm good."

Frustrated, Catherine places the handgun back into her waistband.

"Can we please get out of here?"

Viktor is hunched over the computer keyboard, his hard drive still plugged in on the desk. "Just one last thing."

THEN

Screams and gunshots fade as Viktor hikes as fast as he can, up and away from the military base. The ground is worn and stamped down where the horde passed through. Mud and slush make it difficult at times but he pushes on, heading for a street he remembers when he first arrived while riding shotgun with Tom. He dares not take the road that leads out of the compound in case the soldiers make an escape. Who knows what they would do to him for such a betrayal. This fear is enough to keep him moving through the dark forest.

When soft earth turns to the hard crunch of gravel, he realizes he's made it to the road, its damp surface reflecting the bright moonlight and snow-dusted trees. He draws the handgun from his waist and looks it over. Grabbing for the magazine, he's quick to jam it in and rack the slide. He knows that could have been a deadly oversight but was so focused on putting distance between himself and the base that he forgot to load the gun. He places the barrel back into his waistband, the cold steel biting against his stomach. Viktor pulls his thick jacket down over it but has to do a full unzip as his body temperature has risen from the exhaustive hike.

Tired, wet, and hungry, he knows he has to put as much distance between himself and the base before finding shelter for the night. He plods along the empty two-lane road, moving cautiously as he passes abandoned vehicles. The shapes inside play tricks with his mind. With dawn still hours away, Viktor is relieved when he comes across a driveway. A sign hangs over the single-lane dirt road.

"Blue Ridge Camp," he whispers, but it could be a shout among the dead silence of night.

The road past the sign doesn't have any fresh tracks and the two lamps on either side have long burned out or shut off. He makes his way along the winding driveway which, to his disappointment, goes much further than he anticipated. Viktor might not have gone this way had he known how far back in the woods the camp sat. After another twenty minutes of walking the monotony of the road breaks away into an open campground lit by the moon overhead. He's apprehensive when he sees a half dozen campers scattered across the roundabout road.

Drawing his pistol and comfortable enough to click on a small headlamp that he lifted from the base, he scans the area and moves to the least dilapidated camper. Peeling back the metal door, which hangs open on the hinges, Viktor sticks his head and hands inside, painting the interior with the beam of light and sweeping from left to right. A glint catches the light as two beady eyes lunge toward him. The scraping of claws comes right for him as he runs in place trying to back out of the door. As quick as it lurches at him, the raccoon darts between his legs and out into the night, chattering all the way.

Viktor falls to the doorstep and catches his breath. After a moment of recovery, he pulls himself up and latches the door behind him. The small camper is the size of a child's bedroom. It's cold and damp as the tears in the fabric walls have done little to keep the elements and wildlife at bay. A large cushion sits in the bed frame at the rear and, aside from some leaves and trash, it doesn't look that bad, considering. He even manages to find a rolled-up sleeping bag in an overhead cabinet.

After checking the space for any additional surprises, he climbs into the bag and stretches out in the thin but soft bedding. He falls asleep quick, not waking until the warm licks of sun flash through a tear in the wall of the camper, hitting his face.

Viktor is slow to move as the chill is still present in the morning air, but the sun feels nice and this motivates him to leave the campsite. The more miles he can put between himself and the base, the less chance he'll be found by any survivors. There's no way they could search in every direction, or even know he survived the attack, or so he tells himself.

The door cries as he exits the camper into the campground. Now that he's able to take in the scope of the area, Viktor realizes he will find few supplies here. The place has been picked clean. He even checks the metal grill stations that protrude from the ground. All that remains is charcoal and shards of aluminum foil.

Viktor walks the entire roundabout and is ready to turn back to head down the long driveway when a large disturbed area next to the tree line causes him to do a double-take. The area in question is maybe twenty feet across and half as long. He walks around it, looking at every wet, brown leaf that's stuck to the next. And then he sees it. What his gut knew the moment that his eyes found it his mind now puts together. A small tattered shoe protrudes from the edge of the leafy covering. Viktor brushes the covering away with his boot, knowing it's not just a lost shoe but hoping that he's wrong. The shoe leads to an ankle, which leads to a leg in jeans that twists down into the earth.

He checks his surroundings and finds a long branch with a sprawling fork. Viktor uses it as a rake and clears the covered ground. Dark wet earth, almost black, with a few weeds tangled from where the leaves held back the cold. Underneath, body parts stick up from the dirt. A hand here, a foot there. An elbow or knee over there. Then he hears a voice in his head. Ramirez is telling the story of their botched mission, and the survivors that were executed and buried. Viktor pulls himself up and leans back against a tree. In the far distance, carried through the forest, a faint motor travels along the road and tires hum against pavement.

The sound is unmistakable. A Humvee, at least one, traveling at a high rate of speed. Viktor cowers next to the closest camper, though its tattered fabric doesn't provide much cover. His eyes are fixed on the forest as the vehicle gets louder. As it reaches peak volume it begins fading away.

Viktor looks back to the disturbed earth, body parts now exposed to the sun and air. There isn't enough sticking out of the dirt to inspect them for any personal belongings and the idea of digging up all those bodies for that purpose alone dissuades him. With some guilt, he uses a large branch to rake the earth and leaves back over the corpses, once again hiding them from view and leaving them to decompose and vanish. A crack of a branch echoes in the trees just beyond the tree line behind him.

He stops and listens, waiting for a whoosh of wind to justify the sound. The follow-up doesn't come and he finishes covering the pile. Viktor breaks the makeshift rake over his leg and jams the pointy end into the soil. It has a fork shape at the top that will serve as a cross. He pulls a piece of tan canvas off the camper and cuts it loose with his pocket knife. Viktor flicks the blade in between his fingers, not knowing the last time he'd even opened it, the edge still razor-sharp. The piece of canvas fits around the grave marker and he even tied it into a bow for decoration. As he stands, wiping the dirt from his hands on his pant legs, a blur of motion in the trees catches his eye.

Viktor draws the pistol once more, the barrel following the shape as it darts and weaves around trunks and branches. The movement stops behind a large tree trunk, out of sight. He listens for another moment, waiting for it to reappear.

"Come on out!" he shouts.

He can sense a stir behind the tree but no sign of life, neither human nor animal. Viktor begins taking short, quiet steps toward the trees, the gun still raised in front of him.

"I have a gun. Just step out from behind the tree slowly."

Leaves rustle behind the trunk. He's almost to the end of the grass, maybe twenty feet from the tree.

"Look. I'll put it down. I won't hurt you." Viktor lowers the gun halfway to his side, still ready to hip fire like an old western draw.

"Ok," a soft voice comes from behind the tree. The sound carries little weight and almost feels like part of the forest as it lands on the leaves and vanishes into the open campground.

He's taken aback, not expecting a voice so quiet, or young. Before he can say anything in reply, an arm extends from behind the thick gray bark. It leads into a ragged, blue long sleeve shirt. Matted but tight curly hair, light brown with a speck of leaf stuck in it, emerges next. Viktor drops to a knee when the child reveals her face. She can't be more than twelve, or at least close to the same age as his daughter. Her dark complexion isn't enough to hide the dried mud and soot. A large bruise is swollen on her cheek. The girl stands in the woods, both hands in the air, trembling.

"I won't hurt you." Viktor quickly shoves the gun into his waistband and shows his palms. He's still kneeling in the dirt and gestures for her to come closer.

She's reluctant and he can see she's calculating if she should run.

"I'm Viktor. What's your name?"

The girl doesn't cry and she's not shaking out of fear, he sees. The worn shirt and mud-covered jeans are all she has on. She must be freezing. "You need to come get warm."

"Where did you come from?" the girl asks, her hands still halfway in the air.

"The base. It was overrun and I escaped."

She makes a quick turn as if she's going to sprint into the woods. He knows he would never catch her and scrambles to find the right words.

"Wait! I'm not a soldier."

The girl turns back to him, looking over his outfit, checking out his story. He can tell fight or flight is doing its work on her poor nervous system. Viktor begins to realize who she might be. He looks to the burial site, around the campground, and then back to her.

"They attacked you. This was your camp." He can see her expression as validating his assumption. "And that's your family." Viktor trails off, putting the pieces together.

The girl offers a small nod. Her hands now clenched at her side, she doesn't look at the grave, only at Viktor.

"We need to get out of here, the both of us. You heard the vehicle on the road just now, some of them must have escaped too." He bends his fingers to call her forward.

As she steps behind the trunk, her right arm reemerges with a spear. Or more of a broomstick with a kitchen knife wrapped to the end. But it's not the weapon that surprises him. Viktor has to fight back tears when her other hand comes from behind the tree.

This time a tiny hand grasped in her own. The young boy can't be more than four, his skin fair, brown and red hair caked to one side. Dirt smeared across his freckled cheeks, lines running down cut by rivers of dried tears.

The girl leads the boy from the trees. Viktor stands and motions them toward him. She's cautious, and the boy avoids looking at him. His head is down, watching his own feet as he steps over the forest growth. She stops at the edge of the trees and Viktor takes a step back giving them both some space.

"My name is Basil, like the leaf. This is Jake." Her voice is soft and sweet, but a hint of ferocity that Viktor admires. The boy looks up with pale green eyes, the whites still bloodshot.

"Hi there," Viktor says as he crouches down, extending a hand to Jake who looks right through him.

"He doesn't talk anymore. But he listens good." Basil steps past Viktor using the spear as a walking stick, leading Jake around him. Viktor turns as she guides the boy through the campground. "We're ready to leave this place," she says, not looking back, as if offering it for reclamation to the forest. He allows himself a painful smile and hustles to catch up.

NOW

There wasn't much left behind after Tom and his rebuilt force ransacked the community. Anything of value was stripped and kept, or destroyed by the marauders. Thankfully, long before the attack and even before Viktor's arrival, Jason had ordered all of the residents to turn over assets for cataloging. Every member now dead at least lives on in the hard drive that bounces around in Viktor's backpack.

Knowing that Tom and his soldiers headed south out of the community, Viktor suggested, and Catherine agreed, that they re-climb the hill that heads northwest toward the highway. He knows they'll need to be extra cautious and rethink their plan to travel along the roads. But first, they just need to find camp for the night. It takes them until the late afternoon to reach the highway again, which leaves less than an hour of sunlight.

Viktor leads Catherine to the roadside shack that led to their paths crossing in the first place. It has been two weeks since he first came across the corn hut, but he half expected the carnage to be long gone. Granted, Jason's crew cleared everything out, including the bodies and any supplies, but the large stain of blood on the outside wall was as bright and prominent as the day it happened.

Maybe more so in contrast with the white snow packed around the edges. They peel back the door and step inside as the moon hovers over the mountains in the distance.

Catherine is quick to start a fire. She uses the wood from the blown-out section of the wall, after first dragging a headless frozen corpse out and rolling it down the bank. Viktor uses his axe to knock off chunks of the wood counter to burn for fuel.

"Some home," Catherine jabs, poking at the small fire that flickers on the rafters above.

"I never said this was home. Christ, I was here maybe ten minutes before the doobie brothers showed up." He gestures with his axe at the clear mayhem and destruction that took place. The fire roars up as he places a couple of thick planks at an angle.

"Teepee method. That's one way to go."

Viktor rolls his eyes as Catherine extends her hand.

"By all means." Viktor hands her the axe.

She uses it to knock down his newly built teepee in the fire and stacks them in a square like an intertwined log cabin. She adds more from the pile beside her.

"Think we'll get smoked out?" he asks.

Catherine looks around, following the billowing smoke with her eyes. She points to the roof with the axe before handing it back to Viktor.

"Looks like it's funneling out there, between the aluminum sheets."

They sit in silence for a while. In the process of breaking down the counter, he did come across a couple of bottles of Coke that had rolled underneath, and a bag of corn kernels bound up with a twist tie. He had shoved the Cokes into the snow outside using the hole in the wall so he didn't have to leave the hut. He digs through his backpack and pulls out a small vile.

"Beard oil."

Catherine looks confused. "Will it help you grow a real one?"

Viktor strokes his stubble before pouring out a few drops into a metal hubcap that he had found hanging on a beam over the door. He places the hubcap onto the fire. After a short moment, Viktor pours the entire bag of corn kernels into the oil.

"Don't worry, it's just coconut oil and a bit of lavender," he says, examining the vile and putting it back into his bag. He places another hubcap over the kernels as a lid and sits back.

"Clever." Catherine even looks impressed. "So, how long have you been on your own?"

Viktor is lost in the fire but decides to indulge. They didn't get very far past how he lost his family before she fell asleep the night that she stayed over. He's cold, hungry, and not tired enough to sleep. May as well pass the time.

"Off and on since the beginning. Been solo for three years or so."

"Did they..." She leans in, not wanting to say it.

"Some." He continues to stare at the fire, flicking at the bottom of the blackened hubcap. "What about you?"

She had resisted opening up about anything prior, but something about the night air, the modest hut, and having been through something significant together made a clear difference to her, though he couldn't put a finger on it.

"I was in a medical combat unit of the Pennsylvania National Guard. Once shit hit the fan we were dispatched to another city outside the state. They told us it was protocol that we not serve in our own communities. Which makes sense now, but sounded like bullshit then. They were afraid we wouldn't kill a dead if we recognized its face." A single pop of corn bounces in the hubcap.

"It didn't take us long for our unit to fall apart. Guys started getting word their neighborhoods had fallen, and they disappeared overnight. Who could blame them? Leadership was a mess. We didn't know how far up the orders were coming from or if there was even a unified government overseeing the operations." A few more pops in the fire.

"It wasn't until we were overrun that I finally said 'fuck it'. Some of the guys were headed to a makeshift military base they had heard about but I figured I'd done my time. You've seen by now, there isn't really safety in numbers." Her eyes move to him, the fire's reflection dancing off her round pupils. He could get lost *there.*

"I've been mostly on my own since. A couple of strangers now and again. Had to kill a few when their intentions were finally revealed. Others were strong enough to stay alive past their first fight with a dead, but not much after." The corn begins popping at a steady frequency.

"If you prefer being on your own, why head to Texas?" Viktor asks.

She looks back to the fire. "When I left, I headed back home. I knew that my town would have been long gone and the likelihood of finding family was slim to none. But I found them. Just not how I would have liked."

Viktor looks into the fire as well, understanding her meaning and not wanting to say anything.

"Anyhow, figure life isn't just about survival. If there's not something more than what's the point. Right?"

The corn popping subdues. Viktor is quick to grab his axe and lift off the top hubcap using the blade. A few white kernels fall into the fire and vanish in a bright flash. He uses the tip to pull the bottom hubcap out of the fire and onto the cold floor. The metal sizzles as it cools. Viktor walks to the hole in the wall and grabs the

Cokes from the snow, unscrewing the cap and handing one to Catherine. She smiles. He offers a toast and she playfully taps her bottle to his. They both take a swig of the flat beverage. He grabs a handful of popcorn and takes a bite. She looks at him, unsure.

"Not bad, a bit flowery, and could use some salt." He pushes the hubcap across the dirt with the axe and watches her grab a handful.

"Bon appétit," he says. Her smile is infectious as she pops a kernel into her mouth.

Traveling with an abundance of caution, the pair still made good time along the mountainside highway. They left at first light, both having fallen asleep pretty quick from the strenuous day of up, down, up again hiking. Against his better judgment and persistent reminders, Catherine insisted the highway was the fastest and safest route as they left the shack.

After three days on the same road, once taking a dirt side road to avoid a menacing area, they climbed up a steep onramp and onto another highway.

The six-lane road is dotted with sporadic, rusted vehicles, many charred but some still looking brand new after years in the sun and elements. Viktor was the first to slow down and inspect the cars as they passed, but even Catherine agreed it made sense to scavenge what they could as their supplies were not endless. With two of them to search, the time trade-off was less of a hit to her hurried pace.

He was fortunate to find a few unopened bottles of water, and a half-filled bottle of clear liquor, or what smelled like liquor. The label had long been wiped away leaving the sticky adhesive behind. Worst case, they could maybe use it as a fire starter or disinfectant. The food was scarce, most packaged items already found and torn to bits by unseen critters. In a glove box, he did find a pack of gum that brought them both more joy than he expected. They shared a single piece, Catherine biting it in half first. Viktor watched her for a moment, her chewing movements pushing in her dimples, admiring the late afternoon light that was casting complementary shadows on her feminine features.

"What?" she had asked.

He said nothing, hiding a smile and turning back to loot. While usable supplies were hard to come by, collectibles were not. Viktor nabbed close to a dozen IDs, a few phones that he had yet to inspect, and a single-family photo that he found in a wallet located in a burnt-out tractor-trailer. The remains were beyond human recognition, but it was the shiny money clip that caught his eye. Most of the wallet had melted, including the driver's license, but somehow the folded photo inside had only singed corners. An older, yet very attractive blonde woman, stands with her arm around two grown boys, both with dark brown hair, tall and athletic. The background a green yard and bright trees. On the back, there was writing in faded pen.

"Jean, Daniel, and David. Summer 19," he read.

From the melted ID, Viktor tried his best to sleuth the last name. It appeared to be either Wallace or Williams, something with a W and kind of long. He wrote as much on the back of the photo in pen as well as the rough location of the truck. *Highway 120, what state were they in now? Kentucky.* He scribbled that as well. They spent another three days following the highway east, with no signs of anyone, alive or dead. As the afternoon became evening, they agreed on stopping for the night. A rest stop at mile marker 78 would do fine, he suggested.

Viktor unpacked his sleeping roll first once inside the visitor center. Even though the glass double doors had long been reduced to shards, crunching under their feet as they stepped in, the building was plenty warm in contrast to the past week of sleeping outside. Catherine rolled her mat out next to him, tucked up against the booth at the center of the room. Old information pamphlets were scattered across the floor with empty clothes hangers and vending shelves left barren, save for a thick coat of dust. Both of them were worn down from the arduous trek, and they didn't say much before calling it a night.

Now, just as Viktor closes his eyes to try to fall asleep, Catherine touches his hand and speaks in a gentle whisper.

"I think we'll make it to just outside of Bowling Green tomorrow. Maybe a good a place as any to split up."

He can feel her watching him as he tries to think of what he wants to say. She fills the void.

"No sense you going any further west, right? If you're still headed north."

Viktor acts oblivious to her subtle invitation, despite his reluctance to leave her side.

"Uh yeah, I guess that's a good idea," he finally says.

He rustles for the atlas and unfolds it between them. She leans in close, her hand now brushing up against his arm.

"Looks like I can just follow 65 up to 64, avoiding Louisville, and then hit 79 near Charleston, right up into Pennsylvania," he says in confidence as if this was always the route.

"Sounds like a good plan."

"What about you?"

She slides the atlas, angling it toward her with one hand. With the other, her fingers begin tracing his forearm. Viktor tries very hard to pretend he doesn't notice and all is normal. The urge to tear the atlas away and kiss her is almost unbearable.

"I think I'll just keep heading due west. There's gotta be a boat or something I can take down the Mississippi." Catherine sounds serious, but it could just as well be a joke.

"Sounds dangerous."

"Could be, but I grew up around water. If anything, I'll follow its banks. Then head directly west at 20, all the way into Texas." Catherine slides the atlas back to him.

"Keep it."

"Like hell, plus you've scribbled all over the damn thing," she teases.

Viktor looks around, climbing out of his bedroll.

"What is it?"

"One second."

He digs through some trash and cardboard and comes up with a thick pamphlet, dusting it off by beating it against his leg.

"There you go, miss independence."

Viktor hands her the folded map. He expects her to resist, but her smile is a demonstration of thanks from which he can't look away. She tucks the map into her pack as Viktor climbs back into the warmth of his bedding.

"I thought it'd be warmer in here," he says.

When she doesn't respond, he looks at her and is surprised by her longing stare. He blinks but doesn't speak. Her hand slides into his sleeping bag as she leans in close. Viktor refuses to acknowledge her cold hand, the human contact bringing warmth and chill at the same time. As it slides lower across his abdomen, he leans into her. He can't say who bridged the gap first, but their lips collide with the force of years of pent-up stress, anger, and horror.

This may not be her first post-world encounter, he thinks, but it's his and waves of emotion pour from his mouth and tongue into hers. The encroachment is reciprocated and before he knows what happened, Catherine is inside his bedroll tangled around him. Their hands roam and explore like they're both in high school, figuring this all out for the first time. Viktor pulls back a little to speak, but she bites his lip.

"Don't you fucking dare." She smiles and they plunge into a frenzy of passion that he's both longed for and feared.

He can't say for how long, could be a few minutes, could have been an hour, but as fast as it began it was over too soon. Catherine is sound asleep nestled in his arm, having said nothing once they were finished. He stares at the moldy ceiling tiles overhead and has to wonder; *did she do this so he wouldn't go? Or was it only because he was leaving?* Both thoughts nag at him until late into the night, he knows what he wants.

I'm going with her.

He wants to shout, to wake her and tell her, but doesn't have the heart to disturb her as she breathes shallow exhalations into his chest. With his free hand, Viktor retrieves the pouch from the front of his pack that sits beside him on the floor. He pulls out Francesca's ID, rubbing his thumb across it for the last time.

So stupid, chasing ghosts is the best way to become one.

He tucks the ID back into the pouch and closes his eyes. With peace of mind, it doesn't take long for him to fall asleep against a woman for the first time in years.

THEN

So many questions fill his mind as he watches the young girl lead the boy around the campground and his hatred for Tom grows larger than he thought possible. The atrocities committed, likely in plain sight of these two children, deserve the ultimate punishment. But there's no satisfaction in how Viktor left him, hanging halfway out of the door, blood pouring from his face and mouth. Surely, he's dead, put down by his own soldiers after becoming one of *them*. The idea that he might be out there stealing life as one of those creatures isn't a whole lot different than how he was alive, but it still makes Viktor's stomach turn. He replays the moment over and over, wondering if there was something else that he could have done.

Keeping at a reasonable distance to let Basil do her own thing, he observes her retrieving their belongings. A single backpack each, dirty and torn, hers stuffed full and the boy's just a sagging weight in the bottom. She pulls out a black trash bag from beneath a dilapidated camper, the cylinder shape inside must be lightweight as she slings it over her shoulder with ease and ties the bag to her backpack shoulder strap. With her spear in one hand and Jake's hand disappearing in her other, she does an about-face to Viktor, planting the spear into the dirt.

"We're ready." Her hesitation and blank stare tell Viktor that she means for him to lead.

Up until this point he'd been an observer, admiring her maturity and poise in the body of a child. It's now that he gets a spike to his senses, a parental instinct to take the reins. With a nod, he steps forward and past them. He extends a hand to touch Jake's head but the boy moves just enough to avoid contact. No one says anything, and they wait for Viktor to get a few steps ahead before he can hear them following behind. Basil whispers to the boy, he can't make it out but it feels sweet and comforting.

"I need you both to listen for me. You hear any vehicles or voices, don't be scared but don't question yourself either. Speak up. You've got young ears and can hear better."

Viktor turns around with a smile, thinking the self-deprecation may warrant one in return but only receives a curt nod from Basil. Jake's head still looking at the ground a foot in front of each careful step.

"Right then," he says to himself, turning back to the dirt road ahead. "We'll have to follow the road for just a bit, but as soon as we find a good place to get off, we'll make our way through the trees." He glances back, again wanting some sort of response. "Look we don't have to chat but I need to at least know you hear me or I'll keep looking back."

Basil sighs and does a double *tap* of her spear against the ground.

"That works." Viktor turns forward once again. He likes her. She has no fear of him as an adult or any false expectation of authority to him as a stranger. It's no wonder to him now how she's survived this long. The boy wouldn't be alive without her. They're both stronger than he is though, and in that moment of walking along the empty road, he swears he'll give his life for theirs if it comes to it. He'll do what he couldn't do for Caroline.

After fifteen minutes of road walking, Viktor's nerves take over. Any moment, he fears a Humvee will rush up behind them and either take them out without slowing, or worse. They're all familiar with *worse* by now. At the first manageable clearing, he steps off the secluded road and down a small bank into the thick trees. A game path lies ahead and he means to follow it.

"They were heading south so we'll head north for a while."

Tap. Tap.

They press on for another hour and find a clearing to take a break along the edge.

"Jake's hungry," Basil says, the sound of her voice startling Viktor.

"Here's a good a place as any. Do you have any food?" he asks, reaching into his pack.

Basil retrieves a small colorful bag of something and gives it to Jake, who tears into it with a big smile. She also pulls out a cell phone, turns it on, and hands it to the boy who sits on a stump. He turns it sideways and begins giggling.

"Volume down, remember." The boy nods, sticky red and blue covering his lips.

"How does that thing still work?"

She pulls out a rectangular box not much larger than the phone, a grid pattern on both sides. She unfolds it on the downed tree and it expands about three times its size.

"My parents had this in their camper. It's not enough to use the phone all the time but it lets him play his game and watch a show or two before bed."

"May I?"

She hands him the device with some hesitation.

"Solar, that's brilliant."

He feels somewhat stupid given his experience on the base, but assigns the ignorance to him being lost in the element of the new routine at the time.

"He likes looking at pictures of his parents and brother. From before."

She pulls it back and places it face up into the sun. Jake giggles as he stares unblinking at the small screen. Without looking away, the boy hands the empty wrapper back to Basil, who tucks it into a small bag in the front pouch of her backpack.

"There's only three cartoons on there, but he doesn't seem to get tired of them. Only rule is no repeats, he's gotta watch all three before starting over."

Jake nods as if she were talking to him. Basil smiles for the first time since Viktor encountered them. He can't help but mirror it. They both watch the boy enjoy his cartoon, too distracted to eat anything themselves.

Tap. Tap.

"Where are you?" Viktor whispers.

Tap. Tap.

He steps over branch and stone, calculating each foothold, using his ears to pinpoint the sound.

They had traveled the rest of the day through the woods until dark. As it became time to make camp for the night, they came across a junkyard and conceded to find a vehicle to serve as shelter. Somehow, the kids and Viktor became separated among the metal skeletons. Now he's trying to find them in the pitch dark.

"Again."

Tap. Ta--.

The second tap is cut off. It's not far away but the clouds have covered the moon and the salvage yard he's stepping through is almost void of all light. He rubs his eyes, hoping that they'll adjust and give him a little more to work with. The silhouettes of junked cars and rusted heaps are barely visible, the only guiding light is any dim glow reflecting off of an intact windshield or shiny paint job.

"Hello," as soft as he can manage.

A single *tap*. But it's enough to give him a direction. Viktor moves from car to car, resting his weight on them to soften his footsteps. A low scraping sound gives him another clue. It reminds him of the sound a garden rake makes dragging through dry soil. He steps toward the direction he believes that it's coming from.

"One more."

No tap but the scraping stops. A chill cuts through his bones. Thumping on soil approaches, hearing the vibration in his body more than his ears. It comes from his right as he whirls off the car that he was propped up against. Viktor can see a shape, like a wave of oil rolling across the ground toward him. He stumbles back, rearing his axe forward as he falls on his ass. The mass is crawling up his legs, pulling at his jeans. He feels a compression on his calf and knee and then thigh. He swings at nothing in particular, careful not to strike his own flesh. The blade lands in something as a cloud moves across the sky. Just enough glint of moonlight bounces off the glass and metal to allow his eyes to adjust.

Viktor plunges the axe up and down as three dead crawl up his legs. One has succumbed to his first blow. The other two reach and claw. He lands the axe several times until the mashed pulps, which were once ferocious heads, stop moving. The weight sagging onto his legs and feet. He pulls himself out from under them, wiping his face with his arm, and then the blade of the axe on his bloodied pants.

"Basil. Jake." A tone higher but still just above a whisper. "I can't see you. You gotta make a sound."

No taps, but her voice startles him as they emerge from the darkness from the same direction that the dead had charged him. "Are they--," Basil asks, stopping as she looks down at the corpses. Jake peaks from behind her leg, his cheeks red and damp. "I'm sorry. I couldn't make any sound. They were hunting us. We got into the shell of a car and their scraping was awful. I thought for sure they'd get in."

Viktor, out of breath, gestures for her to come closer. "The light." He bends his fingers to signal she hurry. Basil steps forward, handing him the small headlamp that he stole from his work bag on the base. He had given it to them as they entered the junkyard as Jake was complaining of how dark it was. They had agreed to keep the light off until they found a car suitable for sleeping.

He can't turn it on fast enough, casting the beam up and down his pants. He rubs at the jeans, pushing the blood and gore away, looking for any tears or cuts.

"Were you. Um--," Basil stammers.

"I don't think so. They didn't break the skin." Viktor steps closer to the bodies and shines the light across the ground. "That explains that I guess." Viktor shines on the faces of the dead, all missing their teeth, one missing its complete lower jaw. He moves the light to their hands which are little more than stumps, a couple of partial fingers with no ends.

"Jesus, Lord. That's some sort of luck."

Basil gives him a stern look. "If you're going to invoke the Lord into all this, you best not think it's luck." Her arms folded and as serious as ever.

"Fair enough." Viktor casts the beam down along the bodies and past their torsos. "Well, there it is."

Basil shrugs.

"That's why they couldn't get into the car with you."

He shakes the lamp across the ground where their legs should be. Bloody, stringy, stumps emerging from just below the hips. A partial femur here. A hamstring there.

"Ugh, gross," Basil murmurs, Jake pulling his head back behind her leg. "What did that to them?"

"I don't know." Viktor shines the light around the salvage yard. The light bounces off of the glass and bodies of the vehicles. "There." He gestures with the beam.

About fifty feet away, a large car compactor, clamped shut. From its caged and closed horizontal bars, body parts and limbs hang down almost touching the ground.

"I think it's safe to say that's the rest of them."

Basil looks away from the grotesque scene. "I don't want to sleep here tonight."

"Yeah. Me neither, kid. We can go."

"Come on, Jake." She nudges him out from behind her and grabs his hand. The boy looks down at the bodies as they walk by.

Viktor does a quick sweep of the dead. Finding nothing, he shines the light back to the compactor, speaking to the amalgamation of dead bodies. "Sorry boys. Not happening."

He flicks off the light, allowing their eyes to once again adjust to the darkness. The moon now casting enough ambiance to help lead the way out of the salvage yard.

NOW

Viktor awakens to a cold pressure against his neck. The steel blade rests just below his Adam's apple and he can feel a warm drop of blood traveling down to his collar. His eyes struggle to focus, the morning light just enough to restrict his pupils. He bats his eyes to push out the cloudy moisture. His hands have risen above his head into a surrender pose as he lies still on his back, afraid to move, even breathe.

Catherine stares straight down into his eyes. Her own, bloodshot and full of tears, one races down her cheek and drops to land on his own.

"Cat--"

"Don't you say a fucking word. I'll cut your throat right here."

His lips quiver, but he does as she commands. She sniffles hard, pulling in the mucus that fills her nose. Her other arm rubs across her face as she takes a deep breath, applying more pressure with the blade, but easing up on the point where blood has drawn. Viktor tries to swallow but it's obstructed by the knife. He stifles a cough. Catherine's eyes dart back and forth between each of his, not staying long enough on either eye.

"I'm going to ask you one question. I swear to God, if you lie to me or stutter, I'll bleed you out and watch you take your last breath. Blink if you follow."

He can't blink fast or hard enough. She eases the pressure of the blade, but only a little, as she reaches to the floor beside him and pulls up something with her other hand. His pouch. He's so confused, and the shock of being awakened in a panic isn't helping his clarity. Viktor squints as her hand comes into view. Catherine takes something out of it and tosses the pouch back to the floor. She lifts a rectangle of plastic into his field of vision. Viktor struggles to focus, and it becomes clear.

"Why the fuck do you have my sister's ID?"

Viktor tries to blurt out a coherent response. "I--. I---. She--."

He can feel the knife press back into his neck as more blood oozes from the small wound.

"Speak."

"Listen. Listen. I don't know her. I--I found it. Shortly after I left, just outside of uh-uh--Knoxville."

"Bullshit," she screams, new tears welling in her red eyes. "She was in Pennsylvania! I found her body myself. You did this!" She shoves the ID in his face, pressing it into his nose and cheek.

He can sense her tipping. Any moment now his life will begin spilling from his body. "I swear to you. It's true."

"No. I found her and my dad, turned in their own home! What did you do to them!"

Viktor's breath is rapid and uncontrolled.

"Why do you have this!"

"Come on, please. You've known me long enough now. I had nothing to do with any of that. I swear it. I was going through my collection and her picture struck me. I felt something. And when I discovered the body wasn't hers, I had this stupid hope she could still be alive. Her ID saved me!"

Her blank stare is more terrifying than her screams. "You're lying."

Catherine sits up, straddling him like the night before, the knife not moving from his neck. She sniffs again.

"I promise. I don't know what else to tell you. Why else would I be heading north?"

"Maybe you weren't. Maybe you were headed south when they caught you. All I know to be true is you ended up in that cell and that camp, same as me."

Silence hangs between them. Viktor has given up. His tension fades and breathing slows.

"Just like that, you're ready to die then?"

He can hear the struggle in her voice, trying to sound disconnected, uncaring, a duty that she must follow through.

"Yes."

His answer surprises her. Catherine looks disappointed that he doesn't continue to grovel for his life.

"Do it. I'm sorry."

"So, you're admitting it." A hint of rage flashes in her eyes.

"No," he says. "But I knew hope was a dangerous thing. I knew I would never find her. And I knew nothing could come of what I feel for you. So now that it's all gone and I have nothing left, no hope, no purpose, I'd rather you take me out here than keep surviving in disparity until I break a leg or get mauled to death." Viktor raises his neck, pressing himself further into the sharp edge.

She backs off some to compensate.

"Stop it. That won't work. I won't feel sorry for you."

With a final sigh, he places his hand on hers, pushing the knife back against his skin.

"I don't want you to. I just want it to be over." Viktor closes his eyes, waiting for the flow of warmth and the darkness to follow.

"Just don't let me turn," he whispers.

His hand is wrenched away and he hears the knife scatter across the floor. The pressure on his abdomen eases as he opens his eyes. Catherine stands over him, looming, wiping her tears away. She reaches down and picks up the knife, pointing the blade at him.

"Don't you fucking follow me! I swear I'll plant this in your head without a second thought." She tucks Francesca's ID into her shirt pocket and grabs her bag and sleeping roll.

She slings her rifle and Viktor watches, motionless, as she backs toward the doors of the visitor center.

"I mean it. Go back east, or south, or fuck it go all the way to Canada. But I swear you'll never see me again. You'll be dead before you know I'm even close." Catherine steps a foot through the broken glass doors and slips through as she calls out one last threat. "And I will let you turn."

The door rattles and a few shards of glass fall from the frame to the floor. Her running footsteps fade and disappear in the cool morning air outside. Viktor drops his head back to the mat, as his hand finds the cut on his neck. He stares at his sticky fingers as he moves the blood between them.

He can't bring himself to move. Minutes become an hour as Viktor lies on his back staring at the same moldy ceiling tiles. This time under much different circumstances and emotions. Where he had looked at the patterns above and thought of the future, now he can see only the rotting mold, eating away and taking over the once white dropdown tiles.

After Viktor can fight the urge to piss no longer, a trip to the outdoor area behind the visitor center is due. He would just lie there and soak himself, but what little dignity he has left stirs his feet into motion. Without a moment to spare he relieves himself into a hedge of bushes, leaning against the cold, jagged concrete exterior of the building. His breath is still visible in the morning hours, but the sun is up and the warmth feels nice. There seems to be a welcome break in the weather. He wishes he could enjoy the day with Catherine.

Viktor moves back inside the visitor center. He packs up his belongings, uncaring and unorganized, shoving everything into his bag as if he won't need it ever again. It's difficult to zip and he knows how frustrated he will be later when he needs something and can't find it. One last stroll around the interior to find anything useful as the effort the night before was done in haste as the cold seeped in through the broken doors.

Maps and brochures are scattered across the scuffed blue concrete floor, the paint chipped and missing in large sections. The vending machines and snack area have long been ransacked by their appearance, but to his surprise, a single bag of wavy chips lies lonesome on the top rear of the machine. Using the back of his axe he's able to knock it onto the floor. He presses and the air doesn't deflate, so there's hope they might not be stale. Viktor puts the chip bag in his jacket pocket and takes one last look around the room. Having no plan or direction, he's going to just walk. Any direction but west. Maybe he'll head east to the ocean and walk the coast north as far as he can.

As Viktor moves to the front doors, a low rumble, like a distant earthquake, begins rattling the metal frames. A hum rises in the distance. Tires. Engines. He backtracks toward the rear of the building. When the sound gets louder and slower, he begins to panic. He hears the rubber and brakes squeal as the vehicles stop out front. He edges out the back door where he took his piss.

Maybe he could run, down into the woods and away from the highway. But it's full light outside and the trees have lost most of their cover. He could be spotted for a mile in any direction. Viktor looks around the back exterior as doors close on the other side and inaudible voices shout commands that echo across the concrete.

There, next to the watered hedge, a large, faded-green junction box rises next to the wall and stands four feet off the ground. He climbs onto it. The roof is reachable and he uses his bag to slip over a vent and pull himself up onto the ledge.

Voices grow louder within the building. Viktor grips the bag until his knuckles are white and rolls toward it. He jams his boot into one of the slats to keep from sliding down and falling on his face.

"Check out here. Sweep the woods." The raspy, angry voice is right below him. Viktor dare not breathe but his heart is pounding, both from the climb and the adrenaline coursing through his veins. The metal roof is freezing against his back and legs, but he's still sweating in his jacket. He counts in his head to try to slow his heart rate. A shuffle and rattle as more bodies burst through the rear doors. Then a familiar voice.

"I know you're not traveling alone, sweet pea."

Motherfucking Tom.

A gasp responds as the soft thud of what sounds like a gun against flesh strikes below.

"Talk, woman. You see all those angry men with guns doing everything I say? Well, they haven't seen a woman quite so pretty as you in a long time. Sure, the ones in the trucks will do but you take the cake. So, it seems I'm your best friend right about now." He speaks as if he's doing the poor woman a favor.

"Speak!" Tom screams, almost scaring Viktor off the roof and onto their heads.

"Fuck off." The voice can't be true.

Catherine.

Viktor rages in his mind, what can he do. He has the element of surprise, but they'd shoot him dead before he was on his feet. *Fuck. Fuck. Fuck.*

"Move it, you dumb bitch. You can't say I didn't warn you."

Just then, through the trees, the voices of a few soldiers return as their boots smack against the grass and then concrete.

"Nothing out there, no prints or trace of anyone. You want us to keep going?" a soldier calls out. There's a silence as Viktor pictures Tom contemplating his next chess move.

"I told you. I was traveling alone, asshole." Catherine's trembling but a fierce voice interrupts his thought. Another thud and soft gasp from below.

"No. Saddle up. Move it, sister." Glass crunches underfoot as boots shuffle into the visitor center.

Viktor pulls himself up the edge of the roof and toward the peak. It's not too steep, but it's cold and slippery. The vehicles on the other side rev up and change gears as doors slam shut and more orders are called out. He moves faster, grabbing the crest with both hands and pulling his head up over to see down into the front of the visitor center parking lot.

The same caravan of Humvees and trucks that raided the compound is now pulling out onto the highway. There's one last truck, it looks more like a tow truck, but the passenger door is propped open.

"Hurry up, Ramirez. Convoys leaving!" the driver yells out from inside the truck.

A soldier rounds the corner of the building, zipping up his fly, his rifle bouncing on his back. Sure enough, it's the same Ramirez, and Viktor can't believe both he and Tom have survived. He feels crushed thinking of how many innocent people must have died that night and those that should have perished, did not.

Was any of it worth it?

As Ramirez hustles toward the passenger side of the truck, Viktor sees his moment and doesn't hesitate. He throws his entire body weight into the move, backpack included, as he slides over the crest of the peak, heading feet first down the front side of the roof. The truck door closes as the ground approaches. He knows this will hurt, but he's ready for it. Viktor flies off the roof and lands hard on the sidewalk below, rolling head over heels to soften the landing. Pain surges through his leg and hip as the truck begins pulling out of the parking lot.

He forces himself back to his feet with his bag in hand. The truck sputters as it shifts manual gears. As it jumps going from first gear into second, it gives him a window of opportunity to toss his bag in the back and pull himself up onto the rear bumper. He hides behind the winch system hoping to obscure any view from the soldiers should they look back.

When the truck doesn't slow down and instead gains speed as it pulls onto the highway, Viktor steps over a toolbox and lies down in an indent next to the rear wheel well. The cold wind snaps against him as it rushes over the truck bed. He pulls his bag close and holds himself in the fetal position for warmth. With no plan of what to do when they stop, and no clue where they're headed or for how long he'll be a stowaway, Viktor curls himself tighter, shivering as he realizes he's now just along for the ride.

THEN

They walked the rest of the night, too shaken to calm the nerves and they dared not sleep anywhere close to that "miserable junkyard," as Basil put it. Viktor did not argue and, though tired and sore with his limp having returned sometime during the scuffle, he powered on knowing there was little chance the children would want to slow down before dawn. Jake tagged along close, holding on to a bit of rope Basil had tied off to a loop of her jeans. Their feet had tangled a few times and so she insisted he would "be ok a few steps back and to just tug on the rope if he needed anything." He resisted at first but then calmed down when he saw it was a couple of feet of rope and he could just tug on her pant leg with his bare hand if needed.

Viktor led them along a dirt road for several hours. He could hear their feet shuffle on the loose gravel which was comforting. They stopped a few times as a rustle in the woods or a faint sound would bring his axe up in a motion suggesting they halt in place. He still carried the handgun at his side but hated the thought of having to use it at night, not knowing how many more dead he might attract with little to dampen the sound of the shots. Plus, he's limited on rounds with only a single 10 round magazine at his disposal.

As a sliver of amber-glow now turns the sky from black to gradients of deep purple, they arrive at a two-lane paved road. Viktor leans against a street sign and retrieves the map he also pulled from the base. There's just enough light to make out the details without turning on the headlamp, though the names are hard to read. He traces a finger trying to find a familiar area. He had already circled where the base was to ensure they moved in a common-sense direction, both away from there and away from anywhere survivors may have been headed.

"It's almost light. What do you say we head into this small town up the road? It'd be safer in the daytime and there may be supplies or a place to sleep for a little while."

"Okay," Basil agrees as Jake lets loose a wide and sleepy yawn. She rubs his hair with the palm of her hand. "Just a little bit longer and we can have a nap."

He picks at the rope that droops between them. Viktor folds up the map and places it back in his pack. He situates the handgun and grips the axe firm.

"This way. Just a couple miles or so."

They walk out onto the road, heading right. A green sign, bent but still upright, stands twisted off into the grass.

"Hawksboro. Two miles," Basil reads.

"Do you know this town?" Viktor asks, unsure of where they were from before arriving at the campground. She shakes her head no. The children seem eager for a break and their pace to town is a struggle for Viktor to stay in front of, though he doesn't let it show. He reminds himself to be strong, but deep down he needs it more for himself than for them.

Thirty minutes later they step onto the sidewalk of a quaint main street. Trees dot the curbing that runs along the outside of abandoned storefronts. A thin strip of grass with a gazebo splits the road in two, right down the middle. Some trash and wrecked cars tarnish the otherwise picturesque view of downtown Hawksboro. Viktor could see himself having a cup of coffee at the shop, sitting at an outdoor table while a pup pants and drools next to his feet and onto the cool sidewalk.

"Do you think there's anyone still here?" Basil speaks up first and he can hear the fear in her voice, though it sounds like she's trying to mask it with caution.

He realizes neither child may have seen much of what the world has become.

"I doubt it," he says as he looks around, noticing open doors but no signs of barriers and little vandalism. "How long were you two at the camp?" Viktor asks as he begins walking down the sidewalk.

"Jake was already there with his family when I got there. But...I remember my mom came and got me at school and we went right there. She already had my clothes packed in a bag. And my dog. She said my dad and older brother would meet us there, but they never did."

Viktor staggers to change the subject and knows he should pivot to something else. At least until Jake can be put down for bed. "What kind of dog was it?"

"A mutt. We got him at the shelter for my 10th birthday. So, two years ago I think."

"What was his name?"

"Sundae. Like the dessert." Jake giggles and they both look back. He mimics being a dog and hops to her side, pretending to lick her hand and wag his tail. Basil smiles and scratches under his chin.

"Cute name. I like it," Viktor adds.

She turns from Jake back to him, all of a sudden more serious.

"When the soldiers came, Sundae tried to help. That's why he's not with us."

"Sounds like a brave boy." He gives a proud expression by furrowing his brow and looks back to the walkway in front of them.

"He's guarding my mom now. In heaven."

"I think you're right. And I bet he's doing a great job at it."

Tap. Tap. He's surprised by the sound but doesn't look as a sniffle tells him everything.

"Wait here."

Viktor peers into the large glass window of a two-story storefront. He doesn't see any movement inside and steps to the large wooden door in the center of the overhang. He tugs and it opens. Warm, musty air funnels out into the street and he covers his face, expecting a foul, rotten stench. When it's just dust and mothballs, he leans in through the open doorway.

The morning sun has risen enough to shine between the opposite buildings, casting light into the front room. Viktor whistles and clanks his axe blade against the metal door frame. He raises it to the ready. No disturbance, no sound, no reason not to go in.

"Let's check it out. Stay close behind me and keep your eyes open."

Tap. Tap. They move inside and let the door latch behind them. After clearing the first and second floor, room by room, they return to the front door. Viktor pulls the deadbolt across and turns the handle latch to the lock position.

"Well, this should do for a few hours. Go pick your rooms, but stay together."

The kids scatter up the stairs, stomping up to the second floor, their feet causing the boards to creak above him. Dust filters down through the cracks like snowfall. Viktor looks through the large bay window and out onto the empty street. His face is obscured by the large green cursive letters that scrawl across the width of the glass.

BAILEY'S BED AND BREAKFAST

A couple of hours passed as Viktor rested his eyes, first downstairs in the lobby and then upstairs in the main hallway closer to where the kids slept. He never did fall asleep and knows he'll pay for it later.

"What's wrong? Is something out there?" Basil's soft voice calls out from down the hall.

Viktor sits on a window bench overlooking main street, the sun now shining down from overhead. He looks back at her, trying to hide his anxiety but drinking in the moment. The young girl leans against the door frame where Jake is still fast asleep. Light beams catch the dust billowing from the carpeted hallway between them. Wood planking lines each wall, with paintings of fruit and animals skipping over the half dozen doors on the second story. Old wall sconces hang next to each door frame, cobwebs stringing down and swaying in the draft.

"No, all is quiet," he reassures her.

"You should rest," she says.

"I'm okay. Never been one to be able to sleep much with the sun up."

"Is it really that, or is there something more?"

Viktor doesn't expect such insight from someone her age. "When I traveled alone, I learned quick that buildings and homes were not safe places to stay." He's quick to continue so as not to scare her. "But we're safe here. I just prefer being outside where I can hear, smell, see everything before it sees me."

Basil walks toward him, her feet creaking the floorboards underfoot. She glides her hand across the horizontal wall molding that reaches almost to her shoulders. "Like the deer?"

"You've seen them?" he asks.

"Our group killed a few, not long after we got to camp."

"Pretty scary, right?"

She nods, stopping at the door closest to him, admiring a painting of a dog hunt that hangs on the wall. The painting shows several hunters on horses as a pack of small dogs chase a deer through the forest. "You've seen them too?"

Viktor nods. "Unfortunately. But I lived to tell the tale."

She sits next to him on the bench, the glow of midday through the glass behind them silhouetting their figures.

"What happened?" she asks, looking down onto the street below.

Few clouds obscure the daylight that battles to warm the crisp weather outside.

"Well, one attacked me, but I was able to fight it off. And somehow I survived."

"You killed it?"

"I did."

"Good." She thinks for a moment. "You think there are more?"

Viktor offers a reassuring smile. "Probably, but I haven't seen one in quite some time."

Basil doesn't seem to buy into the faux consolation so he feels inclined to elaborate. "From what I can tell, their disease is terminal. Which means they can't have offspring either. The longer we survive, the less likely we are to see any more of them."

"How long can they live?"

"Well, I'm no expert, but I seem to remember that when they're healthy maybe ten years. I suspect much less with whatever the disease does."

She seems to like this answer.

"Someone at the camp said they were the reason this all happened."

Basil looks up to him as if this is the one question she's had on her mind for some time.

"I heard something similar. When everything was collapsing and the outbreak first started, news reports were claiming it came from the deer. Like a rabies that humans could contract."

"Or a parasite that takes over the brain?" Basil asks.

Could be. But there are other, worse things to worry about."

"Like the dead."

"Mmhmm."

"And people," she adds with confidence.

"Especially people." Viktor puts his hand on her shoulder. "Why don't you try to get a little bit of rest. I'll wake you in a couple of hours before we head out."

"Where are we going?" she asks as she stands from the bench.

"I think we should try to get a few miles outside of town for the night, just to be safe. We'll find camp before dark and have a nice dinner over a fire. How's that sound?"

"Good."

"Alright, go on," he says, grinning as wide as he can manage. It's not a command, but a note of reassurance. In truth, he feels inclined to take instruction from her. The wisdom and bravery of the child amazes him over and over again. "I'll keep watch and let you know if anything changes."

Basil walks back down the hallway, tracing her hand along the opposite molding on the wall. Viktor looks back to the street until he hears the door close at the end of the hall. The hours pass with not so much as a leaf blowing down the street to draw his attention. His mind travels to so many different times and places. First, he thinks of his daughter, the vivid memories of her death, which he extinguishes with memories from before the worst day of his life. Playing in the park, watching her recitals at school. It doesn't feel like his own life, but more like he's watching a movie of another person's experiences. Only months have passed since the outbreak began, but it feels like a lifetime ago. Someone else's lifetime.

After reviewing his map, he tucks it away and walks the length of the hall to wake the children. He knocks with just his knuckles and the door cracks open not a second later. Basil stands on the other side, her pointy staff in hand.

"I'll wake him up. He'll probably need a snack before we go."

Viktor nods as she retreats into the darkened room. "I'll meet you downstairs."

The boards moan and cry as he walks toward the stairs. He can hear her whispering to Jake as he goes. The steps are even louder, but Viktor lets his feet land sturdy since both kids are now awake. They've already searched the bed and breakfast for anything left behind. No food or water or anything worth adding to their packs except a partial roll of toilet paper and a magnetic figure the boy found on the fridge. A moment later, the kids make their way downstairs, Jake already snacking on something as they walk. The boy rubs his eyes.

Viktor worries that Basil isn't rationing any food for herself.

"Hey, how do you guys like fish?" he asks, out of the blue. The boy doesn't respond, or even look up from his bag of treats, but Basil shrugs.

"Well I saw a river on the map, we'll have to go far enough to cross the bridge but maybe we can camp out there and I can catch us some dinner?"

"Okay," she says.

Viktor turns to the front door, first peering out of the glass, then unlocking the deadbolt. He goes through first, pausing in the entryway. "Everyone ready?"

Tap. Tap. He looks back. Basil stands ready, holding Jake's free hand, and her stabbing stick in the other. They exchange smiles at her tapping, knowing she could very well have spoken.

"Very funny. Alright, away we go."

They exit the comfort of the bed and breakfast, closing the door behind them as if they were paying guests headed out on the town for a day of ice cream and antique shopping. The sun makes the day feel warmer than it is as it radiates off of the concrete sidewalk. In minutes they're already on the shoulder of the road beyond main street and leaving the small town of Hawksboro behind them.

NOW

A rusty green toolbox that stands upright in the back of the tow truck obscures the view from inside the cab and is the reason Viktor has yet to be discovered. The metal container rattles the entire way, the sound etching into his brain so that even when the vehicle slows to a stop, he can still hear the repetitive clamor as if a mechanical woodpecker is trying to pierce his inner ear.

His joints are stiff and face reddened and chapped from the cold wind that cut across his skin at seventy miles per hour. There was little to do except stay curled in a ball for warmth, so he checked his watch, counting the minutes which turned into hours. Three to be exact, and now the complete overcast of gray sky above has the dimness of late afternoon.

When the truck's brakes squeal to a stop, a moment of panic overtakes him. Even though he had thought about this moment for the entire trip, no solid plan has taken root. Without knowing if the entire convoy stopped or just his ride, makes all the difference in what he might do next. From his cramped position, he can see little more than what lies off to the driver's side of the vehicle. He can ambush Ramirez and maybe take out the driver before they had time to radio ahead, he thinks. He peers over the edge of the truck bed, just enough to see beyond the muted camouflage paint pattern that he memorized out of boredom.

While he could see the tops of trees and a piece of hillside here and there as they drove, Viktor had no bearing to where they were headed or where they are stopped at this moment. Buildings. Street lamps. As he begins to eye further toward the front of the truck, the driver's side door flies open and a uniformed soldier steps out. Viktor pulls himself deep into the bed of the truck. If the man walks toward the rear, he'll be seen. He grips the axe, ready to plant it between the driver's eyes before he can call out a scream.

"Fuel up, let's go!" the man shouts, his voice trailing as he walks toward the front of the truck.

More doors open and close ahead of them. *The rest of the convoy.* Soldiers laugh and shout back and forth. The passenger side door opens and Ramirez grunts as he pulls himself from the tow truck. It rocks as he steps out. His footsteps fade as he walks toward the front to join the driver.

Viktor shifts his weight toward the middle of the truck bed. He pulls himself up using the tool chest and peers over the roof of the truck to survey the parked convoy ahead of him. They're on the outskirts of a city, he can't even begin to guess which, and the vehicles surround a large gas station that's cluttered with burnt-out and abandoned tractor-trailers and civilian vehicles.

"Check the big rigs," someone shouts. "Start siphoning the diesel and whatever is left put it in the fuel tanker," commands the same voice.

The soldiers scatter, guns drawn and at the ready as they infiltrate the station grounds, sweeping from truck to truck. Another crew begins the work of pumping out the fuel from the semis. Viktor watches as they carry the containers of diesel to the back of a large flatbed truck. A huge contraption sits in the bed and this is where the soldiers dump the fuel. Three massive drums with hoses connecting them line the bed, each with giant meters and dials that identify levels and pressure.

Like clockwork, diesel is dumped into the storage units causing the dial arms to dance and jump. It takes a moment of watching the men move about like ants, knowing each role with precision and efficiency, that Viktor recognizes the machine they're servicing. It's the fuel converter from the compound, the very one Fez showed off that allowed for reinvigorating stale fuel. *This is why they sacked the community, for a damn machine.*

He scans the area, looking for any signs of Catherine. There must be a dozen vehicles in the caravan total, and he searches each one through squinting lids for clues. His eyes land on a troop carrier up ahead. Three Humvees and some twenty-five yards stand between him and it, where a small group of unknown women is being ushered away and toward a wooded area.

"Piss break. No fucking around," a soldier says as he pokes one of the women with the muzzle of his rifle.

Another trio of prisoners passes them in the opposite direction, being pushed back toward the truck by a guarding soldier of their own. Leading them is Catherine, her hands bound and head down. Her hair cascades over her ears and cheeks as she stomps over the high grass, but there is no question it's her. From this distance she appears okay, despite a large and ugly bruise filling the left side of her face. As she passes a soldier she spits on his boots. Without hesitation he checks her with the side of his gun and dropping her to a knee. He raises the butt of the rifle, ready to drive it into her temple. Viktor is halfway out of the truck when a booming voice stands himself and the soldier down.

"Ease up, Miller. She's just a girl. Never had a little spit on your boots?" Tom emerges from around the troop carrier. He hocks a repulsively moist wad of spit onto the same soldier's boot. "Wanna go?"

The soldier shakes his head.

"Get 'em in the fucking transport or you'll be riding next to them. You do remember how we handle dissidents, don't ya?"

"Yes, sir," replies the soldier, now a comic folly of the tough guy he was playing a moment ago. He places the rifle into Catherine's side and guides the women like a mother duck showing her ducklings to water.

Ramirez's voice distracts Viktor from Tom and the women up ahead. "I'll fill it up, you try and find us something to eat. Who knows when or where we're stopping during the night."

"You got it, *sir*."

Ramirez laughs. "Fuck off, Tozzer."

He can now see the driver, a man he doesn't recognize from his time at the base, walk toward the rest of the convoy. Viktor rolls back to the edge of the truck bed and out of view. He was being risky by just popping his head up. If Ramirez looked back, he would be unmistakable and that would mean certain death. He knows there isn't a chance Ramirez would let him tell Tom how he managed to escape from the base and bring it all down.

With his old friend's back to the truck, Viktor sees this as the moment he must act. Gripping the axe in hand, he pulls himself up onto the driver's side of the truck bed and rolls off the side, keeping the vehicle between him and Ramirez. He uses his free arm to hold his weight so he can set his feet on the cracked asphalt below without a sound. Boots, not his own, clap on the pavement as Ramirez approaches the passenger side of the tow truck. Underneath, Viktor can see a large fuel canister being set down, the faded red plastic shifting with the weight of the sloshing diesel inside. Viktor hears him open the fuel door and unscrew the cap, placing it on the opposite edge of the truck bed.

Moving in silence, one determined foot in front of the other as his back slides against the wall of the truck, Viktor eases his way around to the tailgate. He keeps his head low as Ramirez hums a tune just a few feet away. He hears the gas canister splash and then slides into the fuel tank, gurgling as it fills the truck.

He's at the back corner of the tow truck, an arm's reach from Ramirez.

"Yeah, yeah. Bring me two!"

Viktor recoils for a moment but realizes he's shouting to his driver far ahead, amongst the convoy.

"Fucking idiot," Ramirez mutters. He tops off the diesel and places the empty canister in the back of the truck bed. "What the. Yo, Tozzer. This your bag?"

Viktor jumps from behind the tow truck and lurches for Ramirez, who leans half into the bed as he examines the backpack. Before he can react, Viktor is behind him with the axe blade pressed to the side of his throat.

"Move and your head is mine."

Ramirez is a statue, pressed against the truck with hands bent at his hips to support his weight on the metal frame.

"Not a sound," Viktor whispers.

Ramirez nods.

Viktor unholsters a sidearm from the soldier's waist and presses the barrel into the back of the man's head.

"Rifle?"

Ramirez gestures to the front seat with a head tilt. The passenger door is still open. Viktor leans to the right to have a peek, still aiming the gun at him. He shoves the axe handle into his belt and uses his free hand to reach onto the seat and retrieve the rifle. He slings it over his shoulder.

"Turn around."

Ramirez rests his weight on his heels and turns with a slow pivot, his hands held above his shoulders. The look on his face is a cross between shock and fury.

"Are you fucking shitting me."

"Ah, ah, quiet," Viktor whispers, planting the pistol under his jaw. "We can talk on the way. Get in the truck. And take off your jacket."

Ramirez sighs and unzips and removes his camo jacket, handing it to Viktor.

"Get in. And hands down."

He gestures to the passenger side door and Ramirez steps toward it. Viktor follows him, using his broad shoulders to hide behind in case any soldiers look back in their direction. "In." Ramirez cooperates and pulls himself into the cab, placing his hands on the dash.

"Scoot over to the middle."

He does as commanded. Viktor climbs into the truck and slouches as best he can in the passenger seat. He bunches up Ramirez's coat and crams it against the windshield, further blocking the view from any curious eyes that might look their way.

"Now what?" asks Ramirez.

"Now, we wait."

"Goddammit. I knew I should have killed you."

"On that, we probably agree. Hands to your side, no need to look suspicious." Viktor waves with the gun at his hands that are still pressed on the dashboard.

Footsteps approach as does a terrible whistler. He can see the camo fatigues through the windshield, *Tozzer* printed on the right-side name band. The soldier opens the driver's door without looking in and extends a hand to Ramirez.

"They're cold but not bad."

Tozzer's fingers surround two hotdogs tucked into a single slice of something that resembles bread. When Ramirez doesn't take it, the soldier finally looks up. His mouth hangs open with bits of chewed food tucked in his patchy, dark cheeks.

"Ah, fuck."

Viktor has the handgun aimed at his face.

"You must be Tozzer. Get in."

THEN

Two straight days of uninterrupted sunshine have removed all traces of the snow that blanketed everything on the night of his escape. While the roads and grass have a sheen of dampness, not a fleck of white can be found. The three walk in silence, basking in the warm rays of the afternoon light. A gusty breeze gives a small bite, but it's countered by the feeling of warmth on their skin. So much so that Viktor has rolled up his sleeves and wears his jacket tied at the waist. Basil still wears her light coat, but it's unzipped and she gives herself a cooling wave by fanning the coat flap in front of herself. Jake follows in tow, jumping at the small puddles that remain along the road.

On the way out of town, they pass a mail truck, angled as if the driver parked in the middle of the road and left it with no intention of returning. The back doors hang open, soggy white letters and large yellow envelopes spill out onto the roadway. Viktor is tempted to check it out, and would if he were alone, but thinks it's best to keep moving. Not knowing what they'll encounter when it's time to make camp, moving forward to some sort of shelter has to take priority.

Basil picks up an envelope in their path as they pass the truck.

She doesn't stop but examines it as they continue walking. "Mr. and Mrs. Charles Freeman. Eight Seven Three, West Elmore Road, five, five, two, nine, zero."

Viktor looks over his shoulder.

"I wonder what's inside," Basil says, flipping the letter in between her fingers. She begins to tear the top open.

"Don't you know it's illegal to read someone else's mail?" Viktor teases, half-joking but then turning more serious. Something about preserving the old way feels like an important lesson.

"They're probably not even alive anyhow." Her thumb rests inside the envelope but she stops tearing.

"You're probably right. But even more of a reason to leave it be, I say." It's not a command, and he doesn't look back, wondering if she'll consider his point or if curiosity will get the best of her.

He can't blame her if she opens it, and he doesn't feel strongly enough to lecture her. After a moment of walking, he feels a tap on his right arm. Viktor looks down to see the unopened envelope pressed against his rolled-up sleeve.

"Here. Keep it with the others."

He takes it, examining the outside himself. "What others?"

"The photos and stuff. All the personal things you hold on to."

Viktor thinks for a moment. She must have seen him looking over his family's photo or the few IDs he's picked up along the way. Only now does he consider it as a thing, a mannerism, a task. He hands the envelope back to her.

"You found it, why don't you hold on to it."

Basil takes it back, tucking it into her backpack. "If it's wrong to look at someone else's mail…" She hesitates to ask the rest.

"Yeah?"

"Well, what about their other belongings. Like phones?"

He can hear her rustling in her backpack.

"Like this one. It's not mine. I took it off one of the people at our camp. When they...after they were killed."

Viktor thinks for a moment, then concedes to her point. In principal, the mail is no different than taking photos or IDs or anything belonging to someone else that wasn't intended for his eyes.

"Well, maybe it's not a bad thing if it's something that we need, or if it's something to remember them by. But maybe because it's a letter, and it's still sealed, there can be something special about the unknown words written from when they were still alive. As a way to keep them with us."

She seems to think it over and he hopes that she doesn't challenge him because even he might collapse under his own argument as he's only ever had to justify it to himself.

"Okay."

Up ahead a large metal bridge extends across a sprawling gap. Viktor leads them to the railing and they look between the rusty metal support bars.

"This thing must be a hundred years old," he says, admiring the beams.

"Is it safe to cross?"

"Oh yeah, she's held up this long, she's not going anywhere." He pats the metal, rust flecking off the rivets.

"Good." Basil points down below. The river is dark brown and has swelled up to a few feet below the bottom of the bridge.

"Must be all the snowmelt. Best not get too close to the railing. Let's just get across."

They don't waste any time moving over the bridge. After seeing the water, Viktor did have some misgivings about its structural fortitude against the raging water below, but they managed to get across without incident. A sigh of relaxation is hidden from the children once their feet leave the grated platform and touch the pavement on the other side.

"So much for fishing," he says, looking down from the bank at the raging water sweeping by with ferocious speed.

"We won't have long before dark, but we should find a space to camp out and start a fire for the night. It will likely get a bit chilly."

The ground elevates beyond the river bank and he leads them up into a wooded area. After a few minutes the trees break into a square clearing, the grass low and brown. He admires the perfect tree line and looks down a worn animal trail that leads to the river below.

"This will do," Viktor says, setting his pack down at the edge of the trees. "Look, there." He points to a massive tree with branches as thick as a normal tree's trunk. "We can string up hammocks so we're off the ground. Build the fire down below."

"Do you hear that?" Basil asks.

"I think that's just the river. It should settle overnight. I don't suspect it's going to rain."

"No, that trickle. Over here." Basil leads Jake over the lip of a rise in the trees, roots knotted and tangled over each other. "Another stream."

Viktor looks down on the babbling brook, a large pool in the center that cascades down soft stone and into the brown abyss at the bottom of the river bank.

"Hey, good find. Maybe we'll catch some dinner after all."

This appears to excite Jake. Either it's the prospect of a meal or the task of catching the fish, but either way, it's a good feeling and he means to do his best to deliver. Viktor pulls out his axe and hacks down a few dead trees that are no thicker than his wrist. He breaks them down into manageable sections.

"Here, if you can stack these by the tree up there, we'll burn them for firewood."

Sitting on a stump just above the stream, Viktor uses his knife to whittle a small branch into a shape of his liking. He works at another until both have a notch in the middle, one pointing down and the other pointing up. He places them together, interlocking the notches almost as if they were one branch again.

"Perfect."

Jake watches as Viktor jams one of the stakes into the earth near the stream where it meets the pool. Using a bit of rope, he ties the other branch with a tight knot and runs the line to the nearest tree. He pulls down on a branch hard, testing its strength.

"Yes, this will work."

He ties the other end of the rope to the branch. One notched stake sits firm in the ground and the other sways as it hangs from the sturdy branch above.

"Let's see," Viktor says to himself as he digs through his pack. "Ah, here we go."

He pulls out a bit of fishing line attached to a large circle hook. After tying the line and hook to the middle of the hanging stake he looks back to Jake.

"Your turn, buddy. I'm going to need one of those gummies."

The boy looks to Basil who nods that it's okay. Jake pulls out a red gummy from his pouch and hands it to Viktor. He pats him on the head and skewers the gummy on the hook.

"Here's the fun part. Stand back."

Basil guides Jake away a few steps, and they watch as Viktor pulls down on the branch overhead. He seats the hanging stake with the one in the ground, their notches interlocking. The cuts hold the tensioned limb in place, preventing it from flying up to its normal position. Viktor extends the fishing line and drops the hook and gummy into the edge of the pool.

"That's it?" Basil asks, unimpressed.

"Well. Yeah."

Viktor looks around, proud.

"Now what?" she asks.

"Well uh, we wait. For the fish to bite."

"To eat the gummy? Where did you learn this?"

He watches the fishing line dangle motionless in the pool below.

"Uh, the internet, I think. You know what, let's just get the fire going," he says gesturing back to the stack of wood.

"We're going to starve," Basil says as she pulls Jake back toward the tree.

NOW

“How the hell are you still alive?” Ramirez asks as the tow truck brings up the rear of the convoy.

They've been driving for thirty minutes since they left the gas station and not a single soldier ahead of them seems to be the wiser. It's been all silence, minus the sounds of the road. Aside from the initial commands to "get in and play it cool," there hasn't been a peep from the three men now crammed in the cab of the rumbling camouflage truck.

"You know this guy?" Tozzer interjects.

"Ah, ah!" Viktor points the gun at his hands, which have left the steering wheel. The stubby soldier's face reddens as he re-grips the wheel.

"This is *priority one*." Ramirez shakes his head, saying it almost as a punchline.

"No." Tozzer is astonished.

"The fuck is priority one?" Viktor demands, not knowing if he's being messed with or what to make of it.

"You are, cowboy," answers Ramirez.

"So, this is the little shit who brought down your whole base. Oh, ho, ho, you are sooo fucked buddy, so fucked!" The driver is almost in hysterics.

Viktor scratches his temple with the barrel of his handgun. The rifle is propped between his legs, pointed somewhat in their direction. He would never get a shot off if there was a struggle, but they don't know that.

"You weren't there. What do you know about it?" Viktor asks.

Ramirez raises both hands, palms up, signaling for Tozzer to tell the tale.

"It's doctrine now. Every new batch of recruits has to hear about Captain *Pecker's* arduous journey of survival. He goes into excruciating detail of his big dick adventure from out of the ruins. And the feather in his cap is you. He describes the harrowing mutiny attempt, how he lost ninety percent of his men, present company excluded--"

"Lucky me," interrupts Ramirez.

"Now, as brave nomads, we roam what's left of our world, slaying the dead, and paving the way for the new future." Tozzer's theatrics are tiring, but Viktor doesn't silence him just yet.

"But don't be fooled, Tom isn't some Christopher Columbus prick come to enslave and explore. No, he lives for revenge. Revenge on the dead, for all that they are. Revenge on the weak, for all that they lack. But greatest of all, revenge on you for the ultimate betrayal. This is gonna be great!" He laughs, slapping at the steering wheel.

"Oops, sorry." Tozzer locks his fingers back around the wheel.

"Sounds pretty, but he's got the right of it," Ramirez says. "You're better off cracking that door and tucking out onto the shoulder."

Viktor side-eyes the grass and trees whipping by. "I'll take my chances."

"So then, what's the plan? You do have a plan, right? I mean you must if you've taken us hostage. You're outnumbered in this truck alone. Do you even know how many are ahead of us?"

He doesn't dignify the accusation with an answer, in part because he doesn't have one, but the more they talk the angrier he gets at their shared past. The nerve that Ramirez has to act as if he's just playing his part, a pawn, absolved of any responsibility or obligation to prevent the macabre of Tom's command. Viktor refuses to even consider the possibility that Ramirez isn't all bad. He knows if he allows any doubt to enter his conscience, the seasoned soldier will take advantage and this time it won't be an offering of escape, but a much more violent end. Viktor can even imagine Ramirez using the bolt cutters for something other than the fence and it makes him cringe.

The silence seems to speak volumes. Both soldiers sit tense, eyes forward. Tozzer has done well to keep the distance between vehicles that Viktor demanded when they left. At one point he thought maybe the fool was trying to signal with Morse Code through blinking, and little good it would have done so far away, but realized the man was just inept and so locked into "hands on the wheel" that he wouldn't even scratch his own nose.

As the low rumble of wheels against asphalt fills the cab, Viktor stews in thought. He knows they're right, there's no chance of taking anything by force. The numbers just aren't anywhere near to his favor and any attempts would mean at best a quick death. At worst, he hates to even consider it. He decides to roll the dice and play to Ramirez's weakness.

"Did he blame you for my escape?"

Ramirez stares ahead at the road, long enough to make Viktor think he has no intention of answering. Just as Viktor is about to repeat himself, the soldier speaks.

"He may have, but I was the one who pulled him from the mess you left us. Unconscious, bleeding from his head profusely, thought he was just about dead anyway. I carried him to safety and gathered the survivors to whatever vehicles we could use. We're only all here right now because of me. Yet my reward was being stuck on the maintenance crew. So, I suspect that was my punishment. No offense."

"All good, compadre," adds Tozzer.

"Why did you let me leave and not just turn me in?"

"Look man, I told you back then. It's the same now. I'm here to survive. So, whether it's Tom or you holding a gun to my head, I'm going to do what it takes to see tomorrow. Why don't you quit playing psychiatrist and tell me what it is you want--"

"You know my psychiatrist killed herself?" Tozzer interrupts.

Ramirez and Viktor both glance to Tozzer, who drives as if it's just any other day, minus the firm grip on the wheel.

"I'm only here for the girl."

Ramirez scoffs. "Which one?"

"The last one you picked up. At the rest area, where you had your little piss break."

Viktor can see a hint of rage growing under Ramirez's skin, the familiar red filling his neck and cheeks. *It's working.* But the soldier suppresses it as quick as it was rising.

"What is she, your bed warmer or something?" he asks.

"Ha, nice."

They both ignore Tozzer.

"She's important to me. And I want her freed. Then we're both gone."

Ramirez doesn't react, but Viktor can see the wheels turning. Ever the survivalist, he knows the soldier is contemplating the board, playing many moves ahead, testing every scenario in his mind to see which ones produce an outcome where he comes out alive.

After another hour of silent driving, an audible sigh regains Viktor's attention.

"Daybreak. Or just before."

Viktor shifts in his seat, signaling for Ramirez to go on. Tozzer looks, shifty-eyed, from the road to the pair that are now laying down terms.

"There's another group we're going to sack, just outside of Louisville."

"And then on to Fort Knox!"

Viktor looks at Tozzer, wanting elaboration.

"That seems to be the grand scheme for Tom. Take over Fort Knox and rebuild from a position of power and gold," explains Ramirez.

"Ambitious. Tell me more about the group attack."

"Right before daylight, we'll roll in, just like we do every other settlement. Take what goods we can, recruit who we can, and eliminate the rest."

"Does anyone ever join?"

Tozzer raises his hand and then is quick to grasp the wheel.

"Few," says Ramirez. "So, when we stop, he'll do some big grandstanding Patton speech. That's your window to grab your girl and get the fuck out.

Viktor considers his words. "And how do I know you won't go right to Tom, boost your cred, sell me out as soon as we stop."

"I considered it. But he'll be so amped up for the ambush that he'll either kill us both or I'll have to spend the attack babysitting you with the convoy. The sooner you're gone, the better. And the girl is no skin off my back."

He doesn't believe him, but he doesn't have many options so

he goes along with it for the time being.

"We'll need our rifles back. May look suspicious if we show up to a fight with only fists."

Viktor looks at the rifle resting between his legs and Tozzer's lying against the floor at his feet.

"I think I'll hold on to them for now."

As Ramirez shuffles in his seat, finding a spot of comfort, Viktor shakes the barrel of his gun as a memory comes to mind.

"What happened to Dr. Chan? Did she make it?" he asks.

"Doctor Chan? Only doctor I know is Doc. And nobody has seen him since that night. He's probably eating people now, just like his *patients*." Ramirez air quotes.

"I mean the therapy woman. Cute, Asian?"

Tozzer looks to Ramirez as if he wants to know as bad as Viktor.

"Right, yeah. Becker had a hard-on for her but I think she preferred chicks, to be honest. Anyway, same deal. After you clocked her and they set off the alarm, all hell broke loose. All I know is she's not with us now, so looks like her blood is on your hands too."

Viktor's heart rate rises, a pressure building in his forehead.

"I didn't kill her."

Ramirez gives him a side glance. "Regardless of how she died, *you* killed her."

They both look away from one another. The sun is all but gone and a sliver of orange outlines the shape of the distant hills. As they wind down a zigzagged road from high up on a mountainside, Viktor can see the scope of the imposing convoy. The roaring snake is marked by the uniform headlights as they descend toward an expansive valley. The poor bastards have no idea what's coming for them, he thinks. Ramirez leans his head back and closes his eyes as Viktor trades the gun between hands to wipe the sweat of his palms on his pant leg. His eyelids are heavy and he fights against the lull of the road to keep them open and alert.

THEN

Pops and crackles jump from the fire as Viktor, Basil, and Jake sit around the dancing flames. The orange glow flickers off the large tree branches that swoop over them as they relax, nestled among the sprawling roots. Above, Viktor has strung up their bedrolls and blankets to make hammocks that should prove more accommodating than sleeping on the cold, damp ground. It's hard to resist the urge to go back to the bed and breakfast, but Viktor is stubborn in his apprehension of structures. The soldiers, or worse, could roll up on that town and they would have nowhere to hide.

Here, among the trees, the sense of claustrophobia all but disappears and while the loud rush of the river makes it hard to hear oncoming danger, it should do the same to cover them. A whole convoy could drive past on the road above and be none the wiser, so long as they keep the fire low. In this manner, they leave no trace of their presence except for those that may stumble upon the clearing. The risk is low, lower than the town at least, and the scenery feels inviting.

Basil warms her hands over the modest flame while Jake plays on his phone at the lowest brightness setting. She had convinced him it was to save battery, which wasn't untrue, but both she and Viktor were more worried about the light being seen from afar. A blanket draped over his head helped to quell the glow, and also added a layer of warmth to combat the night chill.

Thwack.

The branches behind them shake briefly, startling the children.

"Haha!" Viktor exclaims as he's on his feet, hobbling past the two kids.

He's wearing the headlamp and flicks the red-light feature on, the crimson illumination bounces as he steps down toward the stream and pool. He was sure to use the red option as the normal white beam would be like a strobing advertisement to anyone or anything nearby.

"Got one!" His voice is ecstatic as if he can't believe it. He holds the fish up to show the kids.

Basil gestures for Jake to stay put as she walks toward the commotion. Viktor works hard to remove the hook from the mouth of the medium-sized fish. It whips its tail back and forth as it hangs in the air from the branch above.

"Looks like we're having fish after all," he says as he wrestles it free.

Grabbing his axe, he flips it over to the dull side and places the fish against a large stone on the ground. Viktor looks back to Basil who watches over him.

"You may not want to--"

She gives him a look that says everything.

With that, he brings down the back of the axe onto the head of the fish. A quick crunch and it stops squirming, now limp on the wet stone. Viktor brings it to the fire where Jake sits, unaware. He puts down the axe and pulls out a knife to begin dressing the scaly dinner. After filleting it, he drops the fish on a flat stone that he had already placed at the edge of the fire. It begins to roast, flesh side up, and his mouth waters at the smell that it releases into the smoky night sky. As the scent drifts toward Jake, he makes a disgusted face then looks back to the phone.

"That's crazy. You caught a fish with a catapult and a gummy bear." Basil places her hand on her forehead. "Why not use a fishing pole?"

Viktor stops admiring the cooking flesh and looks at her, his mouth hanging open like the fish before them.

"Well if you find one be sure to let me know! Plus, who wants to sit next to the pool babysitting the line? Not me," he says in a playful tone.

After a few minutes, he rubs his hands together and lifts the cooked fish off the hot rock using the blade of his knife. Steam and smoke billow from the blackened flesh. He places it skin side down on a large piece of bark from the firewood pile.

He extends it toward Basil who looks at it, uncertain. "Go on! Can't get any fresher than this."

She accepts and looks down on it for a moment. "We should say blessing first."

"Oh. Okay. Yeah, go ahead."

Viktor puts his head down and closes his eyes. After an awkward silence passes, he peeks a glance with one eye open. Both kids have their heads bowed, holding hands. They're waiting on him.

"Right. Um, dear, uh, dear God. We thank you for this meal and uh, providing the fish that I caught, using a uh, catapult and gummy bear as someone put." Jake giggles and Viktor can't help but smile himself. "Uh, keep us safe through the night, God. In your name--"

"Jesus' name," Basil adds.

"Uh, yes Jesus too, uh, Amen!"

He feels silly and a bit embarrassed, but neither child mocks or even looks at him funny. Basil is already pulling a few pieces of flesh off the fish and blowing at them before placing the chunks into Jake's outstretched palms. He blows on them too, acting as if the pieces are hot in his hands.

"Pretend it's chicken nuggets," she says.

The boy continues to blow on his hands and nibbles at the bits of flakey white fish. Basil takes a few small pieces of her own before handing the slab of bark back across the fire to Viktor. He could eat the whole thing, skin and bones and all, but takes just a few small pieces for himself. No more than she had taken.

"Here ya go, finish it up. Maybe we'll catch another for breakfast." Viktor is glad she doesn't refuse and watches as they scarf down the rest of the fish, picking the bones clean.

While the kids finish, Viktor resets the trap, this time using a piece of fish skin as bait. He walks back to the fire and flips off the red headlamp. They sit, tucked into the roots for another hour until Basil tells Jake to turn off the phone and get ready for bed. The boy uses a worn toothbrush, dipping it into his water bottle once, and brushes his teeth, a gaping smile to show how good of a job he's doing.

"Good job. Did you count?" Basil asks. The boy nods. He spits into the grass behind him before curling into her arm and closing his eyes. "Can we stay down here for a bit longer?"

"Sure. We can stay up until the fire burns out," Viktor says as he stirs the flames with a long stick.

They sit in silence, staring at the orange and red and yellow as it grows smaller and smaller until there are only a few lumps of glowing logs and coals left shimmering in the circle.

"What do you say?" Viktor asks.

Basil picks up Jake who is sound asleep, being careful not to wake him, and tip-toes to the tree. Viktor takes the boy and with a free hand helps her up to reach the first branch that's more than six feet off of the ground. She pulls herself up to straddle it and reaches down. He lifts the boy, still asleep, into her outstretched arms.

"Get settled in. I'll be right up."

Basil gets Jake situated in his little hammock and covers him with a blanket. She falls into her own which hangs right beside his, several Y-shaped branches supporting their weight. She turns and curls into her blanket before closing her eyes.

Viktor grabs his bag and tosses it up onto the hammock. He kicks dirt onto the coals.

Thwack.

"Another one?"

He wants to leave it for the morning, but worries it might wiggle itself loose, or attract a wild animal. He clicks on his red headlamp and walks away from the tree and toward the pool. When he sees the stake dangling with an empty fishhook, he curses under his breath. He resets the trap and shines his red light into the water, looking for the culprit. A shriek and scream pierce through the woods from behind him.

"Viktor, help!" screams Basil.

He turns so fast to run back up the hill that his feet slide out from under him. His fingers grasp the wet, cold dirt, trying to pull himself to his feet. His boots dig into the mud and Viktor sprints back up to the tree. He was gone less than a minute and it's already being swarmed by the dead. He can't even guess how many as they pour down from the road above. They bump into each other, scratching at the tree bark. They can reach the lowest branch with fingertips but appear unable or unaware to pull themselves up.

Viktor pulls out his handgun and axe at the same time, double fisting his weapons. He fires a single round into a dead off to the side. The group turns toward him as the children scream above. Jake is terrified, crying out with a shrill that gives him goosebumps. Rotten hands swipe at the cloth of the hammocks just inches beyond reach.

"Just stay up there. They can't get to you!" Viktor shouts among the grumbling and growling moans.

He fires another round into the face of a dead at the base of the tree. It falls flat. The dead step on top of the fallen body, gaining another few inches of reach up the tree. One long finger with chipped nail scrapes at the underside of Basil's hammock. She scrambles back against the trunk, sinking her weight further toward the clasping hands.

"Fuck you!" Viktor yells back.

The dead peel off and lurch toward him. He spends the rest of the magazine dropping the ones closest to him. He plants his axe between the eyes of another. Even more dead stumble down the hill, their quickness and rage increasing as they funnel around the tree. It stands firm against the current, like a boulder in the raging river below.

He looks to the children who have scurried up another branch to put distance between them and the attackers. They hold each other tight. Basil calms the boy who is squealing in fear. Backing away from the tree, Viktor looks around, calculating. The dead flow toward him faster with each passing second.

"Hey! Hey! Down here!" he yells, waving the axe and empty gun in the air.

The last he can see of Basil is her hushing Jake, covering his mouth, and tucking his face into her shoulder.

"Come on! You ugly SOB's!"

All of the dead that surround the tree turn and join the mob that staggers toward him. He back peddles further, still screaming at them. They pick up speed, he can't believe that more are still pouring down from the road but now they're bypassing the tree. Viktor moves out into the field as the moonlight gives him a perspective of the horde that he wishes he didn't have. He keeps moving backward across the grass. What must be a hundred dead filter out of the trees and into the clearing.

"It's working."

He whistles through his fingers. The dead move faster at the enticement and he can no longer walk in reverse. To keep his distance, he's forced to turn and jog as the group of the dead bears down on him. Viktor weaves and dodges branches as he makes his way deep into the trees, moving as far away as he can from the children. He hears the roar of water up ahead as he keeps looking back over his shoulder. They're still following. The entire clearing is full of lumbering corpses, he just hopes the tree has been forgotten.

Viktor runs and runs, his lungs burning with the cold air and the dead ceasing to give up chase. When some fall into pits and roots, the others bowl over them even faster. He can hear the river up ahead and he moves toward it. The trees end and he almost finds himself falling two stories down an eroded bank into the raging brown water. The only evidence of what lies below is the sheen from the moon on the white caps and the incredible roar. He's trapped.

The dead, slowed by the thick trees and uneven ground, have not lost sight and cram in together, merging as a mass of bodies that lunge at him. He sees a large, fallen tree that spans out into the river. It doesn't cross, but it might save him. Viktor steps onto the thick, wet trunk, its roots upended and spiraling into the ground where it fell from the bank. He balances with both hands in the air, the axe waving back and forth.

Afraid to look below, he can feel the rush of wind from the water underneath his feet, the cold mist flicking upward and making the surface of the tree as slippery as ice. The whole thing sways and dips as he's halfway out into the river. He must stop and dares not go any further. Viktor turns and shouts over the volume of the thrashing rapids. The dead seem to have lost him as they meander and bump at the edge of the trees, gnawing and growling. Then the mass surges forward and a few fall down the embankment like a coin game at an arcade. They vanish in the brown surge.

"Yes!"

He tries screaming and waving. More are pushed forward and fall, then are swept away.

When it seems like they won't advance any further, he reaches up to his headlamp and flicks the switch. He presses the button from red to strobe and a bright white light flashes. It's in these strobes he can see the scope of the horde. Countless empty faces bite and clench among the trees as far up and downstream as he can see. The light seems to agitate them. Almost in unison, they begin moving forward to the tree. Some climb onto the massive root structure, but the pressure of hundreds of bodies against each other begins a domino effect. One by one, then dozens at a time, the dead fall into the river. Some grasp at his tree but are pulled away by the current.

He watches in awe as they spill over, like buffalo on the plains. This goes on for minutes, and he never ceases to scream and wave and shout. When the cadence slows and a handful remain, he grants himself a moment of relief. Some are stuck to their waist in the mud of the bank. One hangs by a long patch of skin ripped from its back and stuck to the tree above, the feet dangling inches above the water.

A guttural moan brings his attention back to the bank. He switches off the strobe and peers into the trees, the moonlight still allowing him to see into the forest. A large, dead man with half a beard and torn coveralls thumps out onto the edge. Part of his face is burnt off, as are his clothes. A few letters of a name badge remain sewn to his chest. Yellow and green puss oozes from his scorched chin. The man clamors forward, walking over other dead bodies that claw and twitch in the mud.

The imposing dead man walks up onto the tree and it sways under his weight. Viktor looks around. He's too far from the other side and now his escape is cut off. He grasps his axe tight, hoping it won't take more than a single strike to get the massive figure to fall into the water. Somehow the dead places booted foot in front of the other, moving out onto the log. It creaks and moans as the man bares his teeth at Viktor. For a moment he thinks to throw the axe, the impact could be enough to knock him off, but fears if he were to miss, he would then be defenseless. It's now that he remembers the empty handgun in his waistband. Viktor heaves it with all of his strength. It bounces off of the coveralls and vanishes in the water with little more than a splash. The momentum of the throw almost sends himself off the log.

Unphased by the hit, the predator is closing the gap. Viktor feels his weight shift beneath and he reaches out to find empty air. With a thunderous groan, the large root base of the tree peels out of the earth. He finds a limb, holding on as best he can as his end of the tree plunges toward the water. The dead man is thrown forward by the drop and appears to be flying right at him, unencumbered by gravity. It's all Viktor can do to dodge his mass as the body soars past him. An awful sound of crunching flesh bellows from behind him.

The end of the tree rests in the water, the current pulling and making a claim to carry it down the river. Just a few feet past where Viktor holds on for dear life, the man hangs upright, impaled by a broken branch just above the water. He flails his arms and growls and bites. Viktor looks to the end of the tree as it shifts in the water. He makes a run for it, up the steep grade of the bark toward the last few roots that extend into the muddy bank.

Just as he nears the base of the trunk and is about to jump for safety, the whole tree gives way to the water. He's jolted and thrown into the raging river. Viktor swipes at anything that floats by. He is both above and below the frigid water, taking in mouthfuls and gasping for breath at every chance. Sometimes it's air that fills his lungs, other times it's water.

The large tree snags on the banks ahead of him and breaks into shards. The dead man still impaled on a chunk is whirled toward him. He grabs at the same block of wood for floatation as the dead reaches for him while bobbing up and down in the surf. With one arm on the log, he uses the other to drive the axe blade into the man's temple. His whole body goes limp. The weapon must be glued into his hand as he can't believe it hasn't been lost to the river.

The dead man's weight risks pulling him under, so he hacks at the branch that is keeping them anchored together. With a forceful splinter, the body rips from the chunk of tree and vanishes downstream. The axe is stuck in the wood and provides a strong enough handle to hold. Trees whip by, and in the dark, it's all a blur. He struggles to breathe between fits of coughing. The current carries him in a circle, disorienting his vision and direction. In a flash of white, a tree slams into his head, knocking him unconscious, and leaving him to the mercy of the river.

NOW

Viktor awakens as if the force of a thousand volts of electricity surge through his body, a brain-generated lightning strike to his senses. Somehow, he had allowed himself to be lulled asleep by the quiet sway of the truck and the rumble of the thick tread on the road. He leans into his door and draws up his gun.

"Easy, killer," Tozzer says, glancing between Viktor and the road.

Ramirez is asleep in the middle, mouth hanging open.

"Where are we?"

"Almost there. Been driving all night. Even stopped for a quick refuel and you two sleeping beauties didn't bat a wink. Ha. You're made for each other."

As if on cue, Ramirez lets out a snort and comes to, squinting around the cab. It appears he's as much surprised as Viktor was from having let down his guard and nodded off. Viktor wants to ask why Tozzer didn't take his gun or sound the alarm but resists exposing the gaff to Ramirez who is groggy and unaware.

Is the driver a complete fool or is something else going on?

"Just resting my eyes," Ramirez offers to no one in particular.

"Yeah me too." Tozzer closes his eyes hard and mimics falling asleep at the wheel, even swerving for effect.

"Enough!" Viktor says, gesturing with the gun as if it still means something. "No need to raise suspicion from the guys ahead."

"Ah, good thinking," Tozzer agrees with a tap of his temple.

Through the window, Viktor can see the bright stars in the sky, not a cloud anywhere. A half-moon glows behind them. He checks his watch and realizes sunrise is a couple of hours away. Cursing to himself, he can't believe he slept through the night. His stomach roars and he shifts in his seat to try to hide the sound.

"Sorry amigo, no grub on hand. If I'da known we had company I woulda grabbed you a dog too."

"Just drive, would ya?" Ramirez says.

Viktor digs into his coat pocket and finds the bag of chips. They're a little stale but still retain a bit of crunch and the salt is a welcome flavor to his hunger. He bypasses Ramirez and offers to the driver. Tozzer obliges with an open palm and Viktor dumps a couple of chips into his hand. He withdraws his arm realizing that would be the time if Ramirez wanted to make a move. The sound of crunching fills the car as he finishes the bag and shoves the wrapper back in his pocket.

After an hour they cracked the windows to help circulate the air in the cramped cabin of the truck. Now they begin to slow down. Red wash lights up the interior of the cab as the truck in front of them brakes.

"Looks like this is it. Hope you know what you're doing cowboy." Tozzer almost sounds sincere.

In truth, Viktor is ready to do something. Anything. He's worn down by being a continual bystander without affecting any meaningful change on anything or anyone. He feels like a leaf floating on water, being blown around wherever the wind may wish, no means to adjust or correct course. He's even comfortable knowing that he could be committing suicide, but better now as the result of some valiant, if not vain, mission to save the person who has saved him. It's not Francesca, but Catherine that he made the journey for in the end, he just didn't know it at the time.

"What's it going to be?" asks Ramirez, stretching out his arms and reaching the height of the truck cabin.

"I'll go first before they start unloading. You guys go about your business. Which truck?"

Ramirez rolls his eyes. They both must know that either of them could overtake the man who is in over his head. But neither of them tries, nor do they give the impression it's even a consideration.

"Fourth truck, skull sticker on the bumper." Tozzer sounds proud.

"That supposed to mean something?" Viktor asks.

"Put it there myself. I'm a grunt, so naturally..." He pulls down his collar revealing a neck tattoo of the same skull.

Viktor nods. "Alright. Here's to never seeing each other again." He quietly unlatches the door, gun still pointed at them as he backs out of the truck. It's very dark, and the air bites cold at his back.

"Leave the guns," Ramirez reminds him.

He looks to the floor where the two rifles rest against the seat. He latches the passenger door behind him. There is a soft commotion up ahead as the other trucks have begun unloading. Viktor moves to the rear of the vehicle and crouches behind the tailgate. The parking lights of the convoy cast a wide net of illumination to the trees and road. They're in some sort of cul-de-sac, the tow truck at the very rear where it meets the main road.

If he moves in any direction there's a good chance anyone looking back will catch him in the light. As if Tozzer is aware of this, or because the man is incapable of sabotage, he kills the truck lights. At this moment the surroundings plunge into darkness and Viktor makes a run for the trees. He hears the truck doors open and close as both men get out and move toward the front of the convoy.

From the safety of cover, he observes the gathering of soldiers halfway up the cul-de-sac, on the opposite side of the vehicles as himself. He counts the trucks, but can't see the bumpers because of the glaring tail lights. The murmuring of troops grows louder until they are all hushed by one commanding voice. Tom.

"Men. You know what to do. This is our last supply run before the mother-load. Let's make it count. Don't go killing everyone as we'll need to pad our forces if we're going to take that big bitch in a few days. You know the drill for women, children, and any resistors. Make it quick and efficient. They're heavily armed, but we've got the darkness and element of surprise on our side." He clears his throat, a puff of warm air clouding and disappearing in front of him.

"Our scouts estimate our numbers are about equal, but we know what that means. We've got the fucking advantage thanks to savagery and skillset."

This is it.

Viktor moves from the trees and toward the trucks. He draws the handgun and feels for the axe at his waistband as he props himself against one of the Humvees. The soldiers are locked in on Tom.

"Ready, boys? We move south through these trees for a klick. No lights, no sound. We fire first, we fire last."

Viktor moves to the next vehicle, and then the next. He makes it to the fourth truck in line. There, the skull sticker is faded and scratched on the tailgate of the troop transport truck. He peers in through the canvas. A soldier sits with his back to him, mere inches from his face. His rifle is pointed at the prisoners lining both sides of the transport.

Viktor shrinks back against the edge of the truck. *Fuck.* The sound of the soldiers has gone silent, which is more frightening than a relief. They could discover him at any moment.

"Rolling out," crackles over the soldier's radio from inside the truck.

"Copy. Standing watch. Over," the soldier calls back.

Standing up now, Viktor is breathing hard with his back planted against the truck. He tries to calm his heart and lungs to no avail. Whimpering from inside draws his attention. He peeks through the canvas flap above his head.

"Quiet! Don't think I won't shoot you and leave you for the wolves."

He can see the shape of the soldier lean forward and jab someone with the barrel of his rifle. Another whimper is muffled, then a voice he recognizes.

"Take it easy. Nobody is resisting," says Catherine.

Viktor can't see her face but someone is holding the sobbing woman who was struck by the soldier and he recognizes her jacket.

"Fucking right you're not."

The soldier hocks a wad of spit out the back of the truck, nearly hitting Viktor in the face.

His heart is racing despite his best efforts to bring it down. Placing the handgun in his waistband, he retrieves and flexes the axe in his hand.

When gunfire erupts in the distance, Viktor makes his move. He plants a foot on the hitch of the truck and grasps the side handle as hard as he can. Shouts and screams from the trees are accompanied by flashes of light and a hail of gunfire. It sounds like it's almost on top of them.

"Haha, get 'em boys!" laughs the soldier in the truck.

With axe in hand, Viktor steps up onto the bumper and grabs the soldier's jacket with all his strength, pinching the fabric between his locked fingers and the axe handle. With a kick off of the truck frame, he uses all of his leverage to yank the man out of the transport and onto the ground. The soldier lands face down with a thud on top of his own rifle, his helmet flies off and into the darkness. Before he can scream out, Viktor is on his back and driving the axe down deep into the man's skull. It lodges between his neck and ears. The soldier doesn't even twitch or make a sound.

Warmth pumps into Viktor's ears. His vision grows narrow until the sounds of the prisoners moving behind him bring him back. A wisp of cold air delivers some clarity. Gunfire is still erupting in the forest, as are the shouts and flashes of the fighting. A few explosions, grenades and RPGs, send shockwaves that rock the trucks with a concussive force. He undoes the axe from the man's head and whips open the canvas flap once more. The prisoners sit shocked and terrified as a figure flies toward him. She tackles him back, both landing on top of the body below. She rears up to bring tied fists down on his face but stops, staring into his eyes. Catherine lets out a sigh and drops her still bound and raging hands from overhead.

"I told you not to follow me." It's all she says as she stands from atop him. She pulls a knife from the soldier's belt and flips the handle toward Viktor, extending her wrists forward. Gunfire has become the background track that no longer causes anyone to flinch, even as it grows louder, closer.

He saws at her bindings and without so much as a thank you,

she shakes her hands free, steals the knife back, and jumps into the truck. Catherine works to free the other women. The exchange of gunshots creeps closer still. He can hear the voices calling from each side in between the shooting.

"We have to go," Viktor demands.

"I'm not leaving them here defenseless," Catherine calls out from the dark of the transport.

Viktor scrambles and searches the soldier's body. He yanks a keychain from his pocket and shoves it into the hand of the first woman who hops down from the truck.

"Can you drive?"

She nods, still terrified.

"Once they're free, you get them as far away from here as you can. Got it?"

She nods again looking down at the keys. "Thank you," escapes from her lips.

She runs to the front of the truck, climbs in, and turns the engine over. The whole bed rumbles and the exhaust is thick as it billows around him. Catherine hops down and turns back to the woman behind the wheel.

"Get out of here. Now!" she yells.

He can hear one of the women clap on the cab of the truck. It stutters and jerks forward but the driver regains control and pulls the truck out of the convoy. It leaves the cul-de-sac as gunfire rages closer. Catherine yanks the rifle from under the corpse on the ground. She looks to Viktor for a moment, then toward the woods. The battle is mere feet away. Silhouettes of soldiers shooting into the trees as their muzzles flash. The sky is a light purple as the stars begin to fade.

"How did you find me?" she asks, checking the magazine and chamber of the rifle.

"I'll explain later. We can take the truck," Viktor says, pointing to the rear of the convoy.

"The fuck you can!" a voice carries from the darkness between rounds of gunfire.

Tom emerges from the darkness with a large, imposing gun trained on them from his waist. His face is bloodied, and his eyes narrowed. Gunfire dances behind him, casting a halo-like glow as he approaches. There's a limp in his gait as blood runs down his pant leg.

"Hello, Viktor."

THEN

A blurry shape moves toward Viktor in a bright white room. It hovers as if its feet don't touch the ground, gliding ever so slowly. There's no sense of dimension of walls or floors but there's a notion that it's still a space of some sort. He fights to focus his eyes on the object but can only see the outline.

A young girl in a flowing dress, judging by the waves of hair and fabric, but no more than a manifestation floating through his sight. He cannot turn his head. His view is locked on the confusing picture before him and he has no periphery of any part of himself. No feet or legs or even hands with which he could gesture. The apparition moves closer and stops right before him, though it's no clearer than it was when it seemed a great distance away. The image pulses like an orb of gray against the stark white backdrop.

A *whisper.*

"Daddy."

"Caroline?" Viktor knows he said her name but hears nothing but noise. He screams it again, but static fills the air. The shape seems to vibrate in response to his internal shouting.

"Daddy." The soft voice distorts and he struggles to comprehend what she speaks as it filters through as nonsense. He recognizes the words but they don't make sense in his mind. It's as if he knows what's being said but doesn't understand the language.

"What baby, what is it?"

"Why?" The voice grows in volume, further distorting with static and feedback. There's a booming echo that follows, one that would bounce around an enormous cave, but there are no visuals to explain the reverberations.

"Why what, honey? Come closer." All spoken in his mind, hoping the being can somehow read his thoughts. It pulses and moves closer but with no more clarity to his sight. The blur is the same up close as it is a mile away, it seems.

"Why didn't you--" The low voice fades again as it darts backward like a squid at the bottom of the ocean. The noise of the room elevates, pulsating with the static glow around the shape as it circles in place.

"Please, Caroline. Come closer. I've missed you baby. Daddy's here now!" In his head, he's yelling at the top of his lungs. The orb retreats again a little farther, the cloud now dancing in wider strokes and emitting bellows even louder than up close. "No, no. Don't leave."

He watches for a moment as the shape hovers, the monotonous hum ringing in his ears. Then in an instant, the blur lunges forward into focus, inches from his face. The decayed face and rotten teeth screaming a high-pitched shrill. "WHY DIDN'T YOU SAVE ME!"

The words cut with an icy blast and Viktor is thrust awake into the stark moonlight. Water laps over the log and hits him in the face, eyes, and mouth. He's wedged against the bank of the river in a side pool away from the dashing current. There is water in every part of his clothing to the point where he thinks he might still be under the surface. He wiggles his toes and realizes he can't feel anything below the actual water line that laps at his chest. He begins shaking as his breath casts out steam in front of him. White knuckles are locked around the axe that is still planted in the log.

Fingers ache in their joints as Viktor tries to force his hand to move. With a twist and a grunt, he's able to undo the blade from the soaked and saturated wood, the bloated fibers not wanting to give up the weapon. He falls back into the water and almost goes under, but his numb feet hit muddy stone. Or so he thinks. It's a muted feeling, a sensation of vibration through his legs without any deal of texture. He could be standing on anything, but he's thankful it's enough to keep his head from submerging.

The willpower to tread water is as far gone as the dead that were carried downstream and so, had he gone under, he would have been destined to join them. Viktor grasps at the hedges and roots of the river bank. It takes him several minutes to get his entire body out of the water. He almost plunges himself back in, when the cold air bites through his wet clothes and stings the skin beneath. Drowning may be a more appealing flavor, he thinks.

One hand over the other, and one boot shoved into the muddy bank after the next, he makes his way up the side and onto a grassy ledge above the pool. Viktor lies there a moment, staring at the starry sky, his exhalations billowing white puffs into the open air. He's ready to die, and he believes he will, but he's more terrified of returning to that dream. If he closes his eyes the monster that awaits him is far worse than living here in agony for a few more moments. He keeps wiggling his toes, sensing the movement of his feet but not feeling any feedback from their motion against the inside of his boots.

Somehow, he rolls over onto his stomach. A fleck of light in the distance catches his eye between blades of tall grass. At first, he thinks it's just another star, but knows it's too low to be shining between the trees with such brightness. He crawls forward before propping himself up on his elbows. Viktor bats the water off of his eyelids and tries to discern the light glimmering from across the grassy field. He can't make it out, so he crawls toward it.

The light becomes three and he soon recognizes their purpose. Solar garden lights, the kind he had installed around the sidewalk of his old home. He wonders if they're on right now, while the skeletons of his family are decaying on the living room floor. Still crawling, the dim blue lights are not far away and now he can see the silhouette of a rectangle behind them. A structure perhaps, with a peaked roof.

Viktor reaches to his back, realizing his pack is not with him, and remembers throwing it up into the tree before the attack. And then he thinks of the kids, but as quickly as he allows himself the distraction, he pulls himself back to thoughts of survival. He panics for a moment, knowing if he is to have any chance, he must make a fire or risk succumbing to hypothermia. His one hope is to move toward the lights but he knows, without warmth, he'll soon revisit the nightmare and this time there may be no escape.

He pulls himself to his feet and limps on hollow, numb legs that feel like little more than stubs of flesh against hard earth. Violent coughs double him over. They hurt deep in his lungs and stomach. *Forward, closer to the lights.* He collapses a few yards from his miniature lighthouses that draw his will to push forward.

Again, he crawls as his body begins to shake, but the hacking coughs bring a brief and welcome interruption. It feels like his spine is going to shatter against the intense shivering. Using his elbows and clenched fists, he makes his way past the lights and up to the face of the structure.

The texture is unknown as little feeling remains in the tips of his fingers, but it's soft and wet. He presses against it and it gives, depressing inward and not retreating back. A door, covered in plastic sheeting. Using his axe, he thrusts it into the side of the object where it sticks firm. and pulls himself up onto his knees. In the faint light of the moon, he can make out a latch. Viktor pushes down on it with a closed fist and it creaks open.

A blast of warm air flows out of the crack in the door, the contrast to the cold may as well be a jet engine taking off. It feels like heaven and so he lunges his upper body into the door, forcing it open. Crawling inside toward the warm, stale air, he pulls himself forward and kicks the door closed behind him with all of the energy he has left.

There he lies, convulsing in a fetal position on hard, rough wooden floor planks. They cease for a brief moment and the smell of earth and living things fills his nostrils as he sucks in the atmosphere around him. Moonlight glows through the transparent roof overhead and that is when he notices the shapes all around him. They hang over him, mocking him, looking down on his pitiful body, shaking on the floor. *Plants. Large, leafy plants.* The elation of joy hits him as fast as the urge to sleep.

A greenhouse.

He passes out, huddled among overflowing potted plants and hanging vegetables.

NOW

Catherine is knocked out by a strike from Tom's gun before she can level her own and take a shot. She collapses to the pavement, her rifle dropping at her feet and bouncing before landing close by. Viktor raises the axe but Tom has beaten him to it, and now he's staring down the barrel of the intimidating machine gun. The madman even holds it at his hip like a movie star.

At this range, Viktor would be cut in half from a quick burst before he could land a fatal headshot of his own. The handgun round would fail to penetrate Tom's rugged body armor, so his only chance would be square between the eyes. Viktor is overpowered and knows it. He lowers the gun.

"Good, now drop it." Tom gestures with the jagged muzzle a foot from Viktor's stomach.

With a sigh and glance at the sprawled-out Catherine, he lets the gun spin on his trigger finger and fall to the ground. Gunfire erupts with dangerous proximity in the woods, and for a moment Viktor thinks he's dead, but Tom doesn't so much as flinch as he kicks Catherine's rifle further away from her body. Viktor is relieved as he can see her chest rise and fall. She could be asleep if he hadn't seen what sent her down.

"Back up." Tom steps forward.

Viktor raises his hands and steps back, wondering if he could make a reach for his axe. His eyes dart to every object, path, light, and sound, calculating any way he can counter the one who is about to execute him. Even if he can pull Tom away from the convoy, give her a chance to wake up and escape, that will be enough. He knows she will pursue, and the attempt made folly, but he must try or they'll both be dead in a matter of moments.

Maybe worse than death for her.

Tom edges closer, a limp and wince as blood oozes from his leg and shoulder wounds. Light flashes on his face with every gun that's fired in the battle that rages on behind him.

"Sir, we've gotta evac. We're overrun," Ramirez says as he bursts to Tom's side, out of breath. He doesn't so much as look at Viktor. "Sir?"

Tom turns to Ramirez. "We fight."

He then transfers the mags from Ramirez's front pouches to his own supply, jamming one into the mag well and pulling back to chamber a round.

"Sir, the dead. Ours...and theirs. They're turning. This whole area is about to get out of our control. We need to leave before we're overpowered."

Tom grits his teeth. Viktor can't tell if he's about to murder everyone on the spot, Ramirez and himself included, in one wide sweep of his gun, or if he's going to melt to his knees and blow his brains out.

"Fuck!" Tom thinks for a brief moment. "Give the order."

"Yes sir--" With a scream, Ramirez's body plunges into Tom's, who swats him off, using his gun as a buffer.

Tozzer is on Ramirez's back, teeth clenched deep into his neck peeling back the skin and sinewy tendons. It pulls away like the juicy skin off of a thanksgiving turkey as blood sprays over Ramirez's face and into his wide, white eyes. Tom uses his gun to separate the men from himself, losing balance and stumbling against the rear of the transport truck.

The barrel of the gun is caught on the fatigues of Tozzer and Ramirez as they tangle together on the ground, a horrendous scream coming from the pile. With no patience, Tom squeezes the trigger and blasts through both bodies of his soldiers. *Now. Run!* Not knowing what else to do, Viktor sprints for the far trees across the cul-de-sac, hoping at the very least to draw Tom and the dead away from Catherine.

As Tom pulls his gun from the mangled corpses at his feet, he draws aim at Viktor and fires off several rounds until the gun clicks empty. Viktor crashes to the earth as one of the rounds grazes his side. He looks back across the grass and sees Tom pursuing with a limp, exchanging the spent mag with a fresh one from his chest pouch. Viktor has just made the tree line, and after checking the wound he pulls himself to his feet and pushes into the darkness of the forest. The gunfire softens in the distance.

"Viktor," Tom calls as he stalks his prey. "Come on, little man. Let's not drag this out."

He fires off a couple of bursts into the trees, the bright flash illuminating the woods and echoing for miles.

"Tell ya what. I'll let your sweet butterfly be my personal companion, protect her from the rest of the boys if you give yourself up."

More bursts and flashes of light. Viktor is backed up against a steep rock wall, fifty yards or more into the trees. The essence of blue peeks over the canopy as night and dawn begin to merge overhead. He cowers into a large tree trunk, afraid to step into the growing ambient light. With no retreat, he knows he'll be mowed down without hesitation.

"No? Alright. Have it your way. I'm going to let you turn and watch as you eat your little darling alive. After we've had our way with her for a few days of course." He laughs and fires more bursts. The magazine once again runs dry.

He can hear Tom shuffling out a fresh magazine. Viktor emerges from behind the thick trunk and raises his axe over his shoulder. As Tom racks the slide back, he brings the blade down with full force. The handle glances off a branch and the direction is skewed, and the speed slowed. The face of the axe once aimed for the back of his head now lands angled into Tom's shoulder and clanks against bone. He lets out a howl and falls to his knees.

Viktor yanks the axe from Tom's shoulder and raises it. He can see the movement in his mind and his eyes grow with anticipation. For a split second, he pictures planting it deep into his skull, ridding himself of this degenerate for good. Before he can bring it down, a jolt travels up his thigh. The handle of Tom's knife is the only part still visible from the blood pooling on his pant leg as the blade sits four inches deep into his right leg, halfway between his knee and hip.

He feels warmth fill his face as dizziness overtakes him. He dares not pull it out and collapses to the ground, both men now on their knees in the faint remnants of darkness. He feels for the axe, but it has been lost among the growth.

"You son of a bitch," Tom whispers.

The distant gunfire has ceased as Viktor crawls up tight against the rock formation once again. Tom reaches for his gun. He sways a few feet away as his hand finds the grip. Viktor knows even a fool can finish the job from this distance and so he closes his eyes, wondering if he'll even hear the shots that kill him. He prays not.

A *snort* and *huff.*

The sound fills the forest, followed by an eerie silence. Viktor opens his eyes at the metallic fidgeting of Tom struggling to lift the gun. All he has to do is pull the trigger and turn Viktor into a mist against the rocks. The galloping of hooves against earth grows in the dark. A shadow darts behind Tom.

"You're dead, fucker." Tom bares his teeth and slides his trigger finger into the guard, preparing to squeeze.

Viktor turns his head and pulls himself as close to the rock wall as possible. Tom lets out a gasp of air as a brutal noise escapes his lungs. Viktor whips his head back to see the horror right in front of him.

Tom's body shakes as jagged antlers protrude from his abdomen, just below the body armor. He still holds the gun with one hand and grasps the goring antler that is sticking out from his stomach with the other. Tom screams as the large animal moves back and shakes him like a rag doll. Viktor pulls himself away along the ground in what he hopes is the direction of the convoy, his legs dragging behind him. The knife still planted in his thigh sways as he struggles to pull himself away from the attack.

The sounds of Tom being ravaged are the stuff of nightmares, and there's no time for the feeling of relief. Viktor knows at any moment he could be next. The thought of the antlers piercing through his back has him checking over his shoulder with each dragging movement forward. The dawn light has started to bring up the visibility of the forest and he pulls himself onward for what seems like an hour but is mere minutes.

A short burst of gunfire from Tom's gun cuts through the trees and the echoes dance into obscurity among the forest. Viktor listens but no sound of movement or cries ring out. He claws, one hand over the other, mossy root to sapling to dirt, until he reaches the edge of the tree line and can see the cul-de-sac ahead. Swaying, blurry bodies are obscure among the trucks. He scans he area, looking for any trace of Catherine, but his eyes are beginning to fail him.

Rustling of leaves and branches creep up on him. A low groan and growl, guttural and foul. Viktor reaches for anything, his mind knowing what he'll see before he can even turn around. Tom's mutilated corpse stumbles forward, his dead eyes soft and gray, teeth gnashing as blood runs down to twitching fingers.

Viktor tries to pull himself up, but the knife protruding from his leg wobbles and sends a paralyzing pain in all directions. Tom falls onto Viktor's lower legs. He throws dirt, rocks, leaves, anything his hands find into the face of the biting shell of treachery. Tom scratches at his pants on his way upward, opening wide, a horrific stench permeating from the black hole of his face. His teeth clench and open, and the violent clatter makes Viktor want to puke. At any moment his face will be ripped to shreds.

Writhing in pain with the gnashing jaws now hanging just inches above him, Viktor pulls the blade from his own thigh and thrusts it into Tom's eye socket. The body goes limp. As the blood leaves the wound in his leg his sight goes blurry, focusing in and out on the dead man over him and then on the light through the branches above. There's no confusion like he thought there would be, as somehow Viktor knows the life is spilling out of him faster than could ever be stopped. His femoral artery pumps the gushes of red onto the forest floor. His heart and head pound like a thousand fists beating down on him.

"Shit, shit, shit," Catherine's sweet soft voice sounds like a whisper in the clouds. "Viktor. Viktor. Say something."

He can feel her presence, her soft hand on his face and hair, but no matter how hard he tries, his eyes can't find her. He feels the weight being lifted from his legs and stomach, the awful pain in his thigh turning to little more than a numb tingle. A dark swirl fills in his vision, narrowing, the canopy above now seems like a universe away.

"What do I do?" her voice calls frantically, in a far-off land.

Viktor feels for her, finds her arm, and then her hand that is pressing against the wound on his leg. It takes all of his strength to squeeze her hand, and whisper,

"I'm sorry. Please don't let me turn."

Shapes dance in his vision. He hallucinates turning and killing and eating flesh, the visual increasing with an insatiable appetite that's growing. A brand-new instinct that he is cognizant of and is yet unstoppable.

"I just have to stop the bleeding."

"It's okay," he says, or thinks he says.

He can't be sure. His eyes hurt from holding them open but little light enters. Like a thick black blanket cast over his head, the faintest of senses able to pass through the spaces between the fine threads of fabric.

"No. No. No. I'm sorry, Viktor, I'm so sorry. I should have believed you!"

He can feel the pressure of her face on his shoulder, the warmth of her tears on his neck.

"I would have left me too." He tries to laugh.

With what strength remains, Viktor slides his hand to a pocket and fights to remove a wallet. He brings it up, resting his hand on his chest, fingers grasping the old faded leather like it's his most prized possession. He doesn't need to say anything. Her grasping his hand and the wallet with both of hers as she kisses his forehead is enough for him to know she understands.

As a dark circle collapses around his eyes, he tries to focus on the dawn blue now beginning to emerge between the trees above. Unlike himself, it's winning the fight against the darkness, he thinks. The first ray of sun flickers and flares off of the moisture of a sole leaf dangling above. It dances in his eyes and merges with Catherine's face that is staring down at him. Her face morphs into Caroline's, not dead or decayed, but alive and smiling. It's a beautiful sight. He blinks for the last time as the black takes hold and a final thought rolls over his mind.

She lives on.

THEN

For days Viktor was sprawled out on the floor of the greenhouse, not noticing the change from day to night. A fever had swarmed over him. He would shed his clothes, lying naked on the wooden floor until a freezing cold would send his body into shakes and he would muster all his strength to cover up with a folded tarp. A rain barrel outside, meant to provide irrigation to the plants, was his hydration source as he would drag himself to suck from the black hose as his mouth dried up. He had no desire to eat, despite the nagging ache in his stomach that would growl and rumble nonstop. After a couple of days, he made himself chew on some leafy greens. They tasted bitter and tough but settled the disturbance in his appetite.

After what he estimates as ten days on death's door, Viktor now lifts his thin frame upright. He's able to move with more mobility as he examines the overgrowth around him. He picks a plump tomato, stepping in the rot of its brethren that had fallen to the planks below. It's juicy and sweet and the feeling of the liquid running down his scruffy chin and bare chest is exhilarating. He had hung up his soaking clothes to dry, but they still retained a bit of dampness and a pungent smell of mildew after two days.

With his clothes now dry, but not smelling any better, he gets dressed and makes his way out of the greenhouse. It's a cool but sunny morning, sun shining bright on the open grass field. A hundred yards across the openness, a modest blue house sits nestled among the trees. When he crawled into the greenhouse, he hadn't even noticed that it was there, which is for the better he realizes as he never would have made it that far.

With his axe and what little food he could gather from the greenhouse, he walks toward the main house across the field. He's hesitant by habit, but his brush with death has made him a bit careless on approach. Though he doubts anyone would still be there since they had made no attempts to visit the lush garden where he stayed for over a week. As suspected, no signs of life come from the quaint building. No vehicle tracks in the dirt driveway or anything to indicate people live inside. The door bangs open and closed in the wind, ajar from its latch.

Viktor looks inside and a sour smell hangs in the air. He walks the single-story house, looking among its cupboards and cabinets. To his delight, he finds water and canned goods and a bag to carry them in. There's also medicine in the bathroom cabinet that he's happy to find and it reminds him of Janice and the home of her parents.

It's not until he comes to the sole bedroom that he discovers the culprit of the light stench in the air. Sitting together on the bed, two decayed skeletons sit upright side by side, their bony hands still intertwined. Dried, dark brown splatters cover the wall behind them. A shotgun rests next to one of the bodies. Their skin is translucent and the skeleton beneath is prominent and emerging.

He doesn't go into the room but notices a picture on the dresser beside the door. It's an elderly couple posing together in front of the new greenhouse as if they were duplicating the American

Gothic painting. Viktor can't help but smile. He's able to reach the frame without disturbing the room, so he undoes the back and removes the photo. He tucks the keepsake into the pocket of his new bag, one he found in the closet by the front door, and the medicines inside rattle as he zips up the pack. He closes the bedroom, and then the front door, and leaves the house for good.

Without a map, he has no way of knowing how far he's traveled away from the children. He plans to travel back upstream. He knows it could be hours or it could be days. When he sees the driveway lead out onto a larger dirt road that follows along the riverbank upstream, he decides to follow it rather than walk through the woods. It will be faster and he hopes there may be a street he recognizes from their previous journey to Hawksboro.

Viktor washes the thoughts of the children out of his mind. He's terrified of what he may find and can't grasp the idea of picturing it, blocking it out whenever a flash of a scenario enters his thoughts. *They're okay. You drew the dead away. They're waiting for you. You showed them how to fish. They made it.* It works, and his thoughts travel to the road in front of him.

The long stretch of dirt road is flanked on one side by tall trees and the sounds of the river, now back to its normal flow. The other side is a sprawling grass field with rotting hay bales dotting the area, all sagging and losing their shape. Dust kicks up under his boots as he shuffles over the loose gravel. The sun is high and beats down with inviting warmth.

The dirt road bends and turns. With each intersection, he contemplates changing course. When he can see a paved road in the distance there's a strong desire to navigate toward it, but it would pull him away from the direction of the river so he forges ahead, taking whichever road keeps him closest to the water on his right. The entire countryside is devoid of life, save for birds cawing on useless power lines, or a single woodchuck that he sent scurrying into the field. Viktor contemplated if he could eat it, but the idea of trying to hunt it with the axe and then preparing it with a fire removed any motivation. Keep to the mission, get back to the children, he reminds himself.

Having walked the entire day and the sun now beginning to set, his nerves grow with anxiety. He second-guesses every road he's chosen. Was it possible he was disoriented, is he on the wrong side of the stream, or has he already passed them long ago? When the dirt road he's on comes to an end, he stands at the three-way intersection. The left side splits off into the trees and seems to weave away from the river, the right becomes paved and bends back toward the direction he came. He guesses there may be an hour left of light and he's not prepared to sleep outside. The day is nice but the night will likely drop to a cooler temperature. The memory of his sickness exacerbates his panic.

A raspy growl draws his attention to the trees on the right next to the start of the paved road. He doesn't have the energy to fight off any dead, but he inspects the sound anyway. Just off the shoulder and under a fallen tree, a dead squirms and grabs at the muddy earth. It's clear to him that the log has washed aground during the high water of the storm, and he's elated at the sight. He knows now he hasn't gone past their camp since the dead got washed downstream with him. Viktor steps through the weeds and plants his axe into its skull. A quick sweep of the pockets and he snags a wallet and phone, which go into his bag.

"Thanks," he says to the corpse as he walks onto the paved road.

Viktor can feel it in his bones that he just needs to keep going. After fifteen minutes of walking, the sun now kissing the tops of the hills beyond, he spots a beautiful scene in the distance. An old green metal bridge, the one from just outside the town of Hawksboro. Doing his best to jog and limp, he makes his way to the intersection ahead. He hooks a right and crosses the worn bridge. He's surprised and thankful that it survived the overflowing river.

With the orange and purple glow being the last trace left of the sun, he runs down the bank to the tree where they had made camp.

Viktor calls out to the kids, "Basil! Jake!"

They would have to be back by now, it's dark.

"Hello!" Viktor waits to hear a tap. He plays the sound in his mind and almost believes that he hears it.

"I'm back!" he yells.

Viktor runs up to the tree, hoping to see them asleep above, but all that remains are the torn remnants of the makeshift hammocks they made the night that they were separated. Everything else looks the same as that last moment, which sinks a pit into his stomach. He knows that if they stayed, they would have needed a fire, food, and there would be some sign of them staying here. The fishing line and stick sway empty in the wind over the pool where he caught the fish. He walks back to the tree and almost trips.

At his feet, his backpack sits covered with dirt, muddy footprints all over the dark material. Basil's broken staff jammed into the earth beside the bag, it wobbles as the earth moves as he steps closer. He's devastated and the feeling of disappointment overwhelms him. He's let them down and who knows what horrors they've endured. For well into the night he cries into his hands. Exhaustion takes over and he falls asleep right there in the dirt, cradling his bag. The dead could once again be cast down on him and he wouldn't so much as say a word, let alone put up a fight.

They don't come and the next day brings new light and a fresh perspective. Viktor looks around the tree and stream, examining the large clearing where he led the dead. After surveying the entire area, he leans against a tree and looks out on the clearing.

This can be home.

He vows to himself to build it up so it can be ready for when the kids return. *They will return and he'll have built a safe place where they can all live together.*

Viktor walks through the clearing and back to the massive tree where the tattered blankets swing above. He stands below the sprawling branches that reach out in all directions, the possibilities of what could be filling his mind.

"This is where I'll start."

NOW

"Hand's up," commands a stern male voice.

The sun has peaked over the canopy and dawn has come, but the light under the branches is still dim. A flashlight shines bright in Catherine's burning, wet eyes. She can barely make out the figures behind the beam. The starlike crystals forming kaleidoscopes in her vision made of light and tears.

"I said get 'em up," the same voice instructs.

Catherine wipes away the wetness from her cheek as she releases Viktor's ridged hands, his wallet nestled in her palm. On her knees in the damp earth, she raises both arms toward the sky. Men step in around Viktor's body and lift her to her feet with an upward force, a kindness in their effort. The lights dip down to the ground, illuminating both corpses.

Tom's body is cast aside, a grotesque facial expression with jaw slack, and Viktor's. She had closed his eyelids and it was after she confirmed no breathing or heartbeat that she severed his brainstem with the same knife he used to kill Tom. She wished she had any other method or tool, the thought of sharing the same blade seemed undignified, but shooting him was too violent an end and she promised not to let him turn.

"Jesus," another man whispers.

As her eyes adjust to the light that is now cast away from her face, she can see the half dozen soldiers standing around in a semi-circle. While their uniforms are similar, it's clear they are not part of Tom's outfit. Two female soldiers are among them, both dressed in fatigues like the rest.

"You a combatant?" the first voice asks.

Catherine shakes her head no, unsure of which soldier is doing the questioning.

"Prisoner," she sniffles, the wallet still tight in hand overhead.

One of the soldiers, the commanding officer she realizes, steps forward. "You can put your hands down," he says.

Catherine does so, not out of caution but exhaustion.

"I'm First Lieutenant Ellison. Did you know this man?" The charming, well-groomed soldier points to Tom.

She shakes her head no, refusing to look, but understanding which man he's referring to.

"His men kidnapped me and some others, while I... we, were traveling east."

Catherine nods down to Viktor's body, but can't bear to look.

"Where are the rest of the prisoners?"

"We were helping them escape when they began the attack."

"They on foot?"

"Transport truck," she lets the words escape, too tired to think or articulate.

Ellison turns to one of the soldiers and speaks in a soft tone, but one that commands obedience. "They can't be far, take bravo squad up the pass. Bring those willing back to base."

"And the rest?" the soldier asks.

"Give them rations and fuel. And a map with our base should

they change their mind."

"Yes, sir."

The soldier runs off to the convoy. Catherine looks across the grass and into the cul-de-sac. Dozens of soldiers move about, gathering bodies and taking stock of supplies.

"It was an ambush," she says to no one in particular.

Ellison squints, trying to read Catherine.

"But how did you know?" she adds.

"Walk with me?" he asks.

She agrees but looks back to Tom's body as soldiers check his person. Catherine pushes one of the men aside and reaches down to Tom's chest. With a single swipe, she rips his name patch off of his vest and jams it into her pocket. "Burn that one when you're done."

Catherine follows Ellison back toward the convoy. As she walks away, a soldier jogs to catch up.

"Ma'am. I believe this belonged to your friend."

The bloodied axe is extended toward her, handle-first. She takes it, nodding her thanks, and follows Ellison out of the woods.

"Sir, he's over here." A soldier shows the lieutenant the way. In a neat row, bodies line the edge of the street.

"We had an inside man," Ellison says to Catherine as he points to Tozzer's lifeless body.

She looks confused, not understanding the connection he's trying to make.

"That's how we knew. We send out scouts to make contact with survivors or other groups like ourselves. But some are sent to infiltrate communities that may have nefarious intentions. Like that rotting asshole in the woods back there."

He reaches down and places a hand on Tozzer's shoulder.

"Sergeant Tozzer sent word two days ago that we were in for an attack. The man was a nut, but the hell if he wasn't brave."

They move away from the bodies and the commotion of the soldiers working.

"You can stay with us. We can always use more soldiers. Or doctors. Or anyone with a skillset to be honest," Ellison offers.

"I think I'll pass. I've got other plans." She tries to sound gracious, but it comes out all the wrong ways. Ellison doesn't seem phased or slighted in the least. He has a coolness about him that is calming.

"Fair enough. If you change your mind or want to come back, you can find us here."

He retrieves a folded map from a pouch in his gear. He yanks the lid off a marker with his teeth and makes a circle before handing it to her.

"We've got a heavily fortified base here, lots of people, and not just soldiers. You should think about it."

She tries to look gracious. "Thank you."

"Where you headed, if I may ask?"

Catherine looks around, no longer sure of the answer. All she wanted was to head west, get to Texas, but now she's lost.

"Uh, back south, I think. I don't know actually."

Ellison reads her for a moment, then smiles. "Well, safe travels."

He extends a hand and she meets it with her own.

"Carter, run over some rations and water," says Ellison.

A moment later a soldier appears with a small canvas tote that he hands to Catherine.

"Thank you."

Ellison nods. As Catherine begins walking down toward the end of the cul-de-sac, she passes the tow truck. Her eyes light up, and even though the muscles in her face hurt and ache she can't help but smile. Resting in the bed, Viktor's bag sits propped against the wheel well of the truck. As she slings the bag over her shoulder, she leaves the soldiers and convoy behind her. Catherine puts the map, along with Viktor's wallet, into his bag. She retrieves his atlas and unfolds it in front of her. She traces her fingers along the lines and circles he had made. *There.* She lands on the largest circle, miles and miles away.

After three weeks of intense hiking, evading the dead, and raiding vehicles and small towns for any supplies, Catherine sees the first circle on the map up ahead. She makes her way through the trees to find a modest treehouse hidden amongst the forest. She crosses off the circle on the map and walks to the next. She does this for days, collecting any of his belongings and then checking off each of Viktor's circles, working her way back to the largest circle on the map. One month after she began her newest journey, she walks into a beautiful clearing, the smell of rain and new growth fills her nose as butterflies bounce along the high grass.

In the middle of the clearing sits a large solar panel contraption. From there she follows the worn path into the trees. Weeds have fought to overtake it, but to a trained eye, the route is clear as day. It doesn't take long for her to find home. The towering tree with massive branches still supports the elaborate treehouse that Viktor built by hand. She explores the area and makes her way up and inside via a rope ladder. She's amazed at all of the collections he has stored. Catherine sits in a chair, admiring the locked bins that line the walls.

She feels around in her bag until she comes across Viktor's wallet. It's crusted with mud and dried tears and it cracks as she pries the bifold open. A laugh becomes a cry as it bursts from her mouth. She covers it with a hand, sobbing and smiling at the same time. The wallet is empty, save for a single photograph. The young girl has a glowing smile and a beautiful yellow dress. The back has a scribble of writing:

CAROLINE, 5TH GRADE
BIN COMBOS 451

"Of course," she whispers to herself, somehow unsurprised that the man who spent so much time collecting everyone else's memory, left behind nothing of his own.

She collects the girl's picture as well as the hard drive, phone, and other IDs Viktor carried and stores them in the nearest bin with the rest. If not for the note on the back of the photo she never would have had the heart to break the locks.

As dusk settles in, she builds a small fire in the stone ring below the treehouse. She stares at the flames as they dance, little flecks of yellow escaping to the purple and orange sky above. Catherine removes a crumpled piece of cloth from her pocket and straightens it in her hand. BECKER in black letters over green digital camo. She tosses Tom's name tape into the fire and watches it shrivel amongst the coals. She watches as it curls and smokes before melting away and disappearing into the glowing red.

Tap. Tap.

Catherine grabs Viktor's axe at her side and raises it in hand.

Tap. Tap.

She stands as the fire pops and crackles behind her.

"Who are you?" a soft but stern voice calls out.

Catherine whips around. From the trees, a young girl, maybe fifteen, with dark skin and tight curls steps forward holding a fierce metal bar with a razor point on the end.

"My--my name's Catherine," she stutters as she lowers the axe.

"How did you find this place?" the girl asks, unmoving from her spot a few yards away.

"Uh, a map. From a friend. He uh--used to live here, I think. He built this." She gestures to the treehouse and everything around them.

Footsteps to her right draw her attention away from the girl. A young boy, pale skin and freckled cheeks. He can't be more than nine or ten, she thinks. He carries a baseball bat with a spike protruding from the end.

"Who are you?" Catherine asks.

"I'm Basil," the girl says, looking her over.

Catherine looks back to the boy who grips the bat in one hand.

"And I'm Jake. This is our home."

She looks on at the children standing before her. A flake of charcoal carries a glowing spark from the confines of the fire, up into the night sky to join the stars in the deep blue beyond.

SPRING

PURPOSE

The concrete rectangle looks impenetrable from this distance. Few trees dot the trimmed lawn that sprawls from its base, interrupted by a moat of sand and gravel, like an outfield warning track against the perimeter wall. A lone Blackhawk helicopter descends at the airfield beyond the two-story building, imposing barbed wire and barricades marking its footprint. As they get closer, the sound of the chopper is both a terrifying and a comforting surprise, even though its meaning is still uncertain. This is the first glimpse she has of the dark metal hull as it drops behind the Fort Knox Bullion Depository.

Catherine spent days telling the children the story of how she and Viktor came to know each other. The awful retelling of the attack and his death, she spared little detail once the children seemed to be able to handle the graphic nature of it all. It was clear to her that they had experienced their fair share of macabre. It was only after they opened up during their journey north that she learned the extent of their own tribulation and the impossibility of survival during the night that they were overrun. They explained the last moment they saw Viktor, his heroic actions that they believe saved them, and the desperate attempts to find him afterward.

Hearing Basil explain it, sometimes in too much detail, was almost more than Catherine could take. Like how they were scattered during the horde attack and it took days for her just to find Jake, who was huddled in a chicken coop, shivering and hungry. When they made their way back to the tree and Viktor wasn't there, she led them off in search of him. Encounters with animals, strangers, some friendly and some not, ended up keeping them away for years, having traveled hundreds of miles south into Louisiana.

They waited until Jake was older and able to fight and scavenge for himself to journey back north, once again hoping to find Viktor waiting for them at the tree, though Basil admitted she knew it was a long shot. They came upon the tree, the home Viktor had made for them over the past four years, just three weeks after he left on his trek to find Francesca. They had deciphered this by back timing what Catherine knew of his travels.

Both the kids' goal of reaching the tree before winter and Viktor's desire to do most of his traveling before winter as well, aligned their fates to miss each other by such a narrow window. This was a painfully sad thought for Catherine at the time, though she's glad they stayed put, long enough for her to find them. Basil had described how happy they were once seeing Viktor had built that place, knowing he was alive and could return at any moment. She was willing to wait there as long as necessary until he showed up again.

Now the three stand in awe on the overpass of Bouillon Boulevard, looking down at the massive base that Catherine had followed on the map. It had taken weeks to cover the several hundred miles on foot, but every day the circle on the map that Ellison had given her grew closer. Between Viktor's atlas and that map, she was able to lead them there, and the relief of arrival was a grand thing for them all. Each of them carried a large bag, encompassing all of Viktor's collections. There was no way she could have done it alone and she was thankful the kids were eager to share the load.

In honor of Viktor, no doubt.

"Are you ready?" Catherine asks as they lean against the concrete barrier of the highway, looking down on the base.

Basil and Jake both nod as he adjusts the heavy bag on his thin frame. They walk together, in a line of three down the highway and over the guardrail, descending the grassy bank. They approach the overwhelming fort at its entrance. The safest way, Catherine thinks. Two armed soldiers emerge from the guard shack.

"Hold it there," one shouts, rifle aimed, but finger out of the trigger well and parallel to the barrel.

"Are you well?" the other asks. "Bites, or sickness?"

All three shake their head no, then say it aloud when the soldier only stares at them.

"Weapons?" the first asks.

It's obvious that, with the rifle Catherine carries and still slung on her shoulder, the metal staff in Basil's hand, and the bat pointed to the ground that Jake leans on, they mean concealed. Catherine lifts her shirt to expose a handgun in her waistband, as well as the axe.

"Lieutenant Ellison told me to come here. He gave me a map." She holds it up, unfolded. They both aim their rifles at her quick movement but relax upon seeing the map flutter in her hand.

One guard keeps his rifle up while the other moves to the guard shack. A radio squawks and an inaudible voice emits from inside.

"You can keep the blades and sticks, but deposit your guns

here," he calls out from the shack doorway She looks to the kids and does as commanded.

"I'll need to check the bags," the other soldier adds.

All three sling off the bags and unzip them on the ground at their feet. While one guard sets aside the guns, the other examines the contents.

"An unusual collection you've got here," he states as he shuffles through the bound stacks of IDs, photos, phones, and hard drives.

"Memorials," Basil says, without hesitation.

Catherine smiles at her confidence. The guard steps back and motions to the other guard. The three zip up their bags and struggle to set them on their shoulders again. The guard from the booth escorts them to the fence and unlocks a latch, ushering them inside and then locking the fenced door behind them. The small cage is unsettling, but he's quick to unlock the next door and extends his arm toward the base.

"Follow along this road until it comes to a T intersection. HQ is the big building on your right. Ask for Major Ellison at the desk. And watch for traffic."

Their walk along the interior base road is scorching as the sun shines uninhibited overhead and there's no shade to be found. After a half-mile of pavement and unencumbered radiant heat, they come to the T in the road. Golf carts buzz by with soldiers and guns, none taking a second glance at the newcomers as they drive by. A Humvee's brakes squeal at the crosswalk, allowing them to pass. It drums on behind them as if this was any other day.

Inside the large brick building, it bustles with workers and the noise of productivity. An older woman, with bouncy hair and eccentric glasses, looks up from her computer. Her smile is welcoming as are her bright white teeth.

"Hello there, and to you, handsome sir," the woman greets

them.

Jake's cheeks flush as he looks away.

"Hi uh--, is Lieutenant, or Major Ellison--" Catherine feels cumbersome and awkward as she speaks.

"Yes, dear. He's been notified of your arrival. He's in a meeting but will be down shortly if you don't mind having a seat. There's snacks and water, I'm sure you must be famished."

"Thank you."

Catherine walks with the kids to a waiting area. Comfortable couches and chairs surround a table with dried fruit and nuts, pitchers of ice water, there's even a TV playing cartoons in the corner. They have the area all to themselves.

The hour they spend in the waiting room doesn't seem like a wait at all. To be inside with food, water, and the rare feeling of safety, is a welcome respite from the continuous test of fortitude that the journey required. She longs for uninterrupted sleep.

"I want to be kept in the loop on this, that means daily briefs," a familiar voice echoes into the room.

Catherine looks to the hallway where Ellison emerges, speaking with someone she doesn't recognize but has an unsettling feeling that she knows. Gray-washed hair and wrinkled skin surround thin spectacles and shifty eyes.

"Will do, Major. Thank you for taking me in, I know we're going to do great things here!" The wiry man offers his hand.

"I hope you're right, Doc." Ellison squeezes a handshake and turns to the lobby. The man retreats into the hallway like a mouse.

"I'm sorry for the wait."

Ellison approaches, clean-shaven and in pressed fatigues that display his new rank.

"Major Ellison, you may not remember--"

He extends his hand looking straight into her eyes.

"Catherine, right? I'm glad you made it. And who are these charming warriors?"

He steps to her side and extends a hand to each. They're nervous but reciprocate the handshakes.

"This is Basil, and Jake," Catherine offers.

"I like your choice of weapon there, Jake." Ellison points to the bat the young boy has propped up against the chair. Jake grins and spins the handle, twirling the end on the tile floor.

"I've got to get back soon, but let me show you to our residential barracks. I'm sure you're exhausted from the trek."

All three agree. He leads them out of the HQ building and along a well-groomed sidewalk. Green trees tower over them, the shade bringing a needed obstruction to the relentless sun.

"Can I help you with your bags?" asks Ellison as they move through a courtyard.

"We're okay, made it this far." Catherine and Ellison share a laugh.

"What's this I hear about memorials?" Ellison asks, not accusatory, but of genuine curiosity. Catherine looks a bit distrusting, to which he is quick to explain. "The guards radioed up once you were on your way, thought it might be of importance."

She feels guilty for being suspicious and tries not to wear it on her face as the man has been only kind since they first met.

"How so?"

"Let's take a detour, you might like this."

Ellison leads them through the courtyard and into a beautiful lawn area with dazzling flowers. A large expanse of wall travels the length of the garden. A few people, not in uniform, are scattered along its ivory-white face. The structure stands maybe eight feet tall. As they get closer, Catherine, Basil, and Jake begin to realize what it is they're looking at.

Each section of the wall is separated by decorative etching. Many of the pieces are barren, but the small colorful squares become clear as they step forward. Water pools in Catherine's eyes as a young girl and mother crouch next to the stone slab. They point and trace their fingers across the smooth, glassy surface. The entire face is dotted with photographs and IDs, stacked in rows and columns.

Basil reads the words that are beautifully carved into an ornate stone at the center of the lawn, "Here, they live on."

Ellison takes a step back and speaks in a low voice, "Take your time. But I think you'll find you can lose some of that weight off of your shoulders."

Catherine pulls Basil and Jake close, fighting back tears.

ACKNOWLEDGMENTS

It truly takes a village and without the help of numerous mentors, friends, and well-mannered strangers, this book would still be an adverb-laden, redundant, blubbering mess of thoughts. I am forever grateful for all of the DMs, texts, and emails that kept this train moving. The cliché that it's not about the destination but the journey is as true for Viktor as it was for writing his story. So a heartfelt thank you to the following people and sincere apologies to anyone I may have overlooked.

Jessica, such an amazing wife and mother that *author* sounds so vain in comparison. I value your honest criticisms and sorry there wasn't more of Viktor and Catherine getting it on.

Beta-readers are the true heroes of this business. Thank you all for crawling through my first draft. I was still finding the voice I wanted to use and your notes absolutely shaped this book into what it is today. Jeremy and Cory, I love you both as there was no hesitation to say yes when I approached you with a 115k word doorstop. Tim, I value your pop-culture opinion so much and having you binge the book meant the world. Devon, I was wary of having a fellow creative take a pass but it was completely worth it. Chase, you were a wild card and added countless positives to my revision process. Chris, you are my target audience and receiving your feedback reinvigorated my spirit to make this thing real. Thank you for sharing your service with me and, by extension, the readers. The next book is coming soon everyone, so clear your calendars!

To all of the authors who helped in the query trenches. Joshua Hood, your kindness and talent are unmatched. Yvette Yun, I was at a low before I received your AMM feedback and it was the push I needed to not bury this story. Everyone reading this owes you a debt of gratitude. Danielle Terkhanian, you were the first to view my original query and could have easily made me quit right then. Thank you for your thoughtful notes. Lauren Simonis-Hunter, you helped me to not overthink my query.

The writing community on the bird app is overwhelmingly generous. Mark S., Eric B., Marie L., Jen G., Ryan W., Brett A., Kealan B., SJ C., Brian A. Thank you for each playing your part and being so generous with your time. I'm sure there are more that I bothered so feel free to call me out in a tweet.

If betas are the heroes then editors and proofreaders are their trusty sidekicks. Any errors found within are entirely my own as I probably bumped a key or made a change after their pass. My bad.

And certainly not least all of the reviewers who so graciously agreed to fit my book in before its release. I can't thank you by name as this has already gone to print but indie authors wouldn't stand a chance without people like you.

Thank you to all of the readers who took a chance on an indie book. There are so many talented authors from all paths of publishing who only want to share whatever adventure, trauma, or laughter that is bouncing around in their heads. Your engagement and reviews make the years-long grind at the keyboard worth it. You all rock!

Verba volant, scripta manent.

RYAN YOUNG has been fabricating fiction since he was a kid, but it wasn't until his adult years—when his interest in filmmaking and screenwriting took shape, that he began to also explore the idea of long-form storytelling. He's already working on his next original manuscript, and beyond. In addition to writing, Ryan is an avid reader of fiction and non-fiction, with a particular interest in historical warfare. He is also a recovering post-punctuation double-spacer and an ardent defender of the Oxford comma.

He lives in Orlando, Florida with his wife, daughter, and fur babies but his heart is set on a mountain homestead. Ryan enjoys fitness, traveling, hiking, The Office, and vast amounts of pizza and coffee.